**POISED TO KILL,
READY TO DIE!**

The Marines and PFs hugged the earth, wishing they had proper fighting holes or fighting bunkers in which to hide from the barrage. Fortunately, the mortar rounds were too few, too spread out, and all fell into the hootches behind them—the assault line of Marines and PFs was too close to the trees for the mortar to risk hitting them. Then two whistles shrilled in the trees to their front.

"Hold your fire," Bell shouted. "Wait until they come into the open." They didn't wait long. Suddenly fifty screaming Vietcong burst into the open area between the woods and the nearest hootches where the defenders lay waiting.

"Fire!" Bell and Burrison shouted simultaneously....

A ROCK AND A HARD PLACE

David Sherman

IVY BOOKS • NEW YORK

Ivy Books
Published by Ballantine Books
Copyright © 1988 by David Sherman

Library of Congress Catalog Card Number: 87-92088

ISBN-0-8041-0191-4

Manufactured in the United States of America

First Edition: June 1988

DEDICATION

It's been more than twenty years since the United States of America committed ground combat troops to the war in the Republic of Vietnam. It was a very confused war that we entered, partly a war of national reunion, partly an insurrection against the despots who sometimes ruled in Saigon, partly a war against foreign (translate that to mean European or American) domination. But mostly it was a continuation of the ancient war between Northern and Southern Vietnamese; a war in which the southerners sought freedom to live the way they wanted to, and the northerners fought to keep the southerners under their thumbs. Only this time, the northerners were communist conquerors. Our government, despite disputes from learned members of our free society, understood that later. Unfortunately, our government wanted to avoid too many things: our government wanted not to upset the American public, which was still glowing with its peaceful accomplishments of the fifties and early sixties; our government wanted to avoid showing a bad face to the world at large, which might believe the communist lies about how a giant (us) was picking on a tiny country (Vietnam) and meddling in its internal affairs—which were none of our business. That notion, of course, ignores the outside-backed communist war of domination. So our government never managed to formulate a firm objective for the war and how to achieve it. Instead, our national leaders obfuscated and never told us the truth. Ultimately, because too few of us understood what was happening half a world away, we lost that war. The bigger losers, however, were the innocent citizens of the Republic of Vietnam, who were conquered by the northerners and subjugated as never before.

So this book is dedicated to the kids. It is for the Vietnamese children, whom we knew, we lived with, we played with, we loved. The children whom our government, in the end, abandoned to Hanoi's slavery.

AUTHOR'S NOTE

The U.S. Marine Corps Combined Action Program was real. It was a small project, little noted by the news media and almost unknown to the American public. The official estimate is that only five thousand or so Marines served in CAP during its seven-year existence—of whom about 3,500 came home alive. This small band of Marines quietly trained and fought alongside the South Vietnamese Popular Forces—the civilian militia. Despite its lack of public fanfare, CAP was awarded the Presidential Unit Citation, the Navy Unit Commendation, the Meritorious Unit Commendation, the Vietnamese Cross of Gallantry, and the Vietnamese Civic Actions Unit Citation. And that doesn't count the Medal of Honor, Navy Crosses, and innumerable Silver and Bronze Stars won by individual CAP Marines. A pretty impressive array of awards for a small band of dedicated Marines who didn't have a Barry Sadler, a Robin Moore, a John Wayne, to sing its praises, write its story, or put its exploits on the silver screen. The CAP unit in this novel is loosely based on the combat-outpost CAP the author served with several miles from Chu Lai from May to September, 1966.

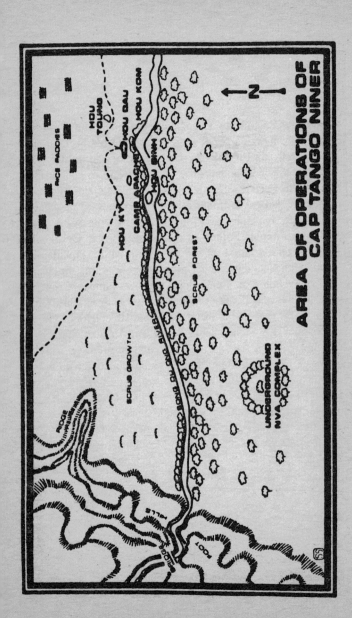

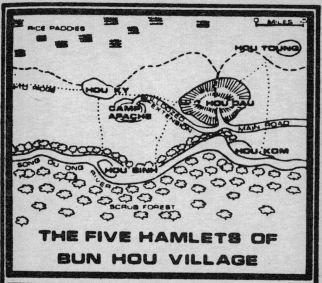

THE FIVE HAMLETS OF
BUN HOU VILLAGE

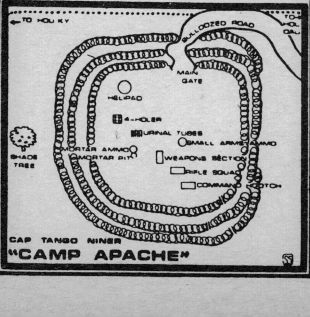

CAP TANGO NINER
"CAMP APACHE"

CHAPTER ONE

Late Night, November 17, 1966

Corporal Jesus Maria Ruizique sighted along the barrel of his rifle at the Vietcong filing past his patrol's position. Ruizique swore soundlessly: two squads of them, too many for his four-man patrol to take on. He cautiously moved his left hand from the forestock of his rifle to his PRC-6 walkie-talkie and pressed the SPEAK button on its side to kill the soft static emitting from its earpiece. At his left, Webster and Pennell saw how badly outnumbered they were and tried to melt into the ground. They thought, they hoped, that Ruizique wouldn't trigger the ambush. Ruizique *always* wanted to tango with Charlie, and so did they, but not when the odds were so bad. Neissi, on the patrol leader's right, stared wide-eyed and slack-jawed at the fifteen VC slipping past in the night and wished with all his heart he was anywhere else. Neissi had only been with Combined Action Platoon Tango Niner for two days and was on his second patrol. The first night he was with Tango Niner, the patrol had had a half squad of the local Popular Forces with it and could have dealt with fifteen VC.

Silently, the killer VC patrol slipped through the trees along the Song Du Ong river, the river's burbling drowning out any incidental sounds they might have made. As suddenly as they had appeared, they disappeared.

I want them, Ruizique said to himself as he watched the VC go by. I want them very badly. Where are my little people now, when I need them so much? Who does that imbecile think he is, taking them away like he did? He should be castrated and then hung as vermin for taking them away. We cannot do our job without our little people.

When the last of the fifteen VC vanished into the night, he released the SPEAK button on his radio and watched the place where they had disappeared. Then a quiet voice came from the radio. "House Flies, House Flies, this is Red House. Do you hear me? Over."

"One," a different voice said over the radio.

"Two," a third voice said.

"Three," Ruizique whispered into the mouthpiece of his radio.

"Who broke squelch, House Flies? Over," asked the first voice, that of Swearin' Swarnes, Tango Niner's radioman.

"Red House, Fly Three," Ruizique murmured. "I did. Over."

" 'Sappening, Three? Over."

"Boo-coo Charlies just walked by. I broke squelch so they wouldn't hear the radio. Over."

"Roger, Three. How many's boo-coo? Over."

"Fifteen."

"Wait one, Three."

Ruizique waited, still watching the place where the VC had disappeared and listening for sounds from other directions. Then a new voice came up on the radio, Sergeant J. C. Bell's. "House Fly Three, this is Red House Five. Do I understand correctly one-five Victor Charlies just passed your position? Over."

"That's an affirmative. Over."

"Are they headed toward one of the other Flies? Over."

"Negative. Yours."

"Are you in danger of being discovered? Over."

"Negative again, Red House. Over."

"Roger, Three. Stay where you are until daybreak. I say again, do not move from your current position until the sun comes up. Then come in. Do you understand? Over."

"Roger that, Red House. Three wilco. Over."

"House Fly Three, this is Red House Five, out." And only the soft sound of static came over the radio.

Ruizique rolled to one side and told Webster they were to stay in place until dawn, then rolled to the other side and told Neissi. Webster passed the word to Pennell. Ruizique didn't bother setting a sleep rotation. He didn't care if all of his men slept at the same time, he would stay awake through the night. He did, seething. He wanted to kill the VC, not let them go by. If that fifteen-man unit had been a supply run he would have sprung his ambush. But not with all fifteen being armed soldiers, not with his patrol outnumbered by nearly four to one. He wanted to kill, not to commit suicide. From time to time his hands lovingly caressed the leather bandoliers crisscrossing his chest. Every loop in the bandoliers held a 7.62mm round at the ready. The leather did not squeak or crack when the Marine moved; he spent many hours polishing the smooth insides of them and working saddle soap into the rough outside so it was soft and pliant. The leather did not shine in the moonlight.

When the sun rose Ruizique led his men back to the hill on which sat the fortified compound the Marines of CAP Tango Niner called Camp Apache.

CHAPTER TWO

November 17, 1966

"Big Louie, get your paddles," Sergeant J. C. Bell shouted. "A bird's coming in."

Corporal "Big Louie" Slover squeezed an eye open far enough to see the sergeant waving at him from the other side of the compound, then scanned the sky to the east. Damn, he thought, how could that thing get this close without me hearing it? The tadpole-shaped UH-34 was less than two minutes out. Slover grabbed the sides of his fishnet hammock and pulled himself out of it to run across the compound to the squad tent his mortarmen shared with the machine gun team. He emerged with a pair of orange Ping-Pong paddles in one hand and ran to the landing pad, a white painted circle in the compound's northeast corner; he ran the way he was built, like an NFL lineman. He checked the wind direction, faced into it across the white circle toward the main gate on the north side of the compound, and waited for the bird to swing into its final approach. As usual when he was in the compound, Slover wasn't wearing a shirt.

The helicopter came in low and fast and Slover held the paddles out to his sides to show the pilot he was level with the ground, then waved him in to a perfect touchdown. It was the copilot's first flight into Camp Apache. When he first spotted Slover directing them he did a double take and said into his throat mike, "Whoa, that crazy fucker better get out of the way before he gets his ass creamed."

"It's okay," the pilot, a veteran of many flights into Camp Apache, answered, "he always brings us in that way."

"You sure?"

"I'm sure," the pilot said calmly, concentrating on bringing his aircraft in smoothly. "I've been out here boo-coo times and I've never seen that dude wear a shirt. He says dark black skin is too tough to get hurt by whatever our downwash throws up."

Big Louie Slover was a very dark black man, with skin almost the color of coal.

The bird swooped over the main gate and the copilot was able to read the hand-painted sign next to it:

CAMP APACHE
USMC
Home of Combined Action Platoon T-9
It Takes Two to Tango
Charlie Gonna Die Here
Barry Sadler, Eat Your Heart Out

"Who do they think they are, John-fucking-Wayne or somebody?" the copilot asked.

But they were landing and the touchdown was too noisy

for the pilot to answer until he idled the rotors. Then he said, "Nah, they don't think they're John Wayne. They say John Wayne thinks he's them."

The man who got off the helicopter was very familiar to the Marines of CAP Tango Niner. He was Captain Hasford, an intelligence officer who had worked with them many times in the past couple of months. As soon as he was far enough away from the chopper that the rotorwash wouldn't blow it off, Hasford slapped on a camouflage bush hat similar to the ones the Marines on the hill were wearing. "Afternoon, Scrappy," he said to the more eager looking of the two men who met him. "Jay Cee," he nodded to the other.

"Welcome back to Camp Apache, Captain Hasford," said Lieutenant Burrison, the one addressed as "Scrappy."

"Hope you got some news for us, sir," said Bell.

"I mostly have bad news for you. That's why I'm here to deliver it in person. Let's go over this way." He led them to the open area in the southeast corner of the compound and sat on a sandbag revetment overlooking the three banks of concertina wire surrounding the compound, with a view of the flood plain south of the hill. The other two sat and Hasford started talking immediately. "I don't have much time so let's get right down to business. First off, there hasn't been any kind of recon over there," he pointed to the rising lines of hills to the west, "and there's not likely to be any in the immediate future. Eye Corps' a big area and Three MAF only has so many recon units." "Eye Corps" was "I Corps," the northernmost of the four military regions of South Vietnam, and Lieutenant General Lew Walt's Marine Amphibious Force, "III MAF," was responsible for it. "They can only be used to check out eyeball reports of enemy action or follow up on other intelligence reports; neither division's G-2 will send a team into an area just because some lowly captain tells them a Combined Action Platoon thinks Charlie has something going on somewhere. They need a report from a different source before they'll spare any resources to check it out.''

"Shit," Bell swore, then squinted at the hills the sun was settling onto. "I know Charlie's got something big over there. That's why he keeps coming this way. We need to know what it is.''

"I believe you, Jay Cee. But recon needs more info before they'll send a team in. And, as far as I can find out, nobody's planning any operations in that area, so we can forget about it for now."

"Captain," Burrison said, "we're sitting smack in the middle of one of Charlie's favorite infiltration routes. What happens if he decides to do something about it and nobody's run a recon to let us know what to expect?''

"Forget it, Scrappy." Hasford shook his head. "Charlie's already tried to wipe this platoon out twice and both times you kicked ass on him. Everybody from General Walt on down knows that. You don't get any special consideration for being on a favored infiltration route because everybody, from Walt on down, knows you've got the Song Du Ong flood plain bottlenecked.''

"But, sir, that was when we had our fay-epps. How soon do we get them back?''

"That's bad news number two, Jay Cee," Hasford said. "You don't. G-5, the civic actions branch, has been trying like hell to get your PFs back. They keep running into the same crock of shit; the Popular Forces are under the direct command of the district chief and he can assign them anywhere he wants. If Major Y wants that platoon to guard his district headquarters, there's nothing we can do about it." He paused and swiveled his head around, looking over the fifteen square miles Tango Niner was responsible for keeping clear of Vietcong. "So G-5 is negotiating with the province chief to authorize creation of a new PF platoon here in Bun Hou.''

"A new platoon!" Burrison yelped. "But all the best

men in the village are already in the platoon we had. Captain, this is the most isolated unit in Eye Corps, we need the best men we can get.''

"I know that, and G-5 knows that. But getting the second-best men is better than not having any. You're going to have to hang on here by yourselves for a while.'' He smiled crookedly. "Hell, Scrappy, Jay Cee—you've got twenty-five Marines sitting here. You should be able to handle anything Charlie throws at you.''

"With all due respect, sir,'' Bell said slowly, "that's bull, and you know it. Some of the shit Charlie's thrown at us, there's no way he couldn't have put us too deep in the hurt locker for us to get back out if those fay-epps hadn't been with us. Not even if the Seventh Cavalry came riding to the rescue.''

Hasford kept his smile and said, "Sergeant, what I know and what I have to say aren't always the same thing. You people are going to have to change your operational scheme of things for a while, that's all. I'll be back in a few days to review it with you and let you know what progress has been made in turning CAP Tango Niner back into a proper Combined Action Platoon. Now—''

"I knew it when you said, 'bad news number two.' Bad news always comes in threes,'' Bell said.

"Cut me a break, Jay Cee. It's not all bad. Most people would think this next thing was good news.''

"We're not most people,'' Bell muttered.

"You've been here for more than six months, right?'' Hasford knew the answer and didn't wait for a reply. "And in more than six months no member of Tango Niner has pulled R&R.''

"Oh no,'' Bell groaned.

"Word has been passed,'' Hasford continued, "Tango Niner rates two R&Rs per week until everybody who has been in-country more than six months has gotten one. That means everybody except a couple of your new people, doesn't it?'' He directed the last to Burrison.

"When you said twenty-five I thought you meant the men under us," Bell said almost to himself. "Now I know you meant including us."

"I think so," the young second lieutenant answered. His face tried to turn pale under its sun-baked bronze tan. "When does this start?"

"Right now. Pick two men. They leave with me."

"You can't do this to us," Burrison and Bell said simultaneously. "Not now, not when we're this short-handed."

"Don't blame me. If it was up to me I'd send the whole damn platoon on R&R until your PF mess got straightened out."

"We can't do this thing," Burrison said. "Instead of sending any of my men on R&R right now I'm going back with you and talk to Lieutenant Colonel Tornado. My men can have their R&R when we get our fay-epps back, but not now."

Hasford shook his head. "No can do. Lieutenant Colonel Tornado's gone away somewhere and, anyway, the R&R orders came from someone with stars on his collar. The lieutenant colonel wouldn't be able to do anything about it even if he was here."

"I'll bet he can do something," Burrison insisted. "Where'd he go? I'll go there and talk to him."

Hasford shook his head again. "I don't know. It was very sudden. I don't think he had a chance to tell anybody where he went. All I've been able to find out is it's out of the country."

Burrison and Bell argued a little longer, but they knew it was a losing effort. They put their heads together and picked two of the men who had been with Bell when Tango Niner had first been formed back in June: Lance Corporal John "Short Round" Hempen from the rifle squad and PFC Willie "Fast Talking Man" Pennell from the weapons section. It wasn't until after they told the two to get ready to go that they remembered Pennell had been reassigned to the rifle squad.

* * *

Hempen and Pennell objected to going.

"You can't do this, Jay Cee," Hempen had said, ignoring the officer. He knew a Marine sergeant wields more real power than a second lieutenant, even when the second lieutenant is the sergeant's commanding officer. "Tango Niner is too fucking short handed, you need us here."

"I can do it and I am doing it, Short Round," Bell snapped. He said it but he didn't want to, he couldn't spare the men now and that made him angry. He couldn't fight with Captain Hasford because it wasn't the captain's fault, and he couldn't fight with whoever it was who ordered the R&Rs for his platoon, so he took the anger out on the men he was sending on R&R.

"Scrappy," Pennell said. He hadn't been in the Marines as long as Hempen and didn't understand as well how things really worked. "Short Round's right, you can't afford to let us go right now. Let us stay until we get our fay-epps back."

"Damnit, PFC," Burrison snapped, "don't you tell me not to tell you what to do! I'm your commanding officer and what I say goes."

"Jay Cee, you need us here, Honcho," Hempen said.

"You're going and that's final."

"Your choices are Bangkok, Hong Kong, Singapore, Taipei, and Sydney, Australia," Burrison said. "Make up your minds where you want to go by the time you get to Da Nang."

"No way we can go now," Hempen insisted.

Burrison fingered the collar of his shirt. "Do you know what I wear here when I'm not in the field?"

"Gold bars. Why?" Hempen asked, confused.

"That means I'm an officer, doesn't it?"

"Yes?" Hempen was still confused.

"What do you wear there?"

"One-and-a-half stripes." The crossed rifles under the chevrons on Marine rank insignia from lance corporal to

master sergeant were usually called "BB guns," but
lance corporals and corporals often called them "half
stripes."

"That means I rank you, doesn't it?" Burrison
snapped.

"Yessir," Hempen snapped back. He was beginning
to catch on and knew what the lieutenant was going to
say next, and what he'd say back to it.

"If I rank you that means I can give you orders and
you have to obey them. Pack your civies, you're going
on R&R."

"Sorry, Scrappy, no can do," Hempen said. "This is
like tunnel rat duty. You can't order a man to do it if he
doesn't want to."

That did it for Bell, he couldn't take any more. "Get
off my fucking hill!" he roared.

Hempen and Pennell jumped back. "What?" Hempen
gasped, blinking at the sergeant's suddenly red face.

"I said get off my fucking hill," Bell shouted, ad-
vancing on them like a fighting pit bull terrier. "If you
aren't off my fucking hill in five minutes on your way to
R&R I'm going to hang your scuzzy asses from the flagpole!"

"B-but Camp Apache doesn't have a flagpole,"
Hempen stammered. He hadn't seen Sergeant Bell act
like that since the first day the platoon was together.

"Hou Ky does, and I'll hang you from it unless you
get off my goddamn hill."

"This ain't your fucking hill," Hempen said. "I dug
the goddamn trenches and bunkers, not you." But he was
back-pedaling to the squad tent to pack for R&R when
he said it. Pennell was right alongside him. The helicopter that had brought Captain Hasford took off five minutes later. Hempen and Pennell were on it, on their way
to R&R.

The helicopter with Tango Niner's daily hot meal was
on its way when Burrison sat at the field desk in the

middle section of the tent that served as the command hootch. One end of the command hootch tent served as radio room and Swearin' Swarnes had his cot there. The other end was a combination storage room and quarters for the CAP's two Navy medical corpsmen. Burrison and Bell slept in the middle section. Burrison studied his topographical map and the acetate overlays for the previous few nights' patrols and tried to figure out what to do tonight. He chewed on the end of his grease pencil until he gnawed all the way through the tightly wound paper to the wax stick inside it.

"Oh God, that tastes terrible," he said and looked around for somewhere to spit out the foul taste. "Where the hell's Jay Cee when I need him?" He went through the radio room to leave the tent. Swarnes was sitting in front of his radios, seemingly so engrossed in his skin magazine he didn't notice the lieutenant go by. Burrison squinted against the late afternoon sunshine and looked around for his number two. He spotted Bell sitting on a newly built bunker on the west side of the compound. Four other men were with Bell; Burrison headed toward them. He guessed the other four men were corporals Slover, Zeitvogel, Randall, and McEntire. He guessed right. Ruizique was laying on his cot in the rifle squad's tent, brooding about how was he going to be able to kill Cong with only two men left in his fire team.

The five Marine NCOs sat talking quietly with long pauses in between. They stared at the rising hills that marched west until they rose to become the mountains of Laos. Laos was called a neutral country, but it was the home of the Ho Chi Minh Trail, a safe passage and haven for the North Vietnamese Army and the Vietcong. Everybody in the world knew Laos wasn't neutral, but they all pretended it was—everyone except the communist forces trying to conquer free South Vietnam. So the South Vietnamese who were trying to stay free and the Americans helping them couldn't go into Laos to stop the invaders before they crossed the border. And cross the border they did, in many places. One of those places was directly to the west of Camp Apache, and they kept coming through the area of Bun Hou village, through and around Bun Hou's five hamlets. Just then all that stood between them and where they wanted to go was twenty-five U.S. Marines.

"What the fuck is over there?" Bell asked rhetorically.

Stilts Zeitvogel slowly shook his head. "Something big," the tall man said. He was very tall. Standing in his tire-tred sandals like he was now, he was close to six-and-a-half feet tall.

"We need to know," said Tex Randall. Randall was shorter than average and built like a wrestler, which he had been in high school.

"Them sons 'a bitches just gotta send Force Recon out there, find out what they got," burly Big Louie Slover said. "Then send in a couple, three battalions of grunts, blow its fucking ass away."

"And nobody wants to spend the 'resources' to find out," complained Wall McEntire. McEntire was a big man who Big Louie Slover had nicknamed Wall because, "He's not tall enough to be a Tree and not fat enough to be a Bear." Slover was the self-appointed giver of nicknames to the men of Tango Niner.

"So what the fuck are we going to do?" Randall said. It was almost a whisper.

"Stay alive any which-way we can," Bell said softly.

Burrison stood behind them, listening for a moment. Then he said, "In the meantime, we have tonight to worry about."

"Right," Bell said. Worry was the right word. They were all worried about tonight.

Burrison looked west, where his NCOs had been looking, and knew what they were all thinking. He slowly turned a full circle, looking out over Tango Niner's area of operations and knew there was no way on earth he and his twenty-two Marines and two corpsmen could cover the entire area—not without the thirty-five man Popular

Forces platoon they had been working with for the past half year. The local VC company that owned Bun Hou village when Tango Niner was first established was long dead, but main force Vietcong units conducted supply runs through the village area and infiltrated reinforcing squads and platoons through it to their combat units east of the village. Tango Niner put out three patrols every night, four Marines plus from four to eleven PFs in each patrol. Most nights at least one of the patrols intercepted Charlie, killed him, and captured his supplies. And recently the VC had tried new tactics to trap and wipe out the combined Marine-PF patrols. So far all that had happened was Charlie got hurt, but the Marines knew that couldn't continue without them getting hurt, too. And now they were on their own, without their little people to fight alongside them.

The lieutenant said what they were all thinking, "No way we can put our patrols out tonight."

The NCOs nodded and grunted their agreement.

"We can do what Captain Hasford did when we were in the lockup," Bell said.

Burrison didn't say anything for a moment, then, decisively, "We're all staying home tonight. One-third alert. Swarnes goes on the perimeter. Tomorrow we'll figure out what to do until we get Houng and his platoon back."

"Good idea," Bell said. "But we can't go for long without putting out patrols. Last time that happened, it only took Charlie two days to figure it out."

"Right," Burrison said.

"Gotta run," Slover said, and suddenly dashed for his squad tent. The helicopter with their hot evening meal was in sight and he had to guide it in.

The helicopter crew chief let go of his machine gun long enough to shove insulated food containers to the Marines on the ground and stow the empty containers from the previous evening's meal that they shoved back at him. The bird was climbing for altitude again less than half a minute after touching down.

They hauled the containers to a table made from a sheet of galvanized metal laid across a bed of sandbags and opened them. Bell assigned himself as chief messman and told Randall to help serve. They had roast pork in gravy with overdone baked potatoes, peas, and some green vegetable that was so overcooked none of them could tell for certain what it had originally been. Dessert was warm apple pie. When all the other enlisted men had their food, Bell let Randall help himself, then filled his own and Burrison's mess kits from what remained. There was enough left over for some of them to have small second portions.

They didn't talk much while they ate. They were all thinking about the Vietcong who were probably going to come through their area overnight, and how those VC would all make it through safely. They wondered how long it would take Charlie to figure out they didn't have any patrols out to catch him, and how long it would take before he decided to try again to overrun Camp Apache. They avoided thinking about what could happen if the Vietcong sent in a reinforced company to wipe them out. Charlie tried that once before, but everyone from Tango Niner was waiting for them; more than sixty Marines and PFs broke that reinforced VC company's back when two helicopter gunships arrived on the scene to help.

"Sure is lonely," Zeitvogel said to anyone who felt like listening.

"Sure is," Randall said. Nobody else spoke, they didn't have to. Every night some of the PFs joined them for evening chow and there was a lot of chatter while the PFs practiced their English and the Marines tried to learn some Vietnamese. What they wound up with was an argot comprised of badly pronounced English, Vietnamese, and French words. It worked for basic communications. The PFs usually brought some food from their homes to supplement the Marines' chow—rice balls, cooked greens, bits of fish, chicken, or pork. And nuoc mam sauce, the ubiquitous Vietnamese condiment made from fermented fish juice that smelled even worse than it sounded.

The night was quiet.

CHAPTER THREE

November 19, 1966

Major Tran Duc Y was the district chief. He had had as his assistant district chief one Captain Phang. Phang was an exceptionally corrupt official who was lying, cheating, stealing, and murdering his way to wealth. Phang's last act of corruption was to sell to the Vietcong a shipment of arms and ammunition intended for the district's Regional Forces. The weapons were stored in a warehouse that Phang arranged to have guarded by three men armed with defective rifles and ammunition. When they came for the weapons, the VC killed two of the three guards. About that time many of the people Phang had harmed in his quest for riches assembled to try him in absentia. Then they lured him to an isolated location and executed him. Major Y hadn't been involved in the arms sale, but he was in with Phang on many other illegal transactions and understood how and why his assistant district chief had been killed. He covered up the murder and the loss of the arms by claiming to his own government and to the Americans that Phang had been killed in a VC attack on the arms warehouse.

South Vietnamese Regional Forces were local militia mustered in a province and under the direct control of the province chief. Popular Forces were civilian militiamen organized village by village and under the command of the district chief, who could assign them anywhere in his district he wanted, though they were normally assigned by platoons to safeguard their home villages. To back his claim that the VC had attacked the warehouse and killed Captain Phang, Major Y had to increase security at his district headquarters. To this end he reassigned the PF platoon from Bun Hou village who, with the Marines, formed the Combined Action Platoon designated Tango Niner. His stated reason for using this particular Popular Forces platoon was it was the best-trained unit under his control—which it was.

His real reason, though, was something else. The Marines of Tango Niner had put a stop to Captain Phang's illegal money-making operations in Bun Hou village and were threatening them in other nearby areas in the district. That put a considerable dent in Phang's income. It also put a dent in Major Y's income, as he had received a cut of everything—well, nearly everything—Phang made. So Major Y wanted to get rid of these meddling Marines, and he pulled Tango Niner's PF platoon. With the unit reduced to less than half strength, maybe the Vietcong would be able to wipe it out. At the same time, he started trying to convince Marine headquarters that Bun Hou village was secure and no longer needed a Combined Action Platoon.

When Tango Niner was first established, a local Vietcong company ruled in Bun Hou village. The Marines wiped it out. That convinced many of the village's men they had nothing to fear by joining the PF platoon. Once properly established, the Marines and PFs of CAP Tango Niner wiped out a second company of local force VC and an NVA sapper platoon sent to kill them, and fought off two major attempts by main force Vietcong units to overrun Camp Apache. That was in addition to Tango Niner's constant interception of VC supply runs and reinforcements being infiltrated through their area. The Marines knew they were an important thorn in Charlie's side, and they knew Charlie wanted to get rid of them. Twenty-five Marines wouldn't have much chance of surviving if the Vietcong made a concerted attempt to kill them all. That was why they were so concerned about losing their little people.

Incidentally, neither the letter nor the sound "P" exists in the Vietnamese language the way it does in English. The letter "P" is always used in combination with the letter "H," "PH," pronounced "eff." The people in Bun Hou village pronounced the separate letters "PF" "fay-epp," which is why the Marines of Tango Niner called their PFs "fay-epps."

Burrison and Bell sat on top of a bunker on the west side of Camp Apache, looking out over the two hundred meters of cleared ground between their hill and a patch of forest beyond it. On the far side of the trees was an area of scrub growth that extended almost to the hills several kilometers distant.

"Last night was no good, Jay Cee," Burrison said. His face wore a worried expression.

"Right the first time," Bell agreed.

"I think what we should do is put one eight-man patrol out every night and keep all other hands on the perimeter until we get our fay-epps back."

Bell nodded.

"Four-man patrols are too small for safety, we know that," the lieutenant went on. "Charlie's out there in units too big for a fire team to take on."

"And we can't afford not to have patrols out there," Bell said when Burrison paused.

"If we don't have any patrols out there for Charlie to run into, he's going to figure out most ricky-tick we're sitting here alone. He'll work that out soon enough as is," Burrison said. Neither man said the other thing he was thinking—if the VC didn't already know. They looked westward in silence for a few more moments.

"I'm going into town," Bell said at length, "talk to Thien, see if he's heard anything." "Town" was Hou Ky hamlet, Thien was the hamlet chief and older brother of Lieutenant Houng, the PF commander.

"Good idea. Take someone with you."

"You know it." Normally the Marines felt comfortable walking alone during the day for the quarter-mile west from Camp Apache to Hou Ky hamlet, or the half mile east to Hou Dau hamlet. But this wasn't a normal time.

Moments later Bell walked through Camp Apache's main gate. Lance Corporal Billy Harold Lewis, better known as "Billy Boy," was with him. Bell and Lewis were the platoon's supposed linguists; they had both gone through a training course in the Vietnamese language. "Big Red," PFC John Robertson, accompanied them. The three men were better armed and more alert than they would usually be taking a daytime walk to town. The bulldozed road that led into Camp Apache turned right at the foot of the hill and, half a mile east, curved south around Hou Dau hill, on which sat Bun Hou's central hamlet, where it connected with a permanent roadway leading all the way to Highway 1 at the South China Sea. The Marines turned left onto a footpath where the bulldozed road turned right. A quarter-mile later the footpath twisted right and emptied under the gateway arch into Hou Ky.

Immediately the three Marines were surrounded by a pack of tiny, squealing children, dressed in all the colors of the rainbow—and some colors that weren't in it. The small children, four, six, eight years old, ran around the trio, screaming and tugging at their clothing and weapons; some of the more adventurous tried to clamber up them. A few feet behind these children many of the hamlet's toddlers toddled about, following the example of their older brothers and sisters—but at a safe distance to avoid being trampled. The little ones wore either shorts or shirts, but not both—shirts only for the boys, shorts only for the girls. Beyond them the ten- and twelve-year-old children laughed and called out to the Marines, but didn't crowd and clutch them—these older children had their dignity to think of.

One particularly small seven-year-old grabbed the stock of Bell's rifle and pulled on it so hard he would have chinned himself if his arms could have lifted his weight. "Me, me carry, Chay Cee," he insisted as he tugged on the rifle.

"You can't carry it, Fart," Bell said, looking down at the boy. "It's too heavy for you."

"Me carry, me carry," Fart insisted and tugged more. They called him Fart because he had reminded Wildman Eastham of his own kid brother whom he called by that name.

"Here, you carry this," Bell said and whipped his camouflage bush hat from his head onto Fart's.

The size seven-and-an-eighth bush hat covered Fart's head and the extended side of its brim rested on his shoulder. He pushed it back with his tiny hands far enough to be able to see from under it and a wide grin split his face. "Me Ma-deen," he squealed, "me need bang-bang," and tried to twist the rifle from Bell's shoulder. His struggles caused the bush hat to plop back over his face and his laughter echoed from under it.

"Here, I'll carry you, you carry my rifle," Bell said, sweeping the child into the crook of his left arm. He unslung the rifle and, without letting go of its pistol grip, lay it across Fart's body so the boy could pretend he was carrying it. The child pealed with laughter and grasped

the barrel guard of the rifle with one hand while holding
the bush hat back with his other so he could see from
under it. This set the others off even more, and they all
wanted to be carried.

It was an odd procession that wandered through Hou
Ky, the three big Americans and a gaggle of perhaps
twenty tiny children. The Marines were festooned with
children; each had two or three in his arms or dangling
from various parts of him at all times, and the children
were vying with each other for the privilege of being
carried. Every time one fell or was dragged off, another
took his or her place.

The hootches of Hou Ky were scattered about in no
pattern easily discernible to Western eyes, but each one
faced on a hamlet footpath. When the Marines first came
to Bun Hou nearly every house in all five of the village's
hamlets were made of grass and bamboo thatch, except
for a few French-built masonry structures. But the Marines hired local people to work for them, to do laundry,
keep their compound clean, dig new holes for the four-
holer, carry water for the fifty-five-gallon drum shower,
and miscellaneous other jobs. They also bought things
from the villagers: their hats; sodas; beer; sometimes
cigarettes, dolls, and bolts of cloth to send home to sisters and girlfriends; and hurricane lamps and kerosene
to burn in them. The infusion of money gave a bit of
slack to the villagers, who didn't have to work as long
and hard at farming and fishing just to make ends meet.
And, once the local VC were wiped out, they got to stop
paying taxes to the VC and that meant more disposable
income for everyone. Some of the families went into
business on the banks of the Song Du Ong river making
sun-baked adobe bricks that lasted longer than bamboo
and thatch. Now most of the hootches in Hou Ky and
Hou Dau had brick sides, and some even had corrugated
tin roofs. Many of the hootches in the other hamlets were
new brick construction as well.

Thien, the hamlet chief, lived in a French-made structure near the center of Hou Ky. The building was laid out in an ell, with the short leg wider than the thinner long leg. Thien and his family lived in the short leg; village elders whom the war had left without adult children to care for them in their old age dwelled in stalls in the long leg. Between the building's wings was a patio of hard packed dirt, surrounded on its other two sides by a low wall. A flagpole flying the scarlet-striped, golden banner of South Vietnam stood in the center of that patio. Thien was sitting alone on a bench that circled the foot of the flagpole.

Bell, Lewis, and Robertson put down the little ones they were carrying amidst gleeful screams for more rides. They talked gently with the children and promised if they left them alone now, they could have more rides later. The children ran away shrieking and laughing. The three Marines looked after them for a moment, then entered the dirt patio square. Some of the children creeped back and watched the men talking inside the walls.

"*Chao, Ong,*" Bell said, and bowed slightly to the hamlet headman. Thien was ten years older than his brother, but too many years of warfare had drawn deep lines in his face and he looked like an old man rather than the middle-aged one he was.

Thien stood and bowed to the tall American sergeant. "*Chao, Trung si,*" he said, then gestured at the bench. He offered them tepid tea, which they gratefully accepted. Rural Vietnamese always drank tea: the heat and humidity forced them to drink quantities of water to avoid dehydration and heat prostration, but because their water was full of cholera and typhus microbes and other such nasty little beasties, they had to boil it before it could be safely drunk, so they flavored the water with tea. Bell sat next to Thien with Lewis on his other side. Robertson sat opposite them.

Vietnamese is a tonal language; the inflections as well as the sounds of the phonemes that form words combine to make sense. A rising vowel sound in a word otherwise spelled and pronounced exactly the same gives the word a totally different meaning. For example: *ro*, with a descending inflection, is the verb to leak; with a rising inflection, it means a type of basket woven from rushes. Tonal languages are very difficult for many speakers of non-tonal languages to master. Nonetheless, it was Bell's and Lewis's limited vocabularies rather than their pronunciation that made it difficult for them to converse with their host. But they did their best and their best was good enough for them to learn what Thien knew—or suspected—was happening. It helped that Thien knew almost as much American English as Bell and Lewis knew Vietnamese. A very loose translation of the conversation they had in a mix of Vietnamese and English would be something like this:

"Houng is very unhappy," Thien told them. "His wife, Cai Lin, has to stay here because his quarters at the district capital don't have room for her—she also is very unhappy about being separated from her husband. It is the same with most of the other members of the platoon, they are away from their wives and families and miss them. All of them are also concerned about the security of Bun Hou; they do not think," he laughed lightly but looked apologetic, "that you Marines can keep Bun Hou totally safe from the Vietcong without their assistance."

"Are any of them happy to be away?" Bell asked.

Thien hesitated before answering. It didn't seem to be a question he wanted to think about. "I think a few of them, some of the younger men without wives. Maybe four or five of them. They are away in what is to them a big city and they are enjoying themselves in it. And they know they are in little danger from the Vee Cee there, because with the Regional Forces and a company of Arvins and four platoons of Popular Forces there, they are too strong for the Vee Cee to attack them. Those few young men are enjoying themselves, I think. But all of them want to come home because they know there is danger here and they know that here, working with you Marines, they can kill many Vietcong soldiers and win the war. But it does not look like Major Y is going to let them come home any time soon.''

''Assuming they don't come back to Bun Hou soon, can we do anything about raising another fay-epp platoon to take their place?''

The old-looking man shook his head. ''Not unless Major Y will give us the money to pay for another platoon. I do not think he will do that, though. What I have heard is, he has told the province chief he was able to take the fay-epps out of Bun Hou because they are so good they have totally eliminated the Vee Cee threat here.''

That last statement made Lewis blink and shake his head. ''Where the hell did he get that idea?'' he demanded. ''We're intercepting Charlie almost every other night, and a week ago they tried to overrun Camp Apache again.''

Thien shrugged with resignation. ''This is not a question I can answer,'' he told them, then stared blank-eyed into nowhere for a long moment. ''I think,'' he finally said slowly, ''that maybe Major Y wants the Marines to go away from Bun Hou the same as Captain Phang wanted you to leave.''

''Goddamn!'' Bell swore and threw his bush hat onto the ground. One of the more adventurous of the children who had come back to watch the Marines talk with their hamlet chief jumped over the low wall and darted in to pick up the sergeant's hat and solemnly hand it back. Bell absently rubbed the boy's head and thanked him. He ran off squealing his delight and laughing at his playmates who were less bold than he. ''We just got rid of one corrupt son of a bitch,'' Bell continued, not really aware of the brief interruption, ''who was trying to get rid of us so he could keep screwing you people, and now you're telling me there's another one picking up right where he left off. That is what you're saying, isn't it? That Major Y is a bad man the same as Captain Phang was.''

The hamlet chief shrugged again and spread his hands wide. "All functionaries wish to become rich," he said. "That is why they become government officials instead of being farmers or fishermen or merchants, who are generally honest men. Government officials are like landlords, they get rich off of other people rather than from their own work."

"Are you sure Major Y wants to get rid of us the same as Phang did?"

"This is what I hear, and that concept certainly makes sense." Bell's questions slightly puzzled Thien, their answers were so obvious. But it didn't occur to him to ask if things were not the same in America. If he had, Bell might have told him they were different where he came from. In America, Bell might have said, lawyers and politicians—who started as lawyers and wrote the laws so that only other lawyers could understand what they meant—were the ones who craved riches from the people rather than from their own work. It wasn't the bureaucrats and landlords who were most corrupt in America.

"Shit." Bell cut the conversation short and thanked Thien as profusely as he could in a hurry. He led Lewis and Robertson back to Camp Apache at a pace barely slower than a trot. They left behind a growing group of disappointed children who didn't understand why they didn't get the rides their Marines promised they'd get later.

"We got us a problem," Bell told Lieutenant Burrison as soon as he found him. "We've got to check it out and, if it's true, get it straightened out most ricky-tick or Bun Hou's going to wind up back in Charlie's hands." Then he told him about his conversation with Thien. Lewis interrupted several times to confirm and amplify what Bell had to say. Robertson only answered the few questions addressed directly to him.

"I'll try to get together with Captain Hasford tomorrow,'' Burrison said when his number one finished. ''But first we've got to deal with tonight. Let's send Tex and Zeke out with Tex in charge.''

''Sounds good to me,'' Bell said.

CHAPTER FOUR

That Night

The sun hadn't set yet so there was no need to light lamps, but the side flaps of the rifle squad's tent were down and lashed in blackout anyway. The kerosene lamps casting feeble light through the tent did nothing to dispel the darkness gathering in the corners of the tent and puddling under the cots and under the makeshift tables set next to them. The Marines didn't want anyone watching from the trees to be able to see what they were doing. Inside the tent Burrison and Bell sat in silence watching Corporal Tex Randall prepare his patrol. Wells jumped in place so Randall could check him for loose gear, making sure he wouldn't clank in the night. Dodd seemed totally disinterested in the entire process. His expression was that of a man who didn't know where he was—and didn't care. Neither man made any sound other than the thudding of his boots on the tent's floor when he jumped. Camouflage paint sticks had drawn lines of green in three different shades across the high points of their faces, necks, hands and arms to break up the outlines and dull the shiny places. Their rifles were loaded with twenty-round magazines and they each carried as many more as their cartridge belts would hold. Their knives and bayonets slid smoothly in their scabbards.

"You already check your people, Zeke?" Randall asked Corporal Ruizique.

"You know it, gringo," Ruizique answered, surly. Webster and Neissi were as silent and night-shadowed as Wells and Dodd were.

"Hop."

Fire danced at the other man from Ruizique's eyes. "Did I ask you to hop for me?"

"No, but I'm going to tell you to listen when I do. Now hop."

Ruizique did without further comment, but it was obvious he didn't like it.

Randall kept his eyes on the crossed bandoliers and listened carefully for them to make noise. They were dull-colored and silent. "Now it's my turn," he said when he was satisfied the other corporal was ready for the night.

Lewis lounged on his cot, watching the inspection with amusement. "Shee-it," he said after the two NCOs finished checking each other, "the way you two acting anybody'd think this was some kind of big deal." He shook his head. "Hell, I did it my own damn self while you were in the brig, ain't no big deal."

"We weren't in no fucking brig, Billy Boy," Randall snapped.

"Okay, you weren't in the brig. You were under house arrest. Samee-same, you were locked up," Lewis said, and rolled off his cot, and before anybody could respond he ducked out of the tent to check himself in the brief twilight. He was the only man in the platoon who was never inspected for noise before going on a night patrol; he inspected himself and was always right. They heard the soft thumping of his boots as he jumped by the side of the tent.

"Is it night yet?" Randall asked. No air moved inside the closed tent and he was sweating, as well as being nervous about taking out the only patrol for the night. Tango Niner's usual three patrols could support each other and sometimes come to each other's aid. One patrol alone, even though it wasn't scheduled to go any farther than a klick and a half from Camp Apache, felt more isolated and endangered.

Burrison looked at his watch. "No. Another fifteen minutes."

"Kill the lights," Bell said. "Start getting your night vision now." It takes twenty minutes for the irises and cones to adjust all the way for the best seeing in the dark, and the patrol was going out minutes after the sun set. Everyone who had a lamp lit blew into its chimney to put out the flame, then damped the wick to stop its smoldering. The darkness in the tent became complete, it was as though they were all suddenly blinded.

"Go over it again, Tex," Burrison's quiet voice slammed through the darkness like a blunderbuss a few minutes later. "What are you going to do out there?"

"We're going to go north and then swing west around Hou Ky," Randall said softly, "then sweep south through the woods until we reach the river. We'll watch over Hou Binh Island for a couple of hours. Any place else I think it's a good idea, we'll lay a hasty ambush for as long as I want to—I'll let you know when and where I set them. We come in at dawn."

"Hou Binh is a waste," Ruizique said, so low he almost wasn't heard. "Charlie hasn't used it in months."

"That's exactly why we have to look at it now, Zeke," Burrison said. Setting an ambush overlooking the deserted hamlet on a small island in the river was his idea.

"Charlie might have the idea we've forgotten how he used to use it as a rest stop."

Ruizique didn't answer.

Gradually the Marines' eyes began to discern shapes in the darkened tent, shapes of waiting men and inert cots and tables and the couple of guitars hanging from the overhead cross beam. Eventually Burrison looked at his watch again and said, "It's time."

"Let's go," Randall said, rising to his feet. They filed out of the blackness of the tent into a night flooded with starlight. The contrast made it seem almost like day. "Billy Boy," Randall said into the shadows next to the tent, "take point."

Lewis emerged from the shadows and nodded. He cradled his rifle in the crooks of his arms, clenched his hands in front of his face, and twisted. When his hands came away the left end of his mustache curled down around and under the corner of his mouth, the right end twisted up in a tight curl. Lewis led the way to the main gate and through it. Wells fell into step behind him and Randall came next with his PRC-6 walkie-talkie radio slung on his shoulder. Then came Dodd. Ruizique followed between Webster and Neissi. When the last of them passed through, Zeitvogel directed his men in rolling the plugs of concertina barbed wire that closed the gate at night into place.

The land was open north of Camp Apache and the patrolling Marines clearly saw starlight sparkling on the rice paddies a few hundred meters ahead. Somewhere to the east a dog barked, causing the Marines to tense for a moment. Another dog answered the first bark, then both fell quiet. By the time the Marines reached the path bordering the paddies they had relaxed again and were paying attention only to their immediate area. Lewis turned left and walked parallel to the paddy path. Ahead of them they saw occasional orange glowing lamps in the hootches of Hou Ky hamlet. Soon those lamps would blink out, either from being put out or from shutters being closed over hootch windows. As they got closer they could hear a radio playing Vietnamese music. That too would soon be turned off. There were no other lights or sounds. When they walked past Hou Ky they saw no movement on the paths between the hootches. The night was quiet in town, just as they expected it to be. Anyone looking from the paddies would have been able to spot the Marines as clouds that momentarily occluded the orange lamp lights visible in some hootches. But there wasn't anybody in the silent, sparkling paddies.

The patrol from Camp Apache's main gate to the paddies and around Hou Ky was less than two kilometers, but the Marines went slowly and took an hour to cover the distance. They stopped frequently to listen to the night. They heard nothing out of place. Before they slipped into the woods south of the trail leading from Hou Ky to the hills, Randall looked to the west. The ridges and hills stood as a ragged-topped black wall underneath the blackness of the sky, which was only distinguishable by the stars glittering sequinlike in it. He wished there was another patrol out in this area west of Camp Apache; he'd go to the foot of the finger ridge that came down from the hills if there was one. He wondered how many VC would come down that ridge tonight, how many he could catch if he had a backup and could go there. Or how many would pass through the cleft south of there, where the Song Du Ong emptied onto its flood plain.

A few meters away from Randall, Ruizique also looked at the black wall of the ridges and hills. He imagined his arm ached where a VC machine gun bullet had torn through it, and the aching made him want revenge. He wanted to go to that finger ridge even without backup. But he wasn't the patrol leader and the decision wasn't his. Cowardly gringo, he thought. Idly, he fingered the bullets in his crossed bandoliers.

Randall sighed almost audibly and signaled Lewis to move into the trees. He gave his pointman his head and

let him lead them on a meandering route through the
forest. Lewis was the best of them at night movement
and had an uncanny sense of danger. He wouldn't walk
them into a trap. A half hour and half a kilometer south
of Hou Ky, Randall pulled his patrol into an ambush position overlooking a little-used trail. If the Vietcong knew
about this trail they might use it, thinking it was forgotten and ignored. He radioed in their position, using dead
reckoning to determine where they were. He gave an az-
imuth and range as a checkpoint for the mortar, a registration point that was sure to miss his position while
still being close enough for him to direct it into where
he needed it. If they needed support from the mortar.
Forty-five uneventful minutes later he pulled the ambush
and they continued southward, this time with a slight
angle toward the east. Two hasty ambushes and four hours
later, they reached the bank of the Song Du Ong across
from the small, sandy island on which sat the deserted
hamlet called Hou Binh.

The river broadened out and slowed down a little bit
upstream from the island and bent in a broad "U" to the
south of it. Sand bars formed and disappeared in the
shallower water until first weeds, and later bushes, flowers, and a few trees took root on one of them and stabi-
lized it. That sand bar grew until it became a small island
in the stream. Eventually, a few families of fishermen
settled on it and quietly plied their trade and flourished.
They built their palm frond and bamboo houses at the
broad, western end of the island and dug their graveyard
at the narrower eastern end. But the war had changed
everything and ended their prosperity. Small bands of
Vietcong traveling east and west along the Song Du Ong
flood plain saw the island as a good place to stop and
rest for a bit. They could see all avenues of approach,
and if government soldiers—or later, Americans—came
along, they could get away before they arrived. It was
also a good place for them to reprovision—the Vietcong
always took fish and other food from the villagers in Hou

Binh. So did the ARVNs who came looking for the VC.
The people of Hou Binh no longer flourished, they became poorer than the farmers and other fishermen who
lived in hamlets near the river. So they moved. Some
went downstream to Hou Cau, the market hamlet, others
went farther downstream to hamlets of other villages.
The Vietcong kept coming, though. Even if they couldn't
get food they could still rest in a safe place. Until the
Marines of Tango Niner moved into the neighborhood.
The Marines developed tactics that enabled them to slip
unnoticed to the river's edge and watch the island. When
they saw movement on it they called in a mortar barrage
and opened fire with their rifles. After a few months
Charlie decided Hou Binh wasn't a safe place anymore.
He hadn't been known to use it as a rest stop for two or
three months now, and the Marines stopped watching it.
It was time to look again, just in case.

"This is a waste of time, Tex," Ruizique whispered
at Randall when he set the seven-man patrol in place to
watch the island. He selected a spot where they could
watch the island, the ford leading from the north side of
the river to the west end of the island, and both ap-
proaches to that ford. "Charlie isn't going to come here,
he knows it's too dangerous for him. He's going to be
somewhere else and we're going to miss him."

"It's not a waste, Zeke," Randall whispered back.
"We're the only people out tonight, we have just as much
chance of catching his ass here as anywhere else. And
it's like Scrappy said, maybe Charlie thinks we forgot
about this place. We wait here." He didn't wait to see
what else Ruizique would say about the ambush site, he
moved on to the next man. They had several hours until
sunrise and were going to stay where they were until false
dawn. He put his men in a circle and divided them into
three pairs. He assigned one pair to watch the island,
one to keep their eyes on the river and the upstream bank,
and the other to cover the downstream bank and the band
of forest behind them. Then he told them one man in each

pair could sleep and one man in each pair had to be awake at all times. He himself would catnap from time to time if he could. The river was black and empty for a half mile upstream. There, clusters of orange lights bobbed on the river—fishermen working at night. If any boats came along without lights, they were considered to be Vietcong and were fair game to be blown out of the water by anyone who saw them. None of the boats came close to the island. The years of war had taught the fishermen to stay clear, even though the fishing might have been better in the shallower water. Reflected starlight danced on the river's rippling waves.

A band of large trees rimmed the river, ranging in width from fifty to one-hundred-and-fifty meters broad. They were heavily foliaged trees that allowed little sunlight to filter through and nourish the sparse undergrowth. The many hard-packed trails paralleling and crossing the area were broad and clear of brush and dried twigs, unlike the narrower, cluttered paths through the scrub forest elsewhere within the village boundaries. The night was blacker under these trees because so little starlight made it through the trees. A man could walk easily along the paths without making noise or being seen by anyone not watching carefully for him. But the Marines were near the river bank and could see more.

Three hours after settling in, Randall finally cradled his head on his folded arms and closed his eyes to sleep. He told Ruizique to wake him in an hour, or sooner if anyone saw anything. It felt like only moments later that he felt Ruizique's tense hand on his shoulder. He flexed his shoulder muscle to tell the other man he was awake and took a few seconds to orient himself to the night sounds before moving. Nothing sounded out of place. He lifted his head far enough to glance at his watch—it was a half hour after he lay down to nap—and looked around. The other corporal seemed to be looking at the river, so Randall swept his gaze across the ford. Oh, shit, he thought. Moving shadows flickered through his view. He looked to the side of where he saw the movement and made out several men wading toward the island. Movement to one side of them caused him to swivel his head again. A line of men was moving from the trees less than fifty meters upstream to ford the river. They were carrying long objects that could only be rifles in their hands. He froze. The men had to be Vietcong, there weren't any South Vietnamese troops or other Marines in the area. There were too many of them for the Marines to handle if they were discovered. Randall froze and hoped all the men in his ambush were also frozen in place. And he especially hoped Ruizique wouldn't do anything. He put a light, restraining hand on the Dominican's shoulder.

He watched and tried to count, but wasn't sure of how many might have disappeared onto the island before he first spotted them, or how many his peripheral vision might have missed. The best way to look at something at night is to look at its side, not directly at it. He estimated twenty-five VC left the trees he was under and crossed to the island. He waited, squeezing Ruizique's arm, for several minutes after the last of the VC seemed to vanish onto the island before he dared breathe easily again.

"I counted twenty-five," he whispered. "How many did you see?"

"About that many," Ruizique answered. There was a tremble in his voice, a tremble born of excitement, not fear. "Let's get Big Louie on the horn and get him to help us waste those mother fuckers."

"You got it. Get everybody else lined up facing the river." He started talking into his radio as Ruizique hurried to prepare the others to fire at the people who had crossed to the island. Bell had radio watch and Randall gave his report to him. "Wait one, Panther Cub," Bell said after getting all the facts. He wanted to wake Burrison as well as prepare the mortar team for its fire mission.

While he waited for Bell to get back to him, Randall checked the new ambush line along the river's edge.

Everyone was watching the island, all were alert and ready to go.

"What's the matter, Tex," Ruizique said, an ironic tone to his voice, "don't you trust me to do it right?"

"Shut up, Zeke. I just needed to see what you did so I wouldn't make any mistakes." Yes, Randall trusted the other man to set them in well, but he was in command and had to know where everybody was placed. Bell came back on the radio before any more could be said between the two.

"Panther Cub, Big Cat. Can you see them on the island?" the sergeant asked.

"Affirmative, Cat." He paused and stared, startled, at the island for a moment. "I don't fucking believe that. They're lighting a fire inside one of the hootches."

The palm frond and bamboo hootches on the island hadn't been repaired in nearly a year. Between that and the frequent mortar and rifle fire they had received in the time the Marines were convincing Charlie Hou Binh wasn't a safe place for them to stay, the hootches all had drooping walls and collapsing roofs. Some had fallen down altogether, leaving only a main support beam or two standing.

"Are they all in the hootch area, Cub? Over," Bell asked.

"As near as I can see, Cat," Randall answered. "I see zero movement in the graveyard. Over."

"Panther Cub, stand by for spotter round. Round two will be a light."

"Standing by."

Camp Apache's hill was due north and one or two hundred meters east of Hou Binh. Tango Niner's 81mm mortar had fired on the deserted hamlet so many times in the past, Randall knew Slover would have no problem adjusting its tube to put the first round smack in the middle of the small group of broken houses. To his rear he heard the *carrumph*ing of two rounds exploding out of the mortar tube. Seconds later there came the distinctive whistling of a rapidly descending mortar round from almost directly overhead. The first round erupted at almost the same instant the second illumination round flashed its eerie, blue light over the island.

Randall didn't even look to see exactly where the spotter round hit, he knew it was on target. "Fire for effect," he said into his radio. "Pick your targets," he shouted to his men. "Let's tango, take those fuckers out, waste them!" He listened for Bell to confirm the mortar was going to fire a barrage of six rounds into the area the first one hit, then looked down the length of his rifle barrel, searching for a target. He saw a black-clad figure running for cover, led it, and rapidly pulled the trigger three times. The runner flopped to the dirt, and he looked for another. He saw three more figures and heard their screams; each was being slammed down by hits from the rifles of his Marines. Then the island exploded with the blasts of the six mortar rounds striking it. Slover spaced them perfectly. The 81mm mortar had a killing radius of 20-by-25 meters; the six rounds landed so that the edges of each round's killing zone overlapped its neighbor's— they blanketed the area of the hootches with a minimal overlap. Randall didn't see anyone else standing on the island after that.

"Cease fire," Randall called to his men. Then, "Beautiful, Big Cat!" he said into the radio's mouthpiece. "Do it again, Big Louie."

"Roger, Cub. On the way," Bell said back.

"How many did we get?" Randall asked his men.

"I wasted one, maybe two," Ruizique said gleefully.

"I think I got two," Lewis answered.

"I got one," Webster.

"I shot at one and he fell down," Dodd said questioningly. "Does that count?"

"Did he get back up?"

"I don't think so."

"It counts," Randall said. "Anybody else?"

"Everyone I saw was already eating lead from somebody else,'' Wells complained. Wells was a tough juvenile delinquent and actually talked that way.

Neissi didn't say anything.

Six more mortar rounds erupted and their shrapnel scythed death across the island.

Bell called again, asking what was going on. He didn't hear the ambush firing.

"They're staying down, Cat," Randall told him, "out of the way of the mortars, and we can't see them to shoot at. Send another light and fire another of the same, over." The first flare had drifted under its parachute almost to the ground. "We got six, maybe seven," he added when Bell told him another flare round was on its way, followed by six more high explosive rounds. The mortar *carrumph*ed on Camp Apache's hill, but seconds before the illumination round reached its pop-open point the first flare hit the ground and fizzed out. The last of the third salvo of six HE rounds left the tube before the second flare popped open. It lit men running to the far side of the small island. The Vietcong had taken advantage of the brief darkness to flee to the south side of the river.

"Get them!" Ruizique screamed and started blasting across the river with his rifle.

"Pick your targets," Randall yelled and fired at the backs of a VC. Then into his radio, "They're running, Cat. Put two groups of six in the river south of the island and then six on the south shore." Then he was too busy trying to knock down the fleeing enemy to hear Bell's answering "roger."

In another half minute it was over. The Vietcong hadn't fired a shot back at the Marines. Burrison told Randall to take his patrol across to the island, count bodies, and treat any wounded they found. They waited until the flare burning above the hootches went out before stepping into the open river and wading through the knee-deep water. While they were crossing the ford to the island, Randall looked upstream. The fishermen in their lighted boats had all headed for shore so they wouldn't be caught in the open during a firefight.

Once they were on the island, Randall set three men on the south side to watch for returning VC, then called for more illumination to aid in the search. They found fourteen VC, all but one dead, half from rifle rounds. They patched up the wounded man, but weren't certain he'd make it through the night, and stacked the dead together. A few more blood trails led to the river. A dozen rifles had been left behind, and they took more than a thousand rounds off the bodies. There were only a few documents on the bodies; Randall pocketed them. He set a watch rotation for the rest of the night, three men awake, three sleeping. He'd catnap if he could.

The wounded man died before the sun rose in the east.

CHAPTER FIVE

During the Next Couple of Days

A heavy haze lay over the island when the sun peeked over the rim of the South China Sea, far to the east. Randall stirred. The noise his men made talking among themselves and searching the island and bodies again in the feeble light of dawn woke him from the light sleep he had finally drifted into little more than an hour earlier. He sat up and groaned. His mouth tasted foul and his back ached from sleeping on the dewy ground. He stood up slowly and stretched, bending forward and twisting his back about, working the stiffness from it. His thighs still felt heavy, but he'd walk that out soon enough.

"A good night's catch, Tex."

Randall turned to see Ruizique grinning at him, eyes glistening. "Yah, a good night's catch," he repeated, then hawked to clear his throat and spat. He walked to the south side of the river, unbuttoned his fly, and urinated into the water while eyeing the south bank of the river. He saw only trees on the other side.

"Radio," Lewis called to him.

He went to Lewis and took the offered PRC-6. This morning, the right side of Lewis's mustache jutted almost straight up, the left swept gracefully down and out in a classic handlebar. "Panther Cub Actual, go," he said into the mouthpiece.

"Panther Cub Actual, this is Big Cat Actual," Burrison's voice said to him. "How did things go? Over."

"Quiet as a church mouse, Big Cat," Randall answered. "Over."

"Glad to hear that, Cub. Do another check of your location in case you missed anything last night. Let me know whether or not you find anything new, then come on in. Do you understand? Over."

"I understand, Big Cat Actual. Wilco, over."

"Panther Cub Actual, this is Big Cat Actual. Roger, out."

"Roger out," Randall muttered. "Let's give this place a last once-over," he shouted to his men. "Line up on me," he said, walking to the west end of the hootch area, near the south side of it. "Keep it on line, five-meter intervals. Look at everything, watch out for booby traps. Call it out if you see anything. Move."

The seven Marines lined up, Randall's own fire team on one side of him, Ruizique and his two men on the other. They went slowly through the hamlet searching its southern half, wheeled around and went back through the northern half of it. They didn't find anything more and he radioed that in.

"Pick up the weapons and ammunition. We're going home. Wells, you've got the point, move it."

Less than an hour later they were back inside Camp Apache. Randall gave Burrison and Bell a brief report while the other men from the patrol went into their squad tent to sleep. When his leaders were satisfied they had enough information and that if they didn't they could get more later, he followed his men into the tent. He stripped down to his skivvy drawers, lay belly down on his cot with his left arm dangling over the cot's side, hand touching his rifle, and fell immediately into deep sleep.

"Yo, Scrappy," Swearin' Swarnes called out from the entrance to his radio room, "that goddamn railroad tracker's hauling ass the fuck back out here. Be here in about fifteen fuckers."

Burrison was sitting in the open air on an upended ammo crate at a makeshift table made from a sheet of galvanized metal laid over a sandbag base. Tango Niner's NCOs were sitting around the table with him, and two topographical maps of the area were open in front of them on the table. Burrison looked blankly at Swarnes for a moment, then his eyes lit up with understanding and he shouted back his thanks. Sometimes what Swearin' Swarnes said came out in a sort of code and needed to be interpreted. He wasn't given his nickname for its onomatopoetic resonance, you know. He got it the old-fashioned way—he earned it, by being the most foul-mouthed member of Tango Niner. His current message was, Captain Hasford was coming back out and would arrive in fifteen minutes.

Big Louie Slover's shoulder and chest muscles rippled under his black skin. "No sweat," he said. "He comes close enough, I got my Ping-Pong paddles in my hip pocket."

The others laughed and shook their heads. None of them would bring in a helicopter without wearing a shirt. Even though they kept the helipad area largely clear of debris, the dust the chopper's downwash kicked up would thickly coat their skin, and they'd rather not have that happen. They returned their attention to the maps.

"You're right," Bell said, picking the discussion up where it had stopped when Swarnes shouted his message, "there's no way from what you saw to know whether they came down the ridge or followed the river down from the mountains."

"Or if they came south from the paddies," Zeitvogel added.

"We don't even know if they planned to go to the other side of the river, or if they just stopped to rest on the island and we made them dee dee in a direction they hadn't planned on," Randall said.

"So much for scientific analysis," Burrison said. "Tonight we have to go for potluck again." He lifted his head and gazed toward the northeast. "Damn, I wish we had our fay-epps back. We could put everybody out and have one bodacious chance of catching Charlie with his pants down."

They mulled over the maps for a few more minutes, kicking about this idea and that. But the only thing they could come up with was an approximate repeat of what they had done the night before. Tonight Zeitvogel and Ruizique's fire teams would be the patrol, with Flood, from the mortar team, joining them to bring the patrol up to seven men. Zeitvogel would be in charge. Then two helicopters were in sight and Slover took his place facing into the wind across the helipad.

Hasford jumped out and ran to Burrison as soon as the bird was close enough to the ground for him to leap out without injuring himself. "Who was last night's patrol leader?" he asked. "Bring him and his fire team, I want to take a look at this."

A few minutes later Lewis and Wells were stomping around Hou Binh, swearing and kicking at hootch walls and everything else standing more than an inch off the ground. Dodd stood off to one side, looking nowhere in particular. Hasford, Burrison, and Randall were standing where the VC bodies had been stacked.

"Well," said the intelligence captain, "I can tell by the bloodstains you had a bunch of bodies here. Those little fuckers sure work fast."

All fourteen VC bodies were gone and someone had started to sweep the earth where they had fallen clean of traces.

"At least we got a dozen weapons to prove it," Randall said.

"That won't convince anybody doesn't want to believe it," Hansford said. "Tango Niner's been doing so much ass-kicking on Charlie you've got a bigger arsenal of Vee Cee weapons than Ho Chi Minh does. How are you going to prove you got those weapons last night and not a couple of months ago?"

"That's bullshit, Captain, and you know it," Randall snorted, but he grinned, pleased at the compliment.

"Why wouldn't anybody want to believe it?" Burrison asked.

Hasford looked at him blandly and said, "Because your friendly local district chief has gone to Division G-2 and told them what a great job Tango Niner's done."

Both CAP Marines blinked at that surprising message.

"He says you've been so damn good at what you do, Charlie doesn't hang on the block in Bun Hou anymore."

Burrison's jaw worked for a moment before he found his voice. "That's a crock," he finally said.

"If Charlie isn't hanging on the block in Bun Hou anymore, who the fuck did we waste here last night?" Randall demanded.

"Where are the bodies?" Hasford asked him.

Randall looked glum and Burrison angry. They both knew the next step for Major Y was to get them pulled from Bun Hou, just like Thien had said he was going to do. They couldn't go yet, the job here wasn't finished, not by a long shot.

"Don't sweat it," Hasford said. "I know as well as you do this is a favorite infiltration route for Charlie's supplies and replacements. I also know some people in Division G-2 and G-3 I can convince of that." He paused before saying, "It'll help me convince them if I can have a couple of those AKs you got last night to souvenir them with."

Burrison looked at the captain. He said in a serious voice, "Sounds like bribery to me," but his eyes twinkled while he said it.

"I prefer to think of it as greasing the wheels," Hasford said in just as serious a voice, but he too smiled when he said it.

"How many do you need?" Burrison asked.

Fifteen minutes later the Tango Niner Marines were back in Camp Apache and Hasford was flying back to Division headquarters with four of the rifles and all of the documents Randall's patrol had captured the night before. Zeitvogel's patrol that night was uneventful. The next day Captain Hasford came back with better news.

"Like I said yesterday," Hasford told Burrison, Bell, and the corporals, "I know some people in intelligence and operations I could convince Charlie's just as active in Bun Hou as he's been for the past several months. They're on our side now thanks to those documents you gave me. And, in part, thanks to the souvenirs you gave them. But CAP comes under G-5, Civic Affairs. They're willing to believe me, but do you have any Vee Cee flags or officers sidearms? The major there says rifles are a dime a dozen and sometimes get caught in contraband searches on the way back to The World."

"Shee-it!" Zeitvogel said. "I'll bet every goddamn little rinky-dink, rear-area, mother fucking pogue in Eye Corps takes home more combat souvenirs than any grunt does." He looked off to the side, out toward the hills and ridges in the west. He screwed his mouth in disgust and added, "Let me get my hands on one of them shitheads, I'll roll him up and turn his fat ass into a roundball I'll dribble on a schoolyard back in Philadelphia and throw them through the hoops a few times. Flatten his ass most ricky-tick."

Hasford laughed. "Cut them a break, Stilts," he said. "Most of the staff officers above the rank of captain don't have any combat experience, the same goes for a lot of

the lieutenants and captains and staff NCOs. They need
the souvenirs because they're missing out on all the fun.
They won't have all the memories you will.''

Ruizique snorted. ''If they think this is fun they should
come out here and go on patrol with me one night when
eight or ten of us find twenty Vee Cee and the Vee Cee
shoot back at us. Then see if they still think being a man
is a game.''

Hasford looked at the corporal from the Dominican
Republic and said, ''I know what it's like out there, Zeke.
Let them have their little dreams.'' Then to all of them,
''The wheels are turning, you're going to get your little
people back and then you can go back to putting a proper
hurting on Charlie. Just be patient, it might take a couple
of weeks.''

The CAP Marines looked at each other, wondering
what the next two weeks might be like if they were left
alone. Especially after Hasford dropped his bad news on
them.

''As for what's over there,'' the captain pointed west,
''Three MAF G-2 knows something's there, but not what.
G-3 says resources are spread far too thin as is with
known high-priority targets. Unless something big
breaks, it's going to be months before so much as a recon
team can be sent to check it out.''

''What about an air strike to mess them up?'' Burrison
asked.

''Do you know exactly where to put it?'' Hasford
asked. ''That's double-canopy jungle over there and they
don't know where anything is. Where the hell are they
going to drop their bombs to make them do any good?''
He shook his head. ''An air strike is out.''

Before he left, Hasford took Randall aside to pass on
a personal message. ''I don't normally put vulgarisms in
the mouths of women no matter what they say, but I was
told to give you this verbatim. Bobbie Harder says if you
don't get your young ass back to Da Nang in a hurry so
she can take you on another picnic, she's going to come

out here to make sure you're still alive. And if she has to come out here to find nothing's wrong with you, she's going to bring a rolling pin and ram it up that young ass of yours.'' Randall turned red at that and Hasford laughed. When he stopped he said, ''She's a fine girl, Tex. As soon as the two men you've got on R&R come back I think you should take a couple days off and go see her.''

''Thanks, sir,'' Randall stammered and blushed even deeper. Bobbie Harder had that effect on him, she could make him turn red despite his deep-baked tan. ''Tell her I'll do that as soon as Short Round and the Fast Talking Man get back.''

Then Hasford was gone and Randall was left alone to face his buddies and try to explain why he was blushing. He didn't explain it very well and turned even redder.

''I do believe that man's going to bust wide open from high blood pressure,'' Zeitvogel said.

CHAPTER SIX

November 21, 1966, Night

"You want Billy Boy on the point?" Randall asked Stilts Zeitvogel while they were inspecting their men before going out.

"Only if you give him to me and you have the short fire team," Zeitvogel answered.

"What do you mean, they get the short team," Mazzucco said. "We get Billy Boy, we have the short one." He started patting the air one-handed and shifting from side to side. "Come on, Honcho, let's do a little one-on-one before we go out."

"Shee-it," Zeitvogel snorted and swiped a huge hand at Mazzucco's head. Mazzucco ducked under it. "You think you're such hot shit on the court, tell you what I'm gonna do. I'm gonna get me a roundball and something to use as a basket. I'll go one-on-one with you," he paused and looked around to make sure everyone was listening to him, "just as soon as I'm sure I got a replacement coming in. Because when I go one-on-one with you, you gonna die, mother fucker."

"Bullshit, Stilts. You're so damn long and gangly you'll trip over your own damn feet, fall down and hurt yourself trying to block me," Mazzucco said, still patting the air and bobbing from side to side.

Zeitvogel stretched to his full height—the crown of his bush hat was more than six-and-a-half feet above the soles of his combat boots—and pointed down at the other man. "You're on, homeboy. I'm getting me a roundball and show your ass up," he boomed. "I'll even spot you Rick Barry." Then he dropped the pointing arm and said more quietly, "You can chicken out any time you want to until I get the basket hung and I won't say anything. You got more balls than brains to say in public you want to go one-on-one against me in roundball. I was a schoolyard champ three years running before I joined this man's Crotch." Zeitvogel called Mazzucco "homeboy" because they were both from Philadelphia.

Mazzucco looked at him quizzically. "I played for Bishop Neumann, what school'd you play for?" he asked.

"Didn't play for no pussy-assed school," Zeitvogel said in an offended tone. "High school league roundball had too many rules and fouling out. I played schoolyard ball." He started a description of a sport that sounded like basketball played with tackle football rules but was interrupted by Randall.

"We got to cut the lights and get ready to move out."

"Right. Everybody put out your lights."

"Or you'll punch them out, right, Stilts?" Mazzucco asked, laughing.

"Shut up, homeboy. Time to get serious, we got to get ready for work."

The lamps in the tent were blown out and the Marines left each other alone, each with his own thoughts in preparation for the night's patrol. Outside they heard the thump of Lewis's boots as he hopped to check himself for noise. Fifteen minutes later the six Marines emerged from the tent to line up for the night's patrol.

"Billy Boy, you got point," Zeitvogel said.

"You're in Stilts's fire team for tonight," Randall added.

Through the long night, Burrison and Bell took turns with Swarnes on radio watch. There were no battle sounds except for a few distant fire fights and some harassment and interdiction artillery fire. None of that had anything to do with Tango Niner. Every half hour, Zeitvogel called in with a terse "situation as before" radio report. Twice he signaled he was moving into a hasty ambush to see if anything walked into his killing zone. Each time Burrison or Bell came on watch, he went around the perimeter to check the defensive positions. Big Louie Slover and two of his mortarmen were in the mortar pit. Otherwise there were six two-man positions looking over the defensive wire, one on each gate, one covering the east side of the hill, and three on the west. One man was awake in each position. Doc Tracker sat with Swearin' Swarnes in one of the three western positions. Doc Rankin, the senior corpsman, held radio watch with Burrison and Bell and served as a supernumerary to replace anyone who got sick overnight.

A three-foot-deep trench, wide enough for a man to walk through without having to sidle, circled Camp Apache a few meters inside the inner of three banks of concertina wire; the wire was filled with trip flares and Claymore mines. Shorter lengths of trench connected the command bunker, mortar pit, and the living bunkers next to the squad tents that housed the rifle and weapons squads to the perimeter trench. A couple of other trenches crossed the compound to allow men to quickly go from one side to the other without exposing themselves to grazing fire across the top of the hill. Every thirty or so meters around the perimeter, the trench was widened to make a position in which two men could fight without blocking the passage of others moving along it. These positions were far too thin to defend Camp Apache from a concerted enemy assault even if they were all manned. Only six of the twenty-six were occupied. All any of them could do was alert the rest of the compound if someone was coming. And each had a front nearly one hundred and forty meters wide to cover. Each rifleman had five hundred rounds and twenty hand grenades. The automatic rifles had more ammunition and the machine gun had four thousand rounds.

Burrison woke Bell at 0300 for radio watch. Bell sat up and yawned, rubbed the sleep grit from his eyes, and stood up to stretch. "I'm going to make the rounds," he said quietly. "Notify Swarnes and Tracker I'm coming." Battery-operated ground-wire telephones connected all of the fighting positions and the mortar pit to the command post and to each other.

Bell's first stop was the piss tubes to empty his bladder. Swarnes and Tracker were at the southwest corner of the compound. They were fine, as he knew they would be. They had been through watches like this together before and had decided to stay awake together all night. "If I fall the fuck to sleep on goddamn radio watch tomorrow and miss some asshole calling in, if it's fucking important he'll call back," Swarnes said. He often said people with important calls would try again if he missed a transmission, but so far he hadn't missed an incoming call.

"Call the back gate, let them know I'm on my way," Bell said, and left them. He wasn't having the positions notify the next in line to make sure someone was awake when he arrived; he had them do it so a nervous man wouldn't shoot before checking that it was him instead of a VC. He checked in with the CP when he reached each position to let Burrison know where he was.

Flood and Reid from the mortar team were on the back

gate. "Man, I can't wait until these two hours are up and I can wake Jughead for his next watch," Flood said to Bell. Reid was called Jughead because his first name was Archie, like in the comic books. "This is one slow night out here. Nothing's happening and nothing's going to happen." Then he rang the one position on the hill's east face to alert them to Bell's approach.

Knowles and Vandersteit from the machine gun team held the lone position on the hill's east side. Because that face was too steep to walk up, the Marines felt it was safe to put only one position on that side. Only two banks of barbed wire were there instead of the three around the rest of the hill. Vandersteit had only been with Tango Niner about a week. He was awake and jittery while Knowles slept quietly next to him.

"Damn, I don't like this," Vandersteit said. "This fucking perimeter's so goddamn big we're in shit city if Charlie decides to hit us."

Bell chuckled deep in his chest. "Newby, you talk like you've been hanging with Swearin' Swarnes for too long," he said, and Vandersteit smiled wanly. "Don't worry. If Charlie decides to hit he'll probably probe first to find out where our positions are and get an idea of how many of us are up here." He sat with the new man for a few more minutes, talking quietly, calming his fears. Then he moved on to the main gate. McEntire was waiting for him.

"How's your newby doing, Wall?" Bell asked, tipping his head at the sleeping Kobos.

"He'll do," McEntire answered. "Just wish I got a PFC instead of a lance corporal. Be nice if Knowles could get his BB guns, he's good enough with the gun to be gunner."

Bell shrugged. He agreed with the gun team leader; no one in Tango Niner had been promoted since it was formed—every replacement for men killed or wounded too badly to return had the same rank as the man he replaced—and that wasn't right. But there wasn't anything Bell could do about it. They sat in silence for a few minutes, two men who knew each other well and felt no need to fill the air with jaw noise when they were together. Finally Bell said, "Tell Zeke I'm on my way," and moved to the position near the helipad.

Ruizique was awake while Neissi, his new man, slept. "Staying up all night?" Bell asked. Ruizique had been on watch the last time he came around, and it had been Ruizique's voice he had heard on the ground-wire phone when Burrison had made the rounds in between.

"Charlie's out there," Ruizique said without taking his eyes from the broad area he was watching. "I can feel him. When he comes to tango with us I want to be the first to kill him. The newby," he jerked a thumb at Neissi, "might not spot him early enough to wake me in time to make the first kill."

"Don't push yourself too hard, Zeke. I need you alert and able if we get hit."

"Don't worry about me, Honcho. I was awake all last night and slept well during the day. I'm fine to be awake all night tonight."

Bell stared long at the profile of the corporal from the Dominican Republic. He had changed a great deal after getting wounded. Bell wondered whether the change was for the better. Then he noticed a glistening at the corner of Ruizique's mouth and shuddered: he was salivating in anticipation of a firefight. Bell determined to send him on R&R when Hempen and Pennell came back from theirs, get him out of combat for a few days, give him a chance to return to normal.

He moved on to the last perimeter position, the one he was most concerned about. Malahini Webster and Willard held it. Webster had been the squad's M-79 grenadier until Willard joined Tango Niner. Willard, a lance corporal like Webster, had been a fire team leader in his last company. Bell and Burrison gave him Webster's M-79 and made Webster the automatic rifleman in Ruizique's fire team. That was a reduction in position for each man. Bell thought Willard resented not having a fire team of his own, and he wasn't sure Webster didn't object to having his grenade launcher taken from him. If Tango Niner was going to have a morale problem, these two men would be the first ones affected.

Webster had just woken Willard to take his turn on watch and hadn't yet fallen asleep.

"How's it going?" Bell asked, leaning on the parapet between them.

"Quiet," Webster said.

"No problem," Willard mumbled.

"You two getting along all right?"

"We got enough firepower here to handle anything that comes our way," Willard said, patting the automatic M-14 which was resting on its bipods in front of their fighting position. "Whichever one of us is on watch uses it."

That didn't answer the question. "Good. But how are you two getting along?"

"No problems, Jay Cee," Webster said. "Zeke's a cool dude and Willard's taking good care of my shot-gun."

"Mine," Willard mumbled.

"That's what I said." There was a long moment of silence before Webster added, "No problems, Jay Cee."

"Glad to hear that. Tell whoever's up in the mortar pit the next man he's going to see will probably be me."

Webster reached for the handset of the phone but stopped when he saw Willard grabbing for it. He held his hand in place, halfway between where it had rested on a sandbag and the phone set for a moment before pulling it back. Willard made the call.

Athen and Graham were up in the mortar pit. Slover wasn't leaving his new man alone on watch. He and Athen worked out a rotation where each was up for half of Graham's watches and stood half a watch alone. They seemed ready to use the tube if they needed to. It had taken Bell more than half an hour to check the positions.

"About time you got back," Burrison grumbled.

"Go ahead and get your beauty sleep," Bell said, grinning. "You need it more than any other officer I've ever met."

"Up yours." Burrison grinned back. He closed the flap to their sleeping area and left Bell alone in the radio room.

Vo Hai Bao squatted under the trees east of Camp Apache as night fell. He lifted the captured Starlite scope to his eye when it became dark and counted the seven Marines who exited from the north side of the compound. They traveled west, parallel to the trail leading to Hou Ky. Bao stayed where he was until after midnight, watching the hill. He didn't see any other Marines leave. Then he stood and padded away to where the rest of his platoon waited, halfway between Camp Apache and Hou Cau hamlet.

The Vietcong had mortared Camp Apache, strafed it with machine gun fire, assaulted it with a reinforced company, and attempted to assault it with two platoons. Hitting it with the mortars and machine guns did minimal damage. The reinforced company was met by a defense force that was better prepared and larger than anticipated. The two platoons were detected before they were in position and lost their advantage. Earlier, a squad of sappers from the North Vietnamese Army penetrated the wire only to find the camp undefended. Tango Niner's mortar team then did to those sappers what the sappers had intended to do to the defenders of Camp Apache.

Tango Niner and Camp Apache must be destroyed. It was time to try something different to rid the area of this obstacle. The VC had known of the removal of the Popular Forces platoon from Bun Hou within twenty-four hours after it departed for the district headquarters. They dispatched a scout with a captured Starlite scope, the night observation device that gathered and amplified the light of the moon and stars to see by, to recon the Ma-

rines and see what they were doing in the absence of their
PFs. This was the third consecutive night the scouts
watched a seven-man patrol leave shortly after sunset.
Careful counting of the Marines indicated that Camp
Apache was defended overnight by about eighteen men.
On both of the first two nights that seven-man patrol returned after dawn. There was no reason to think that
tonight the seven-man patrol would return earlier than on
the previous two nights.

Two hours before dawn a platoon, divided into two
sections, would slip into the barbed wire surrounding
Camp Apache. Two squads following a man skilled in
penetrating defensive works would enter it on the south
side of the camp, and a single squad following another
man would penetrate the wire from the north. Infiltration
of the outer and middle banks of wire were thought to be
routine. Infiltration of the inner bank would take place
under the cover of a mortar barrage. Inside the wire, the
first group would split into two squads. The single squad
from the north and one from the other group would move
around the perimeter in a counter-clockwise direction and
kill everyone in the defensive positions. The third squad
was to head straight for the mortar pit and the command
post and dispatch the men in them. The seven-man patrol
would be killed when it returned after dawn. Of course,
that patrol might make a radio check after the command
post was destroyed and would be alerted to trouble if the
base failed to acknowledge their calls, but even if that
happened those seven men would be fairly easy to track
down and kill once the camp was taken care of.

That was the plan.

In 1964 Vo Hai Bao had gone north, where he under-
went extensive training in infiltration techniques, explosives, sabotage, in the use of a wide variety of individual
and crew-served weapons, and other high military skills:
he became a sapper. On his return to the south in late
1965, he was assigned for a year to train other Vietcong

guerrillas as sappers. It was only within the past two weeks that he had been reassigned from a training command to a combat unit. This assault on Camp Apache was his first combat mission in nearly two years, and his first as a sapper. He was leading two squads plus the platoon commander from the south. The best of the men he had been training for the past week and a half was leading the third squad, along with the platoon sergeant in from the north. All he had time to do in that week and a half was teach some basic techniques of penetrating barbed wire and disabling booby traps.

Vo Hai Bao reached the first bank of wire a few minutes after 3:00 A.M. So far the lightly armed men following him had moved in a silence so absolute he had had to look back a few times to be certain he had not lost them. Their ability to move so quietly reassured him of their ability to make it through the wire without alerting the Americans waiting on top of the hill—providing he widened the small openings he would find in the wire enough to admit them. He held no illusions that any of them could slip undetected through the wire with anything approaching his skill.

He stripped off his uniform and lay prone facing the wire. His body was covered with grease, his only garment a loincloth. A bare knife was thrust through the waistband of his loincloth and a small sack filled with cotter pins hung from a cord around his neck. The coils of concertina were tight, but even in the dark his eyes quickly picked a path that would only take him ten minutes to slither through this first bank. He looked more and saw a second path that he couldn't negotiate as quickly, but which had strands of wire he could shift to the side to allow the men behind him to follow without getting hung up. He started through it. The passage was quicker than he had expected, hardly more than fifteen minutes. He had only had to stop once to disable a trip flare by inserting a cotter pin into it. There were two other trip flares he similarly disarmed, because someone else might trip them. He saw no noisemakers or Claymore mines along the path he followed. Twenty minutes after he reached the open ground between the outer and middle banks, the last of the two squads following him was through. By then he had picked his route through the middle bank.

On the north side of the hill another squad did the same in slightly more time.

The middle bank of wire took Vo Hai Bao longer to traverse because the trip flares and Claymores were more numerous in it. He had to disarm five trip flares and three mines. He would have preferred to turn the Claymores around and aim them at the hill's defenders, but the men following him weren't skilled enough to be certain of traversing the wire without accidentally setting the mines off. Vo Hai Bao was at the inner bank of wire ahead of schedule and had to wait for the mortar barrage to start. On the north side, the other squad progressed more slowly because of the inexperience of the man leading it.

Ruizique suddenly became more alert after Bell's visit. There was nothing in particular he noticed, he just had a feeling about the night that he hadn't had before. He looked around more carefully and found his attention more and more focusing on the area between the helipad and the main gate. It was far too dark for him to see anything, and he heard nothing other than the normal night sounds. He picked up his phone and rang the main gate. McEntire answered.

"Wall, do you see anything out there?"

"Not a thing, Zeke," McEntire answered. "What do you got?"

"I don't know. Look at the wire between your position and mine. All I have is a feeling."

The phone in Ruizique's hand was silent for a long moment, then the gun team leader came back on it. "I don't see a damn thing, Zeke."

Ruizique swore under his breath and kept up his visual

search of the wire and the area north of the hill. Still, he found nothing to justify his feeling of something not being right. He got on the phone again and called the mortar pit.

"Athen, I want to take a look out there. Pop a light about fifty meters north of the hill," he said.

Bell's voice broke in before Athen could answer, "Negative on the illum. What's happening, Zeke?"

"I don't know, Jay Cee. I've just got a feeling and I want to take a look."

"Stand by, I'll be there in a minute." Bell wasn't going to authorize the mortar to fire a flare on the basis of a feeling, not unless he was on the perimeter and had the same feeling. He woke Doc Rankin to take over watch while he checked out the situation. It happened before he reached Ruizique's position.

The last of the Vietcong filtering in on the north side of the hill left the middle bank of wire and took his place at the end of the row of men laying along the inside bank to wait for the mortar barrage. A seemingly random piece of wood lay across a small, flat rock, one end inside the coiled wire, the other in the cleared space outside it. When the VC rolled onto his stomach along the wire, his hip rolled onto the upraised end of the piece of wood. The flat rock served as a fulcrum, lifting the other end of the stick. A taut wire lay across the upper end of the stick. One end of the wire was attached to an anchor post holding the barbed wire in place, the other end to the firing pin of a trip flare. The additional tension on the wire caused by the stick rising under it released the spring-loaded firing pin to smack down on the fuse primer. There was an audible pop and fizz and then a glare of light as the trip flare went off, exposing the VC squad. One man, the platoon sergeant, started shouting orders.

"Holy shit," McEntire shouted. He pointed his machine gun sharply to his left and opened up on the small group of VC clustered against the inner bank of wire. He kicked Kobos, rousing him out of his sleep. Luckily for the new man in the gun team, he wasn't new in combat and knew to roll over rather than sit up if he suddenly woke to the cacophony of gunfire. If he had sat up he would have been directly in front of the gun's muzzle. It took him less than a second to realize that his proper position was at the side of the machine gun where he could feed belts of ammunition into it. He moved to that position. The first man cut down was the sergeant shouting orders.

"I've got you," Ruizique said. His voice was a rumble somewhere deep in his chest. He sighted on the loin-cloth-clad man who was now scuttling back toward the middle bank of wire and pulled the trigger. The almost naked VC screamed and jerked when the bullet slammed into his lower back and tore through his kidney and spleen. Ruizique knew he'd hit his target and swung his muzzle to the others who were trying vainly to dodge McEntire's machine-gun bursts.

Bell dropped into their position at the same instant Neissi snapped awake and flattened himself against the outer wall of the defensive position to look for targets. The sergeant looked over the hillside and saw only the one flare burning. He picked up the field phone and called into it, "Mortars, give me three illum. Light up the entire north side of the hill, understand?"

"You got it, Honcho," Athen said back.

The mortar coughed three times and Bell knew Slover was awake and guiding his tube. The first mortar flare flashed to life over the foot of the hill midway between its corners, the second and third were on the corners where they would also shed light over parts of the east and west sides. The small group of Vietcong, who now lay like rag dolls tossed down by a child tired of playing with them, were all that could be seen.

"Cease fire," Bell shouted. Ruizique, Neissi, and the gun stopped shooting. Bell listened for sounds from the enemy soldiers sprawled under the dancing glare from the gently swaying flares. There were no audible groans, and no noise from anywhere else around the hill.

Vo Hai Bao would have frozen in place on the hill's south side if he hadn't already been laying motionless. He thought quickly and realized the Americans would probably soon illuminate his side of the hill; most likely before he and the men he was leading could get through the two banks of wire between them and the foot of the hill. They would be sitting ducks and suffer many casualties before a few survivors could escape—if any did. He didn't wait to see if the platoon commander agreed with him, or was going to give any orders now. Instead he slithered into the last concertina barrier and hoped to make it to the top before the Americans' mortar lit up where he was. He also hoped his own mortar barrage would start now, to distract the defenders and cover his final approach. It did.

"All positions, look alive," Bell shouted into the phone when the first enemy mortar round hit on the hill. "Keep your eyes and ears outboard. This might be a cover for an assault from a different direction." Either that, he thought, or the VC thought some of the Marines would be above ground after the VC infiltration squad was wasted and they hoped to hit someone in retaliation. He waited and listened. The mortar rounds came slowly, but they seemed to be concentrated on the south side of the perimeter, near the two positions that were manned. "Louie," he said on the phone, "light up the south side."

The six seconds it took Slover to turn his mortar to fire in the opposite direction felt like six hours to Bell. When he heard the *carrumph* of the first illumination round kicking out of the mortar tube he breathed deeply, as though he had been airless for minutes. The first mortar round was quickly followed by two more. Then the three flares spat to life over the south face of the hill, one in the middle, the others at the corners. "Do you see anything on the south side?" Bell asked into his phone.

No one answered immediately, they were too busy looking. Then Swarnes's voice came softly over the wires. "Mother-holy-fucking-shit," he said, "the goddamn hill's crawling with cocksucking gooks." His last words were drowned out by the booming of the M-14s of the four Marines who could see Vo Hai Bao and the two squads he was leading through the inner wire.

The sapper had only a few more strands of wire to pass when the first flare lit the sky above him and cast its sharp glare onto him. Behind him, five of the seven men in the first squad were inside the barbed wire. The other ten men in his infiltration section, including the officer, were still hugging the downhill side of the wire bank. The Vietcong specialist lunged through the wire and scuttled to the trench a few meters to his front and rolled to his right. He waited a few seconds for any others who might have made it through to join him. Two men did. They told him the others who were in the wire were dead, and the lieutenant was trying to maneuver the rest of his unit back through the wire a few men at a time while the others lay down covering fire. He nodded at the report, said curtly, "Follow me," and led them along the trench to one of the places where he heard American rifles firing.

Burrison had listened quietly on the phone to Bell's orders. As soon as Swarnes reported enemy inside the wire on the south he said into the phone, "Chief, Swarnes, I'm joining you." It was more than a hundred meters from the CP to where Swarnes and Tracker were fighting for their lives, and Burrison sprinted it faster than he had ever run before. If someone with a stopwatch had timed his dash he might have been invited to try out for the U.S. Olympic team. Two mortar rounds hitting along the trench flashed brightly but harmlessly during the time it took him to sprint from the CP to Tracker and Swarnes. Then the VC mortar stopped firing.

He dropped into the trench and flattened himself against its forward edge. "Oh shit," he said when he saw VC crawling through the wire and others covering them. He grabbed the field phone and said into it, "Big Louie, put some Hotel Echo in the middle of the inner wire." Without waiting for his order to be acknowledged he continued, "Jay Cee, I'm moving to my left with Chief and Swarnes. Move Malahini and Willard to this position and shift Zeke around for coverage. Go." He dropped the handset and led his two men fifty meters back along the trench. Bullets cracked overhead as they ran. Burrison stopped at an unmanned fighting position mere yards from the exact point where Vo Hai Bao and his two men had entered the trench, and started firing downhill with one hand while he reached for that position's phone with the other. He saw five motionless bodies laying in the wire and a couple more between the inner and outer banks. A small group of VC was crawling backward toward the middle wire while continuing to fire uphill. "Big Louie, more HE on my adjustment," he said and gave new firing directions. Then he noticed only one rifle shooting next to him. He turned his head and looked beyond Swarnes. "Where's Chief?" he asked.

Swarnes turned his head back the way they had come. "Goddamned if I know where that fucking Injun got his ass off to."

"Shit." The young lieutenant looked downhill again and called for more illumination because the flares lighting the hillside were nearly out. Seconds later another flare that flashed to light overhead revealed no one moving downslope from them. "Cease fire," Burrison shouted, "cease fire."

Ears throbbed in the sudden silence following the fury of the small firefight. Burrison broke the silence by shouting for Doc Tracker. A moan came from the trench between where he and Swarnes were and the position they had been in. They ran to it and found Tracker bleeding from a head wound.

"Get back to your radios and send Rankin out here," Burrison ordered. Swarnes grunted and ran to the CP. Burrison headed to the closest fighting position and picked up its phone. "All positions, count off," he said.

"One," McEntire said at the main gate.

"Two," Ruizique.

"Three," Webster.

"Four," Burrison said for himself.

Silence.

"Back gate," the lieutenant said. "Flood, Reid, count off."

Silence.

"Oh, shit. Six count off."

"Six," Knowles said without hesitation.

"Watch your flank in case anyone got in and is coming your way," Burrison told Knowles. "Everybody, look sharp until we find out what's happening on the back gate. Webster, Willard, join me right now."

"Seven," Slover said from the mortar pit, but Burrison wasn't listening anymore.

Vo Hai Bao and the two men with him used the gunfire and mortar explosions to conceal the noise they made crawling hurriedly along the trench toward where they heard two rifles firing at their companions. Feet short of where the rifles were firing, he halted, drew his knife, and gestured at one of the men with him to do the same. When the other had put down his rifle and readied his knife, Bao signaled with his hands and the two VC rose to a crouch, then charged into the fighting position. They caught the two Marines by surprise and silenced them almost instantly. The three VC put their heads together for Bao to give orders, then continued along the trench. They moved more quietly now because an American had shouted behind them and to their left, and silence fell over the battle scene.

* * *

Rankin had arrived where Burrison was standing over Doc Tracker, and had checked his medical partner's vital signs by the time Webster and Willard reached them.

"He's still alive," the senior corpsman said.

"Patch him up then join us at the back gate," Burrison said to Rankin, then to the others, "Let's go scope it out." They ran to where he knew, but was afraid to say to himself, they would find two more men dead or dying. He was right on both counts. PFC Archie "Jughead" Reid was crumpled on the trench floor, eyes staring blindly at the sky, throat gaping like a second mouth below his chin. Flood was curled in a tight fetal ball, clutching his belly and gasping for air. Willard looked on emotionlessly while Webster swore and uncurled Flood enough to slap a pressure bandage onto his wound.

Burrison grabbed the position's field phone. "All hands, now hear this," he said, more formally than any of his men had ever heard him speak before, "we have uninvited visitors on board. Both men on the back gate are down with knife wounds," his voice almost cracked with the emotion he struggled to keep out of it, "so the people snooping and pooping with us know what they're doing. Everybody, hold your positions and blow away any fucker you see moving toward you."

Rankin, who hadn't heard Burrison's order to stay in place, pounded down the trench to them and gasped out, "I don't know if Tracker's going to make it. What do we have here?"

"Reid's dead and Flood's belly's cut open."

Rankin briefly probed Reid's throat with one finger to confirm the diagnosis, then bent over Flood to see what he could do for him.

Burrison picked up the phone again and ordered Slover to light up the entire top of the hill. When the illumination rounds from the mortar lit the hilltop like day he looked it over. "Does anybody see any movement anywhere?" he asked. Everybody answered no. The lieuten-

ant brooded over the situation for a moment. He needed
to cover the entire perimeter in case of further assault
and he had men down in two different places, men who
needed protectors. And he needed to send someone along
the trench looking for whoever was in it. He decided.
"Doc, can Flood be moved?"

"Not a great idea, but possible," Rankin answered.

"You and Willard carry him to where you left Chief
and guard both of them. Malahini and I are going along
the trench the other way."

"Aye-aye," Rankin said. He carefully picked Flood
up in his arms and followed Willard to where they had
left Tracker.

Burrison spoke into the phone again, telling his men
what he was doing. He finished with, "Knowles, they're
probably coming your way. When we get close to your
position I'll let you know it's us. Blow anybody away
you see before then." He hung up the phone and signaled
Webster to follow him. They hadn't quite reached the
next fighting position when gunfire broke out ahead of
them. It sounded one-sided, all they heard were M-14s.
Burrison grabbed the next phone along the way and
waited until the firing ahead of them stopped before asking what was happening.

Knowles's excited voice came back, "My newby saw
someone in the trench and blew them away. We're going
to check it out now."

"Negative that," Burrison snapped back. "There may
be more waiting for you to show yourselves. Stay where
you are, Malahini and I are close, we'll check it from
this side."

"Roger," Knowles said. "You're the honcho."

Burrison smiled briefly at that. It hadn't been that long
ago when nobody in Tango Niner had enough confidence
in him to do anything he told them to.

When he was ten meters from Knowles and Vandersteit, Burrison called out to them.

"We see you, Scrappy," Knowles called back.

Burrison and Webster stood erect and eased forward under the light of another flare. They found the three VC who had penetrated Camp Apache's defenses piled in a heap in the trench.

"Somebody get me a rope," Burrison shouted. "Everybody else stay down in case there's more of them somewhere. I'm going to check the bodies for booby traps before I search them." VC raiders would sometimes stuff a grenade under their bodies and pull the pin from it before dying, which meant the only safe way to search a body was to tie a rope to it and move it from a safe distance first. A minute later Athen ran over with a thirty-foot length of quarter-inch nylon rope. The Cong on top of the pile, naked except for a loincloth, was laying on his back with his feet in the direction he had been heading, his head toward Burrison. The lieutenant tied a loop of rope around the corpse's neck and backed off, feeding the rope out until he was around the next bend in the trench. "Fire in the hole!" he shouted and jerked on the rope. With Webster's help he pulled the dead man halfway to where they were. There was no explosion. "One down, two to go," Burrison called out. He checked the other two bodies the same way. None had booby-trapped themselves before dying.

While Burrison was checking the three bodies, Bell returned to the CP and radioed a request for a med-evac for Flood and Tracker. He also called Zeitvogel on the radio and told him to return to base immediately. When the patrol came back in Bell and Burrison organized a search under the light of more flares. They didn't find anybody else.

It was dawn before the med-evac bird arrived. Captain Hasford came in on it and stayed behind when it left with the casualties.

CHAPTER SEVEN

November 22, 1966

The dirt near the back gate of Camp Apache and in the southwest corner of the compound looked like Paul Bunyan had been breaking ground for an excavation but couldn't make up his mind where to start. A few of the Marines were mending some tears in the canvas of the tents or filling in the mortar craters. All twenty of the rounds that had hit Camp Apache during the aborted assault had landed near the two manned positions covering the south side, but they hit behind the trench and none of them had done any actual harm. Apparently, the gunner wasn't positive where the men he was covering were, and overshot to avoid hitting his own people.

Captain Hasford surveyed the damage with Burrison and Bell in the early morning light.

"Charlie sure knew where our defensive positions were," Bell said.

"Those were the only places you had people on this side of the hill?" Hasford asked, looking at the two chewed up areas.

"That's right," Burrison said. "Those sappers were coming in right between those two positions, and they were doing the same on the north side when one of them tripped a flare."

"The mortar didn't fire on the north side?"

Burrison shook his head. "They probably realized they didn't have anyone left there to cover and wanted to conserve their ammunition, that's my guess."

Hasford looked at Bell and the sergeant nodded agreement. The captain's eyes swept the hilltop once more, then he gazed out over the land to the south and swung around to the west. "Charlie sure wants you out of here," he finally said. "I think you better cancel your night patrols until your fay-epps come back. Keep everybody on board here so maybe you've got enough strength to fight when he hits again."

"When are we getting them back?"

"Like I said last time, it'll take a couple weeks. Be patient, it'll happen."

"Does Major Y know it?"

"He knows it. He wants everything to go through channels, all the 'i's dotted and 't's crossed. Don't sweat it, he's just jerking your chains."

"Shit," Bell said, "we don't have a couple of weeks. We lost three men last night. If Charlie keeps hitting us like that, in one week there won't be any of us left. Can't you do anything to get them back sooner?"

Hasford shook his head sadly. "Lieutenant Colonel Tornado's still gone and I don't swing enough weight to get anything that big done." He looked at Bell with a helpless expression. "When it comes to something like this, I don't have any more power than a three-stripe sergeant does."

"How about sticking a grunt company out here until our fay-epps come back like they did with Echo Company the last time we were in deep shit?" Burrison asked. "Hell, a platoon would do."

Again, Hasford shook his head. "Can't do that for the same reason Echo Company got pulled out. That operation they got sent to turned out to be bigger and hotter than anybody imagined. Every ground combat unit in three provinces that isn't in contact with the enemy on another operation or essential for security at an American installation has been sent into it."

"This is an American installation," Bell said.

"True enough," Hasford nodded sadly. "But if this one gets overrun and wiped out, we don't lose any aircraft, artillery, armor or major equipment or ammunition stores. This installation is very small potatoes in the grand scheme."

Burrison grimaced at being called small potatoes and changed the subject. "Still no change on scoping out what's over there?" he asked, indicating the ridges and hills to the west.

"That's right," Hasford said. "You may as well forget about what's over there because nobody's going to be looking. Unless it's the spooks. And if the spooks are looking, they aren't telling anyone who's talking to me."

"Spooks," Bell snorted. "Fucking CIA doesn't talk to anybody. Sometimes I think they don't even talk to themselves."

"All right," Burrison said, moving right along, trying to salvage some aid to help in the mess Tango Niner was in, "what about the R&R? Can I at least postpone any more R&Rs until the fay-epps come back? Until Flood and Tracker make it back and I get replacements, Tango Niner's short three men even without anybody gone on R&R."

"Scrappy," Hasford sighed, "everybody in Eye Corps is short three men. I already checked on this. You have to send two men per week on R&R until every man in this platoon who's been in-country for more than six months has had R&R.''

Burrison looked at the captain levelly. ''Sounds to me like Tango Niner's between a rock and a hard place,'' he said, ''and they're winning.''

''It does sound that way, doesn't it?'' Hasford looked to the west again, his brow knit in thought. He didn't want to say what he had to say next, but he had to offer these Marines something. ''Listen, there is one thing I can do. If things get too tough out here, I can probably pull some strings and get you out of Bun Hou until your little people come back.''

''Bullshit,'' Burrison snapped. ''Pull us out of here and it'll look to the people like we're deserting them. Charlie'll walk right back in and take over again. When we come back we'll have one hell of a time trying to get the people to trust us again.''

''That's what I thought you'd say.'' Hasford smiled ruefully. ''You're right, you're between a rock and a hard place. And I'm about to make it tougher.''

The CAP leaders blankly looked at him. They couldn't imagine how their situation could get any worse than it already was.

''You don't have artillery support anymore. The one battery that was close enough to Bun Hou to give you some help if you needed it is taking off this morning for that same operation that has everybody else involved.''

Burrison and Bell didn't seem to move, but they visibly sagged. They were truly on their own, twenty-one Marines and one Navy corpsman isolated, without hope of assistance or relief, opposed by an unknown number of Vietcong who wanted them out of the way.

''I don't think I can take any more good news in one day,'' Burrison said hollowly.

''Just as well I don't have any more to give you.''

Swarnes poked his head out of his radio room and shouted to them that the helicopter coming to pick up Hasford was only four minutes away.

While the three of them walked to the helipad, Hasford had a few last things to say. "Improvise. You're Marines. We Marines never have as much of anything as we need, so over the generations we've become expert at improvising. Whatever you have to do to stay alive and effective, I don't think anybody's going to come down on you too hard for it later."

The helicopter was making its final approach now, aiming at Big Louie Slover's orange Ping-Pong paddles. Hasford held out his hand to shake and shouted, "Good luck," over the roar of the landing bird. He ducked under its spinning rotors and jumped aboard. The helicopter didn't even settle to the ground before it was climbing for altitude again.

As soon as his job at the helipad was over, Slover ambled to where Bell and Burrison stood watching the retreating bird. He knew by their expressions Hasford's news was bad, and could guess what most of it was. He didn't say anything, just stood near them. He could wait until they were ready to talk about it.

After a long moment Burrison looked at Slover and said, "Tango Niner up, Big Louie. I want to talk to everybody."

"Aye-aye, Scrappy," Slover said and turned toward the tent area. His eyes widened and he took a few deep breaths to get the sudden shaking in his limbs under control. The news must be worse than he thought.

In a few minutes all twenty members of Tango Niner were gathered around the makeshift tables where they ate most of their meals, facing the lieutenant and sergeant who were their leaders. Nobody cracked any jokes.

"All right, people," Burrison started, "we've got problems." He gave them all the bad news and finished with, "But like Captain Hasford said, we're Marines. We will improvise. Jay Cee and I are going to figure out what to do next, how to get us all through these next two weeks. If any of you have any ideas, let us know. Your ideas will carry as much weight as ours, we're all in this together."

"Scrappy," Stilts Zeitvogel said and stood up, taking full advantage of his height to get everyone's attention, "When Captain Phang tried to fuck with us, we faced him down. The little son of a bitch might have been a real corrupt bastard, but he had too much respect for us as fighters to take us on directly. Maybe that Major Y feels the same way. Captain Hasford says we're getting our fay-epps back anyway, it's just that it'll take a couple of weeks to do it through channels. What I think is, since it's going to happen anyhow, we should skip channels, go straight to the district headquarters and take them back now."

Stunned silence greeted Zeitvogel's proposal, but it only lasted a few seconds before the others started seconding it and cheering his idea. Mazzucco was the loudest and Billy Boy Lewis, the shortest man in the platoon with Hempen away on R&R, reached up to pound him on the back until the tall man threatened to use him as a tent stake. It took Burrison and Bell several minutes to quiet them down.

"That's probably not a legitimate course of action for us," Burrison said when his men were finally quiet enough for him to talk to them again. "But it's worth thinking about."

"We get them back, we don't have to worry about the rest of the shit," Randall said. "And like Hasford said, whatever we do to stay alive and effective, probably nobody's going to bust our balls too hard for it. Doing that will sure as shit keep us alive and effective."

"And we can go back to work wasting Charlie," Ruizique added.

When there were no other suggestions, Burrison promised to consider Zeitvogel's suggestion and dismissed them. He and Bell retired to their room in the command hootch.

"It'll work," Bell said as soon as he and Burrison were alone. He couldn't quite control his excitement. "If Houng and his people want to come home, we can just walk right in and take them and Y won't be able to do a damn thing about it. This is just too damn bodacious not to work."

"I agree," Burrison said. "Let's figure out how to do it."

Burrison also thought they were alone. They weren't, but it was easier to ignore the fact that Swearin' Swarnes in his radio room on the other side of the canvas divider was listening to every word they said and passing it to the rest of the platoon than it was to find a way of preventing him from hearing anything.

Later that morning Thien joined them and they started serious planning. Important questions had to be answered and decisions had to be made.

"We have to take everybody so we look impressive enough that Major Y will take us seriously."

"But we have to leave a few people at Camp Apache for radio watch and to keep unfriendly visitors out. I'd hate to come back and find the place booby-trapped."

"What if not all of the fay-epps don't want to come back yet?"

"They will, Thien. Let's not think about that."

"Do we try to do it all in one day, or do we plan on going there one day and stopping somewhere overnight before we spring them? It's pretty far to walk both ways in one day, especially if it takes any time to locate our fay-epps and talk them out of Y's hands."

"Who says we have to walk? What can we do about transportation?"

"Helicopters are out, Jay Cee. We wouldn't be able to get them even if any were available."

"Me know. We get boo-coo truck, car."

Burrison and Bell stared at Thien. "We can't get military vehicles for the same reasons we can't get helicopters," they told him.

"No, not Ma-deen truck," Thien said, shaking his head vigorously. "Me know that not good. Me know where get people truck, car, bus."

Burrison and Bell shifted their stares from the hamlet chief to each other. If they could get a civilian convoy together that would not only solve their travel problem, it would also give them a bunch of friendly witnesses in case the district chief tried to make trouble. They turned back to Thien. "How can we put this convoy together?"

Thien beamed with pleasure as he told them of relatives and friends he had in the bigger villages and towns closer to the district headquarters, people who owned motor vehicles and would be glad to lend them to the cause.

By the time they broke for noon chow it was decided. Seventeen Marines would make the trip, some in Tango Niner's Jeep, the rest in a bus Thien said he could have at Camp Apache in the morning. Four Marines, the remaining three mortarmen and Swarnes, along with Doc Rankin would stay behind. Thien would also procure enough vehicles to transport the thirty-five members of the PF platoon back to Bun Hou.

"Thank you, Thien," Burrison said gratefully. The civilian vehicles would make the whole operation easy— well, possible at any rate. "We are going to eat now. Please join us."

"Thank you," Thien said, bowing. "Me no can do. Me go now, get bus, get truck. No time eat now."

Burrison bowed back and thanked Thien again. He said he understood about the time pressure, then stood watching the hamlet chief trudge back to Hou Ky to fetch his bicycle. Thien, in turn, appreciated the offer of lunch, but he didn't turn it down because he didn't have time to eat. He turned it down because he couldn't stand the bland taste of C rations. Thien was never able to understand how Houng and the other PFs could eat that terrible, tasteless American food when they had good food to eat at home, food like rice cooked with fish heads and greens and smothered in nuoc mam sauce.

Tango Niner didn't put out any patrols that night, and Charlie didn't come visiting.

CHAPTER EIGHT

"Down Show at the OK Corral."

"All dressed up and no place to go," Zeitvogel complained at ten A.M. "The story of my fucking life."

"Yours and mine both, homeboy," Mazzucco said, and laughed at the offended expression Zeitvogel affected.

The Marines scheduled to go on the expedition to the district headquarters in Phuoc Nam town were dressed up, or at least as dressed up as was possible under field conditions. They were wearing clean, though mended, uniforms, and had buffed a fresh coat of polish onto their boots. As soon as they'd finished their morning chow, they all shaved and cleaned their rifles and cartridge belts. Their camouflage bush hats were all properly squared away on their heads. These Marines of Tango Niner were

as close as they could get to parade-ground sharp. Even
Billy Boy Lewis's mustache was almost symmetrical; the
left side drooped down Fu Manchu style and the right
swooped in a Western marshal–style handlebar. Each of
them even had rank insignia stuck in his pocket to put
on his collars when they reached Phuoc Nam.

All dressed up and no place to go. The only vehicle
they had was their own navy blue Jeep. Thien hadn't been
seen since he left before noon the previous day, and they
had no word on the bus he promised them.

"We have to made a decision in the next couple of
hours, Jay Cee," Burrison said. "If Thien doesn't show
up with that bus by noon, either we hold off another day
or we hump this afternoon and go in to get our fay-epps
tomorrow morning and hump back."

Bell nodded. "I think he'll be here this morning like
he said he would. If he isn't, I think we should hold off
another day and expect to see him then. If we ride, we
will do this thing in style and it'll be easier to pull off."

"The vehicles would impress Major Y more than if we
walked in, that's for sure," Burrison said.

They waited, growing impatient and nervous about the
success of their mission, until Tex Randall shouted,
"Here comes somebody." He pointed at a cloud of dust
rising from the bulldozed road south of Hou Dau hill.
The Marines gathered on the east side of their compound
and watched the progress of the dust drifting above the
top of the scrub forest the road cut through, until they
saw a vehicle break free of the trees and head toward
them.

"What in the fuck is that?" McEntire asked.

For starters, it was pink and fire-engine red and sky
blue. As it came closer they could see it was an old
French-built flat-bed truck. Its hood and the cab roof
were painted a bright baby pink, the sides of the motor
housing and the doors were red. The back of the truck
had wood slat sides painted light blue. A giant eye was
superimposed over the grill to guide the truck safely, the

same eyes as were painted on the bows of sampams. The way the truck bounced on the road's ruts, it was obvious its springs were long gone. When it got close enough they could make out two people in the cab and see that the windshield was missing. If the door windows had glass, that glass was rolled down.

One cylinder was knocking loudly when the ancient truck turned to climb the Marines' hill. Then the driver thought better and backed down to make an awkward seven-point U-turn. Thien jumped out of the passenger seat, dragged his bicycle off the back of the truck, and walked the bike up the hill.

"See," he shouted gleefully, "me get truck. Ma-deen ride truck. Other bus, car wait for us. We go now." He gestured wildly, urging the Marines to follow him.

"What's the matter, Jay Cee," Zeitvogel said, "don't you like old Stilts anymore? You want me to ruin my kidneys riding that sucker? How about you put Tex in charge of the men in the truck, let me ride in the Jeep. Tex is so full of shit he won't notice the bouncing."

Bell's mouth hung open as he looked at the truck. It snapped shut at Zeitvogel's questions. He swallowed and said, "Sorry about that, Stilts, but you're the senior fire team leader. I'm driving the Jeep and Scrappy's riding shotgun. That means you're the next most senior man and you have to ride in that . . ." his voice trailed off while he looked for the right word, "contraption."

The other Marines stared and joked at the brightly-colored truck.

Burrison shook his head at the truck. "Does it work well enough to get us where we're going and back?" When no one answered he decided it would—he hoped it would—and called out, "Tango Niner, saddle up." He turned to Slover and the others who were staying behind and said, "Good luck. We'll be back before sundown."

"If that cockatoo Arvin major don't slam you all in the brig for dressing too loud," Slover said, nodding at the festive-looking truck and grinning. He took the hand

Burrison held out to be shaken. "Luck, Honcho," he said, and shook his head, thinking, Better you than me.

The young lieutenant glanced over his small expeditionary force as he walked to the Jeep. Bell was already sitting behind the wheel of the navy blue vehicle, and Randall and Willard were sitting in the back with a PRC-20 radio to maintain communications with Camp Apache. Zeitvogel was busy herding the other dozen men onto the back of the truck. Burrison dropped into the passenger seat of the Jeep, and Bell put it in gear and rolled through the gate and down the hill. Zeitvogel finished loading his men onto the truck and went to the front to climb into the cab. Thien had already retaken his place next to the driver. The front seat wasn't wide enough for three men, and the hamlet chief refused to relinquish his seat in the front. Bell stopped the Jeep next to the cab.

"Problem, Stilts?" Burrison asked, standing to see through the cab. He noticed for the first time that Thien was armed with an AK-47.

"No goddamn problem," Zeitvogel said, disgust evident in his voice. "I'll ride in the fucking back of the bus."

Randall laughed and said, "It ain't a bus, Stilts, it's a Mardi Gras float."

"Fuck a bunch of Mardi Gras," Vandersteit said from the back of the truck. "Can't you see it's pink and red? This sucker's the South Vietnamese entry in the Tournament of Roses parade." Vandersteit was from California.

"Let's move it out," Burrison said. He raised his right arm and brought it down in a sweeping motion to the front. "Go slow enough so that thing can keep up with us," he added in an aside to Bell.

The Jeep moved smoothly ahead of the truck and headed toward Hou Dau. Behind it, the red, pink, and blue truck belched, bucked, shuddered, roared, and finally jerked forward. They were on their way. The Jeep traveled at a stately fifteen miles per hour; it seemed a moderate speed to its driver and passengers. Behind it the truck roared, hiccuped, jerked, rattled, and rolled, and seemed to be going at something greater than its maximum speed—sort of as though its driver had turned on its afterburner and was headed for Mach five. The truck managed to keep up with the Jeep. They passed the turn-off for Anh Dien and continued for another two miles before reaching a hamlet that held what looked like a small junkyard. Or an Appalachian front yard, or something.

Parked to one side of the hamlet square were a gaudy, three-wheeled Vespa and a hybrid vehicle consisting of a Rolls-Royce grill, hood, and front seat, and a pick-up truck bed. The third vehicle was a bus with serious body cancer. Somehow, Bell heard Thien's thin voice shouting over the uproar made by the truck and stopped. The Rolls was bright orange, the bus was pale blue, white, and yellow where it wasn't rusted.

"We here," Thien said when the truck ground to a stop and its engine noise abated. "Fay-epp ride Bun Hou them." He waved his arm at the vehicular mortuary. He shouted something in Vietnamese and the three vehicles' motors reluctantly awoke.

Burrison cocked a disbelieving eye at them and said to Bell, "Didn't I hear you say something about traveling in style?"

Bell didn't look at the lieutenant when he answered, "Beats all hell out of humping."

And then what seemed like all the children in the world descended on the Marines in the Jeep and the truck.

U.S. Marines rank high among the world's most fearsome, fearless fighters. Theirs is a reputation that has been earned in blood over many generations and in many wars—the blood mostly belonged to whoever the Marines were fighting. Not everybody believes that reputation, but the Marines do, and that's the important thing. Believing your own reputation is at least fifty percent of making it real. After that it's easy. The Marines have an expression, "Old Marines don't die, they go to hell and regroup.'' The implications of that are: Marines are too nasty to get into heaven; they never give up; and Old Nick himself better watch his tail if the Marines ever go after it.

And there's hardly a kid in the world who can't see through the bluff and bombast to the sweet, homesick heart lying underneath. The world-class, fearsome, fearless fighters and the kids love each other. Some wise old heads who were never Marines themselves have pointed out the simple fact that these fighting, teenage Marines aren't much older than the kids they give candy to and play with, claiming that the small age difference explains the affinity they have for each other. There could be some truth to that, half of the men in the Marine Corps actually are nineteen years old or younger. Don't ever tell a Marine the kids love him because he's also a kid, though; he just might make you wish you had died and gone to hell.

The children laughed and giggled and ran around, and the Marines laughed right back and mock-chased the children and tickled them when they caught them. The bemused parents and grandparents watched their children playing with these warriors who were so like children themselves. Burrison was partly immune to it all. At twenty-three he was an old man, the second oldest in Tango Niner. He let his men and the kids enjoy themselves for ten minutes before telling them to knock it off so they could get on with their mission.

Bell assigned two Marines to ride in each of the odd assortment of vehicles. Zeitvogel sourly watched the six men board their assigned rides and sincerely wished he wasn't senior fire team leader; he really wanted off that truck.

The convoy took off again. The Jeep led, followed by the parade-painted truck, the afflicted bus, and the gaudy Vespa. The Rolls-Royce pickup was tail-end Charlie. The truck moved a little less rheumatically this time.

* * *

Phuoc Nam town was a great metropolis. Metropolis is a relative term. In this part of South Vietnam, Phuoc Nam's population of eight thousand, nearly nine thousand if the ARVN soldiers, Regional Forces, and Popular Forces assigned there were included, made it not only the biggest town in the district, but the biggest in more than a day's walk from any hamlet in the district. Hardly any of the farmers and fishermen in the district had ever seen a larger town, and many of them had never even been to this one. It was common for a Vietnamese peasant to be born and die in the same hamlet and never travel more than ten miles from his home during his entire life. Phuoc Nam bustled, and was splashed everywhere with bright primary colors and lively pastels. It had actual dirt streets instead of only dirt footpaths, and the buildings in the heart of town were all masonry or wood construction. The thatch and bamboo hootches, homes for the peasants and workers, were part of a shantytown on the outskirts. Some few of the shantytown hootches were made of sun-baked brick, while more were built from the ubiquitous cast-offs of the American-supported war machine. Walls were cobbled together from broken shipping crates and empty C ration cases. Falstaff, Schlitz, and Coca-Cola cans were split open and hammered flat to make shingled walls and roofs.

For nearly the first time, the Marines saw women wearing *ao dais*, the traditional Vietnamese dress, high-throated, body snug, slit up the sides to the hips, and worn over pantaloons. These graceful dresses were in every color of the rainbow, and some the rainbow wished it had thought of. Half of the non-uniformed men wore shirts and shorts so colorful they would have embarrassed a tourist in Hawaii. The kaleidoscope stunned the Marines, used as they were to the sedate black pajamas of the farmers of Bun Hou and the greens and browns of their village. But they got used to it quickly enough, just like they got used to the motor vehicles—mostly Honda motorbikes and military Jeeps and trucks—that roared along the streets.

Burrison clipped his bars to his collars and saw that everyone else also pinned on his own rank insignia. Then he found a place for the convoy to park and left Zeitvogel in charge while he went with Bell and Randall in the Jeep to find the PFs and Major Y's headquarters. Major Y's headquarters was in a building larger than most, one of the few two story structures in the town. It was marked as being special only by the sharply starched and creased guards standing at parade rest in front of it, and the American half-track with Vietnamese markings parked by the entrance.

"We'll come back here after we find Houng and his men," Burrison said. It didn't take long to find them. Just beyond the next side street was a rambling L-shaped structure that resembled more than anything else a Spanish stable. A low wall surrounded the structure, and the PF squad leader the Marines called Collard Green was squatting to the side of an ornamental gate set in the wall. As usual, Collard Green's face was twisted in an expression that told the world his stomach was filling with bile and he was about to throw up.

Bell stopped the Jeep a few feet from the PF and said, "*Chao ong*, Collard Green. Vietnam numba one."

Collard Green's eyes shot up at the familiar and unexpected voice and a huge grin split his face when his eyes confirmed what his ears had heard. "Chay Cee," he exclaimed, bounding to his feet, hand extended to shake. Despite his smile, he still looked like he was about to lose his lunch.

"Are you ready to go back to Bun Hou?" Bell asked in faltering Vietnamese.

"I've been ready for the past week," Collard Green answered in Vietnamese, slowly enough for the Marine to follow it.

"Where's Houng?"

"You come me," Collard Green said in English for

the benefit of the rest of the Marines. He waved them to follow, Oriental style, fingers down rather than up.

They dismounted and started through the gate, but Bell took a quick glance around and noticed a few people eyeing the navy blue Jeep. "You stay here and guard our wheels, Tex," he said. "This place looks like there might be some horse thieves around."

Randall grimaced and said, "If I have to stay here I'm driving back." He settled himself behind the wheel.

"We'll see about that," Bell said, and followed the PF squad leader with Burrison.

More than a hundred men were lounging in what patches of shade they could find, or walking slowly about inside the wall. They were the night security crew, Collard Green explained, off duty now but on stand-by, which was why all of them were there instead of out in cafes or bars. The rest of the Bun Hou PFs were together at the far end of the long ell of the stablelike structure. The others largely avoided them because they were such country bumpkins, not urbane and sophisticated like the RFs and PFs who had been in Phuoc Nam for a month or even longer. The Bun Hou PFs shouted and hollered when they saw their Marine leaders and clustered around them, grabbing at them, slapping their backs, shaking their hands, and chittering questions faster than the Americans could possibly understand.

Houng pushed his way through his men, stood at attention directly in front of Burrison, and smartly saluted him; this was the first time he had saluted any Marine officer. "You come, got good news?" he asked.

"If you're ready to go home, I've got transportation for you," Burrison answered. "Are you ready?"

"You numba fuckin' one, Scrappy. We go home, see baby-san, boom-boom wife," Houng said and clutched his crotch. The PFs laughed loudly at that. Houng looked happier than Bell had seen him over anything other than killing Vietcong.

"We're going to tell Major Y we're taking you home,"

Burrison said. "Can you meet us in front of his headquarters in—" he paused to figure out how long it would
take them to get the rest of the Marines and the vehicles
to the district headquarters building "—about twenty
minutes?"

Houng looked at his wristwatch and traced an arc one-
third of the way around its face. He nodded vigorously.
"We be there."

"Good. Then we can go back to Bun Hou and kill
more Vee Cee."

"Yes, kill Vee Cee, kill boo-coo Vee Cee." The PFs
laughed again.

Fifteen minutes later, an ARVN corporal behind a
fence divider inside the headquarters building looked up
from his old Underwood manual typewriter long enough
to tell Burrison that if he made an appointment he could
see Major Y in a week or so.

"Not good enough," Burrison said. "Where's his office?" But the ARVN corporal had returned to pecking
one at a time on the keys of his machine and wasn't
listening.

Bell nudged the lieutenant and said, "I'll bet he's in
that room over there." He nodded at a door on the opposite side of the room. Miniature Vietnamese flags dangled from crossed flagpoles on a wall plaque on the door,
a second plaque under that held an American eagle. The
thrumming of an air conditioner seemed to come from
behind it.

"I'll bet you're right. Let's go." They pushed their
way through a swinging gate in the divider fence and
headed toward the decorated door.

The ARVN corporal screamed and almost fell jumping
out of his chair rushing to intercept them. "You not go,
you not go," he shouted at them and made shooing motions with his hands. He had to back up rapidly to keep
from being trampled. "You dee-dee, dee-dee mau. Make
appointment, come back next week."

"Khong the duc," Bell said without looking at the ARVN junior NCO, "no can do."

They reached the door. Bell knocked on it and pulled it open. Burrison looked in, saw Major Y seated at his highly polished teak desk. The major wore a pressed khaki uniform so heavily starched it held its sharp creases despite the heat and humidity. A Sam Browne belt, shined to a mirror finish, crossed his chest and the paratrooper boots visible under his desk were polished just as brightly. Many rows of colorful ribbons and badges adorned his shirt, and a white scarf was artfully draped around his neck. Burrison stepped into the room. The corporal was still trying to stop him and was carried back and over into a sprawl by the much bigger American's forward movement.

Major Y looked up and sneered at the two barbarous Americans who barged into his office uninvited. The lieutenant and sergeant who were now stepping over one of his clerks, who had somehow managed to grovel at their entry, looked vaguely familiar. But who could tell? The crude, graceless men from far across the ocean all seemed to look alike in their oafishness once one had seen enough of them. And these two were sufficiently uncouth as to carry their rifles slung on their shoulders into his office rather than leave them outside. At least they had enough courtesy to carry their hats in their hands instead of on their heads. He let his hand fall naturally to the chrome-plated Walther PPK that lay on his desk, and tilted his head so a lamp placed for exactly that purpose would reflect off his mirrored sunglasses and dazzle these intruders. The lieutenant blinked but the sergeant didn't. "What is the meaning of this?" Major Y demanded in a clipped, British accent.

"This is a courtesy call, sir," the lieutenant said. "We just want to let you know we're here with transportation for our platoon. We're taking them with us now."

Major Y blinked behind his glasses. "Your platoon? What do I know of your platoon? I have nothing to do with it. Go back to wherever you came from or I shall report this matter to your superiors and you both will be burning shit at Phu Bai." He moved his hand from the automatic and picked up a thin sheaf of papers from his "in" basket. These stupid Americans were very useful with their weapons and other war matériels and riches, but they could be such a damnable nuisance when they got underfoot.

"That's what we intend to do," the lieutenant said. "Just wanted to let you know." He and the sergeant about-faced and left the office, closing the door behind themselves.

Major Y looked at the clerk who was still sprawled where he had fallen. "What are you doing on my floor?" he asked. The clerk lurched to his feet, sputtered something, and dashed out of the office, almost hitting himself with the door in his haste. The major sighed deeply and leaned back in his chair, wondering if there was any point in trying to find out who those two Americans were. Then it hit him, the hats they had carried in their hands: they were camouflage bush hats. There was only one American unit he knew of that wore them. These Americans were from that Marine Combined Action Platoon in Bun Hou! They must be here to take the Bun Hou PF platoon away from him. Major Y roared like a wounded tiger and bolted from behind his desk, shoving the silver-colored automatic into his patent leather holster. On his way through the outer room he shouted orders.

He roared again when he reached the street and saw the two Marines supervising the boarding of a PF platoon into a series of vehicles that looked like refugees from a circus. He looked to his right and saw a platoon of his infantrymen boiling around the corner of the building. He shouted a command to the bewildered lieutenant leading the platoon, watched it form up blocking the street, and stepped in front of it to face the caravan.

"Stop!" he bellowed loud enough to be clearly heard halfway across the small town.

Burrison and Bell looked at him and the platoon behind him. They stepped into the street facing him, unslinging their rifles as they did. There was a long moment of silence while the Vietnamese soldiers on one side and the two American Marines on the other stared at each other.

"Lieutenant—" Major Y groped for the name "—Burrison, you are not going anywhere with those PFs. They are mine, not your platoon. I say they stay here."

"Sorry, Major," Burrison said. "They're needed back in Bun Hou. We've got too damn many Vee Cee coming through there."

"They will return to Bun Hou when I am finished with them here."

"You're finished with them now. You're only waiting for orders to come from your province chief to send them home."

Y smiled, a tiger's smile, like his roars. "If I do not have the orders, then I am not through with them."

"The orders are on their way. In the meantime, these men are needed at home. They're going with us."

Major Y said something over his shoulder and the ARVN lieutenant snapped an order. His men brought their rifles to port arms and jacked rounds into the chambers. "They stay with me," Y said, and showed his teeth.

"Stilts," Bell said to the side. Fifteen more Marines stepped from behind the vehicles of the convoy and lined up alongside Burrison and Bell. They held their rifles ready.

"Ah yes," Y said, "you Americans have an expression for this. Down show at the Okay Corral. I have," he half turned to gesture at the platoon to his rear, "twenty-five men here, you have fewer over there," he turned back to the Marines. "And I have close to a thousand more men in Phuoc Nam. If I give the order, all of you die."

"True enough," Burrison said. "But if you give the order, you'll die first. Do you want to keep these fay-epps that badly?"

"Maybe I will die, and maybe I won't," Y grinned. "You most certainly will. You and your Marines should leave now and I will send these PFs home when I am through with them. If you leave now, perhaps I will not report this to your superiors.''

Something said in rapid Vietnamese made Y jerk his head to the side. Houng then repeated what he had said in English, for the Marines. ''Me say him give order, him die most ricky-tick. Him and boo-coo Arvin.''

While the others had been busy facing each other down on the street, Houng had led his platoon off their vehicles and around to the side of the ARVNs. They had their weapons aimed at the ARVNs; Houng and three of his men had theirs pointed at the district chief.

Y's smile vanished and he glared at the PFs on his flank. If he called their bluff and they weren't bluffing, he would most certainly die. He turned back to the Americans, his face dark and his body trembling. ''You may go now and take these scum with you. But do not think you have heard the last of this incident. You will pay.'' He spun and marched stiffly back into the headquarters, leaving the platoon he had ordered to back him up standing confused and frightened in the street.

Bell and Houng both shouted orders, and the Marines and PFs of Tango Niner piled into their convoy and drove away. They hooted and hollered all the way back to Camp Apache. All but Burrison and Bell, who wondered what mischief Y would make for them. That night they put out three patrols of ten men each, and all the PFs who weren't on patrol manned the Camp Apache perimeter. The only excitement for the next couple of days was Thanksgiving dinner.

CHAPTER NINE

It Ain't Stuffed Turkey with All the Trimmings, But . . .

The sun had been up for several hours by the time Tex Randall's eyeballs stirred under their lids. He let his other senses absorb the sounds, smells, and feel of his environment before his eyelids creaked open. He lay mostly on his stomach on his canvas folding cot and his left arm dangled over its side. The comforting bulk of his rifle was under his hanging hand. The air inside the tent was very warm, but enough air moved across his body, naked except for skivvy drawers, to tell him the sides of the tent were up. Muffled stirrings from nearby told him the other members of his fire team were also waking. No one had sounded reveille, or anything. No one had tried to wake them together. It was simply that when four men were on an all-night patrol together and went to sleep at about the same time and in the same place, they tended to wake at about the same time. That's how tuned in they were to each other.

High-pitched shouts and soprano giggles from beyond the tent told Randall children were in the compound playing with the other Marines and doing odd jobs for them. The occasional baritone voices were few. Randall knew many of the Marines were off somewhere, visiting in one of the hamlets or on one of the frequent walks in the woods they took during the day as informal patrols and to keep themselves fully aware of the countryside they patrolled in for real at night.

Gradually, Randall lifted his hand from his rifle, rolled onto his back, and stretched a mighty, back-arching, yawning stretch. He rolled into a sitting position with his legs over the right side of the cot, one foot resting lightly on his rifle. Lewis was already pulling on his utility uniform and slipping his feet into his tire-tred Ho Chi Minh sandals. Wells lay supine, scratching his bare belly, his eyes still closed. Dodd lay scrunched into a fetal oblong—the cot was too narrow for a fetal ball—and held his thin pillow tight over his head.

"Chow," Lewis mumbled as he finished dressing. He slung his rifle over his shoulder, picked up his mess kit in one hand, his shaving kit in the other, ducked under the raised side wall of the tent, and headed toward the command hootch. Once there he stood staring at the four C ration boxes laying upside down alongside the command hootch, trying to figure out which one was the ham and limas so he could take one of the others. He held his mess kit over the boxes and moved it slowly to-and-fro, side-to-side, like a one-handed dowsing rod. He flipped one box right side up and sighed in relief. Its lid was labeled "Beefsteak."

Randall suddenly realized the odds of his not getting the ham and limas were rapidly diminishing, pulled on his trousers, and darted to the side of the command hootch without his rifle or mess kit. He grabbed one box at random, ran back to the tent to gather his shaving and mess kits and his rifle, and headed toward the sweating Lister bag hanging from a tripod to get water to brush his teeth with. It wasn't until he was brushing his teeth that he looked to see which C ration meal he'd gotten. When he did he reflexively spat out a mouthful of toothpaste water. His toothbrush went with the toothpaste water. He looked at the wet toothbrush lying in the red dirt of the hilltop and swore. As if it wasn't bad enough he had to get stuck with the ham and fucking limas. Like everybody else in the Marine Corps, Randall hated C ration ham and limas.

If Hempen had been there, though, he could have told the corporal about one time he had ham and limas and it had been just about the best tasting meal he'd ever had. That was at the end of the First Marine Brigade's thirty-day-long Guerrilla War School in Hawaii. The students were on their final training patrol, three days deep in the jungle valleys that branched out from the east side of the Pali. The food they carried for each four-man fire team was: one pound of rice per fire team, one pound of raisins per fire team, one pound of tuna fish per man. Unless someone in the fire team was carrying hot sauce, sugar, pepper, or other condiment, it was a gawd-awful dull diet. They also ate whatever ripe fruit they could find growing wild, mostly guavas, mountain apples, not-yet-ripe grapefruits, and small bananas. The squad Hempen was in captured a three-man "aggressor" team that happened to be carrying C rations. They took the aggressors' C rations and gave them a can of tuna and the rest of their rice in exchange. Hempen got stuck with the ham and limas. He warmed the food up over a heat tab and stoically dug in. His eyes grew wide. This, the most universally despised meal in the entire military cuisine, tasted delicious. But let's face it, after three days of hard humping in the tropic jungle, eating unflavored rice and unripened grapefruits, almost anything with flavor will taste good.

But Hempen wasn't there to tell Randall about the time ham and limas was just about the best tasting meal he'd ever had. Besides, Randall hadn't just gone through several days of unflavored rice and unripened grapefruits. Ham and limas were the pits. Randall swore again when he picked up his now muddy toothbrush, and swore again when he tried to clean it in fresh water. Its bristles never did lose the red stain they got from landing in the red dirt of the hilltop. Naturally, he wasn't in the best of moods a few minutes later when he joined Lewis—after a brief stop at the piss tubes.

Wells moved at a more leisurely pace and visited the command hootch, the Lister bag, and the piss tubes in a different order than Randall had. When he arrived at the sheet metal-on-sandbag table, Randall was still opening his can of ham and limas to cook over his field stove—a small C ration can with its top cut off and the open end bent out of a circle and triangular holes cut in its sides along the bottom. Water was in his canteen cup on the stove, heating to make C ration instant coffee. Wells was smiling. He had boned chicken breast.

Lewis was starting to eat by the time Dodd, stretching and yawning, stumbled out of the squad tent. He emptied his bladder, brushed his teeth, rubbed a hand over a jaw that didn't need shaving and, finally, went to the side of the command hootch to pick up the last C ration box. Getting the beans and franks didn't impress him, he looked as blank and unaware as ever.

Randall swore while he stirred the powdered coffee, the sugar, and the powdered creamer from his C ration box into the almost-boiling water in his canteen cup to make a beverage that didn't quite approximate the taste of bad coffee, and swore when he put it aside to cool off before he put its hot metal rim to his lip. He swore again when he put the ham and limas on the stove to heat up, and he swore while he stirred the ham and limas.

Lewis and Wells joked back and forth in their fake Southern accents and laughed at each other's jokes. Dodd seemed to be just going through the motions of heating and drinking his C ration hot cocoa and heating and eating his beans and franks. Randall looked jealously at Dodd's food and said, "Swap you, you don't care what you eat."

Dodd shook his head. His head shake didn't say, "no way Jose," it said, "I don't care what I'm eating, why should you care what you're eating?"

Lewis finally broke off joking with Wells and said to the other two, "Ya'll got sum hairs up you asses or some'pin? What's 'a madda, you doan know today is Thanksgiving?"

Dodd looked at Lewis. His look seemed to ask, "so what?"

Randall stopped swearing at his ham and limas long enough to glower at his automatic rifleman. "What's there to be thankful about?" he asked. "I'm not at home in Texas with my father and my brothers and my uncles, eating turkey. There aren't any pretty girls around here for me to have wet dreams about. I'm stuck here on a goddamn red-dirt hill with a bunch of smelly-ass Marines so damn close to the equator I can never cool off and I'm eating ham and fucking limas? Bullshit, Thanksgiving." Then he went back to swearing at his ham and limas.

"Come on, Honcho," Lewis said, dropping his fake Southern accent. "They fucked us over on the Marine Corps Birthday, you just know they're going to fly out turkey and all the trimmings for evening chow today."

Randall shook his head. "No they aren't," he said through a mouthful of ham and limas, and almost gagged in the process. "Jay Cee told me last night we aren't getting turkey today."

"Say what?" Lewis's voice rose several octaves.

"You got a hearing problem? I didn't stutter." Randall dug his mess kit fork violently into his ham and limas and swore at them.

"That's fucking bullshit," Lewis shouted and jumped to his feet. He stomped off to corner Bell in the command hootch. He was back in less than three minutes. His lower lip pouted over his upper lip, engulfing one whole side of his mustache and half of the other side.

"Jay Cee said we don't get no fucking turkey for Thanksgiving chow," he blurted, and dropped back onto the empty ammo crate he was using as a stool. "Fuck. It ain't fucking fair. They fucked us over on the fucking Marine Corps Birthday and now we don't get no fucking turkey on Thanksgiving, neither. Fuck. I was really looking forward to fucking cranberry sauce and giblet gravy, too."

Randall looked at Lewis without lifting his head. "I'd say you was hanging with Swearin' Swarnes too much, except he swears better than that."

"Fuck," Lewis said again, and lost himself in thought.

Randall grimaced and decided he'd had enough ham and fucking limas. He scooped the remains of his meal into the C ration box and carried it to the trash pit. This felt like a good day to feel sorry for himself, so he went back to the squad tent and lay back on his cot with an arm over his eyes to shade out the light. He hadn't been lying there for more than five minutes before Lewis rushed in and started shaking his cot.

"Come on, Honcho," Lewis said excitedly, "drop your cock and grab your sock. We're running a med-cap into Hou Cau."

"Fuck a bunch of med-caps. This is a goddamn holiday, I don't run no med-caps on holidays."

"You're going on this one, get up." Lewis grabbed the foot of Randall's cot, lifted it up a couple of inches and slammed it back down.

Randall pointed his arm that wasn't covering his eyes at Lewis and said, "You do that one more time, shithead, and your ass is grass."

"Okay, I won't do it one more time," Lewis said. He

did it twice while shouting, "On your feet, Marine, we got a med-cap to run."

Randall started to jump to his feet, but before he could Wells grabbed the head of his cot and, with Lewis, tipped it over, dumping him onto the duckboard deck of the tent. He bounded to his feet, roaring and swinging. Doc Rankin stepped inside his swing before he could connect with anyone and shouted the angry corporal down.

"I'm running a med-cap into Hou Cau and you're driving the goddamn Jeep," Rankin finished. He wasn't a particularly tall man, but he was taller than Randall and stood chest-to-chest with him, shouting down into the other's face.

"I'm going to kill that scrawny fucker," Randall snarled up at the corpsman. "Lemme by. I'm gonna put one bodacious hurting on that little cocksucker."

"No you're not, Marine. You're my driver and you're driving for me, not kicking ass on other Marines." There are times when a medical corpsman outranks a Marine, regardless of their actual ranks. This wasn't one of them, but Rankin was betting Randall wasn't thinking clearly enough to realize that.

Randall stepped back, sputtering at the corpsman, eyes bulging at him.

"Come on, honcho," Lewis said from his safe position behind Rankin. "We got to go into Hou Cau so I can visit the marketplace, get the fixings for Thanksgiving chow."

Randall blinked a few times and stared past Rankin at Lewis. "What?" he asked.

"My famous Cajun cooking. Jesse James is going to help. Come on, honcho. We need you to drive."

Randall craned his neck forward. "Your famous Cajun cooking? Billy Boy, I heard you say famous Cajun cooking one time before, but you didn't do the cooking. Besides, you never left The Bronx before you joined the Crotch, and Wells is from Indiana. What the fuck do you know about Cajun cooking?"

"Come on, Tex," Lewis said, a wide grin splitting his face under his asymmetrical mustache. "Me and Jesse James, we're both good ol' boys from down home. All good ol' boys from down home know all about famous Cajun cooking. Malahini and Big Red are digging a roasting pit for when we get back. Stilts is supervising them, he used to be in Hawaii and knows all about pit roasting. Let's go." He turned and left the tent, heading toward the Jeep parked next to the command hootch.

Randall blinked a few more times and looked up at Rankin, his jaw hanging in bewilderment.

"You trying to catch flies or something, Tex?" Rankin asked. "Shut your damn mouth and let's dee-dee. You're the driver on my med-cap." He shouldered past Randall and ducked out the side of the tent to take his place in the passenger seat of the Jeep. Lewis and Wells were already seated in the back of the Jeep.

Randall stared at them for a moment, then shrugged and sat to pull on his socks and boots. Then he plunked his bush hat on his head, fastened his cartridge belt around his waist, grabbed his rifle, and headed toward the Jeep. "You sure we're supposed to do this?" he asked when he sat behind the wheel.

"Goddamn it, Tex, stop wasting time and get your ass off my hill to run that med-cap," Bell's voice came from inside the command hootch.

"Aye-aye," Randall said, and swallowed. He twisted the ignition switch, released the hand brake, shifted into first, and eased away from the command hootch. He stopped by the table he had eaten at with his men. Dodd was still sitting there looking morose, staring into the distance, seeing nothing. "Dodd, get the fuck in the back," Randall said, half-disgusted.

Dodd turned hound dog eyes toward his fire team leader and, with no noticeable movement, rose to his feet, crossed the short distance, and climbed into the back of the Jeep where he sat on the floor with his legs around Rankin's medical bag.

* * *

It wasn't a regular market day in Hou Cau, so the marketplace square wasn't jammed with people selling dry goods, foodstuffs, and spices. Randall had no problem driving the Jeep into the square. Dogs, chickens, a few skinny-looking hogs, and clutches of tiny children ran around the square and in and out of the hootches that radiated like spokes from it. Randall parked in the middle of the square and the Marines piled out of it while Doc Rankin started setting out his medical materials in the Jeep's back. The corporal opened his mouth to call the villagers to the med-cap, then closed it. Everybody recognized the corpsman and everyone with any ill, real or imagined, rushed to be first in line to be treated by the "bac si."

Lewis headed straight for the people who had food and spices for sale. Wells and Dodd followed close behind. A number of children equal to the number who lined up for treatment by Doc Rankin followed in their wake. A few children were torn between going to the bac-si or following Lewis and were left stranded in between. They wouldn't be able to get close enough to Lewis to clearly hear his words, and they'd have to stand in line for too long to see the bac si. So some of them went back to their play. The rest decided to try to push their way through the hordes of other children surrounding Lewis.

The Marines didn't visit Hou Cau as often as they did Hou Ky and Hou Dau. So the villagers here didn't speak the pidgin the Marines normally used to communicate with the people they saw more often, and weren't accustomed to the American accents the Marines used in talking Vietnamese. But they all knew Lewis by sight and knew how he spoke their language. Many adults joined the children to listen to how this foreigner would grotesquely mispronounce their beautiful language. It never ceased to amaze them how much trouble the Americans had understanding which of the many simple inflections of their language gave a particular sound its meaning.

The adults tittered behind their hands at Lewis's mangling of their language. The teenagers giggled. The children shrieked with unbridled glee.

Lewis ignored them. He knew they were just putting him on about having trouble understanding what he was saying. Besides, he could always use, and did use, his fingers to point at what he wanted and to haggle.

Lewis was finished with his shopping long before Rankin was through treating all the villagers who wanted treatment, so he and Wells found a slightly higher spot along the river—it was drier than the rest of the bank—and sat to wait. Sitting down might have been a mistake; they immediately had twenty or thirty small children and tots climbing on them to play. The two didn't want it to be a mistake, so they played with the kids.

Dodd returned to the Jeep and sat on its hood, looking nowhere blankly.

Eventually everybody who wanted treatment had been treated—Rankin had to shoo a few away when they came back for thirds, having already been back a second time for the same thing—and they got back into the Jeep to return to Camp Apache.

"What'd you get?" Randall asked Lewis on the drive back. He was no longer feeling sorry for himself.

Lewis showed his purchases. He had vegetables that looked like romaine lettuce, thin yams, mutated celery, and an odd-looking white nut. There were a few small bags of not-quite-positively identified spices. The main catch was a half-dozen chickens, which he'd had someone kill, gut, and pluck while Rankin finished the medcap. The chickens were small, but they'd do.

Firewood had burned down to coals in a roasting pit on top of Camp Apache's hill by the time they got back. Palm fronds went over the coals, and the chickens, stuffed in secret by Lewis and Wells, went on top of the fronds, then more fronds and more coals. Most of the PFs showed up when the evening chow bird left. They didn't particularly want to share the flown-in food, but they were very curious about what Lewis and Wells were cooking. They brought some food from home to share. When the chickens were done they all feasted on Lewis's famous Cajun cooking, the flown-in hot meal, and the offerings of the PFs.

It wasn't stuffed turkey with all the trimmings, but . . .

CHAPTER TEN

November 25, 1966

The next day when Captain Hasford flew in on the same helicopter that brought Hempen and Pennell back from R&R, not too many of the Marines had residual stomachaches from Lewis's cooking, and only a couple of them had diarrhea from the (very) unaccustomed food. All things considered, they were in good shape. When Hasford left he took Tex Randall with him. Not for R&R; Bobbie Harder was making a lot of noise about Randall getting his young ass back to Da Nang to see her, and Hasford wanted her off his case. Hasford had two official reasons for visiting Camp Apache, however. The one he didn't need to come out for was:

"Tomorrow a Revolutionary Development team is going to visit Bun Hou," he told Burrison and Bell.

"A what?"

The intelligence officer shrugged. He had seen RD teams in action before and wasn't much impressed, then again he was a New Yorker accustomed to what Broadway had to offer. "It's a sort of small time, home grown Peace Corps. They come out and do entertainments for the locals, talk a lot of support-Saigon propaganda and pass out patriotic literature. In most places they also run a med-cap, though I don't think they'll bother with that here."

"Entertainments?" asked Burrison. "What kind of entertainments?"

Hasford rolled his eyes. "Low-brow Punch and Judy shows, stuff like that."

"Patriotic literature?" Bell asked, amazed. "Don't they realize most of these people are semiliterate at best and won't be able to read it? And what's this shit about support-Saigon propaganda? These people don't give a good goddamn about Saigon, they just don't want Hanoi to take over."

"Look," Hasford protested, "I'm not the one sending them to you or writing their script. All I'm doing is telling you they're on their way."

The CAP leaders looked at each other. What they had just heard didn't make much sense. "Okay, I'll go along with the gag," Bell heard himself say. Burrison nodded agreement.

Hasford also had something he had to see them about personally:

"Remember that reputation Phang was building for you?"

"You mean the one where we were some sort of marauding bandits, going around the countryside raping and pillaging?"

"That's the one," Hasford nodded. "Well, you're getting a new reputation. The latest rumor is you're going into Phuoc Nam any time you want and taking whatever you want from our dauntless district chief at gun-point.''

''What?'' Burrison said, his voice squeaking with guilt.

''I didn't make that up, it's what I heard.'' Hasford looked around the compound, said, ''Nice to see you got your little people back,'' and drew two sheets of paper from the map case hanging from his belt and handed them to the lieutenant. ''Will these help if there's an inquiry? These are legitimate documents for you to have, by the way. They have to do with the disposition of your troops.''

Burrison's hand only shook a little when he took the papers from the captain. The top one was a letter from the Division G-5 to the province chief requesting that the Bun Hou PF platoon be returned to its village to work with the Marines. The second was a letter from the province chief to Major Y telling him to return the PFs to their home village immediately. Bell read the letters over Burrison's shoulder and pointed to the date on the second letter. ''I don't have any idea what there might be an inquiry about, sir,'' Burrison squeaked through his dry throat. ''But if there was anything that someone might want to investigate, something like that reputation of ours, yessir, these'll help.'' The province chief's letter was dated the day before the trip to Phuoc Nam.

Tex Randall's eyes were glowing when he boarded the helicopter with Captain Hasford. Of course, if he had known what would happen in Bun Hou during his absence, he might not have gone. But then, he would have missed something else very important if he didn't go.

The heavy-set gunnery sergeant picked the cold stogie from the elephant-foot ashtray on his desk and lovingly played a match flame over its end while puffing it back to life. His gaze wandered out the window before he returned to his paperwork and focused on a grunt walking smartly in the direction of the entrance to his building. "Bobbie," he drawled, "you expecting that boy you're so sweet on to come calling?"

"You mean Tex?" Bobbie Harder asked.

"I do believe that's the one."

"Gunny, I keep telling you, he's not a boy, he's a twenty-year-old Marine corporal."

"Ah-yup," the gunny drawled around his cigar, "that's what I keep saying."

The door to the office swung open and Randall stepped in. "Hi, Bobbie." He looked and sounded bashful saying those two words.

"Hi, Tex." Bobbie Harder didn't look or sound at all bashful greeting him.

"I got the word you wanted me to haul my young a . . . ah, uh . . ." He stammered and couldn't get any farther.

Bobbie's laughter filled the office. She brought herself under control and said through giggles, "I still can't get over how you can blush through that deep tan of yours." His face was a deep red all the way down his neck. She wondered if the blush extended to his chest. "Yes, I wanted you to haul your young ass back here—" She burst out laughing again at his expression, hearing the words from her "—so I could see you," she said when her laughter stopped. "Now go away and do something with yourself until 1600, that's when I get off work."

Randall fumbled a few words and almost tripped over himself turning to leave. Bobbie smiled at him. She had the kind of control over Tex Randall a good woman has over a good man.

"Now you wait just a goddamn minute there," the gunny growled. "This is my office and I give the goddamn orders around here." He gave them each a hard look in turn.

"Good afternoon, Gunny," Randall said, finally noticing Bobbie wasn't alone in the office.

The gunny grunted a reply and kept looking from one to the other. Tex Randall was slightly shorter than average, blond, and had a wrestler's build—he had been one in high school, as well as a football player. He had the appearance of a big cat ready to pounce, the manner of a combat Marine who intended to survive. He looked out of place in the relative civility of this military office. Bobbie Harder was a beautiful young woman with nearly perfect features and thick, dark hair that flowed across the top of her shoulders.

The gunnery sergeant jabbed his cigar at them and snarled, "Both of you, get out of my goddamn office." He turned back to the papers on his desk, muttering about how "she ain't going to be worth dick-shit the rest a the day, knowing that boy she's sweet on's in town." He heard them leave and looked out his window to watch them walk away hand in hand, oblivious to where they were, and he sighed. He wanted to get into her pants himself. Bobbie Harder was the most beautiful woman he had ever been that close to, and he had probably the fiercest letch for her that he had ever had for any woman. Before she met Corporal Tex Randall, he had tried and kept trying. He thought that she'd eventually give in, if for no other reason than to get him to leave her alone. He saw the way she was immediately attracted to the younger Marine, and he to her, and gracefully backed off. Not because he thought that was the proper thing to do, understand, but because it was common sense not to mess with the woman of a combat grunt, especially not if he's in the habit of carrying a loaded weapon every time he walks into your office.

Neither Tex nor Bobbie could later say with much certainty what they did that afternoon. They knew they walked and talked and held hands and talked some more. At one point Bobbie's flirtatious smile and batting eye-lashes stopped an Air Force lieutenant from chewing Tex out for not saluting him. They remembered that and shared a laugh about it. The other things they remembered were that Bobbie checked out a Jeep and they went shopping for picnic supplies. French bread, cheddar cheese, cold cuts, cookies, several bottles of soda pop, a can of ripe olives, and a six pack. Then a quick side trip to her quarters where she changed from her work dress into Bermuda shorts and a loose blouse (''No peeking, Tex''), raided her roommate's latest care package from home for some chocolates—she left a note promising to pay her back—took some leftover roast turkey from the previous day's holiday dinner, and picked up a blanket. She drove them to a secluded piece of beach, not too close to the Vietcong caves of Marble Mountain and out of sight of the new helicopter facility in the mountain's shadow. She drove close to the water's edge so the waves lapping on the sand would wash out their tracks.

''I spent two weeks scouting this place out so we'd have some privacy,'' she told him when she turned away from the South China Sea and parked in a cul-de-sac formed by two dunes that overlapped but didn't quite meet. She cut the ignition and stared through the windshield, gripping the steering wheel with white-knuckled hands for a long moment before twisting toward him and saying softly, ''I need to see you, Tex. I want to be alone with you.'' Then she hopped out of the Jeep and grabbed the blanket from its back. ''You bring the rest of the things,'' she said, and trotted to the ocean side of the dunes. He followed with his arms full.

She spread the blanket with one edge riding up the foot of the dune so they could lay with their heads pillowed by the sand if they wanted to. She sat with her knees tucked under her chin and her arms wrapped tightly around her legs, and she talked to him. He sat and listened quietly: most of what she said he could understand because he felt the same things. Bobbie Harder talked of the loneliness of being in a foreign country, half a world from home and all she had known her entire life. She shared a comraderie with some of the other women, civilian and military, who worked at Da Nang, but it wasn't true friendship, and always left her with an empty feeling somewhere deep inside. She talked about the constant, gut-gnawing fear of life in a combat zone, of always knowing each second might end with a horrendous blast that would leave you maimed or dead. She knew there was little real danger for her being in Da Nang, or at least she had always been aware of the existence of danger, but it had never bothered her. Not until she met Tex. She knew where he was and what he did and she was afraid for him, and that made her afraid for herself. And she talked about the insecurities and stresses of being a woman in a nearly all-male environment. The cat calls, the leers, the touches, the crude propositions.

"Let's eat," she said abruptly, and rolled onto her knees to sort the picnic things. "What'd you say?"

Randall had muttered something about the harassment she felt. "Any son of a bitch does anything to you, I'll kill him," he repeated. His face was grim.

She laid her hand gently on his arm. "I know, Tex. Don't worry about it. Let's eat." She returned her attention to the food.

They made sandwiches and ate them and drank soda and fed each other olives and laughed and talked. After they ate, they went for a barefoot walk in the surf and wished they'd brought bathing suits. "But we'd have to wait an hour before going in the water," Bobbie said, "or we'll get stomach cramps and drown." They held hands and walked close to each other, and after a while they wandered back to the blanket. When the sun went down they climbed the dune to watch it drop behind the mountains.

"Too bad the ocean's in the east," Bobbie said. "It would be nice to watch the sun set into the water."

Randall didn't answer. He was staring at the mountains, his jaw was set hard. "Charlie's over there and we need to know more," he finally said.

She waited until they were back lying side-by-side on the blanket with their arms between them barely touching before asking what he meant by that. He told her what the Marines of Tango Niner suspected about an enemy installation on the other side of the hills west of Camp Apache. She shuddered when he was finished and clutched his hand. They were quiet for a while. Suddenly she rolled onto her side, her breast pressed against his arm, her legs against his. Her mouth was almost touching his cheek.

"Tex, look at me."

He turned his face to hers and their noses brushed against each other. They held their positions for a long moment before she sighed softly and asked, "Aren't you ever going to kiss me?"

He did. Softly, gently caressing her lips with his. She kissed him back, less softly and gently. He rolled onto his side and they hugged each other tightly, each a mooring for the other in a world gone mad. Their kisses became harsher and deeper, more demanding and more giving. Their hands roamed each other's backs and sides, their legs twisted and intertwined. She grabbed his hand and pulled her chest from his to draw the hand to her breast.

"Here, touch me here," she gasped. "Squeeze it, make my nipple stand up." He did and she emptied her moan of pleasure into his open mouth. "Make love to me, Tex. Now."

"But I don't have any . . ." he stammered. He'd never before made love with a woman he respected and didn't know how to talk about sex with someone like that, didn't know how to tell her he didn't have any condoms with him.

"It's okay, Tex. I have a diaphragm, I'm using it."

That done, they undressed each other with trembling hands and touched each other and kissed all over each other's bodies. When she lay back and he entered her they both screamed, hers high and clear, his low and guttural. They spent themselves in a passion that removed them totally from where they were, they became one universe unto themselves for that timeless moment.

When they were sated, they lay naked on the blanket, tenderly touching and softly kissing. The night was too dark for their eyes, but their fingertips saw their smiles. It wasn't the first time for either of them, but it was their first time together and that gave it a specialness neither had experienced with anyone else before. They slept briefly, then woke and made love again, more slowly and languidly the second time. Then they lay back and watched the stars wheeling across the sky and made up stories about them.

After a long while Bobbie sat up and said in a low voice, "I have to go back."

Randall pulled her back down. "Don't. Let's sleep here tonight."

"No," she whispered into his face. "We can't, some-one might find us. Besides," she laughed, "I have my reputation to think about. It won't do for me to be out all night when people know I was with a man."

"But it's okay to come in at—" he looked at the lu-minous hands of his watch "—almost three A.M.?"

She nodded, her hair brushing his face. "Nobody checks to see what time you go to bed, but everybody watches to see where you wake up." She kissed him quickly and pulled away. He watched her silhouette against the sky as she dressed and wanted to make love again, but made no motion toward her. She dropped to her knees and sat next to him with a hand on his stomach.

"Oh my," she mock-gasped, "there's a naked man on my blanket." He rubbed her arm and they kissed again, then she stood up. "Get dressed."

He did. They folded the blanket and gathered the re-mains of their picnic. Bobbie drove slowly back to the transient barracks where he was staying overnight.

"Don't come to my office until 1600 today," she said when she stopped in front of the Quonset hut. "We shouldn't see each other before then, it'll make the day impossible for me to get through. Come to me when I get off work, Tex. We'll do it again."

"I will, I promise, I'll wait until then." They kissed again, and he got out of the Jeep and watched until she turned a corner and was out of sight. Then he went inside and lay fully dressed on the cot assigned to him. He didn't think he'd be able to sleep, but the next thing he knew someone was shaking his cot to wake him up. He spent the morning in a jittery daze, not knowing what to do with himself. A cold shower didn't help at all. Finally he baked his brain into numbness by going for a long run in the just-past-noon heat. Two more cold showers brought him back to something resembling normality—at least he was able to read a *Sgt. Rock* comic book without losing his place ten times on the same page.

Randall was carrying flowers when he met Bobbie at 1600 hours. They spent the evening and most of the night on the same deserted piece of beach. There was less anxiety this second night and it was somehow even better than the first.

CHAPTER ELEVEN

Meanwhile, Back at Camp Apache

The first interesting thing that Tex Randall missed happened while he and Bobbie Harder were wandering around not remembering what they were doing.

"You sure these things work?" Zeitvogel asked.

"Sure I'm sure, what do you think, I'm gullible or something?" Hempen replied.

"I don't know, Short Round," Mazzucco said. He twisted a sheet of paper in his hands one way and the other, puzzling over it. "The pictures in these directions don't look anything like this shit."

"You get off my little buddy's ass, new boy," Big Red Robertson said. "He belongs to me and nobody else gets to fuck with him."

"Go fuck yourself, Big Red," Hempen said, then

113

looked musingly at the sky. "On second thought, don't. Your asshole's so big you're liable to fall in and get lost."

Before Robertson could respond, Zeitvogel put down the sticks and metal clamps he was fumbling with and looked at the men of his fire team. "Red," he said, "all of you little fuckers belong to me. Now I think what I'm going to do now is just sit myself back and supervise."

"Can't sit back, Stilts," Hempen told him. "Damn hammocks aren't set up yet for you to sit back in."

"I don't believe these hammocks are going to be set up. I think you got screwed."

"I got screwed, all right, but it was a little Chinese girl who worked in a bar around the corner from the Presidential Hotel who screwed me," Hempen said, grinning at the memory. "When she took me home with her. The store I bought these hammocks from didn't screw me. They even showed me how to put them up in the store." He had brought back four collapsible frames, hammock, from R&R.

"How drunk were you when they showed you how it's done?" Zeitvogel asked. Hempen shrugged but didn't answer.

"You really got these in Hong Kong?" Mazzucco asked. "That explains it then. What happened was some Chinese guy who doesn't know any English used a bilingual dictionary to translate the directions into English, that's why they don't make any sense."

"You see that?" Zeitvogel asked.

"Yah," Mazzucco said, "I've seen lots of Japanese stuff where the directions were translated that way. They never make any sense and you have to figure it all out the hard way."

"I bet they were made someplace else and some Chinaman made up the directions," Robertson said.

"No, they're made in Hong Kong, all right," Hempen said.

"What makes you so sure?"

"See? It says so right there," Hempen said, leaning

over to point to the legend on the instructions Mazzucco was trying to figure out, " 'The Pearl and Ruby Constriction Company, Ltd., Hong Kong.' "

"That's construction, not constriction," Robertson corrected.

"No it's not, it's constriction. Look."

Robertson and Mazzucco looked at the words under Hempen's finger and both said, "Son of a bitch."

"That's not what I meant, you dipshits." Zeitvogel shook his head sharply. "I meant out there." He pointed a long arm to the southeast.

"What?"

"That, see it?"

"What the fuck?" Hempen said. "Yah, I saw it too."

"What?" Robertson and Mazzucco wanted to know.

"A light, like someone's signaling with a mirror."

"What?"

"That's what I said. Watch."

They watched and the flash of light came again. Hempen held loose fists to his eyes like binoculars. Zeitvogel noticed and did the same. "I'll be dipped in shit," Hempen said.

"Probably," Robertson said.

Zeitvogel said, "Keep an eye on him, Short Round," and ran to the command hootch. He looked into the radio room and said, "Swarnes, let me hold Scrappy's field glasses for a minute."

"Why?"

"Don't argue with me, do it." He accepted the binoculars and ran back to his team. "Where is he now?" he asked.

"See that tree standing by itself there about two fingers left of the bend in the river?" Hempen told him. "He's standing next to it."

Zeitvogel located the tree Hempen pointed out and lifted the glasses to his eyes. He quickly adjusted the focus of the glasses and stared through them for a long moment before whistling and saying, "What the fuck'd he do, take a bath in lard?'' Next to the tree a man with a glistening torso stood slightly hunched over facing the hill.

"Lemme see, honcho." Hempen reached up and tugged on the glasses. Zeitvogel slowly lowered them and let go. Hempen sighted on the distant tree and re-adjusted the focus. He didn't whistle. "I'll be dipped in shit."

"Probably," Robertson said again.

"I do not believe that fucker. He must be hurt or something. What do you think, Stilts?" Hempen handed the field glasses back.

Zeitvogel looked at the figure again. "Could be heat exhaustion. Man's not wearing a hat or shirt." He lowered the glasses and said, "Let's go check him out. Rifles and cartridge belts. I'll tell Jay Cee while you're getting your gear. Short Round, bring my belt." He slung his rifle and headed back to the command hootch. He glanced back toward the lone tree before ducking into the tent and saw the stranger heading west, loping toward the wide band of trees bordering the river.

Bell was laying on his cot reading a paperback copy of Plato's *Discourses*. Burrison was asleep, *The Bride of Fu Manchu* lying open on his chest. Marine infantrymen will read anything they can lay their hands on. The most popular books among Tango Niner's Marines at the time were the most recent Travis McGee book and J.R.R. Tolkien's *Lord of the Rings* trilogy.

"Jay Cee, I'm taking my people out for a walk. Some chuck dude's down toward the river, I think he needs help." The tall man's eyes were unfocused, looking slightly confused. "He seems to be alone, he's not wearing a uniform, and he's carrying an M-60." He shook his head, then looked at Bell. "Dude's probably sick. Have Doc Rankin stand by in case we need him." He grabbed a PRC-6 radio and pointed out to Bell where he had last seen the stranger. The sergeant watched through the field glasses.

* * *

"I think we're ahead of him," Zeitvogel said twenty minutes later. They had gone southwest at a rapid pace to intercept the stranger rather than have to follow him. "Spread out, maintain visual contact and let's wait for him."

They only had to wait for a few minutes. They heard the stranger's heavy footfalls and the breaking of branches on the trees he crashed through before he came into view. Zeitvogel and Mazzucco first saw him as a flash of red from his headband. Hempen and Robertson spotted a flash of light from his oily chest. The four Marines converged on his path.

"Yo, man," Zeitvogel said. His rifle was slung on his shoulder and he held both hands up, palms out. "You need help with anything?"

The stranger looked with blank eyes at the tall, black Marine. His Adam's apple bobbed slightly, but he didn't say anything through his full, slightly parted lips. "Pump some," Hempen whispered to himself. Seen up close, the stranger had muscles piled on muscles. He was obviously a body-builder. The muzzle of the M-60 machine gun he held by its pistol grip in his right hand wavered slightly but didn't rise to point at any of the Marines. He twitched his left wrist to toss another loop of belt ammunition around it.

"I hope you don't plan on firing that sucker," Zeitvogel said, looking at the ammo belt wrapped around the stranger's left forearm. "You'll probably tear your arm off if you do." He examined the man some more. There was a gigantic knife in a sheath hanging from the leather belt holding up his pants. He wasn't wearing a cartridge belt or carrying a pack. A black leather tube about five inches in diameter hung from a strap around his shoulders. He had no canteens, first aid kit, food, or extra ammunition for his machine gun—unless they were in the black tube. Aside from the red sweatband, the long ends of which hung low onto his right shoulder, he wore canvas-topped jungle boots like the Army had but hadn't yet reached the Marines, and black pants cut so tight in the hips and thighs they had to chafe if he had worn them for more than a couple of hours. "We live on that hill over there," Zeitvogel said. "What say you come with us? We'll give you some fresh water and a hot meal— you just got to be thirsty and hungry in this heat. You are thirsty, aren't you?" He carefully reached for a canteen with his right hand and held it out. The stranger looked at the canteen and licked his lips, but made no motion to take it. "We can get you cooled off, you're sweating mighty heavy," Zeitvogel continued, still holding out the canteen. "If our doc thinks you need it, we can get a med-evac for you most ricky-tick. If not, we got a bird coming in day after tomorrow, pick up a couple people for R&R. It can take you where you belong."

The heavily muscled stranger's Adam's apple bobbed again and he pumped his jaw once or twice before he said, "I am where I belong." His voice was thick and the words came out slowly, as though he had to think about each one before saying it.

"Whatever you say, man," Zeitvogel said. He was concerned about the machine gun. Even if the stranger would hurt himself if he fired it, he could still get out a burst long enough to maybe hit one or two of the Marines before it jammed. "You say this is where you belong, then this is where you belong. What say you come to Camp Apache with us anyhow? Get a meal, drink some water, take a shower clean that oil off you, maybe cop a few Zs."

The stranger's face showed emotion for the first time. It flickered slowly between puzzlement and confusion. "Oil?" he finally asked. "Camp Apache?"

"Yah. We call it Camp Apache because it's deeper in Indian Country than anybody else. And that's how I first saw you," Zeitvogel nodded at the stranger's broad chest, "the sun reflecting off that grease on your bod."

The stranger slowly lowered his head to look at himself. His brow was beetled when he looked up again; it had never occurred to him that his body oil might give him away.

Zeitvogel carefully replaced his canteen in its pouch and stepped forward with his hand extended. "They call me Stilts. What's your name?"

The stranger seemed startled at this sudden change of subject, but regained control of himself. "Uh, call me Cas," he said slowly. "That's from my initials, Charles Arnold Stabone."

"Good to meet you, Cas." Zeitvogel gestured with his hand to bring it back to the other's attention.

"Uh." Cas was confused about what to do, he didn't want to change his grip to shake hands, but didn't want to be rude, either.

Zeitvogel saw the man's predicament and clapped his shoulder instead. "Come and visit for a skosh bit."

Cas turned down the offer of a shower, but he bolted down three C ration meals and drank a gallon of water before curling up to take a nap in the shade of one of the squad tents. He ate sitting cross-legged on the ground with his machine gun laid across his legs—the ammo belt stayed wrapped around his left forearm—and folded his arms around it when he lay down to sleep. The only thing he said that he hadn't already told Zeitvogel near the river was, "There's a Vee Cee installation over there somewhere that has to be taken out." He wouldn't let Doc Rankin examine him.

"Any ideas of who he is?" Burrison asked quietly when Cas nodded off.

Bell shook his head. "I heard a couple of Americans have gone over to the other side, but not anywhere around here."

"He said he knows there's a Vee Cee installation over there." Ruizique pointed to the west.

"And he said it had to be taken out," Burrison said.

"He didn't act like he thought we were his enemy," Zeitvogel said.

Hempen was more practical. He looked at how the sleeping man was dressed and commented, "Look at how tight he's wearing his trou. He don't cut the crotch out of them most ricky-tick, he's gonna cut off circulation to his balls, be talking soprano." The others ignored him.

"We have to turn him over to Captain Hasford," Burrison said. "He'll be able to determine who the best authorities to give him to are. But first we have to get that machine gun away from him, and then we have to hold on to him until he can be picked up." He looked at the broad chest on the stranger and shuddered deep inside; this was definitely a man he wouldn't want to have to take on in hand-to-hand combat.

"Is it legal for us to hold him against his will?" Slover wanted to know.

Burrison and Bell shrugged, they didn't know.

"I've got some pentathol in my medkit," Doc Rankin said. "When I'm sure he's out deep, I'll give him a shot. I think I've got enough to keep him out until a med-evac bird can make it here." He paused to make a mental calculation of the dosage, then added, "If someone comes soon enough."

But Cas didn't drop into a deep enough sleep for Rankin to administer the pentathol, instead he dozed fitfully. Shortly before the helicopter that brought in a hot meal once a day appeared on the horizon, he stirred himself a final time, rose to his feet, and walked out the back gate. He passed McEntire on the way and said in that slow, thick voice, "You've got your mission, I've got mine." If McEntire had been carrying his machine gun he might have tried to face Cas down. But he wasn't, so he let the muscular man go. Several of the Marines gathered in the southwest corner of the compound. The last they saw of Cas was a flash of sunlight reflected in the trees along the Song Du Ong river.

CHAPTER TWELVE

November 26, 1966

The Revolutionary Development team arrived and set up shop in Hou Cau hamlet during the time Tex Randall was going batty from not knowing what to do with himself in the morning. Burrison, Bell, and the rifle squad went to Hou Cau to provide security.

The Vietcong had small teams of cadre they sent into the countryside to sway the people to the communist side. They did this by putting on small entertainments (no small thing in the isolated hamlets, where the only normal entertainment available other than what each individual family unit did to amuse itself was the one or two battery operated radios the hamlet would probably have— but batteries were hard to come by, and the radios were played sparingly), doing some small work in the paddies or fields to help bring in the crops, propagandizing, and providing some medical attention (if they had the means).

So the South Vietnamese government, at the urging of the Americans, came up with what the Americans called "Revolutionary Development" teams. What the South Vietnamese called them was something very different— the Saigon government didn't want any of its programs called "revolutionary" anything. The Revolutionary Development teams worked as a direct counter to the Vietcong propaganda teams by putting on entertainments, giving agricultural advice and assistance to the people, handing out propaganda literature, and providing medical attention.

While Tex Randall was running his mind into a daze and taking cold showers, the RD team was giving seminars on how the farmers could produce larger rice crops with a new strain of rice and giving the villagers of Bun Hou medical attention. Of course, the seeds for the new strain of rice weren't available to the villagers—but it was agricultural advice. The South Vietnamese doctor had taken a job with the RD rather than be drafted into the army. His experience in the villages had taught him what diseases and ills to expect when he visited them. He couldn't figure out why hardly anyone in Bun Hou had any of the open lesions the Americans called "gook sores." The frequent med-cap patrols run by the Marines and their corpsmen had cleared them up months ago, and the soap the Marines handed out kept them away. But the RD doctor didn't know that.

When Randall and Bobbie were having their second picnic dinner on their secluded piece of beach, the RD team was handing out propaganda literature. Most of the adult population of Bun Hou village was, at best, semi-literate. If they had used paper for that purpose, they would have put the propaganda brochures to the same use for which so many country folk in America have used the Sears Roebuck catalog.

By the time the second interesting thing that Tex Randall missed happened, it was after dark, and he and Bobbie Harder were doing something that he found far more interesting.

The RD team erected a six-by-eight-foot screen at one end of the large market square in Hou Cau and cranked up their portable generator in time to start the movie right after nightfall.

"What's the show?" Burrison asked, eyes gleaming. He hadn't seen a movie in more than two months.

"*Goldfinger,*" said the one English-speaking member of the RD team.

Burrison's eyes grew larger with excitement. He had seen *Goldfinger* when it first came out, and that Honor Blackman, well, she was really something. His eyes returned to normal size and he looked less excited when he heard Bell ask that one English-speaking member of the RD team, "You're putting me on, right? How the hell are these people going to understand what's going on?"

The English speaker looked at him curiously. "No problem. We Vietnamese are an urbane, sophisticated people. Besides, there won't be any language problem. The movie's dubbed."

"Uh-huh," Bell said. He shook his head and went looking for Zeitvogel and Ruizique. "I want you two to take your fire teams out there about three hundred meters and secure our western flank. Just in case," he said when he found them. "Zeke, you take Billy Boy. Stilts, take Wells and Dodd with you. Take Prick-sixes with you. Nothing fancy on the call signs tonight. You're Tango One and Three, we're Six."

Ruizique was ready to go. He'd been afraid there wouldn't be any patrols at all and he'd miss a chance to kill Vietcong. Zeitvogel, on the other hand, didn't want to go. Like Burrison, he had already seen this movie. Honor Blackman didn't particularly turn him on, but some of the movie's other women did. Besides, he wanted to find out how they translated Pussy Galore into Vietnamese. But all Zeitvogel said was, "Jay Cee, leave Dodd here. It ain't fair to make him go out. He's a draftee."

"He's a Marine grunt, samee-same you," Bell said. "He goes."

The one English-speaking member of the RD team was from the southern coastal city of Dat Do. When he said the Vietnamese were urbane and sophisticated, he was referring to the middle and upper classes among whom he had grown up, not the peasants about whom he knew virtually nothing. Talking about the mandarin and merchant classes, he was right. These people often spoke French or English in addition to their own language, were university educated, and had often traveled abroad. In many ways they were more European than Asian in their outlooks. Most Third World peasants are relatively primitive peoples living in what amounts to the early Iron Age. They speak local dialects, which can change radically in ten miles, receive little formal education, and often never leave the confines of their home villages.

But the show must go on. Besides, most of the good people of Bun Hou had never seen a movie before and were tremendously excited about seeing one and getting a clear view of life in America's world. However, they simply lacked the cultural referents to understand *Goldfinger.* They didn't understand what a dry suit was, or an oil-tank farm, or a hidden room inside an oil storage tank. And when Bond kicked the space heater into the bathtub, they had no idea of what happened—having neither electricity nor any need for space heaters. And that was all before the opening credits.

The villagers laughed and cheered and clapped and were awestruck. And totally bewildered. When Oddjob made his first appearance they laughed and cheered and clapped some more—they thought he was a good guy, after all, he was Oriental. But then all the Orientals in the movie turned out to be bad guys. It's just as well the movie got interrupted before Honor Blackman made her appearance; Pussy Galore doesn't translate well into Vietnamese.

The Song Du Ong river made a sharp northward bend at a point south of Hou Dau hill, causing the land in between the bend and the hill to form a bottleneck of sorts. Hou Cau hamlet spread along the eastern side of the river bend on a northwest–southeast axis. Sugarcane fields spread east and north of Hou Cau. The village's central marketplace was a large open area in Hou Cau, facing on the river. Zeitvogel and Ruizique set in between the hill and the river, where they could effectively block passage west to east. Ruizique's fire team went to ground at the edge of a small clearing near enough to the water for his left flank man to keep an eye on any river traffic—they didn't expect many fishermen to be out tonight, they'd mostly be in Hou Cau watching the movie. Zeitvogel's fire team was a hundred meters farther inland. Neither anticipated that anything would happen this early in the evening, the VC normally made their runs later in the night.

Hempen turned his head from side to side, listening first with one ear then the other, trying to get a fix on what he thought he had heard. A week earlier, he thought, he wouldn't have had any doubts about it; either he heard something or he didn't, and he'd know where it was if he had. If he was hearing something, he'd tell Stilts now. But he'd been out-of-country for most of the time in between and was afraid his combat senses were dulled. He fingered the selector switch on his rifle to assure himself it was set on full automatic and kept listening, wondering how soon he should tell Stilts what he thought he heard. A hundred meters to his south, Billy Boy Lewis twisted the ends of his mustache and wondered if he should tell Ruizique now that someone was out there or wait until he could give him an idea of how many were there.

Dodd made the decision for them. Like he did with every order he had received since he got over the shock of his draft board telling him he was drafted into the Marine Corps, Dodd accepted his assignment to Zeitvogel's fire team for the screening action with fatalism. When he got his induction notice, Dodd didn't despair or make plans to run to Canada. He shrugged, tried to laugh it off, and reported for his physical. He'd go ahead and spend his two years in the Army, probably including a tour in Vietnam, though he might get sent to Germany or Korea. Maybe he'd get assigned to the infantry but, hey, less than a quarter of the soldiers in the Army are in combat arms units, the rest are support troops. And the infantry is only one branch of the combat arms. He figured he stood a pretty good chance of spending his two years pushing a pencil.

When his draft board told him he was going into the Marines, Dodd wailed, he cried, he gnashed his teeth. He told them he wasn't cut out to be a hero, all he wanted to do was sell used cars, or insurance, or be an accountant. He'd seen John Wayne in *The Sands of Iwo Jima* and knew this wasn't for him. He tried to cut a deal with his draft board: let him out of this and he'd enlist for four years in the Air Force. Or the Navy. Hell, he'd even sign a four-year enlistment contract in the Army. Anything but the Marines, please, he was just a nice, pudgy, suburban kid who had no business running around with those heroes.

But his draft board wasn't buying any of that. They had a head-count quota to meet, so no deals. And the Department of Defense told the Selective Service they had to select a certain number of young men for the Marines, and it was just Dodd's dumb luck his local draft board had picked everybody inducted the same day he was for that honor. Tough, kid, they'd told him, you're going into the Marines.

As far as Dodd was concerned, he was now one of the walking dead. His fate had been decided, his doom sealed. There was nothing that could happen to him now that was worse than what already had. He did whatever he was told to. Not gladly, not with high esprit, but he did it. What he was told to do now was watch for any Vietcong who might try to come through on their way to Hou Cau, and to kill them. So when he heard someone moving in front of him and saw a shadow move against the shadows of the trees he pointed his rifle at the shadow and pulled the trigger.

Someone screamed and fell loudly. Dodd only fired one round and the other Marines didn't react at once, because they didn't know what he had fired at. After a few seconds there were a few voices shouting near where the man Dodd shot was and the sound of a body being dragged. Zeitvogel shouted, "Fire," and all six Marines in his position opened up.

A hundred meters south, Lewis decided not to wait any longer and rolled to his side to tell Ruizique someone was out front. Ruizique listened for a few seconds to the gunfire coming from the north, then ordered his men to hold their fire until they had something positive. Six Marines, south of Hou Dau hill, were firing into the trees to their front. So far, Dodd was the only one who'd had a target, and no one was shooting back.

The radios Zeitvogel and Ruizique carried crackled to life. "Tango One, this is Tango Six," Burrison's voice said. "Sitrep, over."

Zeitvogel fumbled with his radio and said into it, "Tango Six, One. We're shooting at an unknown number of unfriendlies. We hit at least one of them, over."

"Three, Six. Sitrep."

"Six, Three. I've got people out front, but nobody to shoot at. Over."

Burrison listened to the firefight and looked at Bell, who was also listening to it. They thought the same thing, only their Marines were shooting, and the lieutenant said into the radio, "Tango One, this is Tango Six. Cease fire until someone fires at you. Tango Three, maintain silence. Over."

"Roger, Six. One over," Zeitvogel said, and shouted

cease fire to his men. Ruizique was quieter about telling his men to maintain noise discipline. Silence settled over the thin forest where the Marine ambushes were. In Hou Cau the movie rolled on with no one watching it. In small groups, the villagers started drifting away from the market square, in a direction away from the shooting.

"Kill the projector," Bell ordered. "Cut off the generator." He didn't have anyone to give those orders to though, the RD team was headed for their vehicles to make a run for it. He swore and ran to the generator himself and groped for its master switch in the dark. As soon as it was off he ran back to Burrison and Willard. The lieutenant was still on the radio, trying to find out who Zeitvogel's ambush had fired at. Then a new sound disturbed the night.

"Incoming," Willard shouted, and dove for cover at the side of a well.

Burrison and Bell listened for the whistling of a descending mortar round before deciding Willard was right. They dropped flat and hugged the ground. A 60mm mortar round hit thirty meters from them.

Ruizique called in. Burrison picked up the radio handset and replied.

"The mortar doesn't know we're here," the Dominican said in a hushed but excited voice. "It's only twenty meters away, I can see its flash on the other side of the clearing. We're going to take it. Out."

Burrison tried to ask how sure he was of the distance and did he know how many VC were around the enemy mortar, but Ruizique didn't answer. He didn't answer because he was ignoring his radio, he was going from man to man, telling them what he wanted them to do. The corporal took the point himself and stealthily led his men around the clearing about ten meters inside the trees. The first mortar round had been a spotter round. It was now firing more rapidly, about one round every ten seconds—enough time to make aiming adjustments between shots. Burrison and Bell took advantage of the time between rounds—they were all falling in the square—to run out of the field of fire. Bell bent over as he ran past the well and grabbed Willard by the collar to pull him along.

For the first half of the distance around the clearing to the mortar Ruizique led his men at a fast pace, then slowed down until they were on the mortar's side of the clearing. He could see the tube and three men kneeling around it. Using touches and hand signals only, he put his men on line; Pennell at the edge of the clearing, then Webster, himself, Neissi, and Lewis deepest in the trees. They were to advance cautiously until someone spotted them or he opened fire. Pennell, Webster, and he would shoot the three men operating the mortar before joining Lewis and Neissi firing into the trees behind it. Ruizique stepped off as soon as he was sure his men understood his orders.

When they closed to five meters, he lined the barrel of his rifle on the man reaching for another rocket-shaped round to drop down the mortar's tube and squeezed the trigger. The man he aimed at pitched over and he swung his muzzle at the one holding the mortar's bipods. Webster's and Pennell's bullets were already slamming into that VC and the other one. Ruizique turned back to the first one and fired two more bullets into him.

"Swing around," he shouted, "everybody face into the trees. Get down and fire one magazine." The five Marines quickly wheeled so the clearing was at their backs, and fired into the woods. There was no return fire. Each of them stopped shooting when he loaded a fresh magazine into his weapon. "Talking Man, check the bodies," he ordered when all their rifles fell silent. He peered into the trees, looking for movement or any regularly shaped shadows, but it was too dark for him to see anything in the forest.

Pennell scuttled to the three Vietcong and patted them down for personal weapons and documents. Two carried knives, one had a rifle, and one had a pistol. There didn't seem to be any documents on any of them. "One of them's still alive," Pennell reported when he was through.

Ruizique thought quickly. He knew these three couldn't be alone here, they had to have friends nearby. "Talking Man, drag the warm one to the other side of the clearing. Neissi, take the tube, go with him. Let me know when you get over there. Go."

The two riflemen jumped up and ran to obey his orders. They crossed the clearing in a hurry. They both knew there were probably more Cong in the area and neither of them wanted to get caught in the open if the VC picked then to attack. They shouted when they got back to their original ambush position.

"Malahini, Billy Boy, go. I'll cover you." Ruizique strained every sense seeking sign of the enemy he knew had to be to his front, but couldn't find any. For the first time he wished Billy Boy Lewis was in his fire team full-time instead of in Randall's; Lewis had an uncanny ability to know when someone was nearby. Webster shouted that he and Lewis were with the others, and Ruizique twisted around to his feet and dashed across the clearing. Now he held his radio to his head and broke squelch. "Tango Six, Tango Three, are you there? Over."

"Three, Six. Go," Burrison said at once.

"I got me one big souvenir, Six. Also a live one—" he glanced at the Vietcong who seemed to barely be breathing "—if he lasts long. Over."

"Are there more out there, Three?"

"I believe so, but they're not showing themselves. Over."

There was a slight hesitation before Burrison asked, "Do you think you can make it back here with your big souvenir and your live one? Over."

Ruizique thought about that for a couple of seconds. What he wanted to do was stay right here and wait for the rest of the VC to come looking for their mortar so he could blow them away, but he didn't know how many there might be. More Marines and all of the PFs were back at Hou Cau, and it would be safer for him and his men to rejoin them than for any of them to come out to where they were. "Affirmative, Six. Expect us in one zero. I'll let you know when we are about to leave the trees and walk in. Over."

"Roger, Three, I'll see you in one zero and you'll let me know when you're here. Tango Six out." Then Burrison raised Zeitvogel on the radio and asked if he thought he could make it back to Hou Cau. The tall black Marine corporal hadn't seen or heard any sign of enemy activity since his ambush opened up, he thought they could make it back all right.

While Ruizique was on the radio Pennell tied pressure bandages on the prisoner's three wounds; there was an exit wound under the man's right arm that he missed.

"Talking Man, carry the gook, Neissi, bring the tube," Ruizique quickly gave his orders. "Billy Boy, you got point, Malahini, cover me. We're going back to Hou Cau. Go." Lewis led off followed by the two burdened men. Ruizique brought up the rear, walking backward, watching for the VC he knew were there somewhere. He frequently looked over his shoulder to make sure he was still with Webster.

Bare seconds after the Marines left the east side of the small clearing a line of Vietcong reached its west side. The VC approached it as cautiously as the Marines had. They had known there was a squad of Marines in Hou Cau, but until the first fusilade below Hou Dau hill they hadn't known any were in the forest. The VC commander swore when he saw the mortar tube missing and only two bodies laying where there should have been three men. He sent a half squad running across the clearing, hoping to draw fire from any Marines who might have been on its other side. When they crossed in safety, he had some of his men pick up the fifteen mortar rounds still sitting where they had been stacked; they might have the opportunity to get them to the other mortar. Then he led the rest of his platoon across. They continued to move slowly toward the hamlet. Was there more than the one squad of Marines in Hou Cau? How many were in the woods between here and there? Was it true that the PF platoon had returned, and if so, where was it? There were too many questions this VC lieutenant didn't have the answers to.

A hundred meters north, another VC platoon came across the place Zeitvogel's ambush had lain. A few of them fingered the spent cartridges littering the ground and nervously wondered where the Marines were. The platoon's commander thought the Marines had to be a small unit, set out as a screen and now withdrawing to Hou Cau. He moved his unit less slowly than the platoon to his south; he half hoped to catch a small Marine squad in the forest and kill it before it reached the hamlet.

Four hundred meters to the east and slightly north, two more platoons that had gone around Hou Dau from that direction were already in position outside Hou Cau. They could assault from that direction if needed. Their main job, though, was to blockade the small road leading from Hou Cau to the main east-west road north of the hamlet, and to cut down anyone who tried to flee in that direction.

Lieutenant Houng and the PF squad leaders had started organizing their men when the first shots rang out. When the mortar barrage started, they herded the villagers and RD team members into the long-unused bombing bunkers scattered around the hamlet—in every village where there was fighting or the threat of fighting, the people dug bunkers to hide in and be protected from the bullets, grenades, and bombs of the battles. A couple of the RD team members had had to be yanked out of their vehicles and thrown bodily into the bunkers. As soon as they heard from Ruizique that he had captured the mortar, Bell and Burrison worked with the PFs to prepare a defense against an assault on Hou Cau. Two squads took positions along the northeast side of the hamlet, facing the enemy they knew to be out there. The third squad, under Willy, went to the north side to cover against a flanking attack from that side. A few minutes after the rough defenses were completed, Burrison's radio crackled. It was Ruizique reporting he was about to leave the trees and enter the hamlet.

"Come on in, Three. One out," Burrison said.

Two minutes later, after Bell had inserted the five Marines into the middle and river side of the line of PFs, the radio crackled again. It was Zeitvogel coming in. Bell put Wells and Dodd into the right side of the line while Burrison sent Zeitvogel with his fire team to take charge of Willy and the flank defense. The prisoner was barely breathing, and still no one noticed the exit wound Pennell had missed. They waited.

In between other chores, Bell talked to Slover on the radio. Slover was in command of the nine Marines left in Camp Apache. The big mortarman assured the sergeant that he had and could use registration points to help fight off an enemy assault on Hou Cau. Slover also put his men on one hundred percent alert in case the Vietcong hit the Marine compound.

Two of the VC officers, one on the west, another to the north, had radios. When all four of their platoons were in position, they conferred and decided on the moment they would launch their attack. They decided not to take the time to transport the extra mortar rounds to the second mortar.

Tension mounted in Hou Cau, especially among the RD team members. They had been separated during the initial confusion, and not being together increased their fear of the battle they were certain was coming. Although this was not the first time they had shown a movie in a village, this was the first time they had shown one in a village that wasn't in a "secured" area with many ARVN and American troops around, and they had all heard tales of Vietcong attacks on villages RD teams were visiting; the RD teams sometimes seemed to be magnets for the

Vietcong. None of them had liked the idea of having to spend the night in Bun Hou. Most of the villagers in the bunkers were from the other three hamlets of the village and wished they were home. Some of them wished that because they thought they would be safe at home instead of waiting for an attack. Others were concerned about the safety of their homes and property if the VC were hitting all the hamlets.

The Marines and PFs were more nervous than usual about the coming fight. They were used to picking the time and place of a fight themselves, not sitting and waiting helplessly for the enemy to attack. Only once before had all the Marines and PFs fought as a unit, and that was behind the defenses of Camp Apache's perimeter. They reminded themselves not to stare at one spot, licked dry lips, swallowed to moisten constricted throats, kept fingers loose on triggers. The tension on their lines was palpable.

On a silent signal, the waiting VC northwest of the hamlet rose to their feet and advanced on line. The second mortar, set two hundred meters behind the two platoons north of the hamlet, started firing its covering rounds into the northwest end of Hou Cau.

The Marines and PFs hugged the earth more closely and wished they had proper fighting holes or, even better, fighting bunkers in which to hide from the barrage. Fortunately, the mortar rounds were too few, too spread out, and all fell into the hootches behind them—the Marines and PFs were too close to the trees and the VC assault line for the mortar to risk hitting close enough to them. Then two whistles shrilled in the trees to their front.

"Hold your fire," Bell shouted. "Wait until they come into the open." They didn't have to wait long. Suddenly fifty screaming Vietcong burst into the open area between the woods and the nearest hootches where the defenders lay waiting.

"Fire!" Bell and Burrison shouted simultaneously. The

twenty-two carbines and AKs carried by the PFs and the seven M-14s of the Marines opened up on the attacking VC. They were too close for Willard to be able to fire more than one round from his M-79 grenade launcher, but two VC tumbled to the ground when that one grenade exploded. Then Willard dropped the launcher and drew his .45. A Cong charging straight at Bell was flipped backward by a bullet in the throat from the sergeant's personal .357 magnum. Burrison drilled another VC through the chest with his .45.

The Vietcong screamed their blood-lust and fired back, but they were running and couldn't aim well at targets they had trouble spotting anyway. The Marines and PFs had upright targets to shoot at, and dropped fifteen of them by the time the VC reached the first line of hootches and kept going past them.

"Cease fire," Burrison shouted when he saw the VC had passed through their line. "Report."

"Cease fire," Bell echoed him. While Ruizique, Collard Green, and Vinh checked their men for casualties, the sergeant assigned four men to watch the trees that were now to their rear and turned everyone else to face into the hamlet. They moved to the inward side of the hootches they were among. The VC mortar barrage moved deeper into the hamlet, leading the remaining attackers, who were still firing.

"One, Six," Burrison said into his radio. "Bad guys coming in your direction."

"Roger," Zeitvogel whispered into his radio. He turned half of his men to face into the hamlet.

There were shouts and whistles from the VC leaders inside Hou Cau and the shooting stopped. Then a flame flickered to life among the hootches and was touched to the thatch roof of one of them. The dry roof blazed into fire.

"Ah, shit," Bell swore. "Scrappy, we can get those mother fuckers in a crossfire. Let's do it before they burn the whole damn place down."

Burrison agreed. While Bell directed their men to fire into the hootches in the area of the burning one, the young lieutenant got Zeitvogel on the radio and told him to turn his men and do the same. Zeitvogel left two men facing into the trees and had the rest fire into the hamlet. Two more hootches flared up.

Screams rose from wounded Vietcong caught in the crossfire; their screams mixed with keening from a few villagers who peeked out of the bunkers and saw the flames lapping at their homes. Three more hootches were set aflame before the VC in the crossfire broke and ran for the fishing boats beached on the river bank. Not all of them made it. The survivors pushed and hauled boats into the water and poled off, heading across the river and downstream.

As soon as the main assault force was clear, the commander of the blocking force north of Hou Cau ordered his men to advance on the hamlet at a rapid walk, firing as they went. That wasn't part of the original plan, but nobody had expected enemy soldiers to get caught between the burning hootches and the blocking force. He took advantage of the unexpected opportunity to kill a few of the imperialist Marines and their puppet PFs.

Zeitvogel realized for the first time there were VC in the woods where he had been watching. He swore loudly and ordered his men to open up on them. The order wasn't necessary, they were already all returning the fire. Bell and Burrison instantly guessed this was a diversionary tactic to cover the withdrawal of the assault force. They hoped it wasn't also a diversion to lead them into an ambush, and led their men at a run to hit the new enemy force from the flank.

The second VC force suffered fewer casualties in its advance on the CAP members than the first one had—they were charging a unit only half the size of the other—and quickly closed to hand-to-hand distance. The defenders rose and withdrew among the hootches, firing as they went.

The PFs the Marines called Butter Bar and Pheet were backing up side-by-side when one manic VC, glad of his chance to kill the running dogs, charged them. The VC's rifle was empty and he didn't have time to reload it, but its bayonet flashed out straight and bright in front. He lunged at Butter Bar, and the PF fell over dodging the plunging blade. Pheet swung the butt of his rifle around and caught the VC in the back of the head, staggering him. Then he shot the Cong before he could regain his balance, and jerked Butter Bar back to his feet. One hootch over, Hempen saw a VC holding an automatic pistol in one hand and a whistle in his mouth run by. He fired a five-round burst at the running man and saw him drop. Hempen kept backing up and looking for more targets; he didn't see the officer he had shot lurch to his feet and limp away. A VC luckier than the one who attacked Butter Bar and Pheet saw a lone PF silhouetted against a burning hootch and put a bullet through his heart.

Then the main Tango Niner force hit and the un-wounded VC officer blasted retreat on his whistle. The blocking force VC broke off contact and ran into the cane fields east of Hou Cau.

"Zeke, get your people and Collard Green's squad on line and pursue them by fire," Burrison shouted. "Stilts, check out your people. Everybody else, put out those fires." Bell was already organizing the Marines and PFs into fire brigades. They let the hootches that were already burning go, and concentrated on keeping the fire from spreading to the others. Burrison got Slover on the radio and told him to pop a few rounds into the cane fields. He didn't expect the mortar or Ruizique's pursuit by fire to hit anyone, but he thought it would keep the Vietcong running.

Ruizique quickly led the men assigned to him to the edge of the cane fields and lined them up to fire across the nearly open area. Zeitvogel yelled out, and all three of his men instantly replied that they were all right. He led them into the fight against the fire. It took Willy longer to check his men because not all of them answered and he had to run around looking for them. It was easier than it might have been because the flames from the half-dozen burning hootches gave him light to see by. He found three men down; one dead, one badly wounded, one not so badly wounded but unconscious. He put the rest of his squad to work preventing the fire's spread and started giving first aid to his two wounded men.

By now, Thien and the other hamlet chiefs were leading the villagers out of the bunkers and grouping them by hamlet. They enlisted the aid of the elders in keeping the people from interfering with the Marines and PFs who were working to keep the fire under control. Some of the people, those whose homes were burning down, had to be restrained. The hootches were dry and burned quickly. Several more were struck by sparks, but the sparks were extinguished and the hootches saved by Tango Niner's quick action.

All fourteen of the Marines who'd been in on the battle were standing, so were thirty-three of the thirty-five PFs—the lightly wounded PF had regained consciousness. Six houses were destroyed in the attack, but damage to others was minimal. The RD team's movie screen was shredded by bullets and mortar fragments, the projector was broken beyond repair, the generator was damaged, and some of their vehicles had dents from bullet or fragment hits. None of the people were hurt.

As soon as they thought the fire was safe to leave, Burrison, Bell, and Houng put their men on line and swept through the hootches and the market square looking for wounded VC and anything they might have left behind. In the northwest, where they had faced the first assault, they found eleven bodies—including the original prisoner Ruizique had brought back; he had bled to death from the unfound exit wound. There were also several blood trails where wounded men had crawled away. A half-dozen more bodies were on the north side, from where the secondary assault had come. Four bodies lay near or on the river bank, fleeing men who hadn't made it to the fishing boats in time.

One of the VC was still alive when found. He lived long enough to tell Houng that the VC command had wanted to demonstrate to the people that the Marines couldn't protect them. They also wanted to show the people that only harm could come to them if they entertained visitors from the Saigon government. So this company was sent from the stronghold on the other side of the western hills to attack Hou Cau when the Revolutionary Department team was there.

Thanks to the Marines' light security screen, the VC had lost the element of surprise their assault depended on, and the battle was an unqualified loss for them. Most of the people in Bun Hou had little use for the Saigon government and less for the Vietcong. But there was one man, one of those whose home was destroyed, who had grievances against the government and was waiting for an opportunity to help the other side. But when the VC came into his hamlet and, without provocation, burned down his home, he turned solidly against them. Before dawn he went to Lieutenant Houng and asked if he could join the PFs.

When they finished their search the Marines finally took time to look at each other.

"You're bleeding," Bell said to Zeitvogel.

The tall corporal looked at his squad leader for a long moment before putting his hand on his side and feeling the wetness he hadn't noticed in the excitement of the action. "So're you."

Hempen and Neissi also had minor wounds that they didn't notice until someone pointed them out.

CHAPTER THIRTEEN

November 27, 1966

"That tears it," Bell shouted. Nobody had left Hou
Cau after the Vietcong attack, everybody had stayed for
safety in case any VC were still roaming about. The sergeant hadn't slept all night and he wasn't able to fall
asleep now that he was back in Camp Apache. He was
too furious about what the dying VC had told Houng.
"They're trying to kill innocent civilians now," he
roared, stomping out of the command hootch. He looked
west and pointed. "Those sons of bitches are over there
laughing at us! They need to be taught they can't fuck
with the people of Bun Hou. They've got us to pay if they
try it." He stormed around the compound kicking at everything in his path. His lashing feet sent flying an empty
ammo crate someone had put down as a stool. One of

the piss tubes was jarred out of line by a hard, glancing kick. He staggered the wall-less four-holer. A guyline for one of the squad tents was knocked off its stake, creating a sag in the tent's wall. But some unconscious voice inside the sergeant prevented him from kicking any of the sandbag and sheet metal tables or any bunker walls, or anything else he could hurt himself on.

"The honcho looks kind a like a rabid dog today," McEntire said from a safe distance. "Think we should do something about it?"

Zeitvogel shook his head. "He'll get over it on his own," he said. "Only thing we need to do is make sure if he bites someone, that man gets his rabies shots."

McEntire laughed and looked around the compound. Some of the Marines had been sleeping when Bell started his yelling, the noise woke them up. Everybody was doing the same thing he and Zeitvogel were; keeping a safe distance until Bell calmed down.

It took Bell fifteen minutes of kicking and incoherent ranting until he calmed enough to stop storming around the compound. His body was still quivering with rage when he finally stood on top of a bunker on the west side of the hill and shouted, "You're going to get yours, Mister Charlie Cong. You're going to get yours, I guaran-fucking-tee you that." He punched the air to emphasize his words. When he was through shouting he clenched his fists in front of his belt buckle and shook for a moment. Then his shoulders slumped and he turned and slowly walked back to the command hootch, ignoring the looks everyone in the compound was giving him.

"I'm tired of the shit, Scrappy," Bell said to the lieutenant who joined him in their room. Bell was lying on his cot, his arm draped across his eyes. "We've been here six months, what, seven months? and they keep coming from over there." His voice sounded more weary than Burrison thought a Marine sergeant could sound. "It used to be they came just trying to get people and supplies through, sometimes try to take us out. Now they're going after the people. They got to stop it, Scrappy.''

"You cop some Zs, Jay Cee," Burrison said when the sergeant was quiet for a few minutes. "I'll talk to Captain Hasford again. Now we have independent confirmation of what we already know. Maybe he can use that to convince Division or Three MAF.''

Bell didn't answer. His chest rose and fell slowly and regularly. Burrison thought he was sleeping and rose to tiptoe out. "We don't have independent confirmation," Bell said suddenly. "The fucking gook who told us is dead. G-2 can say we made it up and we can't prove different.''

"Maybe. I'll talk to Hasford anyway. You sleep." He went into the radio room and hoped his number one would get some sleep.

"Got a call from Box fucking Top," Swarnes said in a low voice so he wouldn't disturb Bell. "Railroad tracker's hauling tail out here and bringing the Texas badass with him. Shit should hit in about half an hour." Bell's outburst must have had a subduing effect on Swarnes; he didn't swear as much as usual in giving the message.

"Thanks, Swarnes," Burrison said, and jerked his thumb toward the tent flap. "I'll be around." Bell was right. He knew it and every other man in Tango knew it. Probably all the citizens of Bun Hou knew there was an important Vietcong stronghold of some sort west of those hills. Hasford knew it too. The trick was convincing the strategy makers that it was important enough to take out now instead of next year, but how? Burrison's magic bag was empty. He suspected Hasford's was too.

Bell was in a dead sleep when the helicopter carrying Hasford and Randall arrived, and he didn't wake up. Hasford promised to take back to G-2 the information they had been given by the dying VC, but, "Without a live body to stand there and give the information personally, I don't have much hope it'll change anybody's mind," which was what the lieutenant had thought. "As for Flood and Doc Tracker, the word is they'll probably both be back, but the doctors aren't saying how soon.'' Ruizique—protesting loudly all the way—and Knowles left with Hasford to go on their R&R.

"Tell Uncle Stilts all about it, Tex.'' Zeitvogel bent over to drape his long arm around Randall's shoulders as soon as the noise of the departing helicopter had fallen enough for him to be heard without shouting. "That honey of yours is a real good-looking piece. Is she as good a piece as she looks?'' He skipped away from the roundhouse blow the shorter man swung at him.

"Come on, honcho,'' Lewis said, twirling the ends of his mustache in opposite directions, "don't be so selfish. Tell us how she is in the rack.''

"Man, I ain't had none in so long I forget what end to stick it in,'' McEntire said. "Tell me about it so I'll remember.''

"What're you talking about, 'forgot what end to stick it in,' '' Wells chimed in. "You never knew in the first place, Wall.''

"You want a penicillin shot or anything, Tex?'' Doc Rankin asked, deadpan.

"Tex, I'm mean when I get horny, and I'm horny,'' Slover said. "You don't come out with it right the fuck now, I'm gonna knock you down and sit on you while Wall tries to remember on you which end to stick it in.''

Randall's virtue was saved when Kobos called from his position at the machine gun overlooking the main gate, "Company's coming.'' The four corporals, and the others watching their fun, drifted to the wire near the gate. A lone man wearing a black shirt, black shorts, and a conical straw hat walked toward Camp Apache along the bulldozed road to Hou Dau. He had an AK-47 slung upside down over his shoulder along with a Vietcong type pack, and he carried a white flag. He limped slightly.

"Get Scrappy,'' Slover said to no one in particular.

Wells ran toward the command hootch. He was shouting for the lieutenant before he was halfway there.

Zeitvogel peered hard at the approaching man and turned to Lewis. "Tell Doc Rankin to get over here. I think we're going to need Houng for this, too. Go."

"Can I take the Jeep to get Houng?"

"Long as Scrappy don't tell you not to."

"You got it." Lewis ran to the Jeep, which was parked next to the command hootch. Before getting in it, he poked his head into the back section of the tent, where Rankin and Tracker had their cots, and told the corpsman Zeitvogel wanted him at the main gate. Lewis fishtailed the Jeep, he accelerated and turned so hard. He drove through the main gate with a cloud of dust and spun left to Hou Ky, while the walking man who was causing all the excitement was still more than a hundred meters away.

When the armed man reached the foot of the hill he stopped and knelt to lay his rifle and pack down. Still kneeling, he removed his shirt and lay it on the ground next to the rifle and pack. He stood and held his hands, fingers spread, out to the sides, turned slowly so the Marines could see he had nothing strapped to his back, and walked to the main gate. Burrison, Zeitvogel, and Rankin greeted him. He bowed to the lieutenant and the corporal. *"Chao, ong,"* he said to each. He turned to the corpsman and said, *"Bac-si.* Numba one *bac-si,"* and bowed to Rankin as well. He lifted one leg to display a scar on his calf and slapped it. "Numba one *bac si,"* he said again and grinned.

"Yah, I know who the hell you are, too," Rankin said, smiling back. "Where the hell's Jay Cee when we need him," he added in an aside. Bell and Lewis knew the Vietnamese language better than any of the other Marines in Tango Niner. A month and a half earlier, Rankin had treated an infected bullet wound on this man's leg during a med-cap to a nearby hamlet called Ahn Dien. Burrison, Bell, and Zeitvogel had been on the same med-cap. Rankin had been certain then, and the way the man came to them now seemed to confirm it, that he was a VC who had been wounded in action against he ARVNs or the Marines. What the man said next was the final proof.

"*Chieu hoi,*" he said. *Chieu hoi* translated directly as "open arms." It was an amnesty program for Vietcong who wanted to stop fighting. Any VC could surrender using those words and be set free after a short re-education period rather than be imprisoned as a POW. Some Chieu Hois were accepted into the "Kit Carson" program and acted as guides, scouts, and interrogators for American units fighting the VC and NVA. The surrendering VC didn't turn at the sound of the returning Jeep, not even when the Jeep roared so close it sounded like it was going to hit him.

Houng jumped out of the Jeep and scurried to face the newcomer, whom he also recognized. They talked back and forth so rapidly Lewis's linguistic abilities were immediately overwhelmed and he stopped listening. After a couple of minutes Houng nodded decisively and said something that sounded final. He turned to Burrison and the others and said, "Him name it Do Chot Huu. Him Chieu Hoi." He held up a cautioning hand. "Him Chieu Hoi only him Kit Carson Tango Niner. Me think we say yes, him Kit Carson Tango Niner numba one."

"Can we trust him?" Burrison asked.

A grin that didn't express happiness spread across Houng's face and he said, "Him not boo-coo numba one Kit Carson, me bang-bang him toot-sweet."

"Why did he decide to do this now?"

"Because what Vee Cee do Hou Cau last night. Him say that numba fucking ten thou."

"Does he have anything to offer us to prove he's telling the truth?"

"Him say him know where Vee Cee have something important over there." He pointed to the west and grinned wider. "Him take us there."

"No shit."

Later, after he finally woke up, J. C. Bell was one

royally pissed-off Marine sergeant when he found out Do Chot Huu had come in and nobody had woken him so he could be on hand and find out immediately what was going on.

"What the rules are," Bell said, "the rules are we have to turn him over to the Arvins."

"Jay Cee, I'm surprised at you," Burrison said. "We hand Huu over to the Arvins we may never see him again. This is the first time a Vee Cee has turned himself in to us and offered to help. We need him."

The four corporals were in the meeting with Burrison, Bell, and Houng. They all agreed with the lieutenant. Houng also talked rapidly in badly broken pidgin English, supporting Burrison's position.

Bell didn't argue. He held his hands wide and said, "All I'm saying is what the rules are. Major Y's got it in for us since we took the fay-epps away from him. If he finds out we're holding a Chieu Hoi without going through the system, he'll have something he can go to MACV with and raise some holy hell." He looked off to the side for a moment to think, then continued, "If he's smart, he'll go directly to MACV. The Army doesn't like us and they'd probably put their weight behind him going to Three MAF to do something about this." He was playing devil's advocate.

Burrison smiled at that. "Major Y doesn't have to know we've got a Chieu Hoi."

"How do we keep him from finding out if he decides to have his spies check up on us?"

Burrison smiled more broadly and leaned back. He was about to play his trump card. "After last night, there's two openings in the fay-epp platoon. Houng will hire him as a replacement."

Bell chewed on his lip, mulling that over for a moment. "What about the census rolls?" he finally asked. "Won't it show up on the census rolls that Huu isn't from Bun Hou?"

"Y probably won't bother to check. Anyway, the census data is way out of date and doesn't mean that much."

"Okay," Bell shrugged eloquently. He was excited at the prospect of the Chieu Hoi who would lead them to whatever it was the Vietcong had on the other side of the hills. All he'd wanted to do was make sure the most obvious objections to what they were doing had been considered. "One more thing," he said. "How do we know we can believe him? What makes us sure he wasn't sent to lead us into a trap? Charlie wants us gone, he could try subterfuge since nothing else he's tried worked."

"We don't know," Burrison said, "and this could be a Vee Cee trick. But there's only one way to find out. You know the story of Androcles and the lion? Androcles was a young Greek out traipsing through the toolies one day when he was threatened by an angry, hungry lion. The lion was pissed off because he had a thorn in his paw and it hurt. Androcles felt sorry for the lion and took the thorn out of his paw for him. Later Androcles was captured by the Romans and thrown into the arena to be eaten by lions. The lion in the arena was the same one whose paw he removed the thorn from. The lion remembered him and didn't kill him, so the Romans let him go."

"You're saying because Doc fixed Huu's leg he might be the lion to our Androcles?"

Burrison nodded. "That's what I'm saying."

"Let's do it."

No help was coming from higher headquarters, and they all knew it. The only way they could find out what Charlie had to their west was to go and check it out themselves. Huu said the installation was a long day's march from Camp Apache. And, no, he didn't know what it was, only that it was important. Hell, the Marines already knew that. They had to send out a recon without letting anybody, outside of the people in Tango Niner who had to know, know what was happening. Huu would go as guide. Houng had to be along as interpreter. Billy

Boy Lewis was a natural choice because of his highly developed jungle- and night-fighting skills, and that uncanny sixth sense of his that told him when someone was *there*. The recon patrol had to be kept as small as possible to reduce its chances of being detected, but they decided an extra rifle and cool head would be helpful in a jam, as well as someone who could take command and get the survivors back if things went wrong.

"Tex is going," Burrison said. Bell backed him.

"Bullshit, I'm a badder-ass fighter than he is," Zeitvogel objected. "And I got more TI here, I earned it more than he did." TI—time in. A very important concept to enlisted Marines; time in the Corps, time in rank, time in a unit or duty station. It was seniority, and was often the deciding factor in determining who got the choicer assignments. "Besides, you're going to be in the fucking jungle, and my skin'll blend in easier than his will."

"Tex is smaller than you are, Stilts," Burrison explained. "He's a smaller target, and that'll make him harder to spot. He can hide behind smaller objects than you can. Besides, he just got laid. He'll want to be careful not to get wasted or get his pecker shot off so he can get laid again."

Zeitvogel kept arguing, but it was to no avail. Burrison and Bell had made up their minds, Randall was going. All that remained was to decide who would lead the patrol. They decided to do it by coin toss.

"What we have here, ladies and gennelmens," Swearin' Swarnes said in his best sports announcer voice, "is a gen-you-wine You-Ess-of-Ay quarter dollar. This side here with the visage of George Washington's profile on it is called heads. The other side here," he turned the coin over, "with the American eagle spread-legged on it is called tails. The way we do it is I toss the coin up into the air and while it is up there one of you calls out 'heads' or calls out 'tails.' Whichever way it lands, if the person who called guessed right on the way it lands, that person wins. If it lands with the other side facing up, the person who called it loses. Do you both understand that?'' He looked at each of them. Fortunately, they both already knew how a coin toss worked—if they didn't, Swarnes's directions might have confused them as to how it did. ''So, I think the fair way to do this is to let Sergeant Bell make the call because he's the junior man involved in the calling. Are you ready? Here goes.''

Swarnes tossed the coin at the same time Burrison said, ''Seems to me I've heard that somewhere before.''

The coin hit the ground.

''No fair calling now, Jay Cee,'' Swarnes said and bent over to snatch the quarter off the ground before Bell could look at it. ''You were supposed to call it while it was in the air.''

''You're right, Scrappy,'' Bell said, ignoring Swarnes. ''I got the call last time because you have rank on me. Let's take turns.''

Burrison nodded sharply. He wanted to make the call and was glad Bell agreed with him.

Swarnes looked at the two, wondering what came next.

''Scrappy's making the call, Swarnes. Toss it again.''

Swarnes shrugged. He said, ''Call it while it's in the air before it hits the ground, Scrappy,'' and tossed the quarter.

''Heads,'' Burrison said as the quarter curved into its down fall. The coin hit and all three bent over to examine it. ''Goddamn shit,'' Burrison swore. ''Can we go for two out of three?''

''Sorry, Scrappy. We agreed to decide on a flip of the coin, not on two out of three.'' Bell scooped up the quarter that had landed tails-up and dropped it into his pocket. ''For good luck, you know?'' he said when Swarnes asked for his coin back.

CHAPTER FOURTEEN

November 28, 1966

They gave Captain Hasford another twenty-four hours
to come back with good news. He didn't. Then they put
out three patrols, just like always. The difference was,
one of the three patrols had five men who never patrolled
together: Bell, Randall, Lewis, Houng, and Huu. Mc-
Entire, who also never patrolled with any of them, and
four other PFs went with that quintet. They left Camp
Apache at sunset and roved in a westerly direction just
south of the rice fields until, near midnight, they reached
the foot of the finger ridge leading down from the hills.
They lay in ambush there until Bell made silent signals
and the five going on the recon left the others. McEntire
would lead the PFs back to Camp Apache later. This
whole business of putting out three patrols and having

the five men going on the recon hidden in one of the patrols was a decoy to disguise the fact that someone was doing something different. If anybody was watching with a night vision device, all they would see was the usual three patrols leaving Camp Apache. It would be after dawn before anyone would have a chance to see anything different. And by then the recon would be long gone.

If anyone looked closely enough at the patrols, he might notice that two of the Marines in one of them carried light packs and one "PF" wasn't armed but was instead carrying a VC-type tube pack. These three packs carried two days' food for five men.

McEntire watched Bell and the other four start their trek up the finger ridge and silently wished them well. He didn't envy them where they were going. This Chieu Hoi could be their Androcles' lion, but he wasn't about to trust a lion that might be hungry.

For this early part of the recon run, Bell put Lewis on the point and went second himself. Huu was in third place, followed by Randall, who didn't need orders to know he was to kill the supposed Chieu Hoi immediately if they ran into trouble. Houng brought up the rear. A quarter of the way up the ridge Houng closed the gap between himself and Randall. "Stilts fight here," he told the Marine. "Izzy bang-bang. Me come help there." He pointed a little higher on the ridge and off to the side a little.

Randall nodded his understanding. One night more than a month earlier, Zeitvogel and his patrol had ambushed a VC supply run on this ridge and been attacked in turn by a VC platoon that was coming down the ridge line behind the supply run. Houng had come to their aid with a reaction force, but not before PFC Isidro Perez was wounded badly enough that he had to be sent to Japan and then all the way back to the World for treatment. One PF was wounded and another killed in that same action. This was where it had happened.

They trudged on in silence, higher up the ridge than

anyone from Tango Niner had gone before. The range of the 81mm mortar at Camp Apache set the effective distance the patrols could go. If they went much farther than three-and-a-half kilometers from the compound, they were out of range of the mortar's support. The ambush site Houng pointed out was just beyond the effective range of the mortar, the flares Zeitvogel had called for that night barely cleared his own position on the ridge.

Up front, Lance Corporal Billy Boy Lewis let his mind go blank. He didn't consciously look at anything or listen for any particular sound. He let the gray-on-gray shadows that were the sights of night flood into his eyes, he let all the night's sounds wash into his ears. The breeze wafting over the ridge brushed his skin, and the information it carried was absorbed. The smells carried on that breeze entered his nose and made their own impact on his senses. He tasted the air. Some primordial center in his midbrain gathered the data from all his senses, sorted it, filtered it, analyzed it; all without conscious thought. The soothing message his midbrain sent to his forebrain was "All clear." That all-clear kept his forebrain damped down, kept it calm, allowed the midbrain to continue gathering the data from his senses, sort, filter, and analyze that data. As long as the midbrain message to his forebrain remained "All clear," he was confident there was no danger at hand and kept going forward. His rifle was held ready in his hands, its muzzle pointing without conscious thought wherever his eyes drifted; his finger rested on the trigger with an easy, untiring tension. If the message ever changed from "All clear," he could react instantly to the danger.

The message changed. It didn't flash a red of imminent danger, it was more like a yellow caution light flickering on and off on a control board. It was more like a question mark after the "All clear?" than it was a warning. He cut his slow pace in half with one step, halved it again with the next, and came to a full stop on the third. He cocked his head and listened. He didn't hear anything.

Nor was he aware of his nose and tongue testing the air moving over him. "Someone's up ahead," he thought, and waved his left hand back at Bell, then led the recon off the ridge crest into the brush alongside the well-used trail he had followed. They silently got down behind cover. Unseen by Huu, Randall aimed his rifle at the middle of the Chieu Hoi's back.

Bell edged close to Lewis and whispered, "What?" into his ear.

Lewis made an "I don't know" shake of his head, and tried consciously to understand what had made him stop and go for cover. He couldn't detect anything. He put his mouth close to Bell's ear and murmured one word: "Wait." Then he lay down his rifle and drew his K-bar knife. He thought for a second and decided to take the few extra seconds he needed to withdraw his three ninja throwing stars from their oiled, water-proofed wrappings in the inner pocket of his shirt. Ready now, he slid forward through the brush. He thought himself heavy as a feather and visible as air as he moved through the brush. His feet edged forward slowly, confidently, the nerves in their soles questing downward to examine everything the bottoms of his combat boots came in contact with. The K-bar rested easy in his right hand, held at waist level. Its hilt across his palm, forefinger along one side of the pommel, thumb tip against the other, the blade edge upward on his thumb side. The ninja throwing stars were ready in his left hand.

Fifty meters from where he left the others he stopped again. Now something came to his consciousness in the night, but something so faint he wasn't sure if it was a smell or a sound. He continued uphill through brush so sparse it couldn't hide a man in daylight. Twenty-five meters farther, he knew. He heard low voices. He couldn't make out the words, only that they were Vietnamese. He could tell by their tone that he was close to a VC listening post, a listening post manned by bored soldiers who expected that the only people to come along tonight would be other VC passing through on their way down the ridge to attempt infiltrating through Bun Hou. Silently, he moved forward to see how many there were and how they were situated.

What he found was three men, one sleeping, two awake, on top of a bunker so well concealed he wouldn't have seen it if they hadn't drawn his attention by being on top of it. There might be more VC inside the bunker, he couldn't tell. The bunker was dug into the foot of a fifteen-foot-high sheer rise to the left of the ridge-crest trail. A few feet on the other side of the trail the land dropped off sharply. This place looked like a bottleneck with no way to get to the other side without passing through it. Lewis lay for a few minutes looking for a way around this listening post and listening to the guards. They were talking the same talk all soldiers talk when they are bored and lonely; they talked of home and their families and what they hoped to do if the war ever ended. There were times, the two guards agreed, when it seemed like the war would never end. Lewis looked at the guards again and fingered his blades. He was certain he could take out the two men who were awake with his stars. Even though he had never before thrown them at a living target at night, he had practiced throwing them at night at wood targets he made himself. With those two down he could reach the sleeping man and kill him with his K-bar before he could wake up and do anything. But if there was someone awake inside the bunker, Lewis might not survive his attack. More to the point, if they had a radio and had to check in occasionally, their next report wouldn't be made; or even if they didn't have a radio they were supposed to report in on, the next Vietcong to come along would sound the alarm and whoever was on the other side would be alerted, and this recon would be much more difficult. He had to find a way around or they'd have to give up and go back. He returned to the others to let Bell know what he had found. Lewis had been away for twenty minutes.

All four gathered close to hear Lewis's report. Houng translated for Huu.

"Okay, we can't get past on the right because of the drop-off," Bell said when Lewis finished. He was glad Lewis hadn't taken it on himself to wipe out the listening post. Maybe they could do that some other time, but to do it now would, as Lewis realized, force them to cancel the recon. "What about the left side, can we go over it?"

"I don't know. I thought you'd be worried so I came back to let you know what was up before I checked it out."

Huu said something to Houng after he translated that, and the PF lieutenant looked hard at the Chieu Hoi's shadow for a moment before turning to Bell. "Huu, him say he know way around, him say sometime he come on secret, have to stay away sentry. Him say give him point, he lead us past."

Bell looked at Huu and wished it was day so he could try to read the other man's expression. In the night his eyes barely showed as a lighter smudge on the silhouette of his face. "What do you think, Houng, can we believe him?" he finally asked.

Houng's shadow hunched in a shrug. "Maybe. Me tell him him be first to die him not lead us safe."

"Let's go."

Houng told Huu to lead them, but to be ready to die immediately if he was lying. The Chieu Hoi looked around to orient himself, then waved, "follow me." He led them back the way they had come a short distance before turning right, down the gentle slope of the ridge side. He hesitated where the slope became steeper and looked around. He said something to Houng.

"Him not come this way before," Houng told Bell. "Him say he have to look for secret path."

The darker smudge that was Huu against the dark shadows of the night hills somehow suddenly looked more confident and moved onward. Abruptly, the shadow was cut to half its former height. Huu had found the path he was looking for, a narrow track cut in the steep side of the ridge. He helped Houng down onto it and stepped aside so Houng could help Bell down. Huu, Houng, and Lewis were able to walk on the narrow path, leaning their right shoulders against the wall of the ridge side. Bell and Randall, being much bigger, had to sidestep along it. A short distance along the narrow track, Bell took off his cartridge belt and hung it over his left shoulder so the canteens hanging from its back would stop pushing him away from it.

It reduces my ability to fight if we walk into an ambush, Bell thought, but if we get hit here we're fucked anyway.

Randall saw what the sergeant did and copied him. The going was now much easier for the two stocky Americans.

The ridge above them climbed much faster than the cut track they had followed. Lewis watched the ridgeline above and saw it hump upward. He knew that was the bottleneck he had scouted. Beyond the hump the ridge dropped off gently for a short distance before merging with a long hill running north-south. The track they followed ended at the junction of the ridge and the hill. A flight of narrow ridges too steep to be called stairs were cut into the side of the hill. Bell and Randall hooked their cartridge belts back around their waists, balancing carefully so they wouldn't fall. One careful step at a time— the steps were narrow, allowing only fingerholds and feet sideways—they climbed fifty feet to where the hillside started leveling off and the steep flight turned into stairs until the slope became gentle enough that they could walk without aid.

The wind blew harder on the top of this hill than anything they were used to on the Song Du Ong flood plain. The stiffness of the wind kept vegetation from growing thick and high on the hilltop, made it almost bare of growth other than grass. They huddled close, heads together, to plan their next step. The loudness of the wind made them talk more loudly than they felt comfortable doing, especially since the wind would carry their voices. Only Huu didn't seem concerned by it. The Chieu Hoi would keep the point from here on. He knew where the Vietcong installation was and the main trails to it. He also knew ways around those trails, ways they could follow that would avoid patrols and checkpoints. Houng would follow him, then Bell and Randall, with Lewis bringing up the rear. It was now two hours before dawn; they'd have to find a place to hole up during the day before then.

Huu led them on a circular route across the hilltop and down its western side. At places it was so steep they had to grab onto slender tree trunks or bushes to keep from falling. Off the top, the wind rapidly died, and underbrush grew thick. The trees grew taller the farther down the hill they went, and the higher the trees grew the thinner the brush became. Huu followed a game trail that almost paralleled a heavily used VC path. Three times in one hour they had to stop and get down while enemy soldiers tramped by on the other trail. The game trail went along the side of the hill, gradually hair-pinning its way to the bottom rather than going straight down. On the other side, it angled up rather than hair-pinning. False dawn was beginning to lighten the sky in the east before they reached the top of the second hill. Bell ordered a halt there. They found a slight hollow in the hillside, a ten-foot-wide place that was almost flat. Bamboo grew in a thick, natural fence around it and fanned out overhead to cut out the sun. It was twilight-dark inside. The hollow was obviously used as a sleeping place by animals.

"I hope this isn't some tiger's bed," Lewis said as he settled down.

"If it is and he comes back while we're here, he'll probably smell us in time to go away before breaking in on us," Bell said. "Wild animals are usually more afraid of humans than we are of them."

Let's hope so, Randall thought.

Silently, they set out a cold meal. Huu removed rice balls from his pack, the three Marines each took a C ration meal from their packs. Normally C rations are picked blind, so everyone has an equal chance at getting the good ones and everyone will sooner or later get stuck with the ham and limas. They didn't pick blind for this recon, they only took the good ones that could be eaten cold. Turkey loaf, beans and franks, and scrambled eggs were the menu for this morning after a long night's walk. Everybody shared everything, though Huu didn't eat much of the canned American food. He found it too bland for his taste. They opened the bottoms of the empty cans and flattened them, then taped them together and packed all the refuse into one empty C ration box in a way that nothing would rattle. Lewis put the box in his pack. They weren't going to leave anything for the VC to find.

After eating, they set a watch rotation that didn't include Huu. This meant the man they didn't know they could trust would be better rested than the others, but that couldn't be helped. They'd be here until dark, so they'd have time for everyone to get enough sleep anyway. No one came near during the day—certainly no tigers or other animals obviously looking to sleep where they were.

"We go down the other side of this hill and then over another," Huu explained, with Houng translating. "Then we reach a shallow valley. On the far side of it, in something like a box canyon, is the place we are looking for. It will take us about four more hours to reach it." This was while they were eating another meal. The remains of this meal went into Randall's pack.

Bell thought about that for a few minutes. If they spent two hours reconnoitering the place, they wouldn't be able to get back this far before they had to hole up for the day again. But as long as there was a hill between them and the VC valley, they should have no problems avoiding the enemy the next day—as long as their presence wasn't detected while they were over there. It was enough time, he decided. They would leave this place an hour before sunset.

"Wait here, I'll be back in a skosh bit," Bell said. He slipped through the bamboo and went alone the short distance to the top of the hill. The wind didn't whip as roughly here as it did on the first hill they had crossed, and vegetation grew more lushly. He listened for a short while and didn't hear anything other than the wind and birds coming to roost for the night. The top of this hill was narrow; he crossed it quickly and found a place where he could look through the trees and brush to the next hill. Everything was heavily covered with trees and he couldn't see a thing on the opposite hill or the bottom in between. The afternoon sun had dropped well past the middle of the western sky toward the next hill when he turned back to where he had left his men.

"Let's go," he told them. No point now in waiting until the hour before dark, he was certain they were completely alone in this area. The small column moved out in the same order as it did on the ridge track the previous night. This time Huu didn't look for a game trail, he found a narrow gully down which water flowed during the rainy season and followed it. Its bottom was free of brush, though trees and bushes grew right up to its sides and hid it from view. The irregularities in the bottom of the gully made for good footing, better than the game trails they had followed the night before. They didn't make any noise going down. A wider streambed, littered with fist-sized stones, cut between the hill they descended and the next one to climb. Downstream was to the left. Huu led them upstream until he found a gully going up in the right direction and started climbing it.

His sense of time must be off, Bell thought when they reached the top of that hill. At this rate its not hardly going to take us four hours to get to where we're going. But they didn't go almost straight like he had thought—they took a long dog-leg which took time.

It was still light when Huu found a path that ran along the hilltop and turned south on it. The path was being overgrown by weeds and finger saplings, it wasn't used much anymore. Bell wondered how much of their passing this trail would show in the morning. He didn't let that bother him, though. As long as they didn't leave signs on their way back out, they'd be all right. And if they ever came back here, they'd come in by a different route, too, just as they were going to leave by a different route tonight.

The Chieu Hoi turned off the hilltop path after going along it for a kilometer and managed to find a game trail leading down to the shallow valley below the hill during the day's last light. The descent was only half the distance of the climb on the other side. The valley floor was almost flat, sloping almost imperceptibly down to a stream in its middle. Copses of trees were scattered around the valley, but it was mostly covered with grass, except near its ends where there were cultivated fields— rice paddies at the north, sugarcane and vegetables at the south. Occasionally they could hear isolated dogs barking in the hamlets at the ends of the valley. They avoided the copses.

The grass was man-high, and they had to push their way through it except where someone—or something— else had already passed by. It seemed to be riddled with paths and roughly broken trails. Bell thought even if the pathless places they broke their own trails through were seen, they wouldn't be distinguishable from any of the others in the valley. His only concern was that if someone was watching the valley now with a Starlite or an infrared scope, they'd be visible. But evidently nobody was, or never looked where they were.

The stream in the middle of the valley was about ten-feet-wide now and little more than a foot deep. During the monsoon it would rage far beyond its current banks, but now it was a gentle brook that posed no problems for the five men. Six hundred meters beyond it they reached the trees that spread out from the foot of the next hill. Huu stopped and leaned close to talk briefly to Houng.

"Him say we close now," Houng told the Marines. "Him say now we must go quiet, avoid guards."

Now we have to go quietly, Bell wondered, what have we been doing? He nodded and said, barely audibly, "Let's go."

Huu went twenty meters into the trees before turning north. At this depth they were deeper into the forest than any sentries the VC might have watching the valley; they wouldn't pass in front of any such guards. The undergrowth here was thicker than any they had gone through before, but it was mostly broad-leafed and pliable. The ground underneath was covered with soft mulch that didn't snap when they walked, and as long as they stepped softly their feet made no noise. Huu led them in a weaving path around the bushes under the trees. Where there wasn't enough room to pass between bushes, he held a branch out of his way and kept holding it until Houng took it from his hand. Houng held the branch to give to Bell, who held it for Randall, who handed it to Lewis, who gently eased it back into place. They made no more noise going through the tight spots than they did where the bushes were far enough apart for them to pass without touching them. They went slowly, taking over an hour to go little more than a kilometer, before Huu stopped, looked around, and turned toward the hill on their left.

After a short distance he reached a vertical wall. He felt along it several meters in each direction until he found what he was looking for, then gathered the others to show them what he had found. A thick vine hung down the cliff face from a ledge fifteen feet above them. Toeholds were skillfully hidden in the face of the cliff. It was a bolt path for the Vietcong leaders from the hidden valley Huu had told them was around a corner but obscured from view. The entrance to the hidden valley, he told them, was heavily guarded, but this way wasn't because only the leaders and a few others knew about it. The ledge above them led around and into the VC installation. If they followed it they could come down inside the enemy encampment undetected.

Bell swallowed and looked closely at Houng. In the darkness under the trees he could barely make out a darker blackness where the PF lieutenant stood. Even though they couldn't make out each other's expressions or use words, the two leaders communicated. Houng put his hand on Bell's forearm and squeezed; he didn't think Huu was leading them into a trap. "Let's go," his hand said on the Marine's arm.

Again, Huu led the way as they climbed the cliff and followed the narrow path at the top of the vine-and-toehold ladder. Bell examined what little his eyes could make out in the almost total absence of light. He decided the entrance to this box canyon wasn't more than twenty or thirty meters wide, probably narrower—easy for a few men to hold off a much larger attacking force, as long as the attackers were only infantry without air support. He looked up and saw how the hillside above him continued almost straight for another seventy-five feet or more, and the opposite hill did almost the same; he revised his estimate of air support and decided it would take luck as well as skill for a fighter pilot to give much help to infantry. And the steepness of the hillsides here would make a descent by infantry close to suicide. He'd have to wait to see how the hillsides looked deeper in. Less than a hundred meters along the ledge Huu stopped and talked into Houng's ear.

Houng turned back to Bell and said into his ear, "Him say we there. Him say, do we want go down?"

CHAPTER FIFTEEN

Late Night, November 29, 1966

Down was through a chimney in the face of the cliff. The ledge overhung the chimney. Its walls were reinforced and hand- and toeholds were cut into it, down a few feet and then back under the overhang. They groped blindly with their hands and feet and Huu guided Houng, who guided Bell. Bell found the horizontal part of the chimney very difficult to negotiate because the holds were spaced for Vietnamese. He was nearly a foot taller than the average Vietnamese, which made the grip places uncomfortably close to each other for him. He hunched his shoulders and held tightly with his hands. There was a slight tremble in his thighs by the time he reached the back wall of the chimney, where the distance between the down-leading holes cut into the face of the chimney wall didn't make that much difference. Randall, three inches shorter than Bell, found the going slightly less difficult than the sergeant had, but only slightly. Even the wiry Lewis found his 5'7" an awkward height on the side steps.

It took a quarter-hour for all five of them to climb down the chimney. When Lewis reached the bottom, Bell looked at the luminous dial on his watch and nodded in appreciation at Huu's accuracy about how long the trip would take. It was almost exactly four hours since they had left the place where they had hidden and rested during the day.

The floor of the chimney was bare and clean of debris. They gathered at the front of it. A screen of growing brush hid the chimney from outside. Bell peered through the brush screen and saw under the thin starlight that filtered through the treetops that the small valley was mostly cleared under the major trees, which were left standing high to conceal it from above. Dimly perceived lumps in the night seemed to be pyramidal tents pitched under the trees. Fifty meters farther into the small valley and half that distance from the wall, a low, orange light burned in front of one tent; two men were dimly visible sitting at a table in front of it. No one was obviously nearby. He spread a couple of branches and looked to the sides. The brush screen in front of the chimney seemed to be part of a curtain of foliage that continued around the cliff face.

Huu tapped Bell on the arm and pointed to the ground at the side. The Marine knelt down and saw a low space between the brush curtain and the cliff face. Huu motioned Bell forward and edged into the space. The space was too low for the Americans to stand in, even in a crouch. They could duckwalk or crawl; it was wide enough that they didn't touch the brush. The two Vietnamese were able to walk bent over. The crawl space continued toward the tent with the light in front of it.

When they reached the point closest to the table they stopped and observed.

One of the two men sitting at the table wore a khaki uniform. Several rows of colorful ribbons decorated his shirt above the left breast pocket, red collar tabs held a rank insignia none of the Marines had seen before. His face was thin, as were his wrists where they protruded from the cuffs of his shirt sleeves, but, despite his thinness, he looked well nourished. The other man wore, as his only decoration, a red armband on his black peasant pajamas. He was not as lean as the khaki man. Both men looked middle-aged in the orange light that flickered from the oil lamp on the table, and they both had many ballpoint pens sticking out of their shirt pockets. They talked in voices that weren't too low to be heard by the hiding men.

Bell listened closely. His Vietnamese wasn't good enough to understand everything the two men at the table said, but he could discuss it later with Lewis, and between them they'd figure out much of what was being said. More, Houng would know what they were talking about. Between the poor English that Houng had and the small amount of Vietnamese Bell and Lewis could understand, they would get most of the conversation between the two enemy officers. There were a couple of things said that Bell almost understood; he lacked a few words, but one thing he thought he heard almost made him wish it were daytime so he could get a better look at the hillsides—he thought he heard the two officers talking about this hidden valley being a communications center. Apparently it was being beefed up to improve communications between the Vietcong headquarters, called COSVN, hidden somewhere near the Cambodian border not far from Saigon, and the field units in northern South Vietnam. The other thing Bell caught, but lacked enough words to clearly understand, sounded like they were talking about a deserter. Bell was certain they were worried about information the deserter had in case he decided to Chieu Hoi or was captured, but he couldn't tell what information the deserter had, when he had gone, or if he had been caught. The man had been trusted, a sergeant from Hanoi. He had often been used as a special courier bearing top secret messages to the units fighting the imperialist Running-Dog Marines east of the hills, and the officers couldn't understand why he had disappeared.

Now and then during the hour the five-man recon listened from behind the brush curtain, a black-clad soldier or two walked through their field of vision. Twice someone stopped at the table; one of the ones who stopped at the table was a cook or a steward delivering a fresh pot of tea that the two sipped at. After a while the khaki-uniformed man said he was through for the night, stood up, brushed his hand over the ribbons on his chest, and bowed to the other, then disappeared into the tent behind the table. The black-clad man with the red armband said he would be along a little later, he wanted to think more first. He sat alone sipping at a cup of tea for a few more minutes before blowing out the light and going in to bed himself. Once, during the minutes he sat there alone, the VC chief looked straight at Bell, making the sergeant cringe. But his eyes were unfocused in thought, not searching through the brush to see what was behind it.

They waited ten minutes by Bell's wristwatch after the second officer retired, listening to the night. Other than an occasional muffled throat clearing, it was quiet in the small valley; the only sounds were those of a camp at night when everyone was asleep except a few guards. Satisfied that all was still in the camp and no one suspected their presence, Bell tapped his men on their shoulders and they crept back to the chimney. The climb back to the ledge was easier than the climb down because the route was familiar. It was also harder—for the Americans, not the Vietnamese—because their muscles were stiff from squatting motionless for so long.

They went as fast as possible while being quiet and,

only a few minutes after reaching the hidden ledge, were climbing back down to the floor of the main valley. Huu led them north again, rather than turning back south, away from the valley. He wanted to show the Marines where the entrance to the box canyon was. Trees grew in its mouth the same as along that whole side of the valley—it was indistinguishable from the rest of the hill it was cut into. They angled through the valley grasslands at a different place than they had crossed in the first place. Once, where a hard-packed trail intersected with another, Huu stopped them to point out a camouflaged trip wire. If he hadn't shown it to them, any of them might have set off the flare and the Bouncing Betty mine it was attached to. They didn't disturb the booby trap. No point in leaving anything that would indicate to the Vietcong in the valley that someone had passed through at any time. They climbed the hill on the far south of the valley at a point a kilometer north of where they had first reached its peak.

The sun was peeking above the horizon by the time they reached the first hill beyond where the ridge down to the Song Du Ong flood plain branched out. This time they didn't find a place as hidden from view as the day before, but two thick-trunked trees and a large bush formed a triangle that hid them well. It was on the eastern slope of the hill, not far from the crest. They had an unobstructed view to the east and were shielded from vision on their uphill side.

"Goddamn, I'm hungry," Lewis said. "Let's chow down before we set the watch rotation."

"Sure thing, Billy Boy," Bell said. "But we're going to talk while we eat. You hear what those bad guy honchos were talking about last night?"

"Yah," Lewis said, pulling a turkey loaf meal out of his pack. "Sounded like that place has boo-coo radios that can talk all the way to Hanoi."

"More radio are come soon," Houng said, reaching for one of the rice balls Huu took from his pack.

Despite what Bell said about talking while they ate, the only sounds they made for the next several minutes were the light scrapings of John Wayne can openers slicing open C ration cans and the munching that followed the opening of the cans. They ate ravenously, the long night's walk to the VC installation and back without a food break had given them all huge appetites.

"If I heard them right," Bell said after several minutes, "what they have in that hidden valley might be Charlie's biggest communications center in all Eye Corps. How'd you hear it, Billy Boy?"

Lewis nodded vigorously. He chewed hard and swallowed the mouthful he was eating. "That's what it sounded like to me, honcho. They can talk to the Ho Chi Minh Trail and to most big units in Eye Corps."

"Them say that, yes," Houng said. "This numba one important Vee Cee place, all right. We tell Dai Uy Hasford, boo-coo Ma-deen go there, bang-bang Vee Cee. Fuck up Vee Cee radio pretty damn good."

"Only problem is, how do we give Hasford this intelligence without telling him how we got it. Shit, they do this right, it might even tell them where COSVN is," Bell said, his eyes unfocused in the distance. Once before he had led the Marines of Tango Niner beyond the boundaries of Bun Hou village. Thirty of North Vietnam's best soldiers had been sent to wipe out the Combined Action Platoon. They had established their base camp in an unknown tunnel complex south of the Song Du Ong river. The Marines discovered it by accident when they were pursuing three of the NVA who had just executed one of the PFs. Bell planned and led an operation against that tunnel complex and wiped out all the NVA who were in it. Bell was in charge then because the NVA had badly wounded First Lieutenant Masterman, who was the platoon commander at that time. When Bell reported the action to the lieutenant colonel they called "Tornado," he was verbally reprimanded for staging an operation beyond Tango Niner's area of operations. And the lieutenant colonel put Tango Niner in for a Presidential Unit Citation because the mission was so successful. Bell didn't want to get caught exceeding his authority again. He couldn't tell Hasford, or anyone else, how they got their information about the VC communications center.

"You'll figure it out, Jay Cee." Randall spoke for the first time that day. "You and Scrappy'll work it out." He grinned. "And the rest of us will help you."

"I know that," Bell said, absently nodding his head. "I just don't know how yet."

"Yet," Lewis repeated.

"Shit," Randall said, "maybe you can even tell Hasford the truth. He's cool. Hell, he might even write us up for some more medals."

Bell had no way of knowing it at the time but later that night, before they reached Camp Apache, he would be handed a way to tell Hasford what the Vietcong had in their hidden valley without telling him about the unauthorized recon patrol.

Before lying back to get some sleep, Bell drew a map of the hidden valley, showing where it was and how it was laid out. He had Randall, Lewis, and Houng help with the details. Later he wanted Huu to draw a map of his own to use for comparison.

During the day's last light, Bell and Houng examined from their hiding place the route they would take when the sun set behind the hill they were on. Huu squatted close behind them and pointed out the main VC infiltration trail. It was to their south, and they could barely make it out through rare breaks in the trees. No one seemed to be moving on it. This time they wouldn't use the narrow track cut in the side of the ridge. They would descend the hill north of the ridge and then follow its side to the rice paddies above Bun Hou village. Then they'd have to find another place to hide until dawn so they could avoid any patrols Tango Niner had out in the area they had to pass through.

The sun was still shining brightly on the west side of the hill they were facing when it got dark enough where they were for them to set out. The Marines and the PF lieutenant were used to the flatlands, where night seemed to come almost all at once everywhere, speeding from east to west. It felt eerie to them to be walking at night and still see the late afternoon daylight ahead. But while they climbed down the face of the hill they were on, night climbed the face of the opposite hill until it covered all the land, and they could see bright stars in a black sky through breaks in the treetops. Near its bottom the hill-side became too steep to walk, and they had to grab bushes and branches to keep from falling. A few times the Americans had to turn their faces to the hill and clamber down short stretches like they were on ladders. The next hill was the steepest they had climbed, and they couldn't help but make noise on it. They all hoped no one was close enough to hear them.

Huu still had the point. He stopped after they crossed the crest of the last hill and squatted while he listened and smelled the air. Satisfied, he turned to Houng and spoke for a moment.

Houng told Bell what Huu said, "This one more Vee Cee trail down from hills." He pointed to a faint path through the woods. "Him say no one use it tonight, we go."

Huu waited until Houng was through talking to Bell, then stepped onto the narrow trail and followed it to the lowland below. He must have been right about nobody using it—at least they didn't encounter anyone else on it.

At the foot of the hill, Bell stopped them and put Lewis on the point. The Marines and Houng breathed more easily now, they knew they were out of Vietcong-controlled territory and back where they owned the night.

CHAPTER SIXTEEN

In the Hours Before Dawn, November 30, 1966, and Later

Billy Harold Lewis was a lance corporal and his fire team's automatic rifleman, its second-in-command. He had even acted as an NCO a few times, taking out a patrol with himself as the patrol leader. Pointman was hazardous duty; the pointman's job was to locate enemy soldiers or booby traps in time for the unit to avoid getting wiped out. If he was skilled, he'd do that without getting himself killed in the process. But too often, the pointman found the enemy by walking into an ambush or a sniper's bullet, too often the pointman found a booby trap by setting it off. Pointman was not a good job for someone important, like a fire team's automatic rifleman or a unit's second-in-command.

But Billy Boy Lewis was Tango Niner's best man at night movement, and he had this sixth sense that told him someone was there long before anyone else had any hint of enemy presence. Because of that, he was point-man on almost every patrol he was on. Also, he wanted to be the pointman any time he wasn't the patrol leader. When he was walking the point himself, he felt he wasn't relying on someone else to keep him alive—he was in control of his own destiny. No one was going to argue with him, tell him to let someone else have a turn on the point. There was no one in Tango Niner who wasn't happy to have him walking point; they all knew no one else could do as good a job of keeping them alive long enough to fight back if they ran into trouble. Not that Tango Niner's patrols ran into trouble very often. Usually it was somebody else who ran into them and had the trouble.

Tango Niner's Marines believed in what General Patton said: "No poor son of a bitch ever won a war by dying for his country. He won it by making the other poor son of a bitch die for his country." They thought Patton would have been a great Marine general, and they tried their best to live up to what the World War II hero had said.

Billy Boy Lewis was relaxed as he led the recon along the edge of the rice paddies toward Hou Ky hamlet, he was home again. He knew exactly where he was leading them, where they would settle down to wait for dawn. He was even a little too relaxed. He almost didn't notice the Vietcong soldier in the rice paddy next to the path he walked, lying submerged with little more than his nose above the water. When he did notice, he reacted so fast everything was over before he consciously realized he had noticed. In one motion, he spun to his left, lifted both feet off the ground, landed in the water on his knees, straddling the man in the water, plopped his rifle down on the path, and clamped both hands around the hiding man's throat.

The instant Lewis moved, everybody else dropped to the ground and waited, rifles ready, for gunfire to erupt at them, telling them in what direction to fire. They wondered if Lewis had finally screwed up and they were dead because of it.

Empty hands thrust out of the water and grasped Lewis's forearms, tried to pry them apart or push them up. Lewis pushed down harder, trying to drown this VC so he could grab his rifle and fight back against the rest of the ambush he'd walked into. But there wasn't any gunfire. His back muscles had bunched, steeling themselves against an expected bullet hit. They untensed and he jerked the VC's head out of the water. The VC's eyes bulged and he tried to gasp out *"chieu hoi"* through his closed throat. "What?" Lewis snapped and eased the pressure on the man's neck.

"Chieu hoi," he repeated, more clearly now that his windpipe wasn't cut off.

Lewis levered himself to his feet, hauling the other with him, and threw his prisoner face down on the path, where he quickly searched him. He was unarmed, but carried a small, waterproof bag under his shirt, and a VC tube pack hung from his shoulders. There were a few documents inside the plastic wrapping, and a uniform and several rice balls in the pack. Only when he finished searching the prisoner did Lewis look at Bell. What's going on? his eyes seemed to ask. They'd been in Bun Hou for six months and killed a lot of Vietcong and taken a lot of prisoners, but no one had given himself up before. Now they had two in a few days' time.

"Secure his ass," Bell ordered when Lewis handed him the packet of documents and the pack, "and let's get away from here in case he's got some buddies who haven't shown themselves yet."

Lewis found a stick about two-and-a-half-feet long and hooked the prisoner's elbows around it behind his back. Then he removed the belt from his own trousers—the prisoner wasn't wearing a belt—and buckled it from one end of the stick to the other, lashing the prisoner's arms behind the stick against his back. A handkerchief served as a gag. Randall grasped the back of the man's neck and pulled him along with them. Ten more minutes of hard walking got them to the junction of two treelines, where Bell thought they would be safe until sunrise. They could see in all directions and were hidden from the view of anyone approaching. When they got into their hiding place, Bell took off his belt and used it to tie the prisoner's ankles together so he couldn't run, even if he could get to his feet with the three Marines and Houng watching him. They didn't bother setting a watch rotation, everybody stayed awake.

"Let's look at what we got here," Bell said when dawn lightened the eastern sky and filtered into the treelines. Their prisoner was a skinny man who looked like he hadn't taken the time to knock any dirt off his body in a while. His black peasant pajamas didn't fit him well and were stiff from having been soaked in the paddy water and dried on his body. A thin scum of mud caked his clothes in large spots. He seemed to be a couple of inches taller than the Vietnamese of the village, but Bell couldn't tell for certain with him sitting down. The sergeant grabbed the man under his armpits and yanked him to his feet. "Stand here," he said to Houng, motioning the PF lieutenant next to the prisoner. The stranger was a little taller than Houng, who was one of the tallest men in Bun Hou. Bell grabbed his hands and twisted them palms up. "Look at that," he said, "no calluses. He's sure as hell no local Vee Cee, they all have boo-coo calluses from farming and fishing." City people tended to rely less totally on rice for their dietary needs, they had better-balanced, more nutritionally sound diets, and usually were taller than the peasant farmers who ate little other than rice for their entire lives. The lack of calluses—which could only be earned from a lifetime of stoop labor—on the prisoner's hands seemed to confirm Bell's suspicions.

To the VC he said, *"O dau ong cai nha?"* He demanded, "Where's your home?" and pulled the handkerchief out of the prisoner's mouth so he could answer.

"Hanoi."

"Right," Bell said, shaking his head and grimacing. What was going on, he wondered. Was another unit from the north coming down to try to take out Tango Niner? If there was, this time the Marines and PFs of CAP Tango Niner would be ready for them. "What's your name and what are you doing here? Why are you turning to the government side—especially if you're from the North?"

The prisoner told them. The three Marines and two Vietnamese stared at him for a long moment when he finished, then Bell shoved the handkerchief back into his mouth. "I find that very hard to believe," he said, then turned to the others and said, "We're almost home. Let's go back to Camp Apache and see if he tells us a different story when we get there."

"Yo, there they are," Hempen shouted.

"About fucking time," Zeitvogel said, running to Hempen's side and looking out over the wire at the men approaching from the direction of Hou Ky.

"There's six of them," Hempen said.

"Say what?" Zeitvogel counted. "Sure are," he said. "And one of them is trussed up like a fatback pig. Let's go meet them." He headed toward the main gate at a trot, shouting at all the other Marines in sight that the recon was on its way back and he and Hempen were going to meet it. He held his rifle lightly in his right hand by its pistol grip. Hempen carried his automatic rifle in both hands; the bipods clamped to its barrel forward of the stock made it heavier and altered its balance.

"Yo, Jay Cee," the tall man said when he reached the tired patrol members, "Welcome back. Who's your friend?"

"Billy Boy found him in the paddies on the other side of Hou Ky before we stopped to wait for dawn," Bell explained. "He claims he wants to chieu hoi."

"I found him, I want to keep him," Lewis said. "Jay Cee said I could if I house broke him before we got back to Camp Apache." He beamed, then looked crestfallen. "But the dumb fuck's still piddling on the kitchen floor."

Bell ignored Lewis. He continued to look to the side at the prisoner while walking along the trail. "But if he wanted to turn himself in, why was he hiding in the paddies like he was?"

"Because he was afraid we'd shoot first and ask questions later if we saw someone out there at night, that's why," Randall said. "Wouldn't you hide from us at night if you were one of the bad guys?"

"And, Stilts, man," Bell continued, ignoring Randall, "just wait until you hear the sea story he told us about why he's turning himself in."

"It's that good, huh?" Zeitvogel asked.

"No, it's not that good. It's better."

"Man, I can't wait to hear this. What'd you find over there?" He jerked his head toward the western hills. "Did my Chieu Hoi give us straight scoop?" He looked at Huu.

"He sure did. There's something in a valley three hills over that looks and sounds like the number one Vee Cee communications center for all of Eye Corps. What this dude here—" he indicated the prisoner "—tells us confirms that. But you're not going to believe why he says he's changing sides. That'll blow your ever-loving mind." He shook his head thinking about what the VC had told them. He still couldn't believe it. But on the other hand, it did make a certain sense. "And, Stilts," he added, remembering the discussion the two had had before the recon went out, "it's probably good you didn't go with us. We ran into an obstacle you couldn't have managed because you're just too goddamn tall. Hell, it almost killed me, and I'm not near tall as you."

"Humph," Zeitvogel snorted. "Only thing could've been a tunnel, and I'm skinnier than you, honcho, I can get through smaller holes than you can."

Bell laughed a short, rueful laugh. "This wasn't no tunnel, Stilts." He told him about the wall they crossed going down into the hidden valley. Zeitvogel shook his head in disbelief at the description.

All the rest of the Americans and about half of the PFs in Tango Niner were waiting for them when they reached the main gate. Doc Tracker, whom they hadn't seen since he got hit, had returned and was there, too.

"*Bac-si* Chief, good to see you," Bell said when he saw the corpsman, who had a bandage still covering the side of his head. "When'd you get back?"

"Yesterday," Tracker said, grasping Bell's outheld hand. "I had to get away from those paleface shamen. They told me I was walking wounded and wanted me to clean bedpans. So I escaped like any smart Indian would." Doc Tracker was a full-blood Kiowa who joined the Navy to see the world. He hadn't expected to see it one step at a time with the Marines, though.

"Scrappy," Bell said to Burrison, "we got what we need for someone to go in and do some heavy-duty ass-kicking. Let me tell you about it first, then this prisoner can tell his story. Most of it backs what we found out. Everything except why he left them."

They sat at one of the sheet metal-on-sandbags tables for Bell to debrief to Burrison. Lewis and Randall frequently interrupted to add details or volunteer observations. They didn't spend much time on the trip to the hidden valley or back from it, but telling about the objective took more than fifteen minutes.

"How certain are you those men were high ranking officers if you didn't recognize their rank insignia?" Burrison asked when they described the two men who were sitting at the camp table, drinking tea in the light from the small lamp. "In some of Charlie's units, promotion is slow. They've got some lieutenants and captains who are in their forties and fifties.''

"Each of them must have had a dozen colored ball-point pens sticking out of his shirt pocket,'' Bell said. "You know how they are. The higher your rank, the more forms you fill out and the more reports you have to write. So you carry more ballpoint pens to do the job."

Burrison blinked, then nodded like he knew it all along and was just checking. But this was the first he'd heard of how many ballpoint pens a man had sticking out of his pocket being a sign of rank.

"Captain Hasford should be able to get some action when he takes this information in,'' Bell finally finished. "And now we even have a Chieu Hoi who claims to have been in that place for a long time. We tell the captain that one of our patrols captured him, which is true, hand him over, and Hasford takes him in as his source and proof and we're off the hook for running that recon, nobody has to know we did it."

"Sounds good to me,'' Burrison said. "Let's hear what he has to say for himself.'' The lieutenant, through Bell and Houng, questioned the prisoner. They allowed Huu to join their circle, and he occasionally interrupted with probing questions of his own—he also had spent time in the hidden valley and knew when the prisoner was lying or obfuscating.

The story told by the prisoner came out in fits and starts, in bits and pieces, it jumped from here to there in its narrative. Put down straight, this is what he said:

"I am Senior Sergeant Nguyen Van Mai of the People's Army of Vietnam—what you call the 'NVA.' My home is in a village near Hanoi, where my family has lived and farmed since the dawn of Vietnamese civilization. In 1953 I joined the Viet Minh to fight the hated French oppressors of our country. After our glorious victory, I did not return to my village because I saw the partition of our country would lead to more fighting and

I would be needed again, so I became a corporal in the newly organized PAVN. In 1958, when the national elections mandated by the United Nations did not take place, I first came south to help organize cadres of revolutionaries for the battle we now knew was inevitable.

"Life in the decadent south astonished me. There were contrasts in the lives of the people I could not understand. The farmers were kept poor by the wealthy landowners, who collected such high rents the people barely had enough left over to feed themselves and pay taxes to the illegal government in Saigon. Despite their poverty and the close watch kept over them by the landowners and the minions of the government, the people were able to move freely about and seemed to be genuinely happy. I talked with some of the people and concluded their happiness was simply due to their believing the lies told to them by the government and the priests of their religions. Buddhism and Catholicism both have much to gain from the people being held down, you know. The people did not know any better, they did not understand why they should be unhappy under a capitalist system where only a few are wealthy and the rest are poor. They had not been exposed to the truths of the Party.

"Yes," he answered to a question, "it is true that the people are also poor under the Party, but there is a difference. Under the Party everybody is poor, not all but a few wealthy people. There are no wealthy people where the Party is in control.

"I knew that once the people knew the truth of the Party they would quickly come to understand that they were not really happy, and they would come over to our side and join in our battle to unite all of Vietnam under the Party. So I exhorted the people to attend the lectures given by the political cadre. They did and were converted. By the time I returned to the North in 1959, there was a strong Vietcong organization in western Quang Ngai and Quang Tin provinces. Then I was promoted to sergeant and served six years as a trainer for PAVN soldiers

who were coming south to act as military cadre for the
Vietcong, or to protect the political cadre who were pros-
elytizing the people.

"Last year, after the American Running-Dog Marines . . ."

"Not 'Running-Dog,' " Zeitvogel interrupted, grinning with what looked like too many teeth, "Devil Dog."

There was a moment of confusion while Bell and Lewis
tried vainly to translate "Devil Dog" into Vietnamese.
Houng wasn't of much help at first because he had never
heard the word before. Finally, Lewis got out his bilingual dictionary and consulted with Houng over it. Senior
Sergeant Mai looked askance at them when he was given
the word. Then he smiled at Zeitvogel and nodded. The
American giant who looked like a montagnard god did
indeed resemble a demon. Mai resumed his narrative.

"Last year after the—Devil Dog Marines"—another
nod at Zeitvogel—"invaded the South and the war increased, I was sent back south as a senior sergeant to
help establish a major communications center to assist in
coordinating the efforts of the Main Force Vietcong field
units and the PAVN units committed to battle in the areas
the American Marines later moved into. It took a long
time to get the communications center set up because we
had to find an ideal location where the—" he paused for
a beat "—Devil Dog Americans and their puppets of Saigon would not find it. Also, the equipment was expensive
and difficult to acquire. In the meantime, the location of
the center was also designated a logistics center and supplies and limited numbers of replacement troops were
funneled through it." He smiled wryly. "The American
Marines established a program that has been very effective in countering the efforts of our political cadres, the
Combined Action Program. This unit here has been very
effective in blocking our resupply efforts for our com-
rades east of here. You have made life difficult for us."
He said the last with professional admiration in his voice.

"Our communications center is now in operation and

most of the PAVN units in what you call 'Eye Corps' are now hooked into it, as well as most of the Main Force Vietcong battalions and regiments. That communications center will be able to cause great harm to come to you. It has a permanent garrison of one hundred men, of whom twenty-five are communications technicians and fifteen others are service personnel. Of the remaining sixty, ten are officers and sergeants, the rest are fighting soldiers used as guards. It is normally commanded by a major, but right now a Vietcong colonel is there overseeing the hooking-up of the last of the Vietcong units into the network, and a PAVN senior colonel is there seeing to the last details. In a few days both of those officers will leave to take command of combat units elsewhere. Our best fighters are not assigned there because no one expects any fighting there. There are bunkers where the radios are kept in case of bombing or artillery attack and there are bunkers that are placed as fighting positions. But, no, there is no tunnel system. No one feels there will be any need for tunnels. Should you Americans find the valley and attack it with infantry—'' he smiled again ''—our orders are to salvage what equipment we can, destroy the rest, and abandon the valley. We can always establish a new communications center, and the next one will be easier to set up than this one was.

''Now, after thirteen years as a good soldier in the People's Army of Vietnam, a trusted soldier, a senior sergeant, never thinking of anything but defeating our capitalist enemies and uniting all of Vietnam under the banner of the Party, I am a deserter. I quit. I refuse to participate any longer in this war. No, it was not my intention to join the chieu hoi program, I have no use for the corrupt government in Saigon and do not desire to join its forces. My plan when I left my unit was to go to Tam Ky or Da Nang and lose myself in the influx of refugees. Who is going to notice one more person fleeing the ravages of the war? When our side wins, I can hide myself among the heroes of PAVN who were captured and imprisoned by the southerners or the Americans, and become repatriated along with them." His eyes focused on the distance while he added, "If we can win the war now. If we do not, then I will maintain my disguise as just another refugee whose entire family was killed.

"When I was found, I did not want to be killed as a spy," he continued, "and surely the American who was strangling me under the water would have killed me. So I spoke the magic words *'chieu hoi'* and was taken prisoner instead of dying. Now I will be a prisoner of war. Still, I quit. I will no longer fight against the Americans.

"Why did I quit, why am I a deserter? You should know that," he said in an aside to Huu. "I know who you are. I have seen you many times in the communications center. Either you are a spy for us in this imperialist unit or you are a Chieu Hoi. You are the only person here who is not armed, so I think you are a Chieu Hoi rather than a spy. Why did you change sides if not for the same reason I did?" He waited for an answer.

Huu said, "You would not understand, you are too steeped in the myth of the Party. You do not understand that the Americans are much better people than your leaders. I wish to be on their side because they are good. I have too often seen your side commit atrocities against the people. The Saigon government steals from them, that is true. But the Saigon government only steals their food and money. Your Party commands that hands and arms and lives be stolen from the people, in addition to food and money." He shrugged and turned his face from Nguyen Van Mai.

Mai shrugged in return. He did not believe the turncoat, but that was of no consequence. "I quit because the Americans have done something that few armies in the entire history of warfare have done. I quit because the Americans are sending crazy people to fight. This is not a rumor, like the one about Americans eating Vietnamese children. I do not believe that Americans eat children, but this, I have seen this with my own eyes, I know the Americans are sending crazy people to fight. I am not going to fight crazy people, I do not wish to become crazy myself. So I quit.''

The Americans looked at each other, confused. ''What crazy people?'' they asked.

Mai looked at them, amused that they would feign ignorance of their own side's new tactics. He knew the crazy man who had come against the communications center had to have been dispatched from this place. ''I saw your man,'' he said, ''the one you sent alone against us. I was sergeant of the guard checking our defensive positions when I saw the sunlight reflecting from the grease on his skin before he even left the trees on the south end of the main valley. The soldier assigned to watch over the entrance to the hidden valley was suddenly stricken with diarrhea, and I was relieving him while he allowed his bowels to empty themselves. From my vantage your soldier's progress along the valley floor was easy to follow, even though it was highly erratic. I never had to wait long before the sun glinted again off his greasy skin. When he got close enough I could see his red headband against the grass, although he was crouched too low for me to see him until he was fairly close to where I was hiding. He did not see me, he did not bother to look very often to anywhere other than straight ahead of where he was walking. He wore no shirt, only tight black trousers that must have chafed him and hurt him here—if he had anything left here to be hurt.'' Mai rubbed his crotch. ''In his right hand he carried one of your M-60 machine guns, its ammunition belt went from its receiver to wrap itself around his left wrist.'' He shook his head. ''Everyone who has ever fired, or seen fired, a machine gun knows if you try to shoot one with the ammunition belt wrapped around any part of your body, you are going to be injured.

''I stayed where I was, confident I was well enough hidden that he would not see me even if he looked directly at my hiding place. He approached to the very entrance to the hidden valley the communications center is in and did not see it. He stopped and looked both ways along the valley and finally continued his erratic course. After a while he went into the trees along the valley side. The last I saw of him was sunlight sparkling from inside the trees. He was a very muscular man. His muscles were so huge, at first I thought he must be stricken with some terrible disease such as elephantiasis, but his swellings were too uniform and I finally understood them to be muscles, though I have never before heard of a man with muscles shaped and huge the way his are.

"I thought for a long time about what I had seen, and constantly rejected the obvious notion that a crazy man had been sent against us. One does not do that to crazy people, one isolates them so their sickness cannot be transmitted to healthy people. But I could come to no other conclusion as to who this man was or what he was doing there. His torso was naked and covered with grease so it shined in the sun, his pants were so tight they had to hurt—unless he had no feeling around his crotch, or," he shrugged, "unless he has nothing there, I do not know what Americans do to their crazy people when they isolate them. He carried a powerful weapon in a manner in which it could not be used. What would you think if you saw something like him? You would think the same thing I did, you would think he is crazy. I was careful about it, but I asked questions, and the following day I learned I was the only one who had seen him. Then I made my decision, and the day after that I slipped into one of the hamlets in the valley and stole these clothes you see me wearing now. Then I left the valley, and the army, and the war." He held up an arm and grimaced at the shirt he wore, obviously wishing he'd been able to steal clothes that were a better fit.

"I am not going to fight crazy men. Craziness is contagious. I quit. Now you may as well turn me over to the Saigon army." He stopped and looked hopefully at the Americans. "But now I have told you everything I know," he added eagerly. "I am not going to return to fight anymore, not now that you Americans are using dinky dau soldiers. Can I leave now, continue on my way to Da Nang, where I can disappear among the mass of refugees?"

Bell blinked at the prisoner. Burrison looked at him blankly. Houng and Huu giggled. "You've got to be kidding me," Burrison said. "We need you to tell what you know to our intelligence people."

CHAPTER SEVENTEEN

Later That Same Day

Lieutenant Burrison stared at Senior Sergeant Nguyen Van Mai for a long moment before turning to Sergeant Bell. "Right," he said flatly. "That the same story he told you earlier?"

"Basically. He added more details this time, though."

"He sounds real good until he gets to the point of why he deserted."

"Yup."

"Do you believe him?"

"Well, the dinky dau American he says he saw had to be Cas; there's just no way he made that up. But I know what you mean—was that a good enough reason to de- sert?"

The two Americans turned to Houng. "What do you think?"

Houng chuckled. So did Huu—Houng had translated for him.

The PF lieutenant nodded. "Man be dinky dau, you stay away him. You not stay away him, *you* be dinky dau."

"It's catching, then?" Burrison asked.

Houng nodded firmly. Behind him Huu added his affirmation.

"Imagine that," someone said, "insanity's contagious."

"No shit," someone else said. "You gonna hang with cuckoos? Not me, man. I don't want to go crazy."

"G-2 ain't going to believe his story about the crazy American," Bell said.

"I do believe you're right on that, Jay Cee. But the rest of it sounds good, they should believe that. Can we tell him not to tell G-2 why he deserted?" he asked Houng.

The PF lieutenant nodded firmly. But he wasn't as positive that the new *Chieu Hoi* would be as cooperative as he tried to look.

"How fast can we get Hasford out here? The sooner we hand this turd over, the sooner we get some action on that communications center. It'd be good if someone would take it out before those two big birds fly the coop."

While Burrison tried to get Hasford to come up on the radio, Bell and Houng worked with Mai to fill out the map the American had started to draw. Mai wasn't totally enthusiastic about giving the Americans help, but he was afraid if he didn't they'd hand him over to a crazy man, so he did anyway. Huu's knowledge of the secret communications center wasn't as extensive as Mai's, but the Chieu Hoi drew a map of his own. It jibed with Bell's and Mai's and provided a few extra details Bell didn't know about and Mai hadn't wanted to divulge.

"All I've been able to do is find out he's at Chu Lai,"

Burrison told Bell later. "If I can't get hold of him sooner than that, I'll fly back on the evening chow bird and hand deliver Senior Sergeant Mai to him. Time is of the essence here."

That's how a very nervous Senior Sergeant Nguyen Van Mai found himself, arms tied behind his back, riding in a Marine UH-34 helicopter with Lieutenant Burrison riding herd on him.

Two days later Captain Hasford came out to visit.

Hasford shook his head. "It's a no-go," he said. "Senior Sergeant Mai, if he is a senior sergeant and if that is his name, tells a good story, that's for sure. G-2 loved him, this was the best intelligence they'd had on this part of the province yet."

"What about the documents he was carrying?" Burrison asked. "Didn't they say anything to verify what he said?"

Hasford shook his head. "They were mostly letters from his family. None of them had anything to do with the comm-center." He continued his report. "G-2 believed him right up to the point where he told them why he decided to desert. The greasy character with all the muscles blew it for him. Now G-2 thinks he might even be a plant."

"He told them that?" Bell groaned. "Damn it, we told him not to, we said they wouldn't believe him if he did."

"But the greasy guy with all the muscles is real," Burrison sputtered. "We saw him ourselves."

Hasford cocked an eyebrow at the lieutenant. "Maybe, if you file a complete written report on the incident here with the greasy character, you can convince G-2 that he's for real. Maybe. It'll take them at least two weeks to process the paperwork and integrate it into everything else they have. Then they'll believe you about it—maybe. Then probably somebody else will want to spend some time finding out why you didn't immediately make a full and complete report when this Cas character came through here. By the time they decide you didn't do anything wrong by not reporting it sooner, because he's apparently a civilian and not subject to military jurisdiction, another week or two will have passed by. Then the whole mess gets kicked back to the Two Shop and they won't give it their full attention because it'll be stale intelligence by then—not to mention that Mai will probably be buried so deep in the Arvin POW system they won't be able to reach him in a timely manner." Burrison started to interrupt, but Hasford stopped him with an uplifted hand and raised voice. "That's the way things work," he explained, "they have so much intelligence coming in all the time most of what they do is try to deal with the most immediate. They don't have the resources to handle everything that comes into their shop."

Burrison took a deep breath to steady himself. He was grateful for the steadying hand Bell put on his shoulder; it reminded him he was far from alone in this. "We've all known," he said, including Hasford in the "we," "for several months now that the Vee Cee have something important on the other side of those hills. Now we know what it is, where it is, and how it's manned. Are they really going to let a story about a crazy American with a lot of muscles and oily skin keep them from making a raid on that communications center?"

"Mr. Burrison," Hasford said patiently, "the Marine Corps has nineteen infantry battalions in all of Eye Corps. Those nineteen battalions are defending Chu Lai, Da Nang, Hue, and Phu Bai. They're moving into Dong Ha and a few other places in the far north of the country. There are major operations going on all along the entire DMZ: there's a big one near Phu Bai, there's another one taking place in Quang Ngai province. The Marine Corps in Vietnam needs a couple of battalions standing by as reaction forces. Where the hell are the troops going to come from for this operation?"

Burrison grimaced, then said through clenched teeth, "What about the Special Landing Force? We've got a whole goddamn battalion sitting on assault carriers in the South China Sea. They're not part of the nineteen battalions you were talking about. Look—'' he pounded his fist in the air for emphasis ''—this communications center is small and only has about a hundred men, and half of them are technicians or other non-combat troops. All it'll take is one company for one day and, bingo, no more Vee Cee communications center tying all their combat units together. How about it, Captain, huh?''

Hasford whistled silently through his teeth while shaking his head. ''Sorry. G-2 was going for it, until Mai came up with his story about Mister Muscles. That blew it, now they don't believe a word he said. I think they even told the Arvins to check their desertion rosters because he might be one of their own.''

''Hey, Jay Cee, Scrappy told us about it.'' Tex Randall dropped down under the lone shade tree that remained outside the wire in Camp Apache's cleared fields of fire. It was below the hill on the west side of the compound. Bell sat half-lying against the tree's trunk facing away from the Marines' hill.

''Go away, Tex, I'm thinking.''

''Careful, Jay Cee. It's always best to go easy with a new experience,'' Randall said, settling himself more comfortably next to the sergeant.

''You know what we got to do, don't you, Jay Cee,'' Stilts Zeitvogel said, lowering himself to the ground on Bell's other side.

''Go away, Stilts. Tex is already fucking up my chain of thought.''

''Bullshit. Tex couldn't fuck up a wet dream.''

''Shit, couldn't fuck up a wet dream, he is a wet dream,'' Big Louie Slover said after he reclined on his side in front of Bell. ''How we gonna do it, Jay Cee?''

''Go away, Louie, I think I hear a helicopter coming in.''

''No you don't, Jay Cee. That's pineapple bugs Uncle

Ho imported from Hawaii just to bug you,'' Wall Mc-Entire said, dropping only slightly less heavily than an earthquake as he sat next to Slover.

''You people got a hard-on for me or something?''

''Who's Something?'' McEntire asked. ''If Something's a she, damn skippy I got a hard-on for her. I ain't fucked nothing but old Hanna in boo-coo months. Hey, how come for why you ain't sent me on R&R yet, Jay Cee? You afraid I'll fuck all the boom-boom girls so good they won't want you when you get there?''

''Yah, I know what we got to do,'' Bell said, finally giving in. ''That's what I'm trying to figure out, how to do it and get away with it.''

Randall nodded slowly. ''Doing it's the easy part. I know that place about as well as you do, Jay Cee. Be a piece of cake taking it. The tough part's how do we keep from getting blown the fuck away by our own people after we do it.''

''After we did those NVA in that bunker complex south of the Song, Lieutenant Colonel Tornado offered to make me a boot brown bar and he put us in for a PUC,'' Bell said, nodding and looking into a distant nowhere. ''But first he threatened to bust my ass with a general court-martial for taking Tango Niner beyond our area of operations. And we could walk to that place and back in one day.'' He paused, then added, ''And have enough time for one bodacious firefight in between. But this, huh-uh. No way one day this time, Jose. This is going to take three whole fucking days. And we got to take everybody. No leaving a few people at Camp Apache, we can't afford it.''

Nobody said anything for a long minute. They all remembered what happened at Camp Apache while most of them were involved in the fight at the bunker complex south of the river.

''What does Scrappy think about this?'' Bell finally asked.

''He hasn't even thought about it,'' Randall said.

"And nobody's told him yet," Zeitvogel said. "No point upsetting the poor ossifer until we got it all worked out and he can see the wisdom of what we're going to do."

"Shit."

"Got that right, dude. He sure will shit when we tell him."

"We can't wait on this one," Randall said. "Those big birds are about to fly, we have to do it before they leave so we can get them, too."

"Besides," Zeitvogel added, "Charlie hasn't tried to do anything with us in a while. He ain't fucking with us and we haven't caught any of his supply trains in more than a week. I think he's getting ready to pull some shit and we should hit his ass first."

"Keep him from putting a hurting on us," Slover said.

"You see any women in that camp?" McEntire asked. They all ignored him for a moment, then Zeitvogel balled his fist and murmured, "Next time . . ." McEntire was the only one who laughed.

"We shouldn't have one whole hell of a lot of trouble figuring out how to do it without getting caught," Zeitvogel said. "Hell, we got four corporals here, plus a sergeant who should be a corporal."

"What the fuck do you mean, 'a sergeant who should be a corporal,' " Bell snapped. Tango Niner was in a very precarious position because of the VC communications center to its west, and Bell was frustrated because no one except them was taking the threat seriously. The tall, black Marine was giving him someone to focus his anger on.

Zeitvogel explained patiently, as though to someone who wasn't as bright as he looked. The other three corporals looked at each other impassively, although they were all wondering if maybe they were giving their sergeant more credit than he deserved.

"You know how it is, Jay Cee," Zeitvogel said slowly, his face innocent of expression. "They say sergeants run the Marine Corps. Well, that's because the sergeants give all of the impossible orders that get carried out. The reason the impossible jobs get done is the sergeants give the orders to corporals, who take the troops and figure out how to do the impossible. When a corporal gets promoted to sergeant, he forgets how to do the impossible. That's what I meant when I said you should be a corporal. You haven't forgotten yet." He stopped talking and looked earnestly into Bell's eyes. "Understand, honcho?"

Bell took a deep breath and let a touch of pride at being so well respected by his corporals help swell his chest. He nodded.

Zeitvogel poked the sergeant in the chest. "We'll work it out. We got four corporals here and a sergeant who should be one." Then muttered to himself, "I hope you ain't forgot how, 'cause if you did, we up shits creek without a paddle or hip boots."

"Let's go see Houng. He knows that place as well as we do."

"Where the hell have you been, Jay Cee?" Burrison asked the sergeant, who was entering their quarters in the command hootch. Bell had missed the daily hot meal that was flown in for the Marines of Tango Niner. "For that matter, where were the corporals?"

"We went into town to see Houng," Bell said, collapsing onto his cot. "He fed us, no problem about missing chow."

"You weren't here so I drew up the patrol routes myself. Here, what do you think?" He handed over a topographical map covered by an acetate overlay with lines drawn on it in grease pencil.

Bell hardly glanced at the map before handing it back. "Fine," he said. "We got something else to talk about. But I got to cop some Zs first." He lay back with his forearm over his eyes.

Before the lieutenant could say anything about the odd

way his sergeant was acting, Zeitvogel poked his head in and asked, "You got the routes drawn up for us, Scrappy?" Burrison handed over the map and its overlay without a word. He was too busy wondering what was going on. "Thanks, I'll bring it back in a skosh bit." The tall Marine disappeared as suddenly as he had appeared.

"You've got something up your sleeve, Sergeant," Burrison said in a measured voice, trying to make his voice sound authoritative, trying to sound like he was in charge here and the sergeant had to do what he said. "Tell me what you've got coming down."

"Later, Scrappy," Bell said. He noticed Burrison had called him by rank instead of nickname and he understood what that meant, but he wasn't going to cooperate. Not yet. "My mind is too fadoozled right now. After I rest for a while I'll tell you all about it."

Burrison waited with increasingly less patience, but it wasn't until after all three patrols had left the compound that Bell finally told him what was going on.

CHAPTER EIGHTEEN

That Night and the Next Day

The tent flaps were tied down and Lieutenant Burrison's hurricane lamp cast its feeble orange glow in the small room he shared with Sergeant Bell. Through the wall on one side of the room came the low crackle of static from Swarnes's radios, static occasionally interrupted by murmured voices. Swarnes replied with two or three words to some of the radio voices. There was no sound from the wall on the opposite side; Doc Rankin was helping with perimeter watch, Tracker was sleeping—the Kiowa never snored.

"All right, Jay Cee, spit it out," Burrison said in a voice as low as the glow from his lamp, but more forceful. "You're planning something, and it's probably something that's going to get us in trouble. I think I should know what's going on, don't you?''

"You're right, Scrappy," Bell answered, sitting up and rubbing the sleep grit from his eyes. He stretched. "Damn, I needed that nap. Wait one while I take a piss." He rose to his feet and ducked out through the radio room, nodding at Swarnes as he passed him. Swarnes acted like he didn't see him and had heard nothing the lieutenant had said now or earlier.

Bell came back in a couple of minutes and reached for his rifle and cartridge belt. "You checked the lines recently?"

"Fuck a bunch of lines, Jay Cee," Burrison said heatedly. "You sit your ass right down and tell me what the fuck is going on." He didn't normally swear much, but dealing with a sergeant who didn't seem to want to tell him what was going on, it seemed like a good idea to talk tough. "I got back from making the rounds a few minutes ago," he added lamely.

"Whatever you say," Bell said, and sat on the edge of his cot. He reached far over to hook two fingers through the handle of the small cooler sitting under Burrison's field desk and pulled it free. He knocked the cooler's lid back and drew two cans of beer from the water that filled it. With two quick flicks of his wrist he opened one can with an opener and offered it to the other man. Burrison refused it with a brusque head shake. Bell set down the unopened can, leaned back, and tipped the open one over his open mouth. He chugged half the beer and sat up and belched.

"Are you through stalling?" Burrison asked, his jaw clenched. Bell hadn't treated him with so much insolence in several weeks, not since Burrison realized just how green he was and how much he needed to learn from his sergeant and corporals before he could be an officer worthy of leading Marines. He hadn't liked the way he was treated then, but at least he could understand why. Now he resented it and was beginning to get very angry.

"Stalling?" Bell said innocently. "I wasn't stalling, I just woke up from a nap."

"Cut the crap."

Bell shrugged, still looking innocent. "I'm not planning anything that's going to get us in any trouble," he said, and paused for a beat or two to let the suspense build. "What I'm planning is going to save us from a lot of trouble." He downed the second half of his beer and opened the other can before continuing. "Charlie's got a communications center over there, right?"

Burrison nodded—he didn't trust his voice.

Bell held up one hand and ticked off a finger. "That communications center needs to be taken out." He ticked off a second finger. "We haven't been able to convince anyone it's really there—" a third finger went up "—or to do anything about it—" a fourth finger. "So we're going to do it ourselves." All five fingers were up and spread.

Burrison stared at the sergeant for a long moment and chewed the inside of his lower lip before saying, "I thought you said you were planning something that wasn't going to get us into any trouble? Any of us who don't get killed doing this thing will get court-martialed afterward."

"I said we won't get in trouble and we won't. And nobody's going to get killed or court-martialed—nobody on our side," he hastened to add. "Look, if something happens and nobody knows we had anything to do with it, we can't get in any trouble for it."

Burrison kept staring at Bell. "Then how are we going to explain what happened to this communications center when people come around asking about it?"

"G-2 doesn't believe it's there. So when it goes, they're not going to know that, either."

"Captain Hasford knows. What do we tell him?"

"We tell him the truth, most of it anyway. We tell him Charlie isn't as active in coming through here anymore, and we heard the communications center has been moved because we're causing too much trouble for the supplies and reinforcements they keep trying to infiltrate through Bun Hou. We tell him they seem to have decided to move that site to a location where they won't have as much trouble infiltrating. Simple.''

Burrison sucked on his upper lip for a moment, then said, ''I think I'll have that beer after all.'' Bell opened one for him. He took a long pull from it, then asked, ''How do we explain our casualties? We will have casualties, you know.''

Bell shook his head slowly. ''Remember,'' he said, ''I was there, I saw the place. Charlie feels so damn secure there we'll be able to get in and hit him so fast and so hard he won't have time to drop his cock and grab his sock before we put him so deep in the hurt locker he won't be able to fight back. He's going to be too damn busy trying to save his own ass and bug the fuck out of there to put any kind of hurting on us.''

''You sound awful sure of yourself, Jay Cee.''

''That's because I am awful sure of myself. Look, this is the way we can do it.'' He reached into the drawer of his wooden ammo-crate table and took out the maps he had painstakingly drawn of the hidden valley and the route to it. ''The things drawn in black are what we saw, the ones in red are what Huu told us about, things we can't be sure of until we know he's trustworthy. Here's the plan . . .''

''It sounds good,'' Burrison said twenty minutes later, ''but where are we going to get the explosives?''

''Hell, that's easy. We've got boo-coo trading goods and the Sea Bees have more explosives than they know what to do with. We get them from Big Louie's cousin Os. Then you get hold of your buddy Ensign Lily, and his pal the helicopter driver can fly them out to us.''

Burrison stared into space for a long moment. ''Maybe,'' he finally said, ''maybe this'll work. Just maybe. I want to sleep on it.''

''Have another, Scrappy. It'll get the brain juices flowing and help you sleep," Bell said, opening another beer and handing it over. "I'm going out to make the rounds."

Burrison looked into one of the holes in the top of the can as though he could find the answers he was looking for inside it. "You got balls, Jay Cee. I'll say that for you, you got balls."

"Hell, of course I do, Lieutenant. I'm a Marine sergeant. Marine sergeants have balls so big we almost have to carry them around in a wheelbarrow."

"Right," Burrison said, but Bell didn't hear him, he had already left the inner room of the tent to make his rounds of the perimeter security.

"Stilts is in charge here until we get back," Burrison told his assembled men for the half-dozenth time that morning. "We'll be back as soon as we can, tomorrow afternoon at the latest." Then he took the passenger seat in the Jeep. Bell was already behind the wheel, revving the motor. Randall and Slover sat in the back. Two sea bags filled with captured VC and NVA weapons and equipment were on the floor of the Jeep between their feet.

"You know, Scrappy," Zeitvogel said with a smile, "if you let someone other than Tex go to Da Nang once in a while, maybe someone else would get himself a round-eye girlfriend, and Tex wouldn't have to go every time we need to send someone there." He was smiling and his voice was friendly, but this was the second time in little more than a week that Randall had got to go to Da Nang. Zeitvogel hadn't been there since he got wounded in October, and most of the Marines in Tango Niner hadn't been away from Bun Hou for even longer. It somehow didn't seem quite fair.

Burrison didn't hear the complaint. He was thinking about the crazy mission he was leaving on, and wondering how he ever managed to talk himself into joining the Marines in the first place, when he could have gone to work as a trainee manager in his uncle's textile plant when he finished college. "You've got your instructions for what to do if we don't make it back tonight, Stilts," he said. Then to the sergeant, "Let's go."

Bell looked at Zeitvogel and said softly, "Point taken, Stilts. An adjustment will be made," before shifting into first and applying pressure to the Jeep's accelerator. The navy blue Jeep rolled smoothly through Camp Apache's main gate and down the hill. It didn't speed up to faster than an easy walk until it was headed toward Hou Dau hill.

Burrison had made several trips to the east, to Da Nang and Chu Lai, but they had all been by helicopter. He wondered what it would look like from the ground between here and Highway 1, the main coastal road. Beyond Hou Dau hill and Hou Cau hamlet he looked south across the cane fields to the band of trees bordering the river. He had trouble picking out the exact location where he had been involved in his first successful ambush on a Vietcong supply run, the place he'd first seen a man die a violent death, the place where he'd first fired a shot in anger and killed a man. A few miles farther, he recognized the branch road leading to the hamlets of Bun Anh village, and he remembered being ambushed along that roadway. Farther on was a hamlet that no longer looked like a vehicular cemetery.

They rode for a long while without anyone saying anything. Bell was concentrating on his driving along the rutted and often pot-holed road—some of the pot-holes were concussion craters from artillery or mortar rounds. Slover and Randall were watching the sides carefully, looking for any sign of an ambush or other trouble. Burrison was lost in his own thoughts of the insanity of this whole operation. Maybe they wouldn't be able to get what they needed to accomplish their mission, and he could call it off with good grace and no argument from his NCOs.

"Here's where Captain Ronson's roadblock was that he stopped me and Stilts at when we were bringing the

Jeep back the first time,'' Bell said at a place where a brush-covered hill rose on one side of the road and rice paddies spread out on the other. He laughed at the memory. ''Maybe it's a good thing we aren't carrying travel orders this time, he sure didn't believe the letter I showed him that day.''

Burrison's throat suddenly went dry. What if they were stopped? How would they explain what they were doing and where they were going? How on earth would they explain the two sea bags of trading goods they were carrying?

''Don't sweat it, Scrappy,'' Bell assured him. ''We'll put our rank insignia on before we get to Da Nang and nobody's going to stop us until we try to leave base. We won't be carrying any contraband then.''

''I wonder if the Air Force is still looking for their Jeep?'' Slover asked.

''What Air Force Jeep?'' Burrison asked.

''Not real hard,'' Randall said to Slover, ignoring the lieutenant's question. ''Bobbie didn't mention it when I last saw her, and Jeep security seemed less than it was earlier.''

Slover hit him with a jarring slap on the back. ''Shit, Tex,'' he said, ''your eyes were so full of round-eye nooky then, you wouldn't have noticed if she did.''

Randall playfully hit him back. ''You watch your big mouth, Big Louie, unless you want to start wearing your teeth in a bag around your neck.'' He blushed so red the big mortarman burst out laughing too hard to be able to say anything else for several minutes.

When he finally got his breath back, Slover said, ''You'd have to get your pappy and your uncles to help if you wanted to try it, Tex. Even then it wouldn't be a fair fight.'' That started him laughing again, and Randall looked back out over the land on his side of the Jeep—but he didn't see anything he looked at, he was too embarrassed.

When they finally reached Highway 1, Bell stopped the

Jeep and looked for a long moment at a weathered, wooden sign. Two words and a westward pointing arrow were on the sign. It said "Indian Country." "Someone remind me to tell Stilts that sign's still there," he said. There were several bullet holes in the sign. Bell started the Jeep again and turned left onto the highway.

Highway 1, the major north-south highway of French Indochina, started in Phnom Penh, Cambodia, and ran east through Saigon to Phan Thiet on the South China Sea. It turned north there and followed the coast all the way to Thanh Hoa in North Vietnam, where it started drifting away from the sea to Hanoi. After Hanoi, Highway 1 jagged east-of-north as far as the border with China. This vital artery, the most important road in Southeast Asia, was a narrow, two lane blacktop road eroding at its sides. Two '61 Chevy Impalas would have trouble passing each other on it.

Fleets of brightly colored civilian vehicles flowed up and down the highway; Vespas, Lambrettas, Honda motorbikes. Tiny buses, piled high with the belongings of many families who decided they didn't like being refugees in one place and wanted to try another one, passed other tiny buses, piled high with the belongings of more families who didn't like being refugees in the places the first were heading for and who had decided to try the other. Most of the buses and many autos, the ones for hire, had chicken wire covering their paneless windows. The chicken wire was there to stop hand grenades from being thrown in.

A couple of miles after turning onto Highway 1, the Jeep passed a twelve-truck Marine convoy headed south. An Amtrack, an amphibious landing vehicle, led the convoy, and every third truck mounted a .50 caliber machine gun with a sharp-eyed Marine eyeballing the landscape over the gun's barrel. The backs of the trucks were filled with dirty, exhausted, hollow-eyed Marines—a battalion returning from an operation. A few of the hollow-eyed

Marines in the trucks gazed blankly at the four clean Marines in the Jeep. Most of them didn't bother.

Far ahead, a three-Jeep convoy was visible in the traffic. Another was more than a mile to the rear. White sand beaches sparkled on the right; the green water of the South China Sea lazily lapped the beach. Rice paddies shone emerald green on the land side of the highway. Here and there, small clutches of bamboo and thatch hootches huddled together under a few trees that tried vainly to shade them from the tropical sun. Black-pajamaed peasants shamble-trotted along the highway with shallow baskets swinging from the ends of long yokes across their shoulders. Fishing boats bobbed close to shore. Traffic became heavier as they neared the city. It was mostly pedestrian traffic, people pushing bicycles or carts laden with market goods, a few leading water buffalo–drawn carts.

Suddenly Bell laughed. "Big Louie, I wonder what your cousin Os is going to want this time that we didn't bring as trading goods."

Slover blinked, then grinned when he remembered the story Zeitvogel had told him about his cousin, Sea Bee Chief Petty Officer Ossie Slover, turning down trade goods in favor of Bell's bush hat, in exchange for fake registration for their Jeep. "Shee-it," he said, "you just know it's going to be something we didn't think of. Man wants some things for his own self, not for trading, it's probably going to be something we don't want to give up." He laughed a short hard laugh. "I know my cousin Os, he's keeping that cover for his own self. I bet he's gonna have it bronzed he gets back to the World, put it up on his mantelpiece when he retires." He laughed again. "Man'll probably even want to find out what medals and ribbons you got, Jay Cee, have someone enamel them onto it after he has it bronzed."

"Bronze a bush hat?" Randall asked, his face screwed up. "Who the fuck would want to bronze a bush hat and put it on the mantelpiece?" He removed his own bush hat and stared at it, trying to imagine it bronzed. Then he remembered how his mother had had his baby booties bronzed, and how the last he heard she was still trying to talk his father into hanging them from the rearview mirror of the family station wagon. He put his bush hat back on his head and didn't say anything more about it. There was no accounting for some people.

Soon they reached a gate leading into the American military installation at Da Nang. Two Marine MPs in helmets and flak jackets were searching a civilian auto leaving the base. A uniformed American was behind the wheel. One of the two MPs would look up each time he heard a car or truck approaching on the in-bound lane and wave it through. He didn't simply wave when Bell stopped to wait to be admitted.

The MP, who was wearing lance corporal's chevrons on his collars, picked up his rifle from where it was leaning against the car he and his partner were searching and slung it over his shoulder. "Afternoon, Marines," he said, walking over to them. He looked at their bush hats while they returned his greeting. "A word to the wise. Wear regulation soft covers until you get back into the bush, not those John Wayne hats. Also"—he looked at their bare collars and could see the holes where they had worn rank insignia—"you must be field grunts and I know field grunts don't wear rank insignia, but unless you want to be privates for real, wear your rank insignia until you hit the bush again. These people running this base don't know whether they want to be rinky-dink or chickenshit. One thing's sure, though. They're being Mickey Mouse about it."

"Thank you, Lance Corporal," Burrison said politely. He removed his bush hat and drew a regulation hat from inside his shirt. He knocked it into shape and pulled it onto his head. The others did the same. Then he withdrew a pair of gold bars from his breast pocket and pinned them onto his collars. Bell put on his sergeant's stripes. Randall was ready for this but didn't think Slover would be. He figured the mortarman had been in the Bun Hou area too long to remember all the niceties of life in the rear. He pulled out two sets of metal corporal's chevrons and handed one set to Slover.

"Can't let you get busted down to private, Big Louie," Randall said. "You get busted, we got to give the mortar to Athen, and he just ain't as good with it as you are."

Slover snorted accepting the chevrons. "Ain't nobody good as me with a piss tube. Athen's good, though."

When the four men in the Jeep completed their transformation from field to garrison uniforms the MP saluted Burrison and started to turn back to the civilian car—his partner was just finishing the search.

"You do much of that?" Bell asked, nodding at the next car stopping to be searched.

"No, Sergeant," the lance corporal turned back. "But right now we got orders to search all vehicles leaving the base with American drivers or passengers unless they're part of a convoy or carrying a field-grade officer." He smiled the smile of a man who knows he's been told to stick his finger in a crack in a dike when a whole section of the dike is down a few feet away. "It's part of a crackdown on trafficking in captured Vee Cee weapons." He glanced at the two sea bags in the back of the Jeep. "But we're only supposed to search vehicles leaving the base." He shrugged.

Bell laughed and shook his head. "Trafficking in captured Vee Cee weapons," he said. "What'll they think of next!" He shifted into first and rolled onto the Da Nang base.

CHAPTER NINETEEN

Da Nang, December 3, 1966

"What we do now," Bell said, "is you pretend this is a sight-seeing bus and I'm the tour driver."

"Tex and I have spent more time in Da Nang than you have, Jay Cee," Burrison told him.

"Picky, picky, Scrappy. If that's the way you feel about it, pretend I'm giving the tour to Big Louie and you're just along for the ride." He wanted to say more, but the roar of a flight of Air Force Phantom jets taking off from the nearby airstrip drowned him out.

The Da Nang base was big and they were hungry, so Bell gave them an abbreviated tour. They drove past relatively permanent buildings that were administrative or belonged to the Air Force. There were clapboard buildings, some of which were Navy property. And there were

Quonset huts all over the place. Most of the Quonset huts belonged to the Marines.

"Over there," Bell said, parking for a moment a block or two from the bay, "beyond this row of warehouses, is the Sea Bee area. Your cousin Os works there, Louie. Think you can find it on your own?"

"Do fish piss in the river?" Slover asked. "No way one Slover can't find another, once he knows what direction he's in."

Bell drove on and stopped again not too far from where a tanker was being off-loaded. He had to wait for a few moments before speaking because of the scream of Marine Crusaders and Skyhawks using the runway. "That down there is the beginning of the oil and fuel dump, Scrappy," he said when the aircraft noise was over. "Ensign Lily probably works there; if he doesn't you'll be able to find someone who knows where he can be found." Lily was a POL—Petroleum, Oil, Lubricants—officer. "Now let's find someplace that's still serving chow," Bell said. "I'm hungry for some hamburgers and a cold Coke."

"Wait one, Jay Cee," Slover said. "That's work for Scrappy and me. What about you and Tex? What are you two doing here if you don't have anything to do?"

"I'm the driver and tour guide," Bell said, straight-faced, "and I'm the only one who knows where everyone's supposed to go. Tex"—he still didn't crack his Marine sergeant stone-face—"he's here because he's a swinging cock with a girlfriend."

"We'll see if we can make that two swinging cocks with girlfriends," Slover said, poking Randall in the chest. It was meant playfully, but was hard enough that he had to reach out and grab to keep Randall from tumbling out of the Jeep's back.

"Now, like I said, I'm hungry for some hamburgers and a cold Coke," Bell said.

"What's hamburgers and a cold Coke?" Slover asked, his eyes wide. They were able to get warm sodas at Camp

Apache, but most of what they got were bottled-in-Saigon Coca-Colas which were always suspect. The only hamburgers they ever saw were called Salisbury steak, heated over and served in gravy once in a while as their daily, flown-in hot meal.

"It's the kind of shit you always used to want to eat when you were hanging on the block with your high school buddies," Randall said. He was thinking of cold chicken, potato salad, and Kool-Aid on the beach with Bobbie Harder.

"Shit, I didn't have block-hanging high school buddies," Slover snorted. "I dropped out of high school because it got in the way of me making the long green. And the block hangers, man, I owned the block, I was their chief honcho."

It was Randall's turn to play dumb. "What's long green?" The American military in Vietnam was paid in "MPC," Military Payment Certificates, Monopoly-size money that came in a different color for each denomination. It was called "Funny Money" and was used to keep American greenbackers out of the black market. Sometimes it did, sometimes it didn't. The others laughed at the joke.

"Find a PX, Jay Cee," Burrison said. "There's sure to be a geedunk near a PX. Maybe even one that'll let an officer in. After that we can find quarters for the night."

"I can probably get us racks in the same transient barracks I stayed in last time I was here," Randall said.

"And your buddy Lily can probably put you up in his BOQ," Bell said to Burrison.

They found a PX, a big one set aside for staff NCOs. Bell almost ran over a sailor, he was so busy ogling the show windows in the PX. It had somehow never occurred to the CAP Marines that a PX in a combat zone would be selling fur coats, fine jewelry, hi-fi sets, major appliances, cars, and evening gowns.

"Jay Cee, park this sucker before you get a ticket for

vehicular homicide,'' the lieutenant said. Bell parked and the four got out to look more closely at the windows. The one they spent the longest time in front of, and made the most comments about, was next to the window with mannequins sporting strapless, backless gowns. This window sheltered mannequins wearing bikinis.

"That split-tail of yours wear them on the beach?" Slover asked, licking his lips.

"Don't call her a split-tail, she's a nice girl," Randall growled—well, he tried to growl. It wasn't easy, though, when he was blushing.

Sure enough, they found a geedunk nearby. It even served officers. Randall went through the cafeteria-type line first, Burrison last. It was force of habit. In the field, Marines are fed in reverse order of rank.

"Are you sure you want five hamburgers?" the server asked Slover when he gave his order.

"And a triple order of french fries and two large Cokes."

"No Coke. We only serve Pepsi here."

"All right, two large Pepsis."

The server looked at him and decided not to argue. If the dumb grunt wanted to pay for food he couldn't eat, it was his problem. But Slover did eat it all and later went back for more.

They found a table with no one at it and sat down. A few men, junior enlisted men, at adjacent tables glanced at them and then looked again. Then got up and moved away. It could have been because they were field grunts and smelled bad, but more likely it was because they were an officer, a sergeant and two corporals. Corporals can usually be trusted, unless they're bucking for their third stripe. But not officers or sergeants. It's bad luck to sit too close to them while you're trying to eat or relax. Before they left, Burrison to find Lily and the NCOs to find a place to sleep, they made arrangements to meet at 1800 hours that evening at a flagpole near the office where Bobbie Harder worked. Bell kept the Jeep with the two sea bags of trade goods.

Ensign Lily was as easy to find as Bell predicted. After introducing him to the other Navy officers he was working with—they were polite about it, but every one of them had trouble picturing this bright-eyed, bushy-tailed kid who didn't look quite old enough to be an officer as the kind of bad-ass Marine grunt officer Lily said he was—Lily took Burrison into a side office that had a coffee maker and closed the door behind them. He poured them each a cup of strong Navy coffee, and they sat across a desktop from each other. Lily asked what brought Burrison to Da Nang.

"We need your help," Burrison started.

"I'm not even going to ask," Lily said when Burrison finished his story, "I know you're shitting me. You've come up with some wild tales during the time I've known you, Burrie, and they've all been true. And I know, the Lily and Reeves VC and NVA War Surplus Store owes you a lot as its prime supplier, but no way on earth I can believe you on this one. What do you really want the explosives for?" He leaned forward and folded his arms on the desk.

Burrison's jaw dropped and he sputtered. Lily brushed flecks of saliva off his face and waited. "That is the truth," Burrison finally managed to say. "We're going to take out a Vee Cee communications center."

"Without authorization, and you're going to hide the whole operation from higher authorities."

"That's right."

"You're dinky dau. You're out of your fucking mind, Burrie. I don't believe one word of what you just told me. And if I did, what do you think is going to happen to me and Reeves when this gets out?"

"Nothing, because nobody's going to know about it except us."

"Uh-huh."

* * *

At the same time, in a building not too far away, Chief Petty Officer Ossie Slover leaned back in his swivel chair, propped his feet on his desk, took his cigar out of his mouth, seemed to study it like tea leaves or *I Ching* · sticks, and carefully laid it down on the edge of his desk. He folded his ham-sized arms across his massive chest and said, "You out of you fucking mind, Little Louie."

Bell looked uncertainly at the cigar; at their previous meeting, Chief Slover had given him the impression of a man who never removed his cigar from his mouth except to replace a burnt-out butt with a fresh stogie. Louie Slover looked at the big moon face without a cigar sticking out of it, and his spirits sagged. He had known his cousin Os since he himself had been a very little boy, and this was the first time he had seen him without a cigar clamped between his teeth.

"You and these white-boy buddies of yours been too far out in Indian Country for too goddamn long," Chief Slover said. "You done gone Asiatic. What you need is some R&R and a month-of-Sundays' worth of round-eye nookie. I can help you with that last one, by the way. Lots a round-eye tail to be had if you know where to look and got some spare MPC for it. But what you say you gonna do? You even crazier than you think I am, you think I'm going to help you."

"But Cousin Os, we can do this if we get the shit we need for it. We know we can."

At 1800 hours, Burrison looked at his NCOs and they looked at him and they all knew. Bell said "geedunk," and that was the only word anyone said except to place their food orders until they were sitting. Then Bell held his large Pepsi in front of his eyes and said, "I wish this was a beer."

"Got to go to a club for that," Randall said. "And they don't have clubs where officers and NCOs can sit down and drink together."

"Shit."

Eventually they started talking about what had happened since they had parted earlier.

"Lily thinks we're dinky dau, and he doesn't believe what we're going to do. He says he's not even going to talk to Reeves about this because it won't work and he isn't going to risk putting his ass in a sling for it."

"My cousin Os don't believe us. He thinks we gone Asiatic, we been in Indian Country too long."

"So much for Plan A," Bell said. "Now we go to Plan B."

"What's Plan B?" Randall asked, looking confused.

"How the fuck do I know what's Plan B?" Bell snapped. "Look, you're corporals, I'm a sergeant. You know how to carry out impossible orders, I only know how to give impossible orders, remember? Now I'm giving you a fucking impossible order; come up with Plan B."

So Slover and Randall came up with Plan B.

"Damn, Burrie, why didn't you tell me this in the first place instead of coming up with that cockamamie story about wiping out some fictional Vee Cee communications center?" Ensign Lily asked that evening when Burrison went back to him with Plan B. They were in a Navy officers' mess eating dinner. "When we finish chow let's head for the club. I'm sure Reeves'll show up there sometime this evening, and he'll agree with me that the Lily and Reeves VC and NVA War Surplus Company will be most happy to assist you in this Great Humanitarian Venture."

Burrison could actually hear the capital letters when Lily said "Great Humanitarian Venture." He shook his head in wonderment. Plan B sounded to him so much more absurd than the truth that he didn't believe Lily would accept it so quickly.

"Hell, Burrie, instead of hiding your light under a bushel for this, you should be running around getting someone to write you up for a Navy Achievement Medal, at least." Lily gazed briefly into the distance wondering how much more in trade goods an NAM would be worth to Burrison after he finished this job.

Later, in the officers' club, Burrison was getting slightly tipsy, and Lily was somewhat more so, when they were joined by Lieutenant (jg) Reeves, a friend of Lily's who was a helicopter driver. Lily explained Plan B to him and told him how valuable participation in this "Great Humanitarian Venture" would be to the Lily and Reeves VC and NVA War Surplus Company.

"Reeves and Lily," Reeves said. He had already been drinking.

"Reeves and Lily."

"How can we help you, Burrie?"

After Randall and Slover had worked out Plan B, they went with Bell back to the warehouse where Chief Slover worked, but by then it was too late in the day.

"Now, I understand you're one bad-assed Marine field-grunt sergeant and two bad-assed Marine field-grunt corporals," said the seaman who explained to them that the chief was gone for the night and wouldn't be back until the morning. "I can tell that by just looking at you. But I really think you shouldn't go looking for the Chief tonight. You see, what the Chief does when he gets off work is he goes to places where they don't rightly like Marine corporals and three-stripe sergeants. I don't care how bad-assed you is or how drunk they is, since there's only three of you—forty or fifty drunk chief petty officers can swab the deck with your asses."

Bell looked at his companions and said, "I've heard this before. Let's dee-dee before this swabbie talks us to death." He turned to the sailor and said, "We'll come back after 1000 hours tomorrow, when the Chief can see straight," but the seaman didn't seem to hear. They could still hear him happily babbling to himself when they were too far away to make out what he was saying.

Bell led Slover and Randall to a 45 club he knew where they could drink and talk. It was called a ''45'' club because it was for corporals and sergeants, enlisted pay grades 4 and 5. The club was a large Quonset hut, with picnic tables and benches sitting across it in three rows that ran the length of the building. A narrow aisle separated the rows of tables, and there was barely enough space between them for two men to squeeze past. Slover estimated there were at least sixty tables in the room, each could hold a dozen men—more, if they were friendly enough. Most of the tables were occupied, many of them were filled. Three huge window air conditioners chugged high in the walls, one at each end and one in the middle of one long wall. There were three alcoves, with serving counters blocking entrance to them, along the long wall opposite the one with the air conditioner.

They staggered slightly when they entered the club. It was several degrees hotter inside and much more humid than in the open air on the other side of the door. The air conditioners, despite their size, didn't manage to do much more than slowly push around the hot, muggy air.

''Find us a place to sit,'' Bell said. ''The first round's on me.'' He struggled through the crowd to the counter at the end away from the entrance; it had the shortest of the three lines.

Slover and Randall looked over the room. ''How about under that air conditioner?'' Slover asked. ''Maybe it won't be so hot.'' They edged, shoved, pushed, and elbowed their way to an empty table directly under the air conditioner and sat down. Chill air from the unit cascaded down on them and tore them straight from the tropics to the climate of a Minnesota October afternoon. They held their arms out, pulled their shirts away from their sweaty bodies, and twisted side to side, letting the cold air wash over them. If the truth were known, they both wished they could strip naked in the flood of cold air. Since they couldn't really strip, they pulled their shirts open and squirmed to let the air directly cool their

skin. This was the first time since either arrived in-
country that he had experienced temperatures cooler
than the high seventies. Even the office Bobbie Harder
worked in was only air-conditioned enough to take the
edge off the heat.

"Man, a few days of this'll blow my heat rash right
the fuck away," Randall shouted above the grumbly
droning of the air conditioner.

"Shit, the only reason you got a rash is you wear a
shirt all the time. The heat doesn't have a damn thing to
do with it," Slover shouted back, scrubbing his hands
over his chest and belly.

After a few minutes they closed their shirts and drew
their arms close to their bodies for warmth. They started
looking around for Bell. He was halfway between the
counter he had gone to for the fifteen-cent cans of beer
and the middle of the room, craning his neck, looking
for them. Slover stood up and wig-wagged his arms at
the sergeant. Bell spotted him and zig-zagged through
the crowded tables to them.

"I said you were lucky to find a table with no one at
it," Bell shouted when Slover and Randall shrugged and
cupped their ears, asking him to repeat what he had said.
They did that because they couldn't make out over the
noise of the air conditioner what he said when he reached
them. He put six cans of beer on the table and sat down.
His mouth gaped open at the impact of the cold air flood-
ing over his body. He was speechless for a few minutes,
reveling in the coolness, then drew his arms close to avoid
shivering along with the two corporals. "I wonder why,"
he started to say, then tried again in a louder voice, "I
wonder why nobody was sitting here."

"Damned if I know," Slover shouted loudly enough
to be heard over the air conditioner.

Randall didn't say anything.

They quickly downed the two beers apiece Bell had
brought back, then Slover announced, "This round's
mine." He stood and pointed himself toward the shortest

of the three serving lines. "They got anything besides beer?" he asked Bell in a booming voice.

"Greasy hamburgers and overcooked hot dogs," Bell shouted back.

"I mean to drink."

"No got. Beer only." The idea behind beer-only was, beer was served in cans, mixed drinks had to be served in glasses. If a fight broke out in the club, and at least one did on most nights, a thrown empty beer can would cause less injury than would a thrown old-fashioned glass.

Slover grimaced and headed toward the line. Bell tried to make small talk with Randall, but the other didn't seem to notice. His face wore a distracted expression and he shook slightly. The sergeant couldn't tell if the shaking was shivering from the chill or trembling caused by agitation. Slover came back in a few minutes. He plopped six beers and a large pile of hamburgers on the table.

"We gonna do any serious drinking, we better eat," he said. "And we got a long way to go." He nodded at a nearby table where a half-dozen sergeants—they looked like grunts from the red dirt staining their utility uniforms—were busy drinking. They were building pyramids of beer cans on their table—the smallest pyramid had more than a dozen cans in it. Eventually someone at a different table might throw an empty can at one of their pyramids. If that happened, which was likely, it would knock down the pyramid and, also likely, cause a riot. There were only two places to be if that happened; someplace else, or drunk enough not to feel any injuries received in the melee.

"You're right," Bell said, grabbing a beer with one hand and a hamburger with the other.

Bell and Slover were too busy shoving hamburgers into their mouths between gulps of beer to talk for several minutes. Randall ate one burger slowly and sipped at a beer.

Finally Slover wolfed the last burger and tipped his

head back to drain the last of his beer. "Your turn," he told Randall.

"Huh? Oh, yah." Randall stood up and headed toward a counter.

Slover picked up the last beer. "He didn't even touch it," he said. "Want to share it?"

"Sure," Bell said. "Bottom half's mine." Slover drank half of it and handed the can over.

Bell knocked off the beer and said loudly, "I think I know how come nobody's sitting here."

"Why?"

"Too goddamn cold and too noisy to talk." He shivered and realized he hadn't thought he'd ever think any place was too cold after spending ten months of not being able to cool off in Vietnam.

Slover nodded; he was feeling the same. "Let's move."

Someone propped open the back door of the 45 club, allowing a slight cross-ventilation. The two joined the sudden rush of bodies for table space near the open door. Randall got six cans of beer and returned to the table under the air conditioner. He sat down and started drinking one before he realized the other two were no longer there. He jumped up and looked around, half in a panic. What was he supposed to do with six open cans of beer if they had left? He didn't want to drink them by himself. Then he spotted Slover standing on a bench near the back door, waving at him.

More Marines had headed toward the tables near the open door than there were benches and tables to hold. While Slover was sitting back down, someone grabbed the space he was holding for Randall. Randall reached them just as Slover was about to feed a knuckle sandwich to the inebriated interloper.

"That's okay, Big Louie," Randall shouted, grabbing the big man's arm. "Here, you take these. I'm going." He put the six cans in front of Slover and Bell and turned toward the open door.

"Hey, where you going?" Bell demanded before he had time to take two steps.

"Where the fuck do you think?" Randall said, turning back with an agonized expression on his face. I'm in Da Nang and Bobbie doesn't know I'm here. I got to go see her."

Bell grinned and shook his head. "Puppy love," he said under his breath.

"What's a matter, bro?" Slover said. "You afraid she gonna cut your balls off she finds out you're in Da Nang and don't go see her first thing?"

Randall blushed.

Bell waved him away and clapped a hand on Slover's shoulder. "Let 'im go, Louie. Man's in love, and there ain't no accounting for what a man'll do when he's in love."

"Love, shit," Slover snorted. "Man's pussy-whipped you mean. We get back to the World I'm taking that man onto the block in Paramus, show him how we put women in their places and keep them there." There was a twinkle in his eyes that said his words shouldn't be taken too seriously.

CHAPTER TWENTY

The Next Couple of Days, Mostly in Da Nang

Bell and Slover nursed mild hangovers in the morning with too many cups of mess hall coffee to count and three servings of steak and eggs and ten slices of toast apiece. Randall was too distracted to say much; his first cup of coffee grew cold by the time he drank half of it.

"Messman told me I wasn't getting any more, I came through the chow line again," Slover said to Randall. "How 'bout I eat them steak and eggs for you, since you ain't eating them?"

Randall absently pushed his mess tray in Slover's general direction.

"Keep your coffee, pano," Slover said, removing the mug from the tray and putting it back in Randall's hands. "Ain't nobody said I can't go back for more coffee.

'Sides, I don't like it all gunked up with sugar and milk like you do.''

Bell looked at his watch and groaned. "Oh, eight-thirty," he said. "I wish it was later, I'm too sick to have to wait another hour and a half before going to see your cousin Os." He rubbed his stomach and belched loudly, then swirled his coffee and drank what was left in his mug. He grimaced at the taste of the grounds in the bottom of the mug. "More," he said, standing. "Anybody else?" Slover held out his mug for a refill. Randall didn't move. "Puppy love," Bell muttered as he wandered toward the coffee urn.

"Pussy-whipped," Slover said around a mouthful of steak and eggs with buttered toast when the sergeant returned with two mugs of steaming coffee. "Got his balls cut off."

"Tell old Jay Cee about it, Tex," Bell said, slapping Randall on the back. He didn't hit him hard—he was afraid of the effect of a hard blow on his own head.

Randall shrugged. "Nothing to tell," he said. "She wasn't there." He sighed deeply.

"What do you mean, 'she wasn't there'?"

"That's what they told me at her quarters. She went to Saigon for a few days." He turned his face, red with something other than a blush, to Bell. "Bobbie went away and didn't say anything to me."

"Don't sweat it, Tex." Bell tried to sound reassuring. "It probably came up sudden-like, and when we get back to Camp Apache there'll be a letter waiting for you telling you about it. Besides, you dumb fuck," he said in a deeper voice with his face close to Randall's, "you didn't tell her you were going to be here and she didn't have any idea she should be around."

"Besides that," Slover said, and washed down the last of his food with a large gulp of coffee, "you think all she got to do is sit around Da Nang waiting for your young ass to show up out of the boonies?"

Randall shrugged them off and stared into his coffee

without answering. Then he shook his shoulders like a big dog waking up, drank the cold coffee in his mug, and rose to his feet. "Coffee?" The other two thrust their mugs at him.

"I told you boys yesterday I ain't gonna help you with this," Chef Slover said. He sat at his desk leaning forward on his folded, tree-trunk arms, somehow managing to look twice as big and ominous as he did standing up, and aimed a bloodshot eye at the three Marine NCOs. His cigar looked unstable in the corner of his mouth. "Even if you isn't lying to me, this is something can get you in a world of shit. How the fuck you gonna 'splain where you got them explosives if you get caught? Investigation sure's shit gonna land right here on Chief Petty Officer Ossie Slover, and I tell you I'm too goddamn old and too goddamn close to retirement to land in Portsmouth brig and lose that retirement. Boys, I can smell that fifty-percent retirement salary like it was a cunt hair stuck up my nose. No."

"Uh, Cousin Os," Slover said, looking guilty, "I got to admit we're lying to you."

"That's what I said, and that's why the answer's no. I don't deal with no people who lie to me. Especially not when they related to me, and the last I heard you was still my mother's brother's son." He glowered, and looked like he had no more to say on the matter.

"That's why we're going to tell you what we're going to tell you," Slover continued. He grimaced—he hated telling lies.

Chief Slover lifted an eyebrow and waited. It was a trick he had been taught by an old master chief petty officer, it was supposed to put the fear of God in the hearts of seamen and junior petty officers and force them to tell the truth after you've let them know you know they're lying.

Slover squirmed on his straight-backed chair, making it shift and groan in protest. "Ah, what I'm gonna tell you is we aren't going to blow no Vee Cee communications center." His teeth grated and sweat beads popped out on his forehead. Louie Slover didn't only hate lies, he hated the people who told them, too. "What we're going to tell you is we want those explosives so we can go up in the hills and make a dam on the Song Du Ong river so our villagers can have better control over the water that comes to their rice paddies." He fervently hoped his cousin had never looked at a map of the Bun Hou area. The village didn't get the water for its rice paddies from the Song Du Ong, but from a river farther north. "We're trying to fix our little people up so's they got better control of their own lives." He blew out and relaxed slightly—at least that much of what he said was true.

Chief Slover unfolded his arms and leaned back, causing his swivel chair to squeak loudly. He laid a sausage-like finger alongside his nose and tapped it a few times. His cigar bobbed once or twice and seemed to become firmly cemented in the corner of his mouth. "Why didn't you tell me that in the first place?" he finally asked. "Little Louie, I just know your white-boy friends influenced you. No way you would have come up with a cock-and-bull story like that on your own, you would a told me the truth up front." He sat up, businesslike, and said, "Now, tell Os what you need and then we can get down to some serious dickering."

Slover swallowed. "Aren't you afraid of the investigation if somebody finds out about this?"

"Investigation? What investigation? You get this job done, report it up the chain of command, and you'll probably get yourselves a medal." He beamed. "Shit, they find out the Sea Bees, in the person of me, helped out, shit, I might get a medal out of it, too. What do you need?"

Twenty minutes later, two sea bags of trading goods changed hands, and the three Marines left the Sea Bee area with Chief Slover's injunction to "Come back here at 1000 hours tomorrow with your Jeep and I'll send you off with your first load of goods. If you can get yourselves a trailer to hitch up to it, maybe you can do it all in one trip.'' He hadn't asked for any trade items they didn't have, he was too busy thinking of the medal he might get for helping out. He didn't even ask what bangalore torpedoes, Claymore mines, and metal-melting thermite grenades had to do with building a dam.

"Man, I hate lying," Slover said into the pile of California cheeseburgers and french fries smothered in catsup on three paper plates in front of him. Two large Pepsis were next to the plates.

"Don't sweat it, Big Louie," Bell said. "You told him you were lying. If he wanted to believe you meant we were lying yesterday instead of today, that's his problem. Besides, it worked.'' They were eating their noon chow in the same geedunk they had eaten in the day before.

Randall was leaning back, very pleased with what they had accomplished. He had almost as many cheeseburgers and fries in front of him as Slover did. "See what corporals do with impossible orders, Jay Cee?"

Bell snorted. "If it wasn't for us sergeants giving you those impossible orders, there wouldn't be any reason to have corporals," he said. "You'd still be lance corporals, both of you."

"They bought it," Burrison said. "I don't believe it. I told Lily what we were going to do and he didn't want to believe me. I told him Plan B and he swallowed it. Reeves loves Plan B. They're going to fly those explosives out when we tell them to and put them down anywhere we want."

In its own way, this was a better meal than the first one they'd eaten after they arrived at Da Nang. The first time they gorged on civilian food was a great treat after what they ate at Camp Apache. This time they were flushed with victory, and the cheeseburgers, french fries, and Pepsis were a feast.

* * *

The next morning, Bell and Randall loaded crates of Claymore mines into the back of their Jeep and drove to a helipad, where Lieutenant Reeves had his helicopter parked. It took two trips to haul all of the mines. Reeves had his crew load the crates onto the bird while the NCOs went back for more. After they made three trips with the tubelike mines called bangalore torpedos, and hundreds of pounds of plastic explosives, Reeves told Bell he didn't have any more time to wait around—he had to get his bird back to its regular job.

Burrison and Slover had left the day before.

"Your tube needs your guiding hand, Big Louie," Burrison had told the big man. "Jay Cee and Tex can drive back after they finish ferrying our stuff."

One more round trip and the rest of the explosives were stored in a place Lily assured them was safe for them to use for the next several days.

"Well, Tex," Bell said when they were through, "let's grab one more meal at that geedunk. Then we got a long drive ahead of us."

Randall nodded numbly. Three days and two nights in Da Nang and he hadn't seen Bobbie Harder. "I'm going to her office and leave a note," he said when he and Bell were through eating.

"All right," Bell said, and drove them there. He waited outside in the Jeep while Randall went in. Ten minutes later he was back, and they headed out of the base.

"Looks like that same gate sentry we passed on our way in," Bell said as they neared the gate. The MP lance corporal wasn't searching any of the vehicles leaving, he waved most of them through, only stopping some to check ID or passes. Bell pulled the Jeep over to the side and put it in neutral. As soon as there was a break in the traffic the MP walked over to see why they had stopped.

"Morning, Lance Corporal," Bell said. "Not searching civilian vehicles today?"

"No, Sergeant," the MP answered, "they told us to stand down on that. We weren't catching enough to make it worthwhile busting people's balls." He recognized Bell and glanced into the empty back of the Jeep. He looked almost disappointed to see it was empty.

"Shitty duty you're pulling here." Bell shook his head. "Everybody hates gate sentries and you got to worry about snipers and incoming, too." He saw the beginning of offense in the MP's face and quickly went on, "I was an MP at Cherry Point myself before getting my orders over here. Lot's of slack, but a lot of shit too, being a gate sentry."

"You were an MP at Cherry Point? No shit," the MP said, forgetting what he first heard as an offensive statement in the flush of talking to a grunt who understood what it was like being a military policeman. "That was my last duty station before here. I was in H&MS Squadron."

Bell grinned at him. "No shit."

"Yeah. You think maybe you were one of those MPs kept giving me a hard time?"

Bell laughed. "Wouldn't surprise me at all. I was with India Three One at Pendleton before Cherry Point. You were all Airedale pogues at Cherry Point, the MPs were almost all ex-grunts. Believe me, we didn't give a rat's ass about busting your balls because we were bored."

The MP laughed. He understood. "What happened to that lieutenant and the splib corporal you had with you when you came in?" he asked.

"The lieutenant decided he didn't like my driving, caught a bird back because it was more comfortable. He took the other corporal to ride shotgun with him."

"How'd he pick him instead of one of you?"

"Bullshit, Lance Corporal, you aren't that dumb. You saw Big Louie Slover. If you saw a second lieutenant with a bodyguard that big, black, and mean-looking, would you fuck with him?"

The MP laughed again. "I guess not," he said.

"That's why. Listen," he said, reaching to the floor-board between the seats, "I'm not carrying any contraband, but I held on to this for you." He held out a Vietcong tube pack. "Man used to carry this pack don't need it anymore. We wasted his ass last week."

The MP bit his lip; he knew he wasn't supposed to accept souvenirs from grunts passing through the gate, but that tube pack was awful tempting.

"Go ahead, nobody's ever going to know where you got it," Bell said, shoving it at the MP's hands. "Where we're going these damn things are so common we use them for shit paper."

The MP looked around furtively. Nobody was watching. He took the pack and stuck it inside his shirt. "Thanks, Sergeant, I really appreciate it. MPs don't get much chance to get real Vee Cee–type souvenirs when they're on gate duty here. Good luck." He waved them through.

Randall glanced back a short distance away and saw the MP still standing there watching them. A few vehicles were beginning to back up, waiting for him to let them through the gate. "I didn't know you were an MP at Cherry Point," he said.

"I wasn't. But it was a good guess he wasn't either," Bell explained. "It always helps to show sympathy to the other guy's problems—makes him more sympathetic to yours, or at least helps him overlook them. Besides, most Marines hate MPs, but you never know when you're gonna need a cop. It's a good idea to be friendly to them; a friendly MP who remembers a favor might come in handy some day."

The drive back to Camp Apache was uneventful. The hot chow bird had already come and gone by the time they arrived, but some chow had been saved for them. Too bad it had gotten cold, but it was still better than C rats. Slover had supervised installing half of the Claymore mines from the trip into the barbed wire defenses of the Marine compound. The rest of them would be used on the operation. And Bell had been right, there was a letter from Bobbie Harder waiting for Randall. In it she told him that a chance had suddenly arose for her to take five days in Saigon. She'd tell him about her trip the next time she saw him, but she knew the trip wouldn't be as much fun without him along.

Ruizique and Knowles had returned from R&R during their absence. Flood had also returned from the hospital. He wasn't really ready to return fully to duty but, like Doc Tracker, was classed walking-wounded and was given work to do in the hospital. Again like Doc Tracker, he left on his own rather than do the work.

"I had to send two more men on R&R yesterday, Jay Cee," Burrison said. "Flood isn't back to full health, so I sent him. The other was Big Red. I told him he's too old for what we're doing and he needed a rest." Robertson was twenty-six, the oldest American in Tango Niner. He had dropped out of law school to join the Marines after the war started—he even turned down an appointment to the Platoon Leaders School; he wanted to be an enlisted man rather than an officer so he could do his share of the fighting.

Bell nodded. The operation would be over by the time the two returned from their R&R. Flood was a good choice. Tracker would have been a good one, too, but they might need both corpsmen. Picking the second man was tough, but Bell couldn't argue with Burrison's choice. He would have preferred sending one of the new men, but the men who had been there the longest had to be the first ones to go.

"It's been gawd-awful quiet lately," Zeitvogel said when they were preparing for the night's patrols. "Too quiet. We haven't even seen a bad guy since we captured Senior Sergeant Mai. I have this feeling Charlie's getting ready to do something, something big and bad. To us."

"I want to do him first," Ruizique said. His eyes flamed at the prospect of bearding Charlie's lion in his own den, putting so bad a hurting on the enemy he might not be able to recover in this area.

Bell looked at the Dominican and sighed softly. The R&R hadn't seemed to do much to cool his passion for combat. He could only hope Ruizique wouldn't do anything stupid and get someone hurt.

"If he gives us enough time, we will," Burrison said. "The biggest question about what we're going to do is, do we take the time to run another recon, get more intelligence about that comm-center, and let more people get a look at it, or do we get ready and blow it now."

"We've got four men who've been there," Randall said. "I think that's enough. If we go back for another look, it delays the operation and gives them one more chance to spot us."

"Good points, Tex," Bell said. "We'll have to think about it. In the meantime, we've got some patrols to run tonight. We've been entirely too lax on that for too long."

The three patrol leaders took their men out for another mind-wrecking, eventless night. Zeitvogel was right, Charlie'd been too quiet for too long. None of them looked forward to finding out the hard way what he had in mind. Not even Ruizique. Burrison, Bell, and Houng talked late into the night. In the end, they decided to mount the operation against the Vietcong communications center as soon as Burrison could coordinate with Reeves to deliver the rest of the explosives.

CHAPTER TWENTY-ONE

December 6, 1966

"He's going to do it!" Burrison said. "I don't believe it. Reeves is actually going to deliver our explosives to the top of the middle hill." He had just gotten off the radio from making arrangements with the helicopter pilot to deliver the explosives.

"I knew he would," Bell said flatly. "We're out here fighting Charlie and collecting all kinds of souvenirs. We swap them with him and Lily for things we need to accomplish our mission and make ourselves a little more comfortable. Reeves and Lily are trading some of them for luxury items we wouldn't even think of, and selling the rest for more money than we're going to make in our entire tours of duty over here. Besides, he and Lily think we're engaged in a great humanitarian venture here." He stopped talking for a moment and shook his head. "And it hasn't occurred to him to wonder why we want the stuff delivered to the second hill? Or why we want it a klick away from the Song?"

Burrison shook his head. "Nope. Maybe he will when he sees the place, but he accepted my directions without question. He's going to fly in here tomorrow morning and pick me up. If he has second thoughts then, I'll be along to make sure he doesn't think I gave him bad directions and put our stuff down near the river instead of where we want it."

"What time tomorrow?"

"Early afternoon."

Bell tipped his head back in momentary thought. This meant he had to have the landing zone secured by 1400 hours, 2:00 P.M., at the latest. "I'll talk to Huu," he said. "Maybe he knows a safe passage along the river where it cuts through the hills. I'd rather wait until after we knock out the comm center before we take out the observation post on top of the ridge. And that ledge we used on the side of the ridge is too difficult for all of us to use."

"Good idea."

Bell left the command hootch in search of the Chieu Hoi. They still didn't completely trust Huu but were willing to let him prove himself. Houng had promised to hire him into the PF platoon if they took the communications center. He'd be turned over to the ARVNs if the operation didn't work out—and if he survived it. Bell found Huu digging in one of the perimeter defensive positions, improving it. Zeitvogel was supervising him, and Lewis and Collard Green were there as interpreters.

Bell saw Huu look at Collard Green while he said something and gestured. Collard Green grimaced and spoke back. Zeitvogel and Lewis roared with laughter and Huu joined in with them. Collard Green merely looked closer than usual to losing his lunch.

"What's so funny?" Bell asked when he reached them.

Lewis's laughter was dying away and he was brushing at tears on his cheeks.

"Huu just said he feels like he's digging a barf hole for Collard Green," Zeitvogel said, his voice breaking up with laughter.

Lewis began to roll on the ground with renewed hysterics. He stopped only when he rolled over the edge of the trench and fell in.

The PF pursed his mouth and looked away; it wasn't his fault the Americans mistook his somber expression for intestinal distress, and there was nothing he or anyone else could do about the color of his skin.

Bell chuckled, but didn't laugh. He thought it must be one of those jokes you had to be there for to fully appreciate. "Very funny," he said, "but I have to talk to Mr. Chieu Hoi."

In the bottom of the trench, Lewis thought about what Huu said and cracked up again. Bell dropped into the trench and kicked him lightly. "Shitcan it, Billy Boy. I need you to help me question him."

Lewis struggled to sit up. He was grinning broadly. He put a hand on his forehead and brought it down to his chin. When it passed below his mouth his face was set soberly. The he balled his fists over the ends of his mustache and twisted. They came away, and the right end of his mustache pointed straight up parallel to his nose, the left end shot straight to the side. "Whatcha want to talk to him about, honcho?" he asked. "Tell old Billy Boy and I'll talk to the man for you."

"Bullshit, 'talk to him for me'—you're going to help. Get up." He held a hand down for Lewis to grab to pull himself up. He turned to the Chieu Hoi and started talking in slow Vietnamese. Huu listened carefully. Collard Green also listened carefully, and rephrased some of what Bell said when his inflections were wrong and his meanings came out wrong. A few times Bell asked Lewis for a word he wasn't too sure of. Collard Green provided some of the words the sergeant needed.

Huu listened carefully and patiently until Bell was through, interrupting him only occasionally to ask Collard Green to explain a few of the more difficult things to understand. When he finally answered the lengthy question, it wasn't with an answer Bell had hoped for.

"Yes, supply runs and reinforcements often come down along the river," Huu said. "It is one of two favorite alternatives to the route down the finger ridge. About one out of four or five parties coming through Bun Hou uses it. But the gorge through the final hill before the flood plain is narrow and there are no secret paths through it. On the other side of the first hill there are many paths; some are Vietcong paths, some are peasant tracks, some are game trails. If we go through along the river, once we get into the hills we have many possibilities for routes to take, but the beginning is very limited, we have to follow the path directly along the river. Sometimes, but not always, there are sentries stationed along that infiltration route to watch for people coming in along it."

"How long will it take us to get through the first hill to where we can get away from the main trail?" Bell asked when Huu was through with his answer. Lewis and Collard Green had helped him put the answer into English, so he was pretty sure he understood all of it.

Huu looked to the west, toward the cleft where the Song Du Ong came through the first hill. "Once we reach the hill, it should not take more than two hours, if we go quickly and don't meet anybody coming the other way."

Bell also looked toward where the river came through the hills, and chewed on his lip. "They only come through at night, right?" he finally asked.

Huu nodded. "They always start through the final gorge after sunset, to avoid detection by Tango Niner." He grinned when he said the last—he well knew how little success the Vietcong had at sneaking past the Marines and PFs of this isolated combat outpost.

"So if we get through before sunset, there is almost

no chance of running into somebody before we can get away from the river—unless they have sentries posted there?''

''Probably,'' Huu agreed. ''Although if they reach that final hill before the flood plain while it is still daylight, they will wait there until it is dark.''

Bell looked westward a few minutes longer, then announced, ''We're leaving right after evening chow. Collard Green, go tell Houng to get the PFs ready and bring them here.''

''One more problem we have to solve before we do this thing, Scrappy,'' Bell said a little later. ''Nobody's going to be here for the next couple of days. How do we deal with the bird bringing in our daily hot meal? What's going to happen when they come two days in a row and find Camp Apache deserted? There's going to be a grunt company searching all around for us when we get back and we're going to have some hard explaining to do to somebody.''

Burrison looked pleased with himself and sounded very smug when he said, ''Jay Cee, us second lieutenants also have a network for getting things done outside formal channels. I've got a friend, someone I went through OCS with, on the logistics staff of the battalion that's feeding us. They're on a combat operation right now. I got him to tell his boss he talked me into letting them skip us for the next few days so they can give their undivided attention to their own troops.''

Bell looked at the young lieutenant with admiration. ''I'm proud of you, Scrappy, you're still learning. Maybe by the time you make first lieutenant, you'll be almost as good at getting things done as a sergeant is.''

Burrison beamed at the praise.

When the evening chow bird came in, the pilot did a doubletake at seeing the entire Popular Forces platoon inside the wire. Instead of taking off immediately as soon as the exchange of food containers was made, the chopper stayed down long enough for the crew chief to shout a question at Slover.

"What's with all your little people here?" the crew chief asked.

"This is a Vietnamese national holiday, Madam Dragon Butterfly Lady Day," Slover shouted back. "They're here to treat us to a picnic, Vietnamese-style."

The crew chief looked uncertainly around the compound. He had never heard of Madam Dragon Butterfly Lady Day and nobody had told him this day was a Vietnamese holiday. "Yah? Nobody told the Vee Cee that. They're still fighting all over the country."

"That's because Uncle Ho doesn't like Madam Dragon Butterfly Lady Day, it's a capitalist holiday, not a communist one."

"Oh," the crew chief said, still looking at all the armed Vietnamese in the compound. They didn't look to him like they were in a holiday mood or ready to picnic. "Whatever you say." He adjusted his throat mike, said something without shouting, and the helicopter took off.

The PFs had all brought food from home—mostly rice and green vegetables, but three or four chickens had been killed and cooked with some of the rice and vegetables for the occasion. They set their dishes on the serving table along with the food brought by the helicopter. Everyone lined up to serve themselves buffet-style, the PFs first, then the junior Marines, followed by the PF squad leaders and the corporals. Bell was surprised at how much food was still left when he, Houng, and Burrison finally went through the line. They sat to eat in small groups around the compound, Marines and PFs in each group. When about half of the men were through eating, Bell had them all group in front of him and the two lieutenants. When everyone was there, the three outlined the platoon's plans for the next thirty-six hours.

"As soon as you finish chowing down, saddle up," Bell finished the briefing. "We move out in twenty minutes.'' While the men started readying themselves to leave he quickly finished his own meal, then went to the command hootch to put on his own gear. His cartridge belt held two full canteens and a first aid kit with two morphine styrettes, two pressure bandages, antiseptic, and—maybe most important—a bottle of halizone water purification tablets; all in addition to his bayonet and five twenty-round magazines for his rifle. He checked his personal .357 magnum before putting on his shoulder holster. Extra ammunition for his hand weapon went into his front trouser pocket. A pack with two pairs of clean socks, four C ration meals, a poncho, and four smoke grenades—one red, one green, and two yellow—in it and two Claymore mines lashed onto it went on his back. He slung a fifty-foot coil of quarter-inch hemp rope over his shoulder and hefted his M-14 in his left hand. One more quick look around the canvas-walled room he shared with Lieutenant Burrison and he was ready.

Outside the tent he found the rest of the platoon, except for Burrison, Houng, Doc Tracker, and Swarnes, ready and waiting for him. ''Here goes,'' he said, half to himself, then louder, ''Van, take the point.'' He raised his right arm over his head, looked to make sure he had everybody's attention, and dropped his arm in the direction of the back gate. ''Move out!'' his voice rang over the hilltop.

The line of thirty-four PFs and twenty Marines headed in orderly fashion—a Marine fire team was mixed in with each PF squad—for the back gate. Randall's team was with the lead squad; Lewis was the first man behind Van. Every man, in addition to his own weapons and ammunition, food, and necessary gear, carried a Claymore mine and a round for the .81mm mortar—except for Willard, who carried a PRC-22 radio on his back, and the machine gun team members, who were loaded down with their gun and ammunition for it. The three fire team leaders also carried PRC-6 walkie-talkie radios. Bell shook hands with the four men who were staying behind to wait for Reeves to come in the next day, then stepped into the line in front of Willard, between the first and second squads in the column.

"You do a comm-check yet?" he asked the grenadier.

"That's an affirmative, honcho," Willard replied, automatically falling into radio jargon. "Did it while you were chowing down. Me and Swearin' Swarnes read each other five-by."

"Good. We'll run another one after we get into the gorge."

Van led the platoon southwest across the scrub growth, angling to intercept the river midway between Camp Apache's hill and the cut in the hill the river flowed through. They walked at the fastest pace they could maintain without tiring. Everyone understood the need to get through the river passage to the far side of the first hill in the three hours they had left before nightfall.

It took them less than three-quarters of an hour to cover the four kilometers to the cleft where the river came down from the hills. None of the Marines were even breathing hard under their sixty-plus-pound burdens each. But the PFs, being much smaller and not accustomed to rapid walking over distance, were panting heavily. Bell called for a five-minute break to give them a chance to rest while he radioed his position to the four men left at Camp Apache. Then they headed up the break in the hill.

The forest ended abruptly once they left the flood plain. Only a few trees and bushes grew in the steep-sided gorge. At the end of the trees, a small area widened out and was strewn with boulders that had fallen from a sheer cliff-face. There hadn't been many birds in the trees on the flat, but countless insects sang their songs under the trees. There were no birds in the gorge, and the few insects' songs were drowned out by the rushing of the river—it seemed an eerie, disquieting silence. The hill at the top of the gorge rose faster than its bottom did; even though they were climbing, they were getting deeper in the hill, and it felt like deeper into the bottom of a barrel.

It was early twilight where the CAP walked, no sunlight ever shined in its bottom. Everyone in the column of fifty-four men grew still and tense.

A kilometer beyond the broad place, a rope-and-plank bridge crossed the river. Most of the Marines and some of the PFs recognized the bridge. When they had first seen it in September, it had looked too fragile and deteriorated to allow their passage, but they had managed to cross it without incident. Since September it had deteriorated further. A few men shuddered at the thought of trying to cross it now; the bottom of the gorge rose more steeply here and the river ran white underneath the bridge. The noise of the river increased.

Half a kilometer beyond the bridge, the hill above them stopped climbing and the bottom of the gorge leveled out slightly. They were slowly coming out of the well they felt themselves in the bottom of, and that tension eased, only to be replaced by another tension, the tension of entering more deeply into enemy territory. Then they were through.

The cleft broke into the bottom of a narrow valley between two rows of hills. A small stream flowed through it and joined another flowing along the narrow valley from the opposite direction. On the far side of the valley was another cleft, through which flowed a river. The two small streams fed into it for its final push to the flood plain.

"I wonder where it starts," Zeitvogel asked Bell. He had left his position in the middle of the second squad and closed with his leader when the column neared the valley.

"I don't think we'll ever find out," Bell replied absently. He was looking at the hill to his right front. The platoon had to reach a place on its top—before nightfall, if they could.

Huu and Collard Green joined the two Marines—the Chieu Hoi had been temporarily assigned to Collard Green's squad. Huu talked slowly, so Bell could understand him. "Let me take the point now," he said. "I found us a way across before, I am the one man in this unit familiar with these hills."

Bell stared at him for a long moment, trying to decide whether the ex-Vietcong could be trusted. He looked at Collard Green, but the PF squad leader merely shrugged—his shrug looked like a heave, Bell automatically stepped aside to avoid the vomit that didn't come. Bell nodded to Huu. "You've got a point," he said in Vietnamese. Huu was in at least as much jeopardy as anyone else.

"Cam on," Huu said. "Thank you." He headed for Van, hiding in the brush, with Collard Green.

"Him got point," Collard Green said to Lewis.

Lewis looked back at Bell and gestured with his rifle; a question. Bell nodded slowly and Lewis nodded back just as slowly. The sergeant understood the question and Lewis understood the answer. If they walked into an ambush, Huu would die before Lewis turned his automatic rifle on the enemy attacking them.

The sun was about to set behind the hills to the west when Bell called a halt. He thought they were close to the place he and Burrison had picked as their landing zone. Before the night fell, they set a defensive perimeter and established a one-third watch. They ate cold food in darkness; they couldn't risk fires or lights of any kind.

CHAPTER TWENTY-TWO

Overnight into December 7, 1966

The air was cooler in the hills than on the Song Du Ong flood plain—but cooler was a relative term. The daytime temperature was in the seventies rather than the eighties. It had dropped into the sixties overnight, and most of the Marines and PFs shivered until they covered themselves with their ponchos. But the humidity was still high. In practical terms the temperature difference meant that the Americans took a while longer to start sweating, and they didn't drink up their water quite as fast.

Bell was relaxed through the quiet night, he thought they hadn't been detected by the Vietcong and the quietness of the night confirmed that. In the stillness of the night, the thirty-foot wire antenna Willard carried for the PRC-22, a more powerful radio than the PRC-20 normally used by Camp Apache to communicate with the regular nightly patrols, was long enough for him to talk to and clearly hear Burrison back at the compound. In the morning, Bell called the Marine corporals and the three PF squad leaders together for a short meeting while everyone was chowing down and making any necessary morning bowel movements.

"I think this is the landing zone we picked out," he said, indicating the treeless area covered with thin brush they'd spent the night next to. "Just to make sure, and to check for unfriendlies in the neighborhood, I'm going to take Billy Boy, Huu, and Willy for a recon. We should be back in an hour, hour-and-a-half at the outside. Big Louie, you're in charge while we're gone. Any questions?"

There weren't. A few minutes later Lewis led them north, along one side of the hilltop clearing. For this recon, they only carried cartridge belts and weapons; they wouldn't need any of the rest of their equipment.

The wooded hilltop was quiet, except for the hunting and territorial warning calls of morning birds and the singing of diurnal insects. The trees weren't the large-boled trees along the river on its plain; the winds that swept the hilltops prevented those trees from growing on them. Nor were the trees scrub, like those that covered much of the flood plain. Most of them were a foot or so in diameter and covered with smooth bark. Their leaves were large, but not giant. More sunlight reached the ground on the hilltop than did in the narrow valleys between them, or in the stand of trees along the river below the hills. The ground was covered with a thick, rich mulch from fallen leaves. Saplings and young bushes sprouted from the mulch. The covered earth felt spongy beneath their feet and muffled the sound of their passage; they avoided paths and game trails. The undergrowth was pliant and bent to their passing without breaking or snapping. Lewis led the recon on a meandering route along the hilltop, staying mostly to the east side of it. After a half hour of slow, northward movement, Bell signaled Lewis to head for the west side of the hill and return to the temporary camp.

They were gone for more than an hour and saw no signs of human presence, or any other clearings.

"This is it," Bell said when they returned. "Let's get this LZ cleared out enough for the chopper to put down when it gets here. I want four LPs out there, two Marines, two PFs in each. Everybody else clears ground. Let's do it."

Each of the three fire teams and the machine gun team sent out two men along with two PFs. One LP went a hundred meters north, another a hundred meters south. The other two were positioned on the east and west faces of the hill. While everyone else, under the supervision of Big Louie Slover and Stilts Zeitvogel, cut down the saplings and larger bushes in the clearing, Bell radioed Camp Apache.

"Home Plate, Home Plate, this is Shortstop, this is Shortstop, over," he said into the radio's handset.

"Shortstop, this is Home Plate, go," Swarnes's voice came back immediately.

Bell glanced at his watch, 0930 hours, exactly the time he was scheduled to call, whether they were at the LZ or not. "Home Plate, Shortstop. We are at our intended location and are prepping it for you, over."

"Roger, Shortstop. Wait one."

Bell waited, knowing the next voice he was going to hear would be Lieutenant Burrison's. He hoped there were no changes in their plans.

"Shortstop, Home Plate Actual," Burrison's voice said on the radio seconds after Swarnes told Bell to hold on. "I understand you are at our intermediate point, is that correct? Over."

"That's an affirmative, Home Plate. Is your ETA the same? Over."

"Affirmative, Shortstop," Burrison said, excitement in his voice. "All systems are go. Over."

"Glad to hear that, Home Plate. I'll pop a caution if I hear you but don't see you, a go light when I see you. Over."

"Roger yours, Shortstop. See you later, alligator. Home Plate out."

Bell took the handset from the side of his face and stared at it for a long moment. "See you later alligator?" What kind of thing was that to say on the radio? He shook his head; Burrison was acting too bright-eyed and bushy-tailed. Oh well, he'd calm down once he got into these hills. This was neither the place nor the situation to be too eager, and the young lieutenant was seasoned enough now to know that. Speaking of eager, though, where was Ruizique and how was he acting? Bell sought out the corporal from the Dominican Republic.

Ruizique was furiously chopping, without making a lot of noise, at some brush with a machete. He frequently looked up at the treetops above the landing zone and compared their location with the space he was clearing. The other Marines and PFs who were supposed to be working with him weren't, they were standing off at a safe distance, watching him.

Bell joined Pennell, standing twenty feet away from Ruizique. "What say, Fast?" he said.

"Honcho thinks that bush is Charlie," Pennell answered.

"Sure looks like it," Bell agreed. He looked around the clearing. In the other four areas where men were working to clean out the clearing, more men were chopping at the brush and small trees, but none of them had been as opened up as where Ruizique worked alone in a frenzy. They were all cutting with an unexpected quietness—someone fifty meters away in the forest probably wouldn't hear the cutting. "Zeke," he said.

Ruizique stopped chopping and stood erect. He ran the back of his hand across his brow, wiping off the sweat that was flowing heavily down his face. Only then did he turn to look wordlessly at his squad leader.

Bell walked over to him, now that the machete was no longer swinging wildly. "I think you've done enough. Give someone else a turn before you get hit with heat exhaustion."

"I'm not going to get heat exhaustion," Ruizique said seriously. "It's much cooler here than on the plain, and I've never had heat exhaustion since I've been in Tango Niner."

"You never worked this hard."

"Yes I did. When we were digging the trenches I worked harder."

Bell stared at him stone-faced and said, "Shitcan it, Zeke, give someone else a turn with the chopper. You're working too hard, I don't want anyone getting worn out clearing this LZ. We've got plenty of time before they come in. Then we've got a hard hump. I want everybody fresh when we hit that comm-center."

Ruizique glared at Bell, the corner of his mouth twitched. He looked as though he wanted to tell the sergeant off. Instead he abruptly handed over the machete. "Some of us have drunk most of our water," he said. "I'll organize a party to get fresh water from the stream we crossed at the bottom of the hill."

Bell waited a beat or two before answering—he wanted Ruizique to slow down and thought the pause might help. "Take Pennell and Dodd. Get three PFs, take three of these," he indicated the PFs who were supposed to be working in Ruizique's clearing party. "The rest of them can stack the brush you cleared. Make sure you put a halizone tablet in each canteen. I don't care how clear or fast running that stream is, there could still be some bad little beasties in it, and I don't want anybody getting sick from contaminated water."

"Aye-aye," Ruizique said. He turned to his crew and pointed, "You, you, you, lai dai. You too, Pennell. Where's Dodd?" He sent them to get everybody's canteens.

"There probably won't be anything left to cut once they stack what Zeke already cut," Bell said to himself.

There wasn't. A half hour after the Marines and PFs set to work clearing the brush and small trees from the clearing all the work was done, except for what little was left of stacking the cut brush at the sides of the clearing. Bell looked at his watch again, it was just past 10:00 A.M. Now they had nothing to do until 2:30 or 3:00, when the helicopter arrived with their explosives—assuming nothing went wrong to stop the operation before then. Ruizique and his water detail returned about the same time the last of the brush was being stacked.

It would be a good idea to know if anything was going on in the last valley they'd have to cross, Bell decided. "Tex, up," he called out quietly.

"If you were on your own, do you think you could recognize the entrance to that hidden canyon from this side of the valley?" Bell asked when Randall joined him.

"I think so," Randall nodded. "What's up?"

"That's what I want to know. Nothing, I hope, but I want it checked out anyway. Take your fire team to the next hill and go a half klick farther north. Set in an observation post, just watch the valley for activity. Pay attention to how long it takes you to get there, cut out of there early enough to be back here by 1430 hours. Got it?"

Randall nodded again and looked at the west side of the clearing as though he could see through it to the next hill, the last one before the grassy valley they'd have to cross before hitting the VC communications center.

"Take your Prick-six, but maintain radio silence—use it only in an emergency. Huu didn't know, but they probably have directional tracking equipment over there that can pick up any transmissions you make and home in on your position. Understand?"

Randall looked back at Bell. "Got it."

"When you get to where you're going, break squelch and say, 'Short alpha,' nothing more."

"Short alpha, right." Randall nodded.

"Don't say anything else on the radio unless it's the kind of emergency where we're all going to have to shag ass out to you to save your asses."

"You got that wrong," Randall said, grinning wryly. He clearly understood the need for radio silence. "We get into shit so deep the only thing that can save our young asses is the rest of the platoon coming to the rescue, it'll be too damn late for you to get to us in time." He looked west again for a moment, then asked, "Want me to signal when we're coming back?"

"Not until you get down near the foot of that hill. The hill will shadow your transmission. Any other questions?"

"Rifles and cartridge belts only?"

"That's right."

"What about Dodd? He's a draftee, it's not fair to make him do everything we do."

Bell shook his head, half in disgust at Randall for wanting to leave one of his men behind, half at the injustice of drafting men into the Marine Corps. "That's no excuse. He went through Boot Camp and ITR the same as you and every other swinging dick in this man's Marine Corps did. He goes with you."

Randall shrugged; he hadn't expected Bell to release Dodd from the recon. "Whatever you say, honcho. I'm ready as soon as you assign two men to take Billy Boy's and Wells's place in their LP."

"Don't worry about that, just go. Do it quietly."

"Aye-aye, Jay Cee. See you back here at 1430 hours."

Five minutes later, Lewis was leading Randall, Wells, and Dodd down the hill, toward the third one, closer to the enemy stronghold. This time speed was more important than total silence. "Find a game trail leading down and follow it," Randall had told him. He did.

Small animals used the trail; it was a foot-wide strip of bare ground, but the underbrush was cleared out of it only to a height of about a foot-and-a-half. Most Americans could have walked across this game trail—or even followed it for a distance—and not known it was there. Lewis moved along the trail slowly, but more quickly than he would have breaking through the untracked brush around it. His feet trod easily and silently on the bare ground of the trail. His free hand held aside branches blocking his torso, and he handed those branches to Randall, who was close behind him. Randall in turn handed the branches to Dodd, who took them placidly and, placidly, handed them to Wells. The game trail wandered down the hill at an angle northwestward to the narrow defile between the hills. They reached the bottom in twenty minutes. Here, the game trail widened out and the overhead was gone. The tiny stream running between the hills formed a small pool here and the ground around it was beaten by many feet. It formed a water hole for the animals that used the trail.

Lewis stopped at the edge of the miniature clearing and examined its opposite side. His sharp eyes located a spot where an almost hidden tunnel, indicating another game trail, broke through the brush. In a few steps, staying out of the clearing, he rounded the water hole and entered the tunnel on its other side. This trail went more straight-up the hill than the first one, but it still edged in a slightly northerly manner. Though the climb was shorter because it was straighter, it took almost a half hour for them to reach the top of the hill—climbing up is sometimes slower work than climbing down.

On top of the hill, Lewis avoided the game trails and headed due north, not closing on the western side of the hilltop until he had gone three hundred meters. Then he angled across it. The vegetation was less dense than it had been on the side of the hills where it was protected from the wind—young brush had a hard time establishing itself in the wind blowing across the hilltop, and more birds and herbivorous mammals foraged here, eating the seeds before they had time to germinate and take root.

The Marines increased their intervals here, from arm's length to more than five meters between them.

When Lewis thought he had gone far enough north he turned to Randall and his eyes asked a question. Randall nodded, and Lewis cut almost straight across the hilltop. When he got there, trees growing on the west side of the hill blocked his view of the valley bottom. Randall surveyed the situation. An observation post that couldn't see was worthless, and if they went down the hill their field of vision would be less than it should. He pointed north and Lewis moved out again. Less than a hundred meters farther, a storm's wind and undercutting rainwater wash had toppled a large, old tree on the hillside. It took several smaller trees with it when it fell, creating a natural loge box.

Randall looked up and saw how unobstructed his vision was to the sky above. He looked across the grassy valley floor and picked out the entrance to the hidden valley where the VC comm-center was, and everything he saw excited him. This would be an ideal position for Slover and his mortar. He held his radio to the side of his head, pushed the speak button on its side, and murmured, "Short alpha." Then he released the button and listened. The soft buzz of static broke off, then started again—Bell or Willard heard his transmission and broke squelch to acknowledge it. Satisfied, Randall assigned his men areas to watch and settled in for the few hours of observation. At the south end of the valley they could make out what seemed to be peasants working their fields. The hamlet at the north end of the valley was too far away for them to see anything. They didn't see anyone or anything near the hidden valley.

"Charlie owns this valley," Dodd said shortly before it was time for them to return to the rest of the platoon.

"No shit, Sherlock," Randall said.

"No, I mean I'm surprised nobody else noticed before now."

Randall looked at him quizzically. "What do you mean?"

"I mean this valley looks like good farm land, but nobody's farming it. Sure, there's hamlets at each end, but there's no farming in the middle. I bet there used to be farmers' houses under those little clumps of trees, too. Government tax collectors or Arvin patrols coming through this area should have noticed and said something about it. Or something."

Randall nodded. It was a good analysis. Why hadn't anybody noticed it before? He looked over the valley again. "You're right," he said. "Look at the pattern of growth in the grass. It doesn't all seem to be the same, in some places it looks newer than in others, almost like it had been farmed until last season. You're right, how come nobody ever noticed before?" He looked back at Dodd and blinked. The draftee seemed to be staring vacantly over the valley. Randall wondered how he could see anything, much less notice something as subtle as the growth pattern of the grass. He shook his head and decided he couldn't understand the mind of someone who could do anything as incredibly dumb as getting drafted into the Marine Corps.

After a while longer Randall looked at his watch and said, "Let's get out of here, people."

They went in the same order they were in before, but Lewis picked a different route this time. Randall made a quick, visual inspection of his men and decided that giving him the draftee was a good idea after all. He had to keep Dodd close to him for the man's own protection. That meant Lewis and Wells were always separated when they were on patrols. They reached the rest of the platoon moments before the helicopter arrived.

Bell was right about their location; the helicopter homed in on the clearing as though there was a beacon guiding it in. He got the green smoke grenade from his pack, pulled the pin, and stood waiting near the middle of the clearing. As soon as the chopper was visible he tossed the grenade, and colored smoke billowed out of the canister, drifting with the wind. Slover didn't bother with his orange Ping-Pong paddles, the smoke drifting on the breeze would show Lieutenant Reeves the wind direction.

Burrison, Houng, Swarnes with a second PRC-22 radio and a thirty-foot wire antenna, and Doc Tracker piled out of the bird. As soon as the rotors were rotating idly, Lieutenant Reeves dismounted. The copilot stayed in the cockpit and the crew chief remained at his machine gun, suspiciously watching the trees around the clearing. Flying through a storm over the South China Sea was just part of the job as far as the crew chief was concerned. So was dipping low over the choppy waves to pluck a downed pilot from the water with NVA gunboats zipping around firing machine guns at his helicopter, with him unable to return fire because he was operating the winch that pulled up the pilot. But this, sitting on the ground, surrounded by trees so he couldn't see anybody who might be nearby, this was too much, and the sooner they headed back to the big pond, the happier he'd be.

"You sure this is where you want your shit?" Reeves asked the Marine lieutenant, continuing the in-air conversation he'd started as soon as he saw the map location of their destination.

"This is exactly where I want it," Burrison assured him for the tenth time.

"I'm no engineer, but this doesn't look like much of a place to build a dam to me."

"We're not going to put the dam on top of the hill, Reeves," Burrison said in the manner of a man forced to state the obvious to someone looking in the wrong direction. "It's just that this clearing is the closest one to where we're going to use the explosives."

"Hell, you could have blown an LZ right next to where you're going to build the dam." Reeves wondered, but didn't ask, why they were going to build the dam up in the hills rather than where the river came out of them.

"Yah, we could blow an LZ closer to where we're going to be using the explosives," Burrison agreed, "but if we did that would blow the surprise element in it."

"Oh, yah." Reeves wasn't sure why the dam had to be kept secret or why the surprise element was important. But anything to keep the supply lines to the Reeves and Lily VC and NVA War Surplus Company open. "Anything else you need from me?"

"Only if I have a major emergency," Burrison said, and made an effort not to quake at the thought of what kind of emergency would cause him to call Reeves in for a second trip.

"Well," Reeves said, taking a last look around the clearing, "I guess we'll be going then." He held his hand out to the Marine and Burrison shook it warmly. This help from the Navy pilot more than paid for all the souvenirs he'd give him in a few days.

"Let's get 'em saddled up," Bell said as soon as the chopper was gone. "Tex found a good spot for Big Louie to place his mortar."

"And let's get out of here in case Charlie decides to send somebody to investigate that helicopter," Burrison said.

Ten minutes later Tango Niner, all together on an offensive operation for the first time, was filing off the hilltop. Each man was burdened with twenty-five pounds of Claymore mines, bangalore torpedos, C-4 composition, fuses, and other explosives, in addition to what they had carried from Camp Apache.

CHAPTER TWENTY-THREE

The Rest of That Day and Into the Night

Lewis had the point again when Tango Niner left the landing zone. He knew where he was going this time, but it took longer to get there than it had before. That's the way it works; the larger the group of men, the longer the trip takes. One man can move silently at a rapid pace, two men not so rapidly, four men a little slower than two. If fifty-eight men don't go a lot slower than four men, they make an incredible racket. The trip that had taken the four-man observation post a little more than an hour took the entire platoon two hours. Of course, they were all carrying more weight than the original OP did, and that made a difference, too.

While Zeitvogel and Ruizique set the troops in the defensive positions they'd maintain until nightfall, Randall showed Burrison, Bell, and Slover the site he thought would be so good for the mortar.

Slover whistled and his eyes grew eagerly large when he saw the clear overhead and open line of sight toward the hidden valley. Where was it, he wanted to know. As soon as he knew where the hidden valley was, he'd set up his mortar to fire on it.

"It's tough to pick out landmarks here," Bell said, "but you see where there's a narrow notch in the treetops over there?" He held his arm straight out, pointing at the entrance to the hidden valley.

Slover looked along the sergeant's arm. "I see it, there's a red tree to the left of the notch."

"That's the one. The notch is the entrance to the valley," Bell said. "What do you think, Louie, you think you can hit inside there without any registration shots?"

Slover looked at the sergeant quizzically. "Man, do the Pope shit in the woods? Is a bear Catholic?"

"I think you got that a bit mixed up."

"That's okay, you got the idea." The big mortarman turned back to look at the place where the hidden valley branched off the main, grassy one. He muttered, "Do I think I can hit that fucking target without pre-registering my mortar. Who the fuck that man think he be talking to, anyway? I ain't the best mortarman in all Eye Corps for nothing, can I hit something that big. Shee-it! Be different, he wanted to know could I hit a water-boo with my first shot at that range. But a whole fucking valley? Shit." Then he said to Bell, "When you want me to start dropping them in, all you got to do is say how far from the near edge of the trees you want them. Bet my first shot ain't more than twenty-five meters off your mark." He cocked an eyebrow. "Just remember to give me that twenty-five meters."

"That's the way I like to hear you talk, Big Louie," Bell said, grinning. "And if I don't give you that twenty-five meters, I'm in some kind of deep shit." He turned to Burrison. "Where's Swarnes? We need to get that radio set up."

Burrison turned in a complete circle. He didn't see the radioman anywhere. "Goddamn it, where did he get off to?"

A trailing wire caught Bell's attention and his eye followed it. It went up a tree. "I don't know this for a fact," he said to the lieutenant, "but I do believe old Swearin' Swarnes is way ahead of us."

Burrison saw where Bell was looking and followed his gaze. A branch rustled high in the tree, then Swarnes dropped into sight climbing down. "How the hell did he get up there? That tree's lowest branch is almost fifteen feet off the ground."

Swarnes reached that lowest branch, rolled over it to dangle from it, looked for a soft spot of earth and dropped down to it. He rolled like a gymnast and landed on his feet at the end of his tumble. "Antenna's up," he announced, brushing himself off. "Mind you, there's abso-fucking-lutely no way for me to know we got good communications without running a godamn radio check. But, Christ on a crutch, if I run one, somebody's liable to notice our signal's wrong, like it's too far off. If they do, our cherry's popped and we're going to need that fucking crutch." He shook his head in awe of the fact nobody was at Camp Apache. "Shit, if the wrong someone realizes where we are, even Christ himself won't stop us from getting ourselves new assholes torn out of our young bods."

"No sweat, Swarnes," Burrison said. "If we run a radio check, Charlie over there might get a fix on us and rip those new assholes himself."

Swarnes looked in amazement at the lieutenant. Obviously he didn't understand the seriousness of the situation. First sergeants, and majors, and people like that would be involved in their punishment if the Marine Corps found out what they were doing. No way on earth anything the VC could do to them would match that.

Then there was nothing to do until sundown except eat evening chow. And think about the coming night. That afternoon and early evening felt a week long. A few men played card games, but they weren't enthusiastic about it. They had to keep quiet, and that took the fun out of any diversions they could come up with to make the time pass.

"Team leaders up," Bell called softly as the setting sun neared the western hilltops. Houng also called for his squad leaders. Burrison and Swarnes were with them in the command post.

In a few minutes the five Marine corporals and three PF squad leaders joined them.

"It's almost time," Burrison said without preamble as soon as everyone was there. "The mortar team and Swarnes will stay here, everybody else goes. Weapons, cartridge belts, explosives. Leave packs behind, we aren't going to take time to chow down or change socks over there. Only team leaders carry ponchos. If it rains we get wet, that's all. We can move more quietly without ponchos." He saw the corporals' knowing swallows; they understood why they were carrying their ponchos—for litters if casualties had to be carried. And they didn't have body bags to put KIAs in. He glanced at Bell and the sergeant nodded at him, he was giving this briefing like an old salt. "If we can get into that valley without being discovered, we're home free. We'll hit those sons of bitches so hard so fast they'll never have a chance to recover. We should be back here before dawn and back at Camp Apache by noon tomorrow." He looked around the group again before asking, "You all know what your assignments are once we get there. Any questions?"

Randall had one, but he paused before asking it. "There're only three men in the mortar team right now. Shouldn't we leave another man with them for safety?"

Burrison sighed. Bell glared at Randall. They both knew what he was thinking.

"We're going to need every rifle we have once the shit hits, Tex," Burrison told him. "Dodd goes with us."

Randall shrugged and grinned crookedly. "Can't blame me for trying," he said. "Poor son of a bitch."

Burrison looked at each of the corporals and the PF squad leaders one more time, then said, "Get your people ready. We move out as soon as it's dark."

The hours of sunlight had seemed to drag endlessly, now there didn't seem to be enough time to do the few things that remained to do before the platoon set out. Packs had to be laid out in two formations—one for the Marines, one for the PFs—so they could easily be found again by their proper owners. Explosives had to be hung from and strapped to each man's body—made difficult by conflicting demands of silence and ease of removal. Every man had to be inspected to make sure he had everything he was supposed to carry and nothing he wouldn't need, and checked for noise—not only the noise he would make walking, but any noise that would be made removing his explosives. The rifles all had to have a round in the chamber and the safety off. It was dangerous crossing the open valley with safeties off, but fifty rifles taking their safeties off when they reached the hidden valley would make a tremendous racket that would give the Vietcong all the warning they needed to turn the tables on the attacking Combined Action Platoon.

They were ready just as the shadows of the western hills reached them. In the last light of the day, Bell used hand signals to line up the platoon and give the order to descend the hill. Huu was the first man in line. Zeitvogel's fire team, mixed with Collard Green's squad, followed him. Burrison and Willard, still carrying the PRC-22, were between them and Randall's fire team with Vinh's squad. Then came Bell and the machine gun team. Ruizique's team and Willy's squad brought up the rear. Houng was with Burrison and Willard. Bell and Burrison had discussed putting out flankers for security, but decided against them—they didn't want to lose anybody in the night. And Huu had assured them the VC felt safe enough in their comm-center, they didn't put many security patrols or listening posts out in the valley at night. They had to trust their Chieu Hoi—and he had told them the truth so far.

The moon wasn't out, but the stars spread their light brightly across the valley floor. Every man in the column hunched his shoulders and tried to stay ducked below the top of the tall grass. They continually cast anxious glances in the direction of the box canyon, hoping they wouldn't see the flashes of light that would be the first sign of rifles or rockets firing at them. Lizards on the hillside behind them and in the grass near the foot of the hill sounded tauntingly ominous when they cried their "fukyoo" mating and territorial calls. Even though all three of the Marine fire team leaders carried PRC-6 radios, they maintained radio silence.

The night was eerily silent in the tall grass. Huu didn't risk going astray, he found a narrow path across the valley floor and followed it, watching carefully for the markers the Vietcong set out to alert each other and friendly villagers to the presence of booby traps guarding it. Twice before reaching the small stream that cut through the valley's length he found markers. The first time he pointed it out to Hempen, who was following close behind, ready to blast him if they walked into an ambush.

The Chieu Hoi halted abruptly and squatted. He turned his head and shoulders back and gestured Hempen forward. The Marine duck-walked to him. Two feet in front of the former VC, barely visible on the side of the trail, was a pyramid of three flat stones. Huu made a low, guttural grunt and spread his down-cupped hands up and out.

Hempen nodded, he understood the pantomimed explosion. He rose to a half crouch and walked back to let the others know why they had stopped. The men in the column lowered themselves to the ground to wait.

Huu lowered himself to hands and knees and crept forward, one hand brushing the air inches above the trail. A few feet farther he stopped and rocked back for a moment's rest. Then he rolled forward again and extended both hands until he was touching the trip wire he had found. He traced the taut wire to one end and found it anchored to a stake hidden in the grass. He puzzled over it for a moment, wondering if he should release it, thinking it might be set to pull the pin from a fuse, then thought better of it. Because the wire was strung so tightly, it might be a pressure-release–type fuse that would go off as soon as the wire was loosened. Moving carefully, touching the wire lightly to follow it but not hard enough to jar it, he traced it into the grass on the other side.

What he found made him glad he hadn't done anything to the wire. A two pound block of C-4 was in a metal can filled with scraps of jagged metal. Two fuses were inserted into the block of explosive—one was a pressure-release fuse that would have ignited if he had broken the wire, the other was a standard pull-the-pin percussion fuse. They were attached to the wire so that the wire went through the pull-ring on the percussion fuse, then angled back to the pressure-release fuse. Break or untie the line, and it would slide through the ring, and the spring-loaded firing pin on the pressure-release fuse would snap forward. If the wire was pulled, the pin would come out of the first fuse, setting it off. That would also release the tension on the pressure-release fuse, setting *it* off—the mine would have two chances to go off, and it wasn't likely both fuses would be defective.

Huu groped on the ground around the jerry-rigged mine until he found a small scrap of wood he could use to wedge the firing pin on the pressure-release fuse back. As gently as he could, he inserted the piece of wood, then folded back the ends of the cotter pin on the other fuse before slowly drawing the fuse out of the block of plastic explosive. He set aside the first fuse, then removed the percussion fuse from the C-4 and laid it on the ground. Then he rocked back into a squat and breathed heavily for a moment before rising to his feet and walking back to where Hempen was waiting. He left the mine exactly where it was; if there was a hidden fuse underneath it, moving it would set that one off.

The Marine edged toward him and saw sweat beading on the man's forehead and a slight trembling around the corners of his mouth. That was all he needed to know how dangerous disarming the booby trap had been and how frightened Huu was doing it. He stood up, folded his hands in front of himself, and bowed. When Huu returned the bow Hempen grasped his right hand and shook it. "Numba fucking one, Huu," he said softly. "You're okay, man."

Huu's broad grin was dimly visible in the starlight. He tugged on Hempen's arm, he wanted to show him what he had done. When the Marine saw the two fuses and understood their meaning, he whistled silently—the booby trap had to have been very hairy to disarm. Then he signaled back to the rest of the column and they started out again.

The second booby trap was much easier to deal with. Huu merely had to bend back the ends of the cotter pin in the fuse and cut away the trip wire. Again, he left it in place because of the possibility of a detonating device set under it. So what if the Vietcong later found the disarmed mines and rearmed them? Tango Niner would be gone long before then. He didn't find any booby traps or other warning devices on the other side of the stream. When they reached the foot of the hill on the other side of the valley, Huu turned right and led the column two hundred meters along it before stopping. He squatted to wait for Burrison, Bell, and Houng to join him.

When the CAP leaders joined him, Huu talked in a very low voice to Houng.

"Him say we there," Houng told the Americans. "This where we make two groups."

The Marines nodded their understanding, and Bell went back along the column to tell his fire team leaders. Zeitvogel nodded and grimaced; the next fifteen minutes would probably be the most dangerous of his life. Randall swore silently when Bell said, "Send Billy Boy with Stilts." But he gave the sergeant no argument.

"Let me got first with Stilts," Ruizique said.

Bell refused. "You follow him like we planned."

Then they were ready.

Bell, only because he had been there before, led Randall's Marines and PFs to the secret cliff-face exit from the hidden canyon. Burrison and Houng went behind Huu, with Zeitvogel's men and the rest of the platoon following them, to the entrance to the Vietcong installation. When they were fifty meters from where the Chieu Hoi said the sentries were stationed, Zeitvogel, Huu, Lewis, and Hempen silently dropped all of their gear except their knives.

Lewis carefully removed a waterproof packet from the inside pocket of his shirt and opened it. He unwrapped the three ninja throwing stars from the oily cloth inside the plastic, then refolded the cloth and tucked it back into the plastic and into his shirt. He nodded to Zeitvogel; he was ready.

Zeitvogel nodded back, then whispered to Burrison, "I want Pee Wee, too." From past experience he knew the diminutive PF was one of the most deadly and silent night fighters he'd ever been with. The lieutenant agreed, and the five men slipped into the trees hiding the VC's hidden valley.

CHAPTER TWENTY-FOUR

December 8, 1966

Huu led the three Marines and Pee Wee in, skirting the edge between the hillside trees hiding the entrance to the small valley and the grass of the main valley floor. He stopped after several meters and turned to face the trees. He looked back at the four men following him and gestured with his knife, then lowered himself to the ground and crawled into the trees. The others followed directly behind him, blades ready in their hands.

Huu kept one hand moving in front of himself constantly, searching for trip wires or anything that would make a noise. He deftly moved sticks and stones from his path and held tree and bush branches so they wouldn't fly back loudly when he passed. The five men tunneled silently through the underbrush, barely disturbing the insects singing their night songs. Ten meters in, Huu stopped crawling and rose to a crouch.

Next to him, Zeitvogel knelt on one knee—and was still taller than the Vietnamese. The tall American listened and heard what he hadn't heard while crawling; the muted sing-song of soft Vietnamese voices a few meters to the right of the route they had followed. He felt Lewis standing stooped on his right and knew Pee Wee and Hempen were doing the same farther along. He peered through the blackness under the trees, eyes darting from point to point, never stopping to focus on anything, and dimly made out what had to be human shapes a few meters away—the softly talking sentries.

Lewis held his mouth close to Zeitvogel's ear and said, in as quiet a voice as he could, "I see two." He held up his throwing stars.

The corporal thought for half a moment while continuing to visually search the area. He also only made out two forms in the darkness. He said to Lewis in an equally quiet voice, "Let's get closer first." There might be more. If there were he wanted to know it—and he wanted to be close enough that Billy Boy couldn't miss.

Ghostlike, the five men eased through the brush until they were four meters from the sentries. Now Zeitvogel could more clearly see in the dim starlight that filtered through the trees two men sitting side-by-side, facing in the direction of the main valley, talking. Behind them, two lumps lying on the ground were two other sentries, sleeping. They were near the moment of truth. Zeitvogel listened carefully for sign of anyone else nearby, but all he heard were the songs of night insects and a few calls from nocturnal birds. He gave orders with his hands: on his signal, Lewis would take out the two talking men with his ninja throwing stars—this was why he was with the team sent to take out the entrance sentries instead of staying with his own fire team. The instant Lewis threw them, Zeitvogel and Huu would jump the other two sentries and kill them in their sleep. If Huu didn't do the job, they could know he was a plant—but that knowledge might come too late to save any of the Marines or Popular Forces of Tango Niner.

Lewis readied himself to throw the stars. He swallowed and breathed slowly and deeply to calm his trembling. He had killed VC at greater distance than this with the stars, but his only experience throwing them at night was at targets he had made himself. All he could do was trust the untested skill he had gained through countless hours of practice. He held one star in each hand, then twisted his body sharply to the right and drew his right arm back and shot it forward. His follow through brought his hands together, transferring the second star to his right hand. He wound right again and sent the second star flying before its target had time to react to the blood spouting from the first VC's gurgling, torn-open throat. The second star buried itself between the startled eyes of the second VC and toppled him backward.

Zeitvogel and Huu were already lunging through the remaining brush, throwing themselves on the sleeping men, slashing their knives across their throats, opening them to the night air. The dying men convulsed against the bodies holding them down. They clutched and bucked and tried to pound their heels against the ground, but it was too late for them to save themselves. The VC hit in the forehead by the second star died instantly from massive trauma to his brain; the other star-struck VC and the two killed by Zeitvogel and Huu took a minute, while the blood gushed from their throats, draining life from their brains and the rest of their bodies. None of them in their dying made noise that carried far.

Lewis wrenched the star from the head of the second man, but he couldn't find the first star he had thrown; it had continued its flight after slicing through its target. I'll have to write to my kid brother, he thought, get him to send me another one.

The three men who had done the killing breathed deeply, getting themselves back under control from the adrenal rush, while Hempen and Pee Wee moved the bodies out of the way. Then Zeitvogel left his men at the listening post and returned alone to the rest of the platoon.

"We did it," he murmured to Burrison and Houng. "There wasn't any noise." He paused before adding, "Huu wasted one of them with his knife."

The officers, American Marine and Vietnamese irregular, nodded wordlessly. Burrison handed Zeitvogel his rifle and gear, then signaled him to lead the way. When they reached the listening post, most of them stopped while Huu led Ruizique, Neissi, and Willy's squad deeper into the valley and then to the left. He returned and led the rest of them—Zeitvogel's fire team and Collard Green's squad came last—into the valley and then to the right.

Once past the narrow entrance to the hidden valley, the brush thinned out, only the tall trees were left to provide overhead concealment from passing aircraft. Aromas from the evening meal lingered in the air. No lights were lit in the Vietcong camp, but a few of their tents were visible as lighter gray masses against the dark grays and blacks under the trees of the valley. Someone coughed somewhere, disturbing the silence, but it was the only sound not made by insects and night hunting birds. Supposedly, the only people awake at this hour were the night-shift radio technicians and some sentries. What the men of Tango Niner could see and hear indicated that that was the case.

After one Marine fire team and one PF squad were on line facing into the hidden valley, the Chieu Hoi moved a little farther to the right and fifteen meters deeper into it. He pointed to a barely seen tent. Burrison and McEntire looked at it and set up the machine gun to cover the tent—it held the rest of the squad responsible for security at the entrance.

Then Zeitvogel and Collard Green and their men followed Huu a hundred and fifty meters farther through the trees along the hill that formed the steep northern wall of the canyon, until they reached the two bunkers that held the radio equipment. A six-man VC squad lounged near the blanketed doors of the bunkers, maintaining security for them. Wires buried a few inches under the ground led from the south side of the radio bunkers to the southwest corner of the valley, where the hillsides weren't as steep as they were everywhere else.

Zeitvogel lined up everyone with him to face the bunkers at a distance of less than fifteen meters. This close, they could make out nearly inaudible voices coming from inside the bunkers—the technicians doing their communications work. Then the Marines and PFs under Zeitvogel all set to work placing their Claymore mines. Bare minutes later they retired into the trees, where they took cover against the backblast of the mines.

The men to the left, inside the valley entrance, had already done the same thing. Their Claymores faced the tents used by the reinforcement squad that patrolled the main valley during the day and the tents occupied by some of the off-duty technicians and service personnel— cooks and medical personnel and others.

In the meantime, Bell, Randall, and Vinh led the other third of the platoon into the trees along the main valley to the hill. They found the vine rope leading up the hill and climbed it to the narrow ledge that secretly led into the hidden valley. The four Marines and eleven PFs negotiated the ledge without any problems until they reached the chimney that was the beginning of the way to the canyon floor. They waited for a few minutes, looking and listening. Directly to his front, Bell could make out the dim, gray forms of a few technicians' tents—no sounds came from them.

Bell carefully felt the cliff face until he found a tree that seemed sturdy enough protruding from it. He uncoiled the rope from his shoulder and tied it to the root several feet from one end, then gently lowered the other end to the foot of the cliff. There had never been any question of them attempting to climb down the chimney using the hand- and toeholds. It would be almost impossible for fifteen men, only two of whom had been there before, to negotiate that path in the night blackness without someone falling off it and alerting the camp's defenders to the attack. On this mission he had to be the first one down, so Bell handed the loose end of the rope to Randall to secure in case the root broke. The sturdy-built corporal sat cross-legged on the narrow ledge and snugged the rope end around his waist.

Bell looped the rope over his shoulder and through his crotch, stepped backward into the night, and rappeled to the ground, fifteen feet below, with one bounce. The root held. One by one, Randall urged the eleven PFs onto the rope. None of them went down the same way Bell had; they gripped the rope tightly and lowered themselves to the ground hand over hand. When they were all down, Randall untied the rope, leaving it looped around the root, and shook the downward side to let Bell know he was ready. The sergeant responded by pulling it taut. Randall stepped out onto the cliff face and walked down it as Bell played the rope out. He was on the valley floor less than seven minutes after Bell had stepped off the ledge.

They set up their Claymores facing the technicians' tents before moving on. Again, Bell took the point, leading his people deeper into the canyon behind the brush curtain that hid the wall from view. He stopped at the point closest to the VC leaders' tent long enough to drop off Randall, Wells, the PF the Marines called Mike, and two others, then led the rest of them farther. Fifty meters beyond Randall's team, he started lining his men up facing into the small valley. They didn't set up any Claymores here, there wasn't any place for the backblast to go—the backblast would blow out to the sides and injure them. He looked at his watch. Now there wasn't anything to do except wait until time.

* * *

At one minute before 2300 hours, Burrison pressed the speak lever on the side of his radio handset and breathed one word into it: "One."

Bell was ready for it. "Two," he said into his PRC-6. He nudged the PFs on his sides, it was almost time.

Zeitvogel was also waiting for the word. "Three," he murmured into the mouthpiece of his walkie-talkie. He alerted his men.

McEntire was carrying Ruizique's walkie-talkie. "Four," he said. The machine gun was ready.

Burrison watched the sweep hand on his watch swing its way back to the "twelve." When it reached "ten" he said, "Mark." The three NCOs didn't reply with words, they just broke squelch in reply. On the dot of 2300 hours Burrison said, "Mark," a second time and depressed the ignition plunger that electronically ignited the Claymore mines the men with him had set out. A dozen anti-personnel mines blasted out their deadly bits of metal, each hurtling seven hundred flesh-rending steel balls in a cone fifty meters long and fifty wide. If any of his people had been in a similar cone behind the mines, they would have been torn to pieces by the blast that came from the mines' rear. Half of the dozen Claymores blasted into rags the tents housing the sleeping security squad, killing most of them instantly. The other half threw their deadly burdens farther, into the technicians' tents.

At the same instant Bell pushed the plunger on his ignition device. His squad's Claymores added their devastation to the others, and nearly seventeen thousand tiny ball bearings shredded the tents holding the sleeping technicians from the side, killing most of them in their sleep.

To Burrison's right, McEntire slapped Kobos on the shoulder as soon as he heard the second "mark" command and the machine gunner poured twenty-round bursts into the entrance sentries' tent. He kept firing until

McEntire told him to stop because he had killed all of the sleeping soldiers.

On the north side of the valley, Zeitvogel and Mazzucco, along with two of the PFs, each fired a LAW, a light anti-armor weapon, into one of the two radio bunkers. Each of them instantly dropped the empty tube of the fired LAW and picked up another one to fire into another bunker. At the same time, Hempen and Lewis opened up with their automatic rifles on the six-man squad sitting security outside the bunkers, killing two of them instantly. The Vietcong hadn't expected to be attacked in this communications center and hadn't built their bunkers to withstand direct hits from the bunker-busting anti-tank weapons. The LAW rockets blasted through the sandbag walls, sending hot, jagged steel fragments scything through their interiors, shattering equipment, turning living bodies into mincemeat. The survivors ran screaming from the carnage inside the two bunkers. Zeitvogel held his fire for a few seconds, until he was certain they were all out, then pushed his plunger, and the Claymores his squad had emplaced exploded in mighty flashes—no living Vietcong soldiers or technicians remained near the bunkers.

Randall, Wells, and the three PFs with them sprang into action as soon as the Claymores went off. They dashed across the open ground to the commanders' tent, hoping to capture the two high ranking officers before they were awake enough to defend themselves. Wells was the first to burst through the closed flaps of the tent. He swung the muzzle of his rifle in a wide arc, hoping to knock over anyone who might already have risen. His rifle barrel collided with the arm of one of the two senior officers and knocked it aside, but not before the officer's 9mm-pistol had fired.

The soft-nosed bullet slammed into Wells's chest and staggered him. He half turned and said in a strange, high-pitched voice that bubbled, "I'm hit," then crumpled to the reed-mat covered floor of the tent. It was the first shot fired by the camp's defenders.

Randall was already rounding Wells when the shot went off. He dove at the muzzle flash with his rifle held in front of him by both hands. The hard edge of the magazine protruding from the bottom of the rifle hit the point of the officer's nose and smashed it in, driving his septum into his brain. The officer was dead before he could pull the trigger a second time.

"Me have!" Mike shouted. He had stumbled onto the cot holding the other officer and fallen on him. The two men grappled. The Vietcong colonel was bigger and more heavily muscled than the PF, but gave up fifteen years to him. Their wrestling match was even until the other PFs jumped into it. They quickly subdued their shouting prisoner.

Twenty meters from the commanders tent, the new unit senior sergeant awoke in the tent he slept in alone to the terror-creating blasts of the Claymores, LAWs, and machine gun. He heard the screaming of the technicians fleeing the radio bunkers and the second round of Claymores that killed them. Then he heard a single shot from the commanders' tent. He rolled out of his hammock and picked up his rifle in one motion. He darted out of his tent. He didn't run straight to his destination, not until he had some idea of what was happening; instead he flitted silently from the shadow to shadow, keeping out of sight of the entrance to the commanders' tent.

Utter silence dropped like a slamming door over the camp. The entire fight, from the first Claymores to the coming of silence, had lasted fifteen seconds. The VC sergeant had no idea how many attackers were involved, but he had heard Claymores from three different locations and a machine gun in a fourth. The only response was the cut-off screams of the radio technicians and the one shot from the commanders' tent. He didn't think there were many survivors. Now he heard excited voices in the tent, voices he didn't recognize, and saw men leaving it, heading toward the secret escape route. One of the men seemed to be bound and struggling. Another one, too big to be Vietnamese, was being carried by another big man. The sergeant's jaw dropped incredulously when he saw what the men were wearing—bush hats. The only soldiers he knew of who wore bush hats were the members of the CAP in Bun Hou. It couldn't be them, though, he knew that. Could it?

Immediately after Zeitvogel fired his Claymores, Burrison was on the radio asking for a situation report.

"No problems yet," Bell answered.

"I think we wasted them all," Zeitvogel said.

"Security squad's wasted," McEntire reported. He slapped Kobos on the shoulder and grinned at his new gunner. The man was working out well.

Burrison missed the crack of the 9mm pistol in the commanders' tent in the general din of the brief, one-sided battle. "Trash Pit, this is Big Bad Wolf, over," he said into his radio.

"Go, Big Bad Wolf," Swarnes immediately answered, and grinned at Slover. He heard the jubilation in Burrison's voice and knew everything was under control in the communications center. Slover picked up an illumination round in anticipation of Burrison's order.

"Trash Pit, give me a light bulb, over."

"Roger, Big Bad," Swarnes said. He made a signal to Slover and the big mortarman dropped the round down the tube of the already aimed mortar. "One light bulb on its way." The *carrumph* of the mortar drowned out part of his words.

A few dazed technicians were still alive in their tents. Some were wounded—a few badly enough that they'd die without immediate medical attention. Others weren't injured physically, but lay trembling on their sleeping mats, unable to move because of the shock—those who had slept in hammocks were all dead from the Claymores. High on the hill in the southwest corner of the hidden valley, five Vietcong soldiers guarding the antenna farm hidden among the trees froze and wondered what could be happening down below. They waited, frightened, for orders from somebody.

The flare burst above the trees and slowly sank under its parachute. It cast little light into the canyon until it penetrated the treetops, then caught on a branch and hung there, swaying in the treetops, spreading its glaring blue light over the VC camp. The moving ball of light made everything seem to dance as it moved shadows in an eerie manner.

Most of the remaining technicians were galvanized into panicked action by the light. They started shouting at each other and shouting for the soldiers to help them. Some of them jumped off their sleeping mats and ran into the lit night. The PF squad with Burrison saw them and opened up with their mixed armory of M-1 carbines and captured AK-47s.

Ruizique was frustrated. So far on this operation he hadn't been able to do any fighting, he'd had no chance to kill his enemy. When the PFs opened up, he screamed for his Marines to fire, and the M-14s added their heavy booming to the crackling from their companions' smaller weapons.

The panicked technicians, fleeing in all directions, were spun about by the impacts of many bullets and dropped. Then the Marines and PFs poured their fire into the tents until Burrison's shouts, "Cease fire, cease fire," penetrated to them. Ruizique was the last one to stop shooting.

"Give me another light, Trash Pit," Burrison said into his radio when the shooting stopped. It would arrive about the same time the one now hanging from a tree burnt itself out. "Two and Three," he continued, "advance across the area looking for survivors when the next illume pops. Understood? Over.''

''Roger,'' Bell answered.

''You got it,'' said Zeitvogel.

''Trash Pit, keep those lights coming one-a-minute until I say otherwise. Understand? Big Bad Wolf, over.''

''Roger, Wolf,'' Swarnes replied.

The second flare fizzed into life above the trees, and the five Vietcong guarding the antennas slowly realized no orders would be forthcoming from the commanders they were now sure were all dead. Quickly, they set the charges that would destroy the antennas and climbed to the top of the hill to make their way alone to the Ho Chi Minh Trail in Laos.

''Big Bad Wolf, Two, over.'' Bell's voice caught Burrison's attention.

''Go, Two.''

''I have one down.'' Bell's voice was heavy.

A tremble shuddered through Burrison's body at the words. ''How bad? Over.''

''All the way bad.''

The young lieutenant swore bitterly to himself for a moment, then asked, ''Who?''

Bell sighed into the radio and said, ''The Hoosier.''

''Can you deal with it?'' Burrison asked. He didn't mean emotionally, men got killed in combat and the survivors learned how to accept the deaths of others. He meant did Bell need any assistance with the body.

''Affirmative,'' Bell replied. ''I've got the situation under control.''

Burrison thought for a moment about the juvenile delinquent from Indiana, a happy-go-lucky kid who always tried to push things a little farther than anybody would allow. Had he finally pushed his luck too far? Wells and Lewis were best friends. How was Billy Boy going to react when he found out his buddy was dead? ''Three,'' he abruptly said into his radio.

"Go, Big Bad Wolf," Zeitvogel's somber voice said.

"Keep that last under your hat for a while, understand?"

"Roger." Zeitvogel knew Lewis might react badly to the news, better to hold off telling him until they were finished searching the communications center—keep it quiet until they got back to Camp Apache, if that was possible.

The three lines of Marines and PFs, forty-six men, converged toward the middle of the small canyon under the light from the second and third flares. Three PFs stayed along the cliff to watch Wells's body and guard the captured VC officer. During the search the Americans and Vietnamese of Tango Niner found some candles and a few unbroken kerosene lamps. They used them to light their way, and Burrison called Swarnes to stop firing flare rounds before the mortar ran out of them.

Burrison and Bell were inspecting the interiors of the shattered radio bunkers when the night was disrupted again by a monstrous explosion on the southwest hillside—the charges the departing guards had set went off, obliterating the entire area of the antenna farm.

"Tex, take Dodd and a couple fay-epps up there and check that out," Bell shouted when the crashing of falling trees quieted and no one, looking wildly around for an attacking enemy force, saw anyone.

"Let me and Jesse James do it," Lewis shouted. "Don't need to send four men to check anything out when you got me and my good buddy Jesse James." He headed toward the south side of the valley, calling for Wells to join him.

"Belay that, Billy Boy," Bell roared. "Get your ass back to Stilts and help him." He stood rigidly, hoping Lewis would obey him before he realized something was wrong.

"Come on, Jay Cee," Lewis called back and kept walking. "Let Dodd help Stilts. Me and Jesse James gonna run a recon. Hey, Jesse, where you at, man?"

"That's an order, Lance Corporal," Bell bellowed.

"Do as you're told for a change." He had to struggle to keep his voice from catching.

"Shit, Jay Cee," Lewis started, then froze as he realized something must be wrong. "Where's Jesse James? Jesse?" he almost screamed the name. "Where the fuck are you? Answer me, man, goddamn your ass."

Burrison, Randall, Zeitvogel, and the few others who knew Wells was dead closed their eyes, or shook their heads, or talked to themselves, or did whatever they needed to to prepare themselves for Lewis's outburst and grief when it came.

Bell ran to Lewis, grabbed his shoulder, and yanked him around. He shoved his face close to the slender Marine's and said through clenched teeth, "Wells is dead, damn it. Get your ass back to Stilts."

Lewis's eyes were wide with shock and his breath came in rapid snorts. "You're bullshitting me, Jay Cee. No way Jesse James is wasted, we pulled this off too damn good for a good grunt like him to get his ass blown away."

"That's the way it happens, Billy Boy. The best sometimes get it." Light glittered under Bell's eye, a tear he didn't want to let fall.

"No!" Lewis screamed and broke from Bell's grasp. "Where is he?" He ran toward the south, screaming, "Where is he, where is he?"

Randall ran to cut him off and knocked him down with a cross-body block. He rolled onto the smaller man and pinned him with one of the holds that had won him statewide honors as a Greco-Roman wrestler during his high school athletic career in Texas. "Cool it, Billy Boy," he said.

"Where's Jesse James?" Lewis cried. "Where's my good buddy? I got to help him. There's a mistake, he must be wounded, no way he can be dead."

"It's no mistake, Billy Boy, he's wasted. Now get a hold of yourself."

Lewis struggled but couldn't break the powerful hold.

He realized he was going to be held until he stopped, so he went limp. Just like that, no subsiding waves, he went from full fight to full sag. And sobbed.

Randall held him for a moment longer, then slowly released his hold, ready to tighten it again if Lewis tensed to break free. The only tensing he felt was shudders as Lewis's sobs grew louder and more violent. Randall rose to his knees and rested a comforting hand on Lewis's shoulder. "Come on, Billy Boy. I'll take you to him."

Randall was vaguely aware that somewhere in the background Bell was sending Zeitvogel and Hempen with a couple of PFs to check out the explosion on the hillside.

Lewis shuddered again, his entire body trembling violently, then he pushed himself to hands and knees. He accepted the hand Randall offered to help him to his feet. The two walked slowly toward where Randall had left Wells, the prisoner, and three PF guards. They had hardly started when shots rang out ahead of them.

The Vietcong sergeant dove for cover when the first flare lit the interior of the small valley. Sweat beaded his forehead and upper lip. He still had no idea of how many enemy soldiers were present, only that there were both Americans and Vietnamese. He tried to burrow into the bare ground when the fusillade near the entrance to the valley opened up on the panicked technicians. When the firing finally stopped and the flare started to sputter out, he low-crawled to the command tent and slipped into it; he found the dead North Vietnamese senior colonel—at least he knew who had been captured. Then he continued crawling as fast as he could in the direction he'd seen the people from the commanders' tent go. When another flare lit the valley, he rolled under one of the few bushes left when the ground was cleared for the camp. He watched, appalled, when lines of men appeared at three different locations around the perimeter and walked toward the middle. This could be all of them, it looked like about two platoons. If this was all there were, he could easily make his escape alone, perhaps join up with the squad guarding the antenna farm and lead them to safety. If this wasn't all of them, he might have no chance of escape. But the Americans had captured the Vietcong colonel. He needed to do something about that before he could do anything else.

A huge explosion high above on the hill told him he was too late to hook up with the squad guarding the antennas. They had to have already departed, first setting the charges prepared to destroy the antennas if the camp was overrun. He nodded to himself. The soldiers on the hill had done their job well. Now he had his own job to do.

Shouting suddenly broke out in the middle of the camp, Americans shouting angrily at each other. The sergeant sensed confusion and took advantage of it to cautiously crawl closer to where he'd seen the colonel taken. He penetrated the brush curtain fifty meters from where he thought they had gone and slithered along with his right shoulder brushing the earth wall. It was so dark behind the brush curtain, despite the harsh glare of the flare burning in the open, that he was almost on them before he saw them. Three Vietnamese in partial American uniforms squatted around the colonel. An American who looked dead lay near them. The Vietnamese were looking toward the center of the camp.

The sergeant took no more time to think. The shouting was over and the confusion seemed to be gone as well. The colonel knew too much to allow the running dogs of Saigon to have him. The sergeant held his rifle to his shoulder and sighted along its barrel. He squeezed the trigger softly until the rifle bucked against him. The colonel's head jerked and he collapsed. Then the sergeant shifted his rifle's aim and fired at the moving Vietnamese who had just lost their prisoner. He fired three rounds, then spun around to his feet and ran, uncertain whether he had hit any of them.

* * *

Randall and Lewis broke into a run toward the gunfire. It sounded to Randall like it was where he had left the PFs guarding the officer Wells had given his life in taking prisoner. He heard excited jabbering and a few shots from the PFs.

"What's happening?" he shouted at them, but they didn't answer.

"Over there," Lewis shouted, and cut to the right of the direction he was running in. "Somebody's in the brush."

Randall shouted again at the PFs guarding the prisoner. He tried to catch up with Lewis when the excited PFs once more failed to answer him.

"Eat lead, you communist mother fucker!" Lewis screamed, and let loose with a long burst of fire from his automatic rifle.

A thin scream and two wild shots answered the stream of fire and were abruptly cut off.

When Randall caught up with Lewis, he was straddling a crumpled body, pointing his rifle at it and jerking on the unresponsive trigger—his rifle no longer fired because he had emptied all twenty of its rounds at the dead man at his feet.

"Eat lead?" Randall said softly so that Lewis might not hear him.

"Jesse James and me, we talked about it," Lewis said, his voice thick, nearly breaking. "We always knew maybe one of us might get wasted. We swore a blood oath if one of us did, the other would make some communist mother fucker eat lead." He twisted his head to Randall; his eyes were red and his lower lip trembled under his asymmetrical mustache. "So I made this fucker eat lead." He turned away and returned to the search of the camp.

Randall looked after him for a long moment. He thought, I never did want the two of them in my fire team anyway, and now I don't, to cover his own grief at losing a man. Then added, but this isn't the way I wanted to separate them. He shook himself back to the present and trotted to the PFs and their prisoner to find out what had happened. One bullet had gone cleanly through the Vietcong colonel's skull, killing him instantly. None of the PFs were hurt. Wells was still dead.

"Pile it all up here, Zeke," Bell shouted. Ruizique was leading his Marines and PFs in gathering the contents of the tents where technicians and one of the squads had lived. "We'll blow it all together before torching the tents." He turned when someone called to him.

"Jay Cee." It was Zeitvogel returning from his recon on the hillside. "Nobody was up there, honcho. Looked like they had a few people guarding their antennas and they blew them when the shit hit down here."

Bell nodded. "Get your people's explosives to Scrappy at the comm-bunkers so we can blow them," he said after acknowledging the report. "Then check all the bodies around them for weapons and documents. We'll take the documents and destroy the weapons."

"Right," Zeitvogel said, and hustled off.

McEntire and his machine gunners were covering the narrow entrance to the canyon, after collecting the weapons and other equipment from the tent where they killed the gate squad's sleeping members.

In only a few more minutes, Burrison's voice rang out through the small valley, "Is everybody done? Have all weapons and documents been collected?"

A scattered chorus responded yes.

"Jay Cee, let's double check those charges before we blow everything."

All the radio and other equipment in each bunker was piled in its middle. The piles were laced with explosives—three bangalore torpedos under each and ten two-pound blocks of C-4 inside each. A thermite grenade rested on top of each pile. Everything was wired together to explode simultaneously.

Nearer the front of the canyon, all the equipment and personal articles from the tents were stacked in a huge pile that would soon become a gigantic bonfire. Even the reed mats and twine hammocks were in the pile to help it burn. Bangalore torpedos and blocks of C-4 wired together were laid on the pile.

Two bags made from ponchos were filled with documents taken from the bodies, tents, and bunkers, and were ready to be carried away. Wells's body was rolled in Randall's poncho.

"Get some poles so we can make a litter," Randall said to Dodd.

"Don't bother," Lewis said. "I'll carry him by myself."

Dodd looked from one to the other. He'd been given an order by an NCO, but the order was countermanded by another senior man. He waited to see what the corporal would say next before heading to the tents to get poles.

Randall hesitated a moment before saying, "All right, Billy Boy, you carry him." Then to Dodd, "Get a couple of tent poles in case we need them for anything later."

Relieved that he was obeying both of the senior men, Dodd got the tent poles.

The one remaining chore was accomplished quickly; the few surviving, wounded technicians were moved to a safe distance from the bunkers and covered with thin blankets. The camp's medical supplies and two days' rations and water were stacked next to them.

"Do not move from here until after the explosions and you will be safe," Houng told them. "Move before then and the explosions are liable to kill you."

They stared back at him blankly, wordlessly.

"All right, people," Bell shouted when everything was ready, "line 'em up and let's get out of here."

Zeitvogel and Randall got the platoon into line and it filed out of the hidden valley. Bell and Burrison followed, reeling out the wire attached to the demolitions. Back in the main valley, they waited until the platoon was well clear before attaching the wires to the generator and plunging the handle. The ground shook with the violence of the explosions. Fire still blazed brightly behind them when they finally reached the opposite hillside, where Slover waited with his mortarmen, Swarnes, and Doc Tracker.

CHAPTER TWENTY-FIVE

The Trip Back and the Following Day

There were still several hours before dawn when the platoon reunited on the east slope of the valley. The Marines and PFs of Tango Niner were accustomed to operating at night, and they had slept much of the previous day, so they were well rested even after the raid. Burrison and Bell conferred briefly and, after a short chow break, decided to go all the way back to Camp Apache in one forced march. There weren't any Vietcong left in the area now, they were sure about that. They could take advantage of their absence to move rapidly across the hills. This time, they wouldn't follow the river gorge; they were going to walk down the finger ridge that protruded into the flood plain. If its top was guarded, they'd kill whoever was there, that's all.

Huu led the way on well-used VC trails. Most of the food they carried when they left Camp Apache had been eaten, and all of the explosives and some ammunition was spent, so their loads were lighter than before. Except for Lewis, who was carrying Wells's corpse. They made good time.

"Let's make a litter and someone can help you, Billy Boy," Bell said before they set off on the long march.

Lewis shook his head. He and he alone would bear his best friend's body.

Bell looked at him closely in the light of the stars and saw the beginnings of exhaustion in his eyes. He quietly told Dodd to stay close with the tent poles, they'd need them soon. Lewis stumbled and fell under his burden once going down the first hill. He tripped and fell twice more going up the middle hill. Then he reluctantly agreed to make a litter—but only so long as he carried one end of it himself.

The platoon stopped halfway up the final hill while Zeitvogel, Hempen, Huu, and Pee Wee climbed to the top, looking for sentries. They found the guard post. The still warm embers of a fire in the bunker, and scattered remnants of food and gear that hadn't been picked up, were clear evidence that sentries had hastily abandoned their post.

The sun was climbing the morning sky when Tango Niner topped the last hill and started its long tramp to the flood plain. By now Lewis was carrying one corner of the litter, sharing his burden with three men, instead of humping the weight himself. A half hour to the bottom, and another hour to Camp Apache's hill. None of the PFs dropped out of the column when it reached Hou Ky, even though half of them lived there.

A horde of children poured off the Marines' hill and flowed toward them when they broke through the last trees before reaching Camp Apache. Some of the children crowded around returning fathers, uncles, older brothers. But most of them mobbed the Marines. "Me carry pfe-kah," some of them shrilled. "Me carry bang-bang," others squealed—it was mostly children too small to hold both ends of a rifle off the ground at the same time who wanted to carry the M-14s. Yet more cried out, "You pfiggy-back me!"

The tiny children scurrying and shrieking around them brought smiles to the faces of the worn Marines and lifted their spirits. They had spoken no more than absolutely necessary since reaching the flatland, but now they started talking again and joking with the children and among themselves.

Except for Lewis. "Get away from me," he snarled and swung his free arm, swatting at the children, not quite hitting them, just swinging close enough to keep them at a distance. "Leave me alone."

The children screamed in delight at this game and dodged his swinging hand until they saw his expression. Then they scattered to other, more receptive Marines. All but one who hung back and watched him with a somber expression to match Lewis's. That boy, five, maybe six years old, guessed at the meaning of the litter Lewis was still helping to carry. He looked up and down the line of Marines and PFs, trying to determine who was missing. He was used to seeing Lewis with Wells and couldn't make out that Marine in the line. The boy walked to the litter and, looking up at Lewis with the oversized eyes small children always seem to have, asked, "Ches-see Cha-mes?"

Lewis grunted and didn't look down at the boy, who nodded sagely and stepped aside. Lewis reached him in a step or two and the boy reached up to grasp the Marine's hand in his own tiny one. They walked silently for a few paces, then Lewis called out, "Hey, somebody spell me here, I need a break." Someone else grabbed the end of the tent pole from his hand, and Lewis looped his arm around the boy's waist, swinging him up to wrap his legs around the Marine's waist and be carried.

When they entered the compound the Marines and PFs

lined up in ranks in front of Burrison, Bell, and Houng. Even the children quieted their playful screams, though they continued to mill around the men.

Burrison looked toward the west before speaking. The hills looked peaceful, as they usually did. For the first time since Tango Niner had been established, they probably were. Finally he faced the men of Tango Niner, Americans and Vietnamese both, and started talking. "We did it," he said. "Tango Niner just pulled off what might just be the most successful small-unit raid in this war. We have destroyed an important enemy installation and, more importantly, perhaps stopped enemy action in this part of the Song Du Ong basin for good. Every man-jack in this unit should be proud of himself for what he did over the past couple of days—I know I'm proud of all of you."

He paused in his speech and paced in front of the platoon, nibbling on the inside of his lower lip. "Unfortunately, the nature of what we did is such that we can never tell other people about it—this operation has to remain our secret. Nothing that any of us did can ever receive any official recognition . . ." he glanced at the poncho holding Wells's body, and his voice broke. "Except for the one of us who made the ultimate sacrifice. He will be recognized with a Purple Heart." Suddenly, he came to an abrupt, parade-ground attention with his chest fully expanded and said, in the fullest parade-ground voice he had ever managed, "Tango Niner is the absolute best combat unit any Marine officer could ever hope to command. I salute you." And he brought his right hand sharply up to the bill of his bush hat in salute.

There was uncertainty in the ranks until Stilts Zeitvogel barked, "Platoon, Atten-tion!" and the Marines snapped to attention. The PFs immediately copied their American companions. Zeitvogel smartly brought his hand up in salute and the other Marines followed. So did the PFs. Bell and Houng also saluted. They held that way until Burrison, eyes tearing and unable to say any more, cut his salute and about-faced to hurry to the command hootch, where his men couldn't see him cry.

After Bell dismissed the formation, Hempen stood in his place, staring at the southwest corner of the compound. Zeitvogel sighed deeply and tramped past him. The tall man eased his tired body into a hammock suspended on a folding frame and slowly turned his head back toward Hempen. "Yo, Short Round," he called out in a much quieter voice than he had used calling the platoon to attention, "when'd you put this shit up, man?"

Hempen didn't answer, but he did start walking toward Zeitvogel. Not straight, but in an arc to get a view from more angles. Mazzucco looked from one of them to the other, shrugged, and joined Zeitvogel. He lay on one of the other hammocks.

Hempen finally reached them. He was chewing on his lip, tugging on his earlobe, and the butt of his rifle trailed in the dirt. "Not me," he said slowly.

Zeitvogel cocked an eyebrow at his automatic rifleman. "Then who did?"

Hempen suddenly dropped to all fours and started checking the hammocks for booby traps. Zeitvogel and Mazzucco didn't realize immediately what he was doing; when they did they sprang out of the hammocks they were lying in and bounded away. When there were no explosions they came back and joined Hempen in his search.

"Who the fuck did this?" Hempen asked. "Who put these goddamn hammocks up?" He stared at the other men of his fire team, bewildered. "Man, I put these fuckers back in their boxes before we left. I still haven't figured out how to assemble them."

Childish giggling spun them around. A half-dozen children were watching the three Marines crawling on the ground around the hammocks. One of them, a girl of about eleven, her chest barely beginning to bud with breasts, stood proudly. "We do," she announced and indicated the other children with her. "We like Shor'

Roun', Stil's, Mazz— Mazz—'' She hadn't yet picked up Mazzucco's nickname of Homeboy and couldn't figure out how to pronounce his last name. "You," she pointed at him. "We put together, you rest when you come back."

The three Marines looked at her and the other children for a long moment, then looked at each other and snarled. "How the fuck a bunch a little kids, can't hardly even read, gonna put up folding frames when we can't even figure out how to do it?" The children giggled again at the Marines' discomfort. "But they did it, damn it." They turned back to the children and announced, "You numba fucking one." They relaxed, pleased that the kids would do something for them while they were gone. "You come us," they told the children. "We souvenir you candy," and led them toward their squad tent and their personal belongings.

During the Marines' absence, the children had occupied Camp Apache. They not only took pains to assure the Marines, "No Vee Cee come here you gone," they also made a major point of telling one and all that they each had kept an eye on the other children to make sure nothing was stolen. Nonetheless, the Marines did search the compound thoroughly before anyone lay on his cot to sleep. They found the children must have been right about the Vietcong not visiting; at any rate nothing was booby-trapped. The children were less right about keeping an eye on each other so nothing was stolen. Every care package, goodies from home, had been raided and all the candy, cookies, and other food not in cans, was gone. There wasn't anything left for Zeitvogel, Hempen, and Mazzucco to give to the kids who erected the hammock frames.

There was one more detail to take care of before everybody collapsed for a day's sleep after the long night. Bell sent most of the PFs home. Then he, Randall, Lewis,

Dodd, and the half-dozen PFs who remained took a walk down into the trees along the river.

"This is the place," Lewis said. They were a couple of kilometers west of the hill. Pock marks still showed in the ground under the trees from a mortar barrage two months earlier. "This is where Jesse James first showed he was learning to be a good night fighter. Like I was teaching him to be." He choked and almost didn't finish what he was saying.

"The night the two of you got drunk and went on patrol anyway," Bell said.

Lewis nodded weakly. He balled his fists in front of his face and twisted, not so much to change his mustache as to give himself time to recover. When his hands came away, the left side of his mustache drooped down Pancho Villa–style, the right end hung limp—they almost, but not quite, matched. "Yah, we went on patrol anyway," he said weakly. "You was gonna hang our young asses, Jay Cee. We had to redeem ourselves, earn a medal so you couldn't hang us." His voice grew stronger while he talked.

Bell smiled wryly at the memory, especially the ass-chewing he delivered to them the next morning. He chewed on them long, hard, and profanely, and didn't repeat any profanity. It was the most colorful chewing-out he had ever delivered.

"I think you're right, Billy Boy," Randall said, "this is a good place to do it."

The ten men lined up in two rows facing each other and Bell called them to attention. "Do you want to say anything, Billy Boy?" he asked.

Lewis shook his head, then gathered himself and said, "Jesse James, PFC George Wells, was my good buddy and a good Marine. I'm gonna miss him. I'm proud to have known him and served with him." Then he fell silent.

Bell waited for Lewis to say more. When he didn't, the sergeant barked a couple more orders and the two rows of men stepped toward and past each other so they stood back to back, the PFs facing east, the Marines west, and raised their rifles to their shoulders. On Bell's command they fired their weapons wildly for a long moment, each emptying a full magazine. Then they trudged slowly back to Camp Apache.

Burrison met them at the back gate. "A med-evac's on its way for the body," he told them. "Somebody's going to want an After Action Report, but unless someone notices he's been dead for longer than we said, nobody's going to question that he got killed down near the river."

The business in the trees was a cover, to convince higher-ups that Wells had died on a routine daytime patrol in Bun Hou, not on an unauthorized operation in the hills to the west.

Captain Hasford came out to visit the next day. He seemed bemused during his stay, and looked like he wanted to ask Burrison and Bell something. But he didn't ask anything other than what decency and the concern of a commander for his troops dictated. He only gave them information.

"Lieutenant Colonel Tornado is on his way back from wherever it was he went," Hasford told them. "He called me from Saigon a couple of days ago to get updated on what was happening in his areas." He looked toward the hills in the west, but his eyes didn't seem to be focused on them. "I told him about your intelligence about the Vee Cee comm-center in a valley over there." He looked back at the two CAP leaders. "And I told him how unsuccessful I'd been at getting anybody interested in taking a look at it. He told me he'd see what he could do about it." Hasford stopped talking and looked at Burrison and Bell speculatively, as though waiting for them to say something. They looked back at him expectantly, as though they were very interested in what he had to say next.

Hasford gave in first. "He called me again this morning," he said. "He called in a favor and got an Air Force U-2 flight out of Korat, in Thailand, diverted to fly over that valley on one of its recon flights to the North. The fly by was yesterday morning, shortly after 0800 hours." He stopped talking again and walked to the trench on the west side of the hill. He stood on the sandbag-reinforced lip of the trench for a few moments, staring westward. His hands were nervously clasped behind his back. Finally, he continued without looking at the others. "The only thing that looked out of the ordinary in visible-light photography was that there was hardly any farming in that valley, it's mostly growing grass. But on the west side of the valley, there was something very interesting in infrared." Now he turned to look at them. "There's a bowl formation in the hills on that side of the valley, it's not visible from the air because of the vegetation—except for a very recent blast in the southwest corner, a blast that knocked down several large trees, and left a huge, red-earth scar in the hill. But the interesting thing, like I said, showed under infrared. It looked like there had just been a major fire in the bowl." He stopped talking long enough to shake his head. "The infrared didn't show any sign of people in the bowl." He looked back to the west, his brow beetled. "Have you seen or heard anything unusual in the past few days, or heard any rumors about anything that might be happening over there?" he abruptly asked.

Bell shook his head.

"No sir," Burrison said. "The only contact we've had since we captured that NVA sergeant was yesterday morning."

"Ah yes, yesterday morning," Hasford said, nodding sagely. "I heard you lost a man without wasting anyone yourselves."

"That's right," Burrison said.

"Pretty unusual for you to lose someone without taking out a squad or more of them, isn't it." The way Hasford said that, it wasn't a question, and neither Burrison or Bell bothered to answer him. "Odd," Hasford continued, "yesterday morning—or the night before at the earliest—the suspected Vee Cee comm-center gets blown away, and you lose a man during the day without killing any Vee Cee. What a coincidence."

"Are you sure the Vee Cee comm-center got blown away?" Burrison quickly asked.

Hasford set his face in his no-nonsense–Marine-captain's expression and said, "We know, all three of us, that the Vietcong have a comm-center over there. Even if we can't convince anybody else there's anything there worth looking at, we know it. The only thing a U-2 recon flight, complete with every state-of-the-art photo-reconnaissance device available, could find where we know Charlie has an important installation is a bombed-out hidden valley. No, I don't know factually that a Vietcong communications center was destroyed, that is, I can't prove it happened. But I know one got wiped out." His eyes unfocused to the west again. "Now maybe somebody will get interested enough to send somebody for a look-see. Maybe." He looked back at them. "I just wish someone would tell me what's going on."

Burrison and Bell both looked innocently ignorant.

Hasford stayed on the hill for a half hour longer, making small talk, while he waited for a helicopter to come from somewhere else to pick him up. He made it clear that he suspected Tango Niner had something—or a lot more than just something—to do with what the U-2 flight discovered under infrared. But he didn't ask any direct questions.

"You know, Tango Niner just might be out of a job, now that that comm-center is gone. Charlie doesn't have any need to come through Bun Hou anymore," he said right before the landing helicopter became too loud for further conversation. He waved at them after climbing through its door and was gone.

"I don't think he'll tell anybody," Burrison said when

the helicopter was far enough away that its noise was dim. "Do you?"

"Nope," Bell said. "If he did, he'd have to get somebody to believe him. If they did, then we'd be in a world of shit. I don't think he wants to get us into any trouble. He likes us too much and thinks we're doing a good enough job, he doesn't care if we step over the line once in a while."

"A short distance over the line." Burrison qualified what Bell said.

"A short distance," Bell agreed.

"As long as we're discreet about it."

"What does discreet mean?"

"It must mean what we did."

They grinned at each other.

CHAPTER TWENTY-SIX

Late Afternoon, December 9, 1966,
the Aftermath

A long column of men wearing pith helmets and khaki uniforms snaked down from the hills and into the northern end of a valley. They traveled lightly, carrying assault rifles and a hundred rounds per man. Each man had one canteen hanging from his belt and all of his belongings in a tube pack slung over his shoulders. A small farming hamlet nestled in that northern end of the valley, but the farmland didn't extend very deep into it before the valley floor became covered with tall, wild grass. A second small hamlet was barely visible in the distance at the lower end of the valley. The soldiers ignored the hamlet they passed near and walked in the shade of the trees that covered the slope of the hill on the valley's west side.

Some of the people of the hamlet glanced blank-eyed at the passing soldiers, but mostly they tried to ignore their passage.

A third of the way back in the column of soldiers walked a man carrying a large radio on a back-board. He spoke into the radio's handset. He listened for an answer that didn't come, then spoke into the handset again. He repeated the procedure several times, until the man walking next to him asked a question. The radioman answered the question and the other man, the officer commanding this column of soldiers, said something to the man walking directly to his rear. This third man shouted out an order and the column of men stopped. The soldiers sank to the ground, gratefully resting from their long march, glad it would soon be over.

The radioman removed the back-board and twisted a dial on top of the radio, then spoke into it again. When he got no answer, he tried a different frequency. Then a third, and a fourth, and a fifth, all without success. He was about to try a sixth setting when the officer snapped at him; instead, he then reset the radio to its original setting and hung the back-board over his shoulders. The officer spoke to his sergeant, who shouted another order. The men in the column rose to their feet, wanting to grumble but quiet about it—this officer had a reputation that kept men from grumbling where he might hear them. Another shouted order and they moved on toward their destination.

At a point near the middle of the long valley, the soldiers in the column's van turned into the trees and followed a barely perceptible path through the trees. A short distance in they stopped abruptly, appalled and unnerved by what they found. They sent a message back along the column and waited. A few minutes later the officer arrived with his sergeant and radioman. The officer's eyes bulged at what he saw when he reached the head of the column. Then he opened his mouth and ranted. Spittle sprayed. He barged through the cloud of flies swarming around the four dead bodies in his path and broke into an area cleared of underbrush and small trees. It was a scene of utter devastation. The charred remains of tents were scattered throughout. Two bunkers were caved in, strings of smoke still wafted from them. Piles of equipment and weapons were scattered in scraps of wasted metal and plastic. Close to a hundred bloating bodies, densely covered with flies and other insects and carrion birds, littered the ground, stinking and stiff. The officer arched backward and incoherently screamed his anger and hatred at the treetops high above. Then he snapped an order at his sergeant, spun about and quick-marched out of the cleared area, back to the grassy valley. He stood at the edge of the valley floor, swearing and shaking his fist toward the east.

"You thwarted me once before, Tango Niner," the officer shrilled. "And now you have done this. Now you feel secure, you must feel secure after you did this. But you are not secure at all, Tango Niner. I am back, better prepared than before. This time, Running-Dog Marines and puppet Popular Forces of Tango Niner, you will know as never before the wrath of Major Nghu. You will thank me for it when I finally allow you to die."

ABOUT THE AUTHOR

David Sherman served as a Marine in Vietnam in 1966, stationed, among other places, in a CAP unit on Ky Hoa Island. He holds the Combat Action Ribbon, Presidential Unit Citation, Navy Unit Commendation, Vietnamese Cross of Gallantry, and the Vietnamese Civic Action Unit Citation. He left the Marines a corporal, and after his return to the World, worked as a library clerk, antiquarian bookstore retail manager, deputy director of a federally funded community crime prevention program, Manager of the University of Pennsylvania's Mail Service Department, and as a sculptor.